/12

Dawn
Song

Dawn Song

MICHAEL MARANO

A TOM DOHERTY ASSOCIATES BOOK

NEW YORK

This is a work of fiction. All the characters, locations, and events portrayed in this novel are either fictitious or are used fictitiously.

DAWN SONG

This book is printed on acid-free paper.

A Tor Book
Published by Tom Doherty Associates, Inc.
175 Fifth Avenue
New York, NY 10010

Tor Books on the World Wide Web:
http://www.tor.com

Tor® is a registered trademark of Tom Doherty Associates, Inc.

Designed by Nancy Resnick

Library of Congress Cataloging-in-Publication Data

Marano, Michael.
    Dawn song / Michael Marano. —1st ed.
        p.   cm.
    "A Tom Doherty Associates book."
    ISBN 0–312–86432–9
    I. Title.
    PS3563.A6228D3   1998
    813'.54—dc21   98–13211

First Edition: June 1998

Printed in the United States of America

0   9   8   7   6   5   4   3   2   1

To Nancy, this *morgengabe*
as a gift of light and hope, in remembrance of the dark
mornings we have faced, and that we now leave behind.
"You are wholly beautiful, my love."

Although this novel is set in Boston in the winter of 1990, the author has taken certain liberties with the geography of that city and the events of that time.

Man doth not yield himself to the angels, nor unto death utterly, save only through the weakness of his feeble will.

—Joseph Glanvill,
as quoted by Poe, "Ligeia"

Lord help my poor soul.
—Last words of Poe,
October 7, 1849

Qui voltur iecur intimum pererrat
et pectus trahit intimasque fibras,
non est quem lepidi vocant poetae,
sed cordis mala, livor atque luxus.

—C. Petronius Arbiter,
Fragmenta XXV

…spiritus carnem, et ossa non habet.

—*Tratado de exorcismos,*
Anonymous Spanish MS ca. 1720,
concerning incubi and succubi

Amor condusse noi ad una morte.

—Dante, *Inferno* V, line 106

Prologue

L awrence and the Succubus were not drawn to Boston, but carried—like two branches dropped into a swift river. Taken by the same currents and eddies, they eventually piled upon the same embankment. Inevitability, not Fate, caused their lives to become so intimately intertwined.

For both of them, Boston was less an earthly place than a vital idea; it was their focus, the site they each believed would be their place of growth and personal fruition.

The Succubus was newly born, nurtured by the loving care of a horned prince from the pummeled soul of a camp-following whore (who had, in fleshy life, serviced one of Napoleon's best officers). With skilled hand and eye, like a master jeweler, he fashioned his child from this twisted spirit, purifying and distilling her to the fog-translucent whiteness of a glistening *manes,* then burning and sculpting this ghost of a once human thing into a crimson-skinned siren—her form holding the secret fire of cinnabar and the muted light of a November sunset.

Her creation was the alchemical translation of a rose into human form, the infernal transubstantiation of almost undefinable beauty into something alive, breathing, with thought. Her beauty touched the Lesser Furies with mute jealousy and rage. She, who had been one of their charges, soot-blackened and shit-smeared, corrupted to near liquid debasement under their merciless authority, now sat coddled on the lap of their Lord, tasting the sulfur-sweet perfume of his breath and skin. They would have set upon her and rent her, returned her to her despoiled state, were it not for their fear of him.

The Succubus loved her Lord and Patron, and sought to achieve great things in his honor. Thus, she came to the Living World to attain a Name, a rare distinction to be granted upon her taking the soul of her twentieth lover, one for each of the angelic spheres separating the deepest pit of the Abyss from the throne room of God. As a mystic would ascend such spheres through meditation and prayer, she would ascend through blasphemy and death, baptized and fulfilled by the salt-tears of human lamentation and grief.

For her, Boston was a garden of puritanical hypocrisy, a perfect, nurturing environment for the stifled desires that would feed her and make her whole.

Lawrence, too, was in search of a name, an identity free from that which had been imposed upon him. Out of need, he had severed his ties to Providence, his birthplace, and to Jacob, his ex-lover.

He despised Providence for its insular mentality, for its gay-bashing, blue-collar sense of Catholic propriety. The city had been a prison for him since childhood. As for Jacob, Lawrence did not hate him so much as the web their relationship had become. They had been lovers since adolescence, and Lawrence had grown beyond the teenage mind-set that had brought them together. Jacob had made clear his need for Lawrence not to grow, and the resulting arguments were hurtful and bitter. Words were said in anger which were not meant, and later, apologies were given without sincerity.

Their relationship died with autumn's leaves, and Lawrence left the apartment they had shared and moved back to the home to which he'd sworn he'd never return. As the soil hardened with frost, and the grass withered to a dead brown, Lawrence found the strength, and the desperation, he needed to redefine his life. The realization had dawned on him, as he felt himself forced again into the role of the ridiculous child his family needed him to play, that the prison Providence was to him was in part a thing of his own creation.

He could walk away.

For Lawrence, Boston was a center of cosmopolitan sensibilities, a world-class city where he would not have to stay closeted, no longer have to fear being assaulted for who he was or what he wished to be. Boston offered him the freedom and self-realization he had earned.

And so it happened that Lawrence moved into the brownstone by the Charles River one snowy night some weeks before Christmas, and the Succubus settled in on the roof above the next evening, during the quiet hours just before dawn.

PART ONE

The Widening Gyre

Chapter One

Friday, December 7, 1990. 12:51 P.M.

Do you have any Perry Mason?"
 Lawrence looked up from his newspaper.

"Excuse me?"

"Do you have any Perry Mason books around here?" The man in the leather jacket leaned forward as he spoke. The scent of his cologne mingled deliciously with those of yellowing books and clove cigarettes. Lawrence wanted more of that scent, nearer, and more intense.

"Check over there." He pointed toward the mystery section and smiled. "It's alphabetical by author, so they'd be under S for Stanley. We've got about ten or so."

The man in the leather jacket, whose eyes were grey like a November sky, frowned slightly. "They're under Stanley, not Gardner?"

Lawrence shrugged and put down his paper. "You know, I'm really not sure now that you mention it. Let's check." He punctuated the suggestion with a tilt of his head. He felt a nervous twitch in his midsection, like the touch of a fly upon skin; his legs felt too weak to support his weight as he stood.

Lawrence knew how the Perry Mason books were shelved; he hoped it wasn't obvious he knew.

As the two walked toward the mystery section, they disturbed the obligatory used–book store cat from her place by a floor heating grate, as well as two young men hunched like vultures over a box of old *Playboy*s. The young men absently got out of Lawrence and the customer's way, transfixed by the glossy photographs.

Lawrence felt the frustrated arousal of the young men, tangible in the musty air like the anger of a growling dog. It made Lawrence more uneasy that his gambit to get the attention of the man in the leather jacket would fail, that he'd be embarrassed.

Lawrence calmed some as he turned a corner in the maze of shelves and scanned the mystery stacks, trying his best to be friendly and cordial, trying his best to flirt well.

"Yeah. You're right," he said, smiling. "They're under G for Gardner."

In the white winter glow falling from the skylight, Lawrence saw that the man's black hair was touched with soft copper-colored highlights. Lawrence wanted to touch it, wondering what it would smell like in the morning, mingled with the musty residue of lovemaking.

The man in the leather jacket placed his hand on the row of Perry Mason books and smiled.

"Thanks a lot."

He didn't notice how close Lawrence was standing to him, nor how intently he was looking him in the eye.

Then Lawrence smiled again, took a breath, and backed away. "Hey, it's what I get paid for."

"Thanks, anyway."

"No problem at all."

No hope at all, either, he thought as he walked to the counter. The man was very straight, and did not pick up Lawrence's flirtations. If he had, there would have been a wonderful sexual tension between them, something like what the two young men were generating over the box of *Playboys,* yet different: a mutual imbalance more thrilling than disquieting.

If there *had* been such a spark, Lawrence would have pursued his flirtation with a discussion of how in the Perry Mason novels, unlike the TV show, Perry and Della Street were lovers, not just boss and secretary. (He'd not read the books himself, but had heard this from a friend who had.)

This would have hopefully led to a veiled hint or two about hidden sexuality, clandestine love, and then, perhaps, an exchange of phone numbers. Or an invitation for coffee after work.

What would he look like by candlelight?

Lawrence imagined the man's hair tinted with an amber glow, his soft grey eyes made brandy-colored by the shadowy light. The candles would be set on a table in Lawrence's apartment: centerpieces to the meal that would be the culmination of weeks of flirting and intimate dating, the meal that would be the prelude to his first sexual encounter in Boston.

A need to be kissed and held made an ache in his chest.

Lawrence took his seat at the counter and realized he'd left the key in the register. His daydream scenario was snuffed—replaced by the realization that his boss could have walked in and fired him for his negligence. He tried reading the paper again, but the news from the Middle East was too upsetting; he'd already read the features section. Instead, he petted the cat, who had settled upon the counter within a patch of dim sunlight.

She was a black and white cat, named Groucho because of a patch on her upper lip that looked like a greasepaint mustache. She seemed to sense Lawrence's gloom, and gave his hand a quick love nip. He felt her purring as he stroked the downy underside of her chin.

Since he'd taken this job, no one had shown any interest in him except MIT slide-rule types: nerds so hopeless, they couldn't be called *gay*, just desperate for anything from anyone. The lack of romantic prospects disappointed Lawrence. He'd wanted his new life to fill the void Jacob had left; he wanted his new job, in one stroke, to provide a viable future and a new lover as well. Meeting people had always daunted him. In this used-book store, there was always a segue to conversation: one could talk about books. He felt safe here, able to talk to strangers. Hopefully, someone whose eye he had caught would feel comfortable talking to him.

The cat looked up; Lawrence followed her gaze. The man in the leather jacket stepped up and placed *The Case of the Dubious Bridegroom* on the counter. It was a paperback edition from the fifties— on the cover, an hourglass-figured woman in a tight sweater and blood-red pumps brandished a .45 automatic. The picture reminded Lawrence of Faye Dunaway in *Mommie Dearest*.

"Thanks a lot, pal," said the man in the leather jacket. "I've been looking for this one a long time." He flashed a big, friendly, and very asexual smile, which made him all the more sexy.

Lawrence opened the book to where the resale price had been penciled above the teaser, LOST: ONE BLOND HELLCAT. He rang it up and said, "Don't mention it, pal."

Lawrence had never used the word "pal" before.

"See ya later."

"Right."

The man in the leather jacket walked out of the bookstore, the only trace of his passing the dissipating whisper of his cologne. Lawrence sighed and rubbed the cat under her chin before restocking the history section.

When Lawrence left work it was still daylight. A bright sun had come from behind the clouds, melting snow and making the air taste of spring. Winter had come early this year, with sudden frosts and deep snows covering the ground at November's end. Then a bitter cold snap took the city, bringing January weather that froze the Charles River and made the fallen snow crystal-hard and brittle.

The cold snap had broken today. People on the streets were at ease, no longer walking hunched with shoulders high, hands in their pockets, brows furrowed and red.

As Lawrence passed shops and streetlamps decorated with tinsel and lights (as well as a few trees bedecked with yellow ribbons, to show support for the troops) a mild wind blew from the west, warm and dry upon his face. The punk rockers milling in front of the comic book and record stores along Newbury Street had their jackets opened, and children, savoring the first moments of the weekend, ran through the slush, their footfalls making splashes of ice and filthy water.

The false kiss of spring, with all its hidden promises, moved Lawrence to become more active in his search for a lover.

II

As the sun set, drawing with it the warmth and light it brought to the city, the Succubus woke, filling her eyes with the wonder and mystery of a changing sky. The colors awed her, the remnants of the blue day giving way to the burning indigo and violet of dusk, night grey already bleeding from the east.

Even the sky seemed alive here.

Sitting with her knees drawn against her chest, she peered over the brick coping of the brownstone's roof and watched the sun sink in the west until its dying glow bathed the cold city with a color she had thought possible only in dreams. Then she stretched out over the cold gravel and snow and extended her mind out across the city to find suitable quarry.

To find her first lover.

As her mind wandered, her body writhed. She was beautiful, the distillation of men's secret desires, those hidden from their own conscious minds. Snow turned to droplets on her blood-red skin; her black nails raked the broken shale. She stretched her arms and slid them over her head, looking for all the world like a child making a snow angel, breathing deeply yet making no mist upon the winter air.

Her mind traveled over Boston, carried by nonphysical winds, free from the limitations of her body yet still joined to it, as the body of a person in a dream is joined to the sleeping body.

She traveled over the quilt of brick and stone grey buildings, swimming in the dusk, taking in not only the physical aspects of the swarming city but the ethereal, seeing minds and bodies swaying and rippling in patterns they could no more understand than stalks of wheat understand the wind that moves them.

She dropped between the valley walls of buildings as dusk died and streetlamps made ghost rivers through the city. She felt heat and soot rising from traffic below, yet still smelled the clean winds where her body breathed.

And then her mind alighted upon another, drawn to it and joining it as one cluster of milkweed clings to another in a warm breeze.

On her rooftop home, she turned on her stomach, as if throwing herself prostrate. The delicate muscles of her neck and back twitched as she raised and dropped her head in rhythm with the man's consciousness.

She extended herself into the man's mind, parting the tangle of his thoughts gently, so as to make herself unnoticed. She tended the dormant seed of desire she found there that would make him her own, awakening it with a caress, a whisper, that would make his need cross his mind as a momentary flash amid his thoughts and sensations, then make it settle and grow in the shadow area of his consciousness.

She made him ripe for harvest.

The Succubus stood, so achingly lovely in the veil of evening that light seemed unable to touch her. She walked across the roof and took from a plastic-lined box the things she'd stolen since she had been upon the earth. She selected her clothing very carefully, for the proper removal of the proper garments could accentuate the tensions of seduction in the most delicious way.

Clothed in fabric, she dressed herself in earthly appearance and walked to the edge of the roof, to a windowless recession like a well closed on three sides. Hidden from sight, she dropped to the alley below gently as a snowflake, and stalked her lover-to-be, following the scent of his mind.

III

After supper, Lawrence deposited, then cashed, his first paycheck at an ATM machine, and went to a gay bar he'd heard about on Boylston Street. The walk was intimidating, through streets strangely empty and dark for a weekend night, past parks dusted with snow beside ink-still ponds unfrozen and filthy in the shadow of rumbling overpasses—places too draped in shadow to have been touched by the afternoon sun. On Boylston Street, Lawrence passed a small park, like a grove, where shadowy figures milled about as if waiting for a bus. Only the brief flash of match touched to cigarette gave hint they were anything but shadow.

Farther down Boylston, he passed the great sleeping hulk of Fenway Park, the towering lights used for night games cold and grey against the darker grey of the winter sky.

He almost walked past his destination. No sign marked the entrance. Were it not for people smoking cigarettes or taking air along the front walkway, he wouldn't have noticed the building. It looked like a warehouse, a windowless edifice distinguished only by a recessed space in the front wall with Roman columns set into it. The walls were rust brown; a blue light shone above the doorway.

Lawrence was hopeful as he went to the door, and felt eyes checking him out as he passed. In the closet-like entryway, he paid the cover charge and had his hand stamped by a bouncer who did not look at Lawrence's face. He checked his coat with a butch girl whose pale features and bleached hair were made violet by the black-light bulb in her narrow booth. He went down the short hallway, also lit violet, to where strobe lights made false lightning at the doorway of the club itself.

The bar overwhelmed him as he crossed the threshold.

He'd expected a quiet, darkened place with a small dance floor. Instead he was confronted by a sprawling nightclub crowded as a subway at rush hour, throbbing and reeking of close bodies, soured cologne, and sweat-tinged hair spray. The flashing lights over the several dance floors made him feverish; the mist from the fog machines choked him. The concentrated breathing, the babble of the throng inside, and the storm of music invaded Lawrence's nerves and vibrated along his spine. He was suddenly dizzy, as if overcome with flu.

He wandered to the bar, nudging, stepping sideways the whole way. Patrons gave him angry looks as he excused himself with each step.

At the bar, people crowded around the service areas like bees clustered at honeycombs. Some wanting drinks darted around the tight groups like wrestlers trying to find purchase, eyeing where they could edge their way to the bar ahead of others.

Lawrence stood with the smallest cluster.

Three songs played before he got to order.

The bartender was very good-looking, with the sureness of someone who knew he could take home whomever he chose on a given night.

"What ya wahnt?" he barked, his thick Boston accent incongruous with his lithe *GQ* looks.

"Gin and tonic." Lawrence felt as if he were talking in a gale. Madonna's "Like a Prayer" thunder-blasted the air.

"What kind?"

Lawrence frowned.

"What kind of *gin*?"

The bartender's nostrils flared, his eyes narrowed.

"Yeah. What kinda *gin* ya wahnt?"

Lawrence felt the press of people behind him, felt their eyes on his back while the bartender fixed his pissed gaze on his face.

"Uh . . . Beefeater?" He knew the brand only from magazine ads.

"Beefeatah. Great." The bartender made the drink, scowling.

Lawrence's heart raced. His hands sweated. The flu-like dizziness made him feel as if he moved underwater. He thought of Jacob, how if he were here this could be an adventure. Jacob's absence was nagging, like a phantom limb. Lawrence felt he could extend his hand and join it with Jacob's, as he used to, almost by reflex. Though toward the end, when things had gotten bad between them, Lawrence could not bear to be with Jacob in a bar.

The bartender slammed the drink down.

"Four bucks."

Lawrence paid, hurried away. The drink was watery and weak. As the ice melted, diluting the drink even more, Lawrence wandered the nightclub, trying to keep his mind and senses clear, trying to learn and explore and meet people.

Yet the people in the lounge areas were cold and anonymous, drawing the walls of sound blasting from the speakers around themselves like thick blankets, muffling out the words of those around them, taking comfort in the difficulty of speech.

He'd been expecting something else.

In Providence, whenever a new person walked into a bar alone, he was taken aside and introduced to the regulars. It happened with each wide-eyed out-of-town freshman who came in, and every local who stood nervously by the door; it was a ritual to take comfort in.

Here, Lawrence was driftwood among islands of cliques: the groups of sensitive postmodernists, too caught up in their oblique androgyny to have any true sexuality at all; the straight college-age voyeurs, out to do something "different" while Daddy footed the bill; the queens standing in corners, dishing those who passed; the gay yuppies out to score nineteen-year-old frivolous faggots—the sort of easy prey who, after a few lines of coke, a quick screw, and a croissant in the morning would think they'd found Prince Charming. All the sorts of people he'd known in Providence to cruise the bars singly or in pairs were here in groups of five or ten.

He nudged his way to the nearest dance floor. It was less crowded there, movement spreading people out. He hoped to find a corner where he could watch others, maybe finish his drink then dance alone for a while until someone danced with him.

Yet he found that the dance floors were worse than the lounge areas—hostile, not merely alienating. The dancers were uninterested in their partners' movements or anything else around them, as if the entire bar were incidental to their presence, an accessory. Lawrence had never seen people more enamored of their own bodies, giving themselves sidelong glances in the mirrors along the walls. Other dancers postured like birds establishing nesting grounds, claiming parts of the floor as small stages for their choreographed seductions.

He edged away from the dance floors, then noticed a stairwell in the far corner; a stream of people shuffled up the right-hand side, another down the left.

Lawrence went up, careful not to spill his drink. The second floor was a single huge dance area that seemed the size of a cathedral. Here was more of what he'd seen below, save the lights were gaudier and the fog machines made the air even thicker. The stairs still went up. There was no traffic to or from the third floor; Lawrence wasn't sure that part of the nightclub was open.

He decided to go up.

As he climbed the stairs, the mirrored walls of the immense second floor made the dancers a churning sea of humanity; the writhing crowd reflected upon itself. A brief lull in the flashing lights made it impossible to see the far wall, the edge of the human sea lost in the deep gloom and the shroud-bank of artificial fog.

When Lawrence reached the third floor, he thought his luck had changed. It was quieter here, more intimate and very dark. Pool tables stood invitingly within islands of light cast by stained-glass lamps hung from the ceiling. The small crowds around the tables were relaxed; the people were not shouting, nor were they bonded into impenetrable groups. The bars in Providence had pool tables; one could meet and talk to others on the pretext of a friendly game. Often, there was no pretext.

But Lawrence found that, like the dancing, there was nothing friendly about the games here. They were tinged with control, dominance. The players shot for money, more cash riding on single line-ups than Lawrence paid for his monthly rent.

Not only money rode on the games—egos were contested as well. Skilled players received vocal approval from the spectators, while losers were belittled with catcalls and comparisons of their shooting to their performances in bed.

The final shock came when Lawrence saw a man sink an eight ball and grin at his opponent. "Now *I* get to screw *you* tonight," he said in a bitchy drawl.

Lawrence left the bar, afraid of his future and very afraid of what he felt. Would all the bars in Boston be like this place? Was all the gay scene here so ugly? Was he too much of a rube to cope with the life he'd come to experience? He'd left Providence because he was sick of it, yet on his first night out, he missed the bars he'd thought he'd outgrown.

He felt a deep distaste, and a deeper shame for feeling distaste.

He'd moved to Boston to escape the judgmental, twisted "Latin Mass" prudishness his father had imposed upon him for the sake of his immortal soul: all faggots were sick and evil, niggers and Fox Point spicks were out to get the good people of Providence, and Boston (or anywhere but Providence) was no place for a good person to live.

Yet he was feeling prudishness now and the need to pass judgment, some part of him still under the sway of the tyrannical bastard who'd raised him and the hate-polluted city in which he'd grown up. Some part of him had become what Dad had wanted. He didn't want to be what he despised, yet he could not condone what he'd seen this night.

There was a meanness to that bar as brutal as what he was trying to escape. The people there were everything Dad had said they'd be. He hated them for it.

And he hated himself for judging them the way his father would. The way his father had judged him.

"A candlelit dinner," he whispered to himself, the words spoken so softly they came from his lips as ghostlike as the mist of his breath. He'd find the right man to share that dinner with before he shared himself.

More people were on the streets now, trudging in groups and pairs to bars and parties and restaurants. A few of the bolder and saner street people worked the streets for change. As Lawrence neared his brownstone, a light snow began to fall. Thick feathery flakes muffled traffic and filled the air with a clean smell.

When a yuppie couple came out of a Kenmore Square pickup joint, the woman grabbing the man's crotch through his open Burberry coat, Lawrence realized how naive were his expectations. Boston would not persecute him for being gay, but he'd still have to struggle for happiness. Moving here was not a completed act of liberation, but the first step. He was not certain he had the strength to pursue the steps that would follow, if he could find a sense of belonging in a city so alienating, if he could find the right man to kiss while they were both bathed with a golden, flickering light.

When he got back to his apartment, for one moment at least, he thought of calling Jacob.

IV

There were many distractions as she walked.

She overheard the babble of fantasies flashing in the minds of people she passed, fantasies so brief and without cogent thought they seemed like sparks arcing randomly in the night. She felt the gnawing dreams of the few sleepers nestled behind darkened windows, and the delusions of mad people huddled in alleys. Often she had to turn aside the gaze of children who saw her and knew her, but could not name what she was or why she filled them with cold dread and the urge to cling close to their parents.

While she walked, she focused on the mind she'd touched, a beacon guiding her through the labyrinth of the city, calling her like a bird to its nest.

When she found the man reading in a café, she was pleased. He was young and handsome, no more than twenty-five. Here, so close, she felt the quiver of his aura upon her skin. She felt the resonances of the poetry he read in her own mind, felt how it moved him, how it touched his heart and his fragrant soul. She longed to know his soul, to breathe it and feel it course through her, to gaze upon the secrets of what he knew beauty to be and to walk among them as she had walked among the streets of this city. She fought the urge to simply take his face in her hands and kiss him, come to know the excitement of flesh touching flesh and the rose-petal softness of his spirit upon her lips.

The Succubus made herself glow with warmth and soft feminin-

ity as she sat across from him with two mugs of tea. She placed one
in front of him. Startled, he looked up from his book.

"Hi," she said with a nervous lilt.

"Hello." His voice and will faltered as his eyes met hers.

She'd made her eyes deep and brown. She felt his gaze enter her
eyes and touch the facade of the soul she had created for him. His
gaze warmed her. She wanted his love more than anything she'd
wanted before.

"I didn't . . . I wasn't brave enough to ask you if I could buy you
a cup of tea, so I . . ." She broke eye contact and made herself blush.
She stood to get up and leave, as if too embarrassed to stay.

The man's hand reached out, and caught the thick woolen sleeve
of her coat.

"No, please," he said.

Like a fawn returning to the side of her mother, she again sat.

"Please stay," he said. A pause as their eyes again met, his gaze flowing into her, spreading through her like sunlight. "I'd love a cup of
tea with you. Thank you. Thank you so much for bringing me one."

For one moment, they drank in silence.

"My name is Andrew." His hand extended across the table.

"I'm Jeannette." She felt the name stir a memory inside him.

They shook, touching for the first time.

She owned him then.

At Andrew's apartment, they kissed for hours, embracing on his
couch like lovers long used to each other. Yet laced with that comfort and familiarity was the thrill of a new caress, the joy of a new
touch that went beyond the skin to make the flesh itself sing.

They were still mostly clothed, and, as she had planned, this made
the encounter electric, bathing the air with tension. She used the tension as a conduit to bring forth the false soul she'd created, extending it outward to make it touch Andrew's through the fabric of his
body.

He sighed each time she did so.

At other times, she felt like crying out of need to take him suddenly, violently. She tasted the sweetness of his soul each time she extended herself into him.

Andrew was shirtless, while she still wore blue jeans and a white
silken camisole. With the slow removal of each layer came a feeling
of completed lovemaking, soon replaced by reawakened desire as
their skin touched and she again extended herself outward, covering
his spirit and body like a garment, warming him.

Andrew's hand, large and strong, reached under the camisole and touched her naked breast for the first time. He withdrew it when he felt something wet and unfamiliar.

The soft scent of vanilla, like the voice of a ghost, filled the air.

"What's the matter?" she asked, her voice a whisper.

Andrew paused. She felt his fear that the wonderful tension would be broken, lost like the memory of a dream.

"I don't know. I . . ." He showed her his wet fingers.

She gasped. "Oh, my God. I'm so sorry."

"What are you talking about?" The scent of vanilla grew stronger, became meshed with another like that of soft wool. Andrew saw in the dimness two dark spots forming on the camisole over her nipples.

"I have a child, Andrew. I should have told you." The only light in the room came from the halogen streetlight outside the window behind her. It made her a silhouette, darkened against its muted amber glow. "I'm sorry," she said again, her voice drifting from her own substantial shadow.

"It's all right. You don't have to apologize."

"I just feel so . . . embarrassed. It must be so strange to you."

"It's okay."

There was silence a moment. She looked down at her breasts. "I should express the milk out," she said as she withdrew into herself, and stood to walk toward the bathroom. This broke the mood, shattered the tension, the desperation Andrew so wanted to keep hold of. She knew he could not let her go.

"Jeannette. Please wait. Don't." The use of the name was a charm, a talisman to keep her near. It touched her and made her want to cry again, and slowly seep out of her body like fog, like a sigh, and envelop him with her embrace. She saw in the amber light the look in his eyes and wanted him so very desperately in that moment. She drew back to the couch and put her hand over his heart. She felt its quick beating against her palm. Through the warmth of his flesh, she spread her essence over his skin like a mist.

Then, as if unworthy, she asked, "Do you want to take my milk?"

"Yes." The word was barely spoken, an escaped breath.

She lifted off the camisole, revealing the beautiful torso Andrew needed her to have. She took Andrew's face in her hands and kissed him softly (he was so very beautiful), then drew him to her breast.

She kissed his brow. His skin was soft and his hair smelled soothing and wonderful, like something she remembered, but could not place. She let herself wash over him.

Again, she wanted to cry, touching the living pulsing gentleness of his soul.

All was coming together as needed, according to Andrew's deepest wants and her most urgent hunger. She could feel his contentedness, his quiet arousal. He was losing himself to the pleasure, to the fulfillment.

She changed the flow of her loving milk to blood, filling Andrew's mouth with the burning copper taste of an opened wound. He struggled, but her arms were steel as he tried to break away.

She felt his panic and his pain. Then, with gentleness, she made her hand immaterial and thrust it into the back of his head. When she solidified it, she jellied Andrew's brain, working it like wet dough, quieting his fear and confusion. She took his soul, savoring its sweet taste as she cut the silver thread that held it to what was once Andrew.

She lay with him awhile, kissing him, touching him, as his body cooled and his heart fell quiet. At last she did cry, so full of joy she felt for the love she'd shared with him.

The body was perfect and whole when she left it—no wounds, no blood, no remorse. As a final gift to her lover, she sculpted the nerves of his face to a look of quiet beatitude, as he had looked while taking the gift of her milk and her love. That was how she wished to remember him.

Her step was unsteady as she left the apartment building. She'd lost mass while Andrew took from her, yet she had gained so much when she'd killed him. She had yet to reconfigure herself, to adjust her essence from this first feeding. This was the first step of her pilgrimage, the first step toward her Name; the more lovers she took, the more closely her existence would resemble *living*. She rested, clinging to the cold iron railing of the stairs that led from the building's front door.

Snow began to fall, and the Succubus gasped with delight. She felt each flake alighting on her lashes and hair. She looked toward a streetlamp and watched snow flurrying around the light like a halo. Beautiful.

A young couple came up the walk, arms around each other's waists. The Succubus let go the railing. Feeling stronger now, she smiled at the couple as they passed.

As the Succubus walked to her home, she thanked Boston for granting her need. She sensed the city differently, now that she wasn't stalking a particular mind. More people were asleep; the dark air had freed the living from work and weariness. The sound of their many dreams was comforting, like a chorus of birdsongs in a wood. She breathed deeply and opened her mind, just briefly, to the city's ether, its imprint in nonphysical space.

She found the scars of frustration and unfulfilled fantasy, smashed dreams, smothered ambitions, and affectionless bonds chaining blighted hearts. By day, when more minds were awake, their churning emotions would rise like a tide, choking the ether and making the scars of the city much more livid and raw.

To her it was as lovely and inviting as an orchard in a season of harvest. This city created so much hunger and loneliness. She was happy and comfortable here, though touched by homesickness. The falling snow, dropping from the darkened sky, reminded her of the steady rain of dimming souls that fell upon the plains of her homeland.

Although, unlike souls, the snow did not scream.

The Succubus climbed the recessed alley wall of her brownstone to the roof, not like a spider or a fly, but gracefully—like a drop of oil rising through water. At the summit, she undressed, carefully replaced her clothing in its waterproof box, and lay down in her hiding place between a large chimney and a forest of aerials, ducts, and air vents. She made her body cold, so the snow would cover her as it fell, shielding her from the gaze of anyone who might see her from any of the nearby buildings. She'd chosen the tallest building on the block, but there was still the chance someone could see her over the brick coping.

Once settled, she quietly digested Andrew's soul, breaking it into its constituent parts. His warmth and kindness touched her heart, and made her treasure all the more the moments they'd had together. His kindness melted inside her, creating a sensuous contrast to the snow upon her skin. Flashes of Andrew's life, instants of memory, were vividly released into her being and forever lost. She felt his sense of beauty, felt the innocence and poetry of his world and the lovingness of his being blossom within her like the soft fire of brandy. Andrew and his soul were now gone, beyond the hope of resurrection, redemption, or salvation.

"And Jesus wept," she said to herself, and changed to her natural form. The change was erotic, somewhat painful, yet pleasant—like stretching a sleeping muscle. The new materiality her lover had imparted made her exhilarated and tired. An aching glow spread through her body. The pleasure of taking human form had been wonderful. It allowed her to project, to radiate, the sensuousness she had taken from Andrew's fantasy, and to grant this sensuousness to him as a gift for the image and the form she had taken from his mind. Yet what had aroused her most tonight, filled her with an excitement that made stealing her lover's life a desperate need, was taking a name, a false name, true, but a name nonetheless.

Jeannette.

It had been the name of a girl Andrew had loved innocently as a child. The Succubus had used that small memory as a final detail of her mask. The power of the name, how it fueled her lover's desires with a magic he could not comprehend, awed her. Her longing for a true and everlasting Name of her own was reaffirmed, as was her determination to please her sweet Father in the earning of that Name.

Sleep took her as she thought of her maker's kind, saffron-colored eyes . . . while directly below her, in a bedroom still unfamiliar and alien, Lawrence was troubled by dreams of another man's life and the voice of a mother he did not know.

Chapter Two

I

Saturday, December 8, 1990. 4:15 P.M.

U naware of the bewildering beauty of a winter twilight, a young man wonders how he will pay for groceries over the next few days. His paycheck is not due till Friday, and paying rent last week has left his bank account almost empty.

He walks the ice-paths worn into the snow that covers the unshoveled sidewalks of the Somerville neighborhood he calls home. He lives north of the sprawl of Cambridge and Boston, and he hopes that in better days he will be able to move south, to a neighborhood where the sidewalks are shoveled. He has said in the past, only half-jokingly, that the sidewalks are not shoveled in this neighborhood because no one here is well-off enough to sue if someone were to slip and fall. He is walking home tonight because he has decided not to pay the dollar bus fare, thinking that the dollar could be used toward a half dozen eggs and a bit of cheap, preservative-laced bread.

The young man wonders, almost aloud and in rhythm with the crunching pace of his steps, if he has been abandoned, if the work and toil and study he has done in the Name of the One to whom he has given his devotion have been for nothing.

In a whisper he speaks, alone on a street lined with sagging houses that cast flickering blue ghosts of television screens out of darkened windows onto snowy lawns:

"Please help me out of this."

He walks a few more blocks in the wine-colored dusk before he sees it: something strangely regular amid the undulating shadows, half-driven into the snow within a boot-print, something that flaps in the wind like an autumn leaf about to fall from the branch.

He steps closer and picks it up.

It is a twenty-dollar bill.

He goes home to his basement flat, and before he can take off his coat, his beautiful wife throws her arms around him and kisses him. He presses his face into her thick, fragrant red hair that tumbles in tresses like a coppery waterfall to her waist. She pulls the wool cap from his head, and his own, dark hair falls to his shoulders. She strokes it, and crackles of static electricity arc on her fingertips.

He hangs his threadbare secondhand coat on the wall hook and tells her of what happened as he walked home.

Her eyes light with a joyous spark, and, like a child leading someone to where a wonderful gift awaits, pulls him toward their answering machine. She plays back the message from his boss; he can pick up extra hours next week because some of his coworkers are taking early Christmas vacations. This will mean as much as one hundred dollars of overtime pay—one hundred dollars that can be set aside for the heating bill. If they are careful, they can stretch the hundred dollars until spring. They will not have to shut off the thermostat at night, so that if one of their arms happens to fall from under the blankets as they sleep, it will not be numb and unmovable in the morning, needing to be rubbed to life again under the covers until feeling returns to the fingertips.

They have a supper, by candlelight, of canned soup and crackers. Tomorrow, the twenty dollars will buy fresh vegetables and fruit, perhaps even a bit of meat. They turn the thermostat high and drink tea and kiss on the worn couch they had found abandoned on a street corner last summer, feeling happy and safe for the first time in weeks.

When the living room is warm enough, they strip their layers of wool and flannel clothing and begin the foreplay of lovemaking, only to stop after some tens of minutes to light colored candles set about the room and to spread salt on the hardwood floor.

They speak words from Syriac and Koine Greek they have memorized phonetically, and she lies belly down on the salty floor, within a weird, crisscrossing geometric pattern outlined atop the floor by long strips of differently colored electrical tape.

Now they speak a dialogue in two other dead languages: Latin and Aramaic. Over the course of this dialogue, they perform the Rite of Sodom, an act of consecration and thanks to Him to whom they have devoted themselves, to Him who has provided for them this night. Originally a rite of devotion to another, they adopted this act long ago to honor their provider, the Unbowed One, who had been well known in Sodom and in other cities of the Dead Sea, and who had been was the enemy of the Sons of Light in Qumran.

With sighs and groans, they finish their act and lean against a ply-
wood dais set against the north wall of the room. Atop the dais sits
a wooden chair, decorated and painted gold to suggest a throne.
Usually, the throne is used for rituals in which one or the other of the
couple assumes the metaphoric role of King or Queen. Tonight the
throne is empty—symbolically occupied by the Unbowed One, their
provider whom they honor.

The young man brushes salt from his wife's torso and arms, then
cups his hand over her left breast. He kisses her softly and says: "I
love you."

"I love you, too," she says as she strokes his face.

For all their happiness, they each feel a tinge of worry. The Unbowed One is rarely this dramatic or obvious with his benedictions,
usually preferring to act slowly and carefully over weeks, years, and,
if some texts are to be believed, centuries. Their provider may be en-
acting a grand scheme, putting into effect something so complex, so
intricate, on such an unfathomable scale of thought, that they may
never live to comprehend it. Or something dramatic may be planned
for them, some task they may be called upon to perform that they
may not be able to rise to meet.

Everything has its price.

She stands, now, and takes a comforter from the back of the
couch, then spreads it over them as she again leans against the dais.
It would be more comfortable to rest and touch each other on the
couch, or in the bedroom, but they both need in this moment to
be near their place of ritual, to bathe in the ethereal energy they
have generated. This is their place now, symbolically at the feet of
the One who has been so kind to them tonight.

Some time later, when they both stand to leave, she draws the
comforter around herself like a cloak. Her heart skips a beat as the
comforter nearly knocks over a fragile, precious thing she has crafted
herself and placed at the far left of the dais.

Quickly, she crouches to steady it.

It is a figure abstractly sculpted to represent a woman, made by
pouring a mixture of salt and rubber cement into a handmade mold.
The twisted shape of the thing is taken from Munch's *The Scream*.
Unblinking doll's eyes have been set into where a face should be, to
suggest wide-eyed horror.

This miniature of Lot's wife is balanced by another figure at the far
right of the dais: a lead figurine of a sharp-faced woman with bat
wings, an accessory for a fantasy role-playing game, supposed to represent a succubus.

A gaze that had been old when the sun was young fixes upon the husk of what had been the soul of a young man named Andrew.

The first blow has been struck; the churning, obscene idiot-beast will fall.

The husk smells of the sweet and nourishing treasure that it had held, the way a fresh rind smells of rich fruit. The Unbowed One crushes it with what would suggest a hand if human eyes could see it; the residual dust is carried away by a current that will be reborn as the föhn winds upon reaching the world of the living.

The scent causes panic upon the vista of ruined souls boiling like a plain of maggots in the lightless, starless place to which the husk has fallen. A hump like the back of an immense sea-beast rises up: thousands of flecks of dead humanity, each crying and hungering and climbing and clawing for the reminder of innocence and life the scent represents.

They do not reach it.

Flying things with fluting, discordant voices swarm like angry fish upon the husk-scraps, tearing, rending, slashing one another to savor the sweetness of the floating morsels.

Soon, she who took Andrew will not leave even the husks of her lovers' souls behind: even these will be taken into her, and not dropped to this place. As she becomes stronger with each lover she takes, so will her hunger . . . a burning concupiscence that will make her better able to take lovers the more desperately she needs them.

Even what she had been able to take into herself from this first lover may have been too much for her to retain. Part of what she had devoured has no doubt leaked out of her in a honey-thick sweat while she slept.

A waste. But no matter.

The first blow has been struck.

She will not fail him.

II

As he left the theater Paul realized he'd taken part in an act of mourning.

With that realization came the guilt that he'd squandered grief, no matter how trivial, that he owed to another, that he'd shirked his obligation to the dead, and so added to the heavy burden he bore.

Shuffling, ghostlike, with the crowd that flowed through the lobby, he felt the patient sadness take him again. It crept on him like dull winter fog, making him stoop slightly, as a flower does, first touched by frost. The sadness was a thing to be endured: a sickness that would pass, until it again clothed him in the gauze-shrouded mist of loss and a darker, velvet-textured regret.

It had been almost a year since his mother died, entombed in the darkness of a hospital room. The pain he had felt the night she died blossomed at times into the deep depression that held him now, the remorse so pervading it felt as if it could stop the beat of his heart.

At times, he was uncertain the depression could pass, when it suffused his blood as a numbing ether. But the sadness would be gone come morning . . . sometimes, in a rare blessing, by late evening. In the meantime, he had learned not to fight it.

He lost when he did.

Josephine spoke brightly beside him. She walked with a slight spring between Paul and Bill, the gold lion's mane of her hair swaying with her step. Her voice was clear, like mountain water; its cadence cut the dull murmurs of the crowd.

"So . . . you guys up for espresso, or beer, or should we go for ice cream?"

Now Paul, Bill, and she were passing through the lobby doors. Patrons dispersed around them as bees leave a hive at first light. Through the brittle air, through his whispery sadness, Paul felt Bill's gaze upon him. Bill and Jo had joined arms; Bill leaned forward slightly, expecting Paul's answer.

Paul wished to not answer; he wished to keep quiet, and give the sadness no voice through his own. He made himself speak, trying not to expel the breath he'd taken to form the words as a sigh.

"I think I ought to get going. Sort some things out." His tone was as soft as one would use to read a storybook to a child, at the time when shadows change from greys to deeper blacks.

The three were an island in the stream of foot traffic. Jo looked at Paul, looked through him, fixing her powder blue eyes upon him.

"You'll be okay?" Even when she spoke quietly, her voice was bright.

"Yeah. I'll be okay."

Bill, tall and elegant, looking, as always, as if he wore a fine suit instead of casual clothes, said, "You sure you don't want to come with us?"

"Yeah. I need to clear some cobwebs out of my head."

Bill gave a slight nod.

Jo asked, "You'll be home, later?"

Paul saw passersby give Bill and Jo sidelong glances and scowls. Boston, for all its liberal pretenses, was a racist town; its people did not hide their disapproval of a Black man joining arms with a White woman. Bill and Jo never seemed to notice the contemptuous looks. But Paul did whenever he went out with them; it made him angry, it *offended* him.

"Before too late, yeah."

Hands in his pockets, alone in the dark wood of his thoughts, he drifted along the Brookline streets, climbing hills steep as staircases, rock salt crunching underfoot. Under the blue-grey dome of night sky, the glow of downtown Boston made a false dawn to the east.

True winter night invaded the light of evening. It was second twilight in Boston, when people left the streets to huddle in bars and restaurants and living rooms as foxes huddle in dens: places thick with the scent of damp wool, cigarettes, and close, heated air. Once Paul could find such comfort on these very streets, among these very houses—once, but no more.

This neighborhood had changed since he was young. The battered VWs and rusty GM four-doors of fifteen or ten years ago had given way to BMWs, Porsches, and the odd Mercedes. Cheap apartments had been converted into condos. Local delis and bodegas were now pasta stores and gourmet shops.

He used to play here with kids from school; bikes were left unlocked in front yards, and on any block, you could find a game of touch football or street hockey, even in winter if the plows had been through. In the thick heat of summer, when sweat would lie upon you like moist velvet and the cicadas sang their incessant songs and fresh-cut grass filled your lungs with the smell of green, growing things, clusters of kids sat on stoops and porches, talking the nonsense of their few years' worth of wisdom, or reading and swapping comic books.

The neighborhood he knew—where long ago he'd had his first kiss, his first beer, and his first cigarette—was dead, replaced by stacked boxes of rental space, harsh track lighting filling windows so that they stared at one another in vacant gazes across streets, yards, and alleys.

To walk here was Paul's tribute, part of a night of mourning Paul had realized was inevitable when he saw the flyer in the lobby that proclaimed that the double feature was A TRIBUTE TO THE MEMORY OF JOHN LENNON.

Of course . . . ten years ago tonight, Lennon had died. The movies Paul had just seen were a testimonial conducted before an altar of flickering images, a testimonial offered to a stranger while he owed his mother so much. Tonight he had squandered his grief by trying to defer it.

By trying to escape it.

Since early this afternoon, he'd been aware of sadness near him as some are aware of coming storms. Paul threw himself into his work: correcting papers, cobbling lesson plans. He could not focus. Yet the pretense of work filled his mind with white noise so the depression couldn't take hold—the depression, and the accusing guilt that walked with it from which he could find no redemption.

Sitting at the kitchen table, he'd picked up his battered copy of *A Christmas Carol,* looking for seasonal material to use in class. His eye touched a line of the text, a plea from the old miser, Scrooge, to the Ghost of Christmas Past.

"Spirit . . . show me no more."

Paul's mind . . . with trains of thought crossing, touching, like a tangle of branches in slow wind . . . was awakened to a memory of a prayer that he had made in silence to a Spirit he could not see or comprehend, made over and over again as he watched his mother die cell by cell, as a rosary of tumors blossomed through the flesh of her chest and along her lymph nodes.

"No more."

A prayer that had been in his mind with the constancy of his own name.

"No more."

As the chemotherapy ravaged his mother's face.

"Please, God. No more."

As her flesh evaporated after the double mastectomy and her skin became translucent as tissue paper.

"God, I beg You. No more."

Thoughts and the memory of prayers, touching, crossing, under the shadow of his grief.

He'd been angry when his father died, suddenly, of an embolism when Paul was eight. Angry, not grief-struck. After his father's funeral, his mother had told him: *"Remember him, Paul. Everything. The good and the bad. Because as you get older, he will slip away from you. . . ."*

And memories of his father, vibrantly alive, the good and the bad, Paul had etched into his mind before the first dew had formed on his father's headstone.

Yet his mother died slowly, so very slowly. The memory of the woman, so proud and vital, had been long stolen from Paul when she finally left this world.

"Spirit . . . show me no more."

A paralysis took Paul as he read the line. To acknowledge the sadness as it nuzzled him, cracking the shell he'd put around himself to keep it away, would overwhelm him in a flood of remorse for what he had failed to do for her before she was forever taken from him. To try to suppress the sadness would make it worse. He'd entangle himself like an animal in a net.

He stared at the page—thinking of nothing yet feeling the sadness close like the wing of a dark angel—until the page became only dark markings on a white background, the spaces behind the print flickering lines of candle flame.

Transfixed, he did not hear Jo come home, nor was he aware of her behind him until she gently put her hand on his back.

"Paul," she said.

He started, as if suddenly woken, then turned to meet her gaze.

"Please come out with Bill and me tonight." Her voice was almost a whisper. "You need to get out of here."

She had freed him from his tangled thoughts, let him focus on something else. It was like dawn breaking.

He was about to speak when she drew her hand away from his back and placed it upon the downy skin at the base of his neck. Her palm felt cool and soothing as she took the chair next to his.

"Please come out with us. *A Hard Day's Night* and *Yellow Submarine* are playing at Coolidge Corner. It'll be fun. You need to get out."

Paul smiled, and placed his hand upon her neck. He drew her gently toward him and kissed her brow.

"I'd love to go out with you and Bill."

She hugged him and kissed his cheek.

Then she made him tea. As the kettle boiled, they talked about work, about how a customer had come into the antique store today and asked Jo if they sold big-screen TVs. Paul complained about his privileged, apathetic students and the willfully ignorant principal.

Bill arrived as they sipped the tea. Then the three took a winding route to the theater, stopping a moment to reaffix bits of coal and bottle caps to the face of a snowman they found on a neighbor's lawn.

Paul was happy to be out of the house. He enjoyed the movies, was distracted from his bleak thoughts and feelings. Then he saw the flyer, and his night of mourning, without the possibility of atonement, had begun.

Paul was walking through Allston, now, past Beacon Street. While his mind had been wandering, he had backtracked around the way he had come, taking the route he had walked hundreds of times in his youth to go home to his mother's house. Some instinct was bringing him home, like a bird or a fish.

"Don't come back."

Either instinct, or a longing for expiation.

"Don't come back."

The words stepped from the shadows of his thoughts, from where they were forever inscribed and forever whispered.

They were the last words his mother spoke to him, said to his back as he left her hospital room. Good insurance had afforded her the dignity of dying in privacy.

"Don't come back."

He froze as he placed his hand on the door. He wanted to turn and ask why he shouldn't come back, why he shouldn't be here when she died.

Then he realized that these were the last words she wished to speak to him.

He could not deny her that.

He left the room. Brutal light from the hallway flooded the quiet, dark place behind him.

"Don't come back."

A final gift from her, perhaps. Absolving him of having to be here when she died, ending his duty, as her son, to help her die as well as she could. But now it was plain her death could not be dignified or honorable, despite the care of nurses and the ministering of shots that could numb earthly pain, but not the unworldly agony of her very body betraying her, not the crucifixion of cancer destroying her with each breath she took.

He would obey her, and not come back to complete his death vigil.

But to come back, he would first have to *leave.*

And this he did not do.

Paul waited in the hospital as his mother slipped into her final coma. He slept on the waiting-room couch, washed in the bathroom, and drank bad and bitter coffee given to him by nurses who let him stay despite regulations. Paul was never more than twenty feet away from her.

When life quit his mother's ruined body, he went to her room before she was removed. Numb, yet knowing grief and pain would sunder his world completely once the numbness passed, in the presence of a kind, older nurse who wore a silver cross upon her uniform, he drew back the sheet and kissed his mother good-bye.

Paul was walking his mother's street now.

Barren oaks arced above him, treetops touching across the avenue. Every fiber of his being cried that this was the way *home,* that to walk down this street and pass through the threshold would be the end of a pilgrimage. But the house was not his home anymore. A young couple with a baby lived there now. Nice people. They still forwarded mail to Paul's apartment.

He resented them.

Paul wished he could have preserved his mother's house as it had been just after her death—before her siblings, whom she could not stand, had come to take away the things Paul could not—and sit there now and mourn in privacy.

And try to atone for his betrayal.

Paul stood across from his mother's house. Christmas lights made the windows glow, as if from a hearth fire. He saw relics from the time it had been his home: plant hangers, glinting in the silvery light of the streetlamps, attached to the window frames facing the small yard to the side of the house.

Paul's mother had hung bird feeders off them: seed feeders in the winter and nectar-filled hummingbird feeders in the summer. Did Uncle Joe, the greasy bastard, take them, along with what had been his father's favorite chair? Along with so many other things Paul held dear?

His mother had gotten the feeders for him, to teach him about wonder, the handiwork of God.

When Paul was twelve, just old enough to become jaded and lose a child's sense of the marvelous, she had hung the feeders from the living-room window. Always the poet, always the teacher and the guide, she took him to the window when the birds came, and showed him how to truly *see* the birds, to *see* the splendor of natural things living within a city.

"Look, Paul! Look at the jay." Her voice would lilt and have cadence like a birdsong. *"Can you see all the blues and the whites and the greys in the feathers? . . . Look at the robin's breast, it's so fine and red and velvety. Can you imagine touching it? . . . See how the sparrow opens and closes its eye?"*

And in summer, when the hummingbirds came, she taught him how the tiniest things held the greatest miracles.

Everything stopped when a hummingbird came to the feeder. The whole world became grey, insignificant shadow beside the tiny, magnificent bird.

"Paul. Look at the feathers!" She whispered as she did in church, before this creature that seemed crafted of intricate stained glass. *"They're like fish scales, or shiny metal. The red under his throat burns like a little coal. . . . It's so little! Its heart beats a thousand times a minute, can you imagine that? Can you imagine being so beautiful? See it sip the nectar? Its tongue can lap thirteen times a second."*

Years later, Paul could articulate what his mother had taught him: that miraculous things are *intrusions.* Welcome intrusions of the Divine that push aside the mundane and the dreary, the things that dull our senses and our minds. And miraculous things could be found everywhere—in the blues and subtle shadings of a jay's feather and in the burning, passionate sheen of a hummingbird's throat.

She taught him of the obligations we owe to marvelous things, to treasure them and preserve them, to accept them as the gifts they are.

And to give them gifts in return.

In the last months of her life, when Paul had moved back to her house to take care of her, she gave him a cloth bag filled with the hair she'd lost from chemotherapy.

"Give it to the birds, Paul."

It had been November. A cold day. She was too weak to go outside.

"I saved it, because it seemed wrong to throw it away. But it's too brittle to give to a wig maker. Give it to the birds, Paul. They look for soft things to line their nests with when it gets cold. Spread it out in the yard. They'll fly away with it to line their nests."

Her way to enter and be part of the world of miraculous things, to know some part of herself could live past her, giving comfort to the things that had comforted her.

Paul sowed her hair upon the grassy yard, placing swirling patterns atop the etched-glass patterns of frost.

He felt her watching him do this through the window.

His mother's hair was still in the trees above him, more than a year later, keeping the birds warm in the midst of this awful winter. He'd seen the birds fly off with the hair, strands of it trailing behind them like streamers.

The Christmas lights in the window had been shut off. Flickering blue suggested a TV on somewhere in the house. He'd been standing so long in the snow, his feet had gone numb.

He should not have come here, in the hope of finding solace. Paul could atone for nothing by being here tonight.

Because he *should have been here* when his mother died, not defying her by keeping a death vigil she did not want him to make.

"Don't come back."

He had betrayed her, and all she had taught him.

For when he did return here from the hospital the night she died, thinking, absently, of when to move his things back to the apartment, Paul became aware . . .

Aware of something in the air of his mother's house.

Of something resonating, vibrating, just barely in the realm of his senses, like the faintest residual ringing of a distant church bell.

Of something *changed,* made electric. The senses and perceptions his mother had honed within him burned and thrilled and reached out to grasp at . . .

Nothing.

An intrusion of something marvelous had taken place, a lifting of the veil of the mundane world.

Something he was not here to experience.

"Don't come back."

His mother's scent was thick in the house. Not the scent given off by her dying, traitorous body saturated with killing medicines. But the scent of her when she had been alive, truly alive . . . vibrant and full of kindness and love.

She had been there.

And he had not.

And remembering what he had felt coming home that night, feeling again what he had felt knowing that his mother's desecrated body slept on a cold metal table in the hospital morgue, Paul wept.

His knees fell from under him, and tears burned his face in the cold air.

His mother, discorporate, free from the agony of her body, had searched for him.

But he had not been where she could find him.

It was past midnight when he left, still crying, to wend his way back to the apartment.

The greatest Beast in Hell, violently formless as a raging sea suspended in the sky, unthinking, obscene, smells something It perceives to be a threat. In the dim, screaming riot of idiot voices inside Its essence, It begins to awaken some form of order, the idiot voices aping thought. Cadences swell as if the many thousands of idiot voices were falling into chanting clusters, each intent on shouting the other down.

It is in this way the thing reassembles Its mind. It does not like to do this, as It finds thought repugnant, something that interrupts the dull seeping pleasure It feels churning in a cloud of Its own waste. Usually simple *reaction* is enough for It to deal with threats, yet if the Beast indeed smells a threat of the nature it seems to be, ugly, ugly thought will be required to solve it.

A long time passes before the thing's mind has congealed enough for It to remember Its name.

Chapter Three

Sunday, December 9, 1990. 7:05 P.M.

Y ou want to play pool?"
    The voice came from behind Lawrence's left shoulder, startling
him like the buzz of a wasp by his ear. He turned to see a tall, ashen-
skinned man with green eyes gesturing toward an unused table. He
had a nice smile, and was very good-looking.

"Sure."

Why not?

Early Sunday evening, and the bar was not as overwhelming as it
had been on Friday night. It felt more like the bars back home—no
blasting music, no packs of postmodernists or grinning studs. The
place was wonderfully warm in contrast to the weather outside. The
bitter cold was returning, temperatures dropping to the low twenties,
and a marrow-chilling dry wind cut the air. Lawrence felt cozy here,
as if he were visiting someone's home.

Groups of people sat sipping drinks and nursing beers, chatting or
watching videos on the big-screen TV in the far corner. Trapped in
a smeary picture, Whitney Houston pranced in a shower of confetti
and sang of her need to dance with somebody. Two men sat at one
of the far tables talking, eyes fixed on each other, steaming glasses of
Irish coffee beside them, holding hands.

The pool tables weren't crowded with spectators making Roman
circus catcalls. Just a scattering of people quietly playing. There was
a comfort in the smell of stale beer and old cigarette smoke. He was
glad he'd pricked up the courage to come back, forsaking a night of
watching romantic movies from his videotape collection. Lawrence
still felt on edge, though, on unfamiliar territory.

"Nine ball?" asked the tall man.

"Sure. Let's play for drinks. Best of five wins." Lawrence felt stupid and phony, his words a put-on. He couldn't choose a cue. He'd

had a favorite cue at each of the bars in Providence, and used to reach for them out of habit. He scanned the rack and grabbed the one closest at hand.

The tall guy took a cue absently and stepped to the table.

"Nine ball it is. You got it." The man's voice was too clear, too carefully enunciated, for him to be at ease. He didn't look at Lawrence, and fumbled as he racked the balls.

Lawrence relaxed; he'd found a kindred soul.

"From around here?" the tall guy asked as he dusted his cue, smiling.

"No. Pretty obvious, huh?"

"Not really." The tall man smiled at Lawrence as he fired the cue ball home; his brown aviator jacket, shiny and stiff, creaked as he moved. "You sound pretty New England to me."

"I'm from around an hour away." Lawrence put chalk on his hands, not to help his handling the cue but to dry his palms.

Crack.

The tall man sank the two ball.

"Hour away, huh? Then you're from around here in my book."

Crack.

He sank the three ball.

"Shit," he said. "Where *I'm* from, we don't think twice about driving two hours to see an hour-and-a-half-long movie. When I was a kid, I spent two hours a day with my butt on a lumpy school bus seat. By the time I graduated, I had calluses on my ass shaped like the springs that poked up through the cushions."

The tall guy never stopped smiling.

Crack.

He missed his shot.

"All yours," he said, sweeping his hand over the table. The green eyes glinted, the grin never faded. His teeth were pearly white and only slightly crooked.

His mouth was very kissable.

"So where's that?" asked Lawrence.

"Where's what?"

"Where you're from."

The guy grinned wider as he stepped from the table. The light from the stained-glass lamps cast a red glow on his face.

"Some shit hole in Kansas you've never heard of and you never will. To us, going to Topeka was a thrill a minute, and Kansas City . . . whoa, now *Kansas City* was fuckin' *Disneyland*."

Lawrence leaned over the table and sighted the cue ball. He couldn't imagine such a place.

Crack.

He missed his shot.

"I say now, son!" the tall guy bellowed.

Lawrence started.

"I say now, *son!*" the tall guy yelled again, imitating Foghorn Leghorn. "You're doin' that all wrong, boy! Let me show ya how!"

He stepped to where Lawrence stood, nudging him out of the way. Then he placed the balls as they had been before Lawrence's shot.

"You gotta just tap it," he said, pantomiming a light shot with his cue. "Try to hit it dead center. Picture there's a bull's-eye in the middle."

Lawrence did the shot as he'd been shown.

Crack.

The ball sank.

The tall man leaned against the table. His lankiness and easy posture made him seem a cowboy loitering in front of a saloon, an imaginary Stetson tilted to one side and a match hanging out of the corner of his mouth.

"Easy as pie. Name's Tom, by the way."

"I'm Lawrence."

They didn't shake. Instead, Tom nudged Lawrence with his shoulder. Lawrence could smell the clean leather of the aviator jacket, like new shoes nested in a box with tissue paper.

They played two games; Tom would often stop to give Lawrence pointers or explain how he himself lined up his shots. He would also touch Lawrence's hands, to help him hold the cue at just the right angles to make his shots. Each time Tom touched him, Lawrence felt a jolt of excitement shoot up his arms, through his torso, to his crotch. Tom saw what his touch did to Lawrence, and kept on touching him.

They drank two rounds of drinks, chatting, telling jokes and anecdotes about their respective hometowns. Lawrence paid for the first round, of course. Then Tom threw the second game to pay for the second.

A half hour after their second round, the two men arrived at Lawrence's apartment, spilling across the threshold as a single person, arms entangled around each other's waists. They acted as one person as well—Lawrence throwing the light switch as Tom closed the door—kissing as they did so.

Lawrence had never picked up a man like this before, not so soon after meeting. His mind was fragmented, butterflies in his stomach and weakness in his knees. His pulse raced with excitement and fear and need and worry. In the midst of this storm of anxieties was one stable thing he could focus upon. And that was the thing that was *not* happening: the fantasy he'd had for months about his first encounter in Boston, how it would come about, what kind of man it would be with, the first gentle bedding culminating after weeks of flirtation and dating and that single, wonderful candlelit dinner.

Lawrence knew, as he stood in the front hall of his apartment kissing Tom, the hardness of their crotches pressed close together, that this fantasy was nothing but stupid romanticism. Fluff. Jacob had been his only lover. Lawrence had never had a candlelit dinner in his life.

Yet he clung to the fantasy, holding it close. He mixed memory and desire, imposing the comfort of the dream upon the arousal of his body, trying to keep himself calm as he came to grips with the looming fact that he was going to sleep with this man.

The fear was too strong; his steadiness buckled. He didn't want things to happen this way, not yet, not so quickly.

"You want a drink?" he asked as their lips parted. Lawrence had no alcohol in the apartment, only soft drinks and juice in the fridge. Perhaps they could drink coffee and talk for an hour before going to the bedroom.

Tom slipped his hand low over Lawrence's ass and pulled him closer; his long, wiry arms were surprisingly strong. "I want what you want," he said as he placed his mouth over Lawrence's.

Lawrence stifled his fear, made himself think of this encounter as a rite of passage, a confrontation with the shameful prudishness he'd felt two nights before. He felt outside himself, seeing his actions as another person's. He wanted to be a witness to what was about to happen as well as a participant; he needed to remember the event clearly, in the smallest detail.

Lawrence lost this detachment in bed, bathed in the pleasure of Tom's touch, the feel of his firm, knotty body against his own. His fear dissipated like smoke as he and Tom kissed, caressed, tasted each other, the perfume of pre-ejaculate thick in the air.

Lawrence's certainty shattered when Tom balked at using a condom.

"What the fuck are you doing?" he said as Lawrence reached into his nightstand drawer.

Lawrence didn't speak. He only showed Tom the foil-wrapped prophylactics.

Tom drew his hand off Lawrence's skinny chest, as if he'd just set it down in something unsightly and corrupted.

"You're ruining the mood."

Tom's eyes seemed a shade deeper green and the shadow of a sneer crossed his face. There was a heavy silence, broken by the hissing clank of the radiator as steam from the boiler far below wound its way to the top floor.

Lawrence was stunned. His friend Martin had died of AIDS, twenty years old when his own blood poisoned him and left him dead like the husk of a fly. He'd died *alone* in a ward, rejected by his parents, who were too steeped in the judgmental ire Providence bred so well to care for their son, who'd shamed them by being a *sinner.*

Lawrence could not bear the thought of dying alone.

"I'm not wearing one of those fucking things." Tom propped himself up on one elbow and absently looked down at his own sparse chest hair, running his fingertips through it as if combing it into place.

The radiator continued its hissing chorus.

Lawrence wanted to cast the condom aside, to comply with Tom's wishes. To please Tom. To be *liked* by Tom.

He felt like a child again, remembering the times he'd buckled in the hope of gaining approval, remembering when his older cousin Fred had dared him to sled down a steep hill without holding on tight to the reins, had told him not to be afraid, had laughed as Lawrence trudged up the hill bloodied and, later, had been so very silent as Lawrence's father slapped Lawrence for being careless.

Not again.

Not now, at this point in his life when he was trying to shed his childhood. Not now, when the shadow of this night could walk behind him, haunting him—giving him six months of sweating anxiety until he could get an accurate HIV test—and possibly one day killing him.

Lawrence made himself a witness again to his actions, to give himself the distance to stand up to Tom and his own need to please Tom.

"Then I guess you can go home." The words felt unreal, sounds he as a witness created that intruded upon what he observed.

Tom stopped his catlike grooming of his chest and flashed Lawrence a look. Lawrence saw that Tom was used to his looks getting him what he wanted. Lawrence called on the witness, his other self, to take advantage of Tom's surprise.

"Unless you want me to wear the condom."

The sex was horrible.

Lawrence tried to imagine he was with Jacob, but Tom was an overwhelming presence, angry and frustrated, needing to punish Lawrence for forcing the condom issue and forcing him to wear the fucking thing.

Tom did not wipe the excess K-Y jelly from his hand on the sheets, but left it there as he placed his palm on the small of Lawrence's back, bracing himself as he entered.

Afterward, the two retreated to opposite sides of the bed, no words spoken as the sounds of the radiator died.

Each clung to his share of the covers, marking his own space.

His own territory.

"Faggots."

Lawrence heard his father's voice saying the word with a contempt that seemed to have physical weight. He relived a moment when he was sixteen, first experimenting with his desires with a guilty weight in his chest. He'd been watching the local news with Dad. In a report about gay organizations on Brown's campus, a spokesperson was interviewed about frat members demolishing the large pink triangle placed on the quad in honor of Gay Rights Week.

"Faggots," his father snorted as he separated his mouth from a bottle of Narragansett beer. *"Listen to that little shit whine. They ain't got no fuckin' guts or spines. All they fuckin' do is whine and want things their way. Little shits, every one of them. . . ."*

The voice of his father . . .

Every time he felt bad about himself, it spoke to him.

Lawrence was furious, sad, lonely . . . homesick.

He wanted the comfort of familiar places; even when Jacob was at his drunken worst, Lawrence hadn't felt this shitty or belittled. He was exhausted, but was too on edge, too nervous about Tom to drift off.

Violation burned inside him, beyond the physical intrusion of Tom. He'd been forced into the same power games he'd despised at the bar Friday night, here, tonight, within his own home.

Within his own bed.

And he felt cheated, trapped, by stumbling into a scenario that fit his father's conception of faggothood so perfectly. Now Lawrence lay next to a man to whom he'd given his body, whom he never wanted to see again. Emotional fatigue, not physical, made him drift off. His tiredness was a hollowness in his chest, a buzzing ache in his head.

His mind dimmed, drawing darkness over itself like a blanket for warmth and welcome numbness.

And then the nightmares took him, much worse than they had two nights before.

No clear image or continuous form revealed itself. Lawrence knew only a heap of broken images, a sleep-riot of subtle sensations and a burning fear of death. The dream was alien, intrusive, probing deep with roots that clutched at his most basic sense of self. His perceptions were distorted, warped by the weight of the dream. His mind folded upon itself, like the surface of a pond in the instant a thrown stone touches it.

Lawrence dreamt of an arm draped over his face, with skin soft as rose petals that smelled of incense.

The kind that is burned in church.

The flesh of the arm trapped its scent in his lungs as it suffocated him.

Quick, strobing images of eyes like a doe's crying.

The taste of tea and milk.

The feeling of holding a woman's hand on a scarred wooden table, the smell of air that had been breathed too many times in a crowded place.

The sense of being surrounded by chatting people who did not matter.

All that mattered was the feel of that hand against his own.

A waxen grey shadow, hot and viscous like filthy bathwater, broke over him in a wave, erasing his smallest sense of self, his smallest sense of awareness.

Neither living nor dead, knowing nothing, Lawrence floated like wet rags in the void. There was no time in that dead place, no sight or word. Then a shrill tone beckoned him. He focused on it, went toward it, a moth to flame.

The tone had a silvery materiality, like the glow of clouds near the moon.

He broke the surface, his eyes seeing only the snowy whiteness of the sheets.

The alarm clock had brought him from the dream, its electronic drone like the chirp of a mechanical bird.

Lawrence started to reach for the alarm . . .

. . . but couldn't move.

Limbs knotted, he was frozen in fear, his body unable to answer his mind. He heard the throb of blood rushing in his ears. The alarm. The flow of air into his lungs.

He blinked twice and tried to move again.

Nothing.

As if he were fixed by the gaze of a snake.

The alarm kept beeping.

Lawrence took as deep a breath as he could, forcing air into his lungs.

That broke the spell.

Clenched muscles fell lax, as if the cords holding him taut had been cut.

He reached over and shut off the alarm.

His arm was tired, sore and weak, his fingers tingling and numb; the joints of his legs and feet ached.

Tom was gone.

He was relieved.

And disappointed.

Disappointed that there was no chance of a good-bye, no chance to try to stay on good terms.

To try again.

Then Lawrence was angry at himself for being such a goddamned Pollyanna.

Tom was a creep.

End of issue.

He got out of bed, feeling shaky and sick.

And hating himself for caring, he searched the room for a note, a slip of paper with a phone number, an article of clothing, anything to mark Tom's passing.

Soft light of winter dawn filled the room as Lawrence searched. The warped resonance of the dream was still with him, making his vision vibrate. His gaze fell on the condom, cast aside by the bed like the skin of a snake.

That was all Tom had left behind—only that, and an empty space in the living room where Lawrence's VCR had been. It had been a gift from Jacob. All the cash was gone from his wallet as well.

Lawrence went to his bed and quietly sat, waiting for his limbs to stop quaking.

II

Monday, December 10, 1990. 11:51 A.M.

The Succubus smelled the church before she saw it. The scent cut through the quilt of stenches made by traffic, dirty ice, misting human breath, and steam churning from manholes. It lodged on the back of her palate like dust, acrid and sickly sweet—a combination that echoed cinnamon and hot ash, touched with the taste of still air in the moment before a lightning strike.

The smell startled her, snapping her thoughts from the new weight of Andrew's soul inside her and the first angelic sphere his soul had afforded her, from daydreams of her promised Name, her Father, and the lovers she'd configure within herself to gain greater materiality, and so ascend the angelic spheres still separating her from her Name. She looked upwind toward the source of the smell and gasped.

For the church was dead, a deconsecrated hulk, office space and high-rent apartments built into what had been cathedral, modern architecture of red brick growing as geometric cancer from the Gothic edifice. The additions rose high as the main spire, yet the place still had the angry cold aura of a living church. The grey stones seemed held in check by the additions grafted atop them.

The structure was a confabulation of deadly sanctity and grotesque banality, dominating the corner it stood upon despite being the smallest building there.

The Succubus walked toward the church, crossing Beacon Street to see it more closely, with the aspect of her vision that transcended the physical.

The husk of the place's holiness remained; the sickening intrusion of its sanctity into the ether was visible to her like the ghost of the sun etched upon the retina. The husk was the shape and color of a robin's egg cupped over the church and its grounds.

Yet the shell was *dead*.

Inert.

It could not harm her.

She felt a mild, quaking nausea from being so close to the thing. The shell of sanctity had a sundering power about it—like a wave frozen at its crest.

She walked the periphery of the church grounds, along the side that faced Massachusetts Avenue. The place was very near the Charles River. The river's strength was like a living presence standing by her shoulder. She watched the church as she would a snake coiled under a bush, uncertain if it would strike, uncertain if its death was a sham to lure her close so it could devour and obliterate her.

And then the Succubus saw the scars.

The church had been *burned*. Gutted by cleansing flame. Striated marks rose from the church like waves of heat from a forge. Yet they were *still*, frozen in the air.

The nave, once filled with wooden pews and prayer-mumbling

hypocrites, was now open to the sky, made into a courtyard visible through archways that had once held stained-glass windows. The wall stood like a disconnected rampart, reduced to a tall stone fence marking the western boundary of the courtyard.

In the courtyard, new brick walls faced old stone walls mutely. The ground of the courtyard was marked with a crisscross pattern of dirty brown paths trod into the snow connecting the structure's courtyard entrances. Bits of trash, carried by the cold wind, danced and scuttled where parishioners had once lined up for communion.

Leafless, dead-looking trees grew between the icy sidewalk and the soot-blackened nave wall, making the place all the more desolate and pleasing to her eye. There was a squirrel's nest among the naked branches, yet the tree gave shelter to no living thing. She smelled no life; the animal that had made the nest was dead, frozen or starved by the brutal cold that had taken the city. The skeletal fingers of the branches held the nest as an offering to the dead church. As she stared at the tree's offering, she covered her mouth prettily to suppress a giggle.

For a bronze statue of a very feminine angel stood atop the nave wall: a lonely sentinel frozen in midstep on the rampart, dusted with soot and snow. Tears of ice ran down her face. The angel looked down at the passersby, who, with their eyes fixed before their feet, took no notice of her.

How abandoned she looked.

How forgotten.

The Succubus would never be forgotten, like this nameless, blasphemous cousin. The Name she'd earn would be hers for eons, long after this graven image whose face was taken from that imagined by men for the mother of the *Kristos* fell—no longer able to hold on tight with mortar to the top of her wall.

She looked at the corpse church for an hour, watching tumor-ridden pigeons perch upon the spires, their images warping slightly as they passed through the dimmed shell of sanctity. People's images warped too, as they passed through the shell, coming and going from their work in the new office space, which buzzed like a hive in contrast to the stillness of the areas that still had the semblance of a church. At times she retreated to the opposite side of Beacon Street when the death smell became too strong for her.

She was very much a child, with a child's sense of the wondrous, unaware of her past life and damnation. She believed her pilgrimage now to be the first time she'd walked the earth, ignorant that she'd once been a living woman of unchanging flesh, that she was not conjured from the essence of her Patron like a homunculus. She did not know that her form had as the base of its substance a dead soul.

A damned soul.

She had no memory of another burned and gutted church in her past—before her death and her second birth through her Patron's hand—where two centuries before and half a world away she had serviced an officer of the New Caesar atop an altar stinking of oily smoke. He paid her in stones pried from the looted chalice. She had no memory that the smothering of the child born of that union had dropped her to Hell. She did not know that the hybrid demons she looked upon with aristocratic disdain once shat into her screaming mouth, a mocking re-creation of her own crime against Heaven.

All this was forgotten.

As a child she saw herself.

As a child she saw the world.

As a child she moved and dreamed.

And so she had spent this day wandering the city, in the body she'd used to kill Andrew, testing things dangerous to her, seeking them with a fascination like that of an infant's with flame.

She'd gone near a synagogue and a mosque; within each place prayers were held that made the air around her sting like sour pollen. She retreated from the sickness and pain those places caused her.

She wandered to a graveyard near the old center of the city. The cemetery had been given over to tourism because of its age, and was now barely sacred, holiness trampled from the soil. Traces of holiness emanated from the tombstones that leaned like rows of crooked teeth through the snow.

The cemetery rose to a hilly place where the stones were scattered among a handful of sepulchres that had cracked under the weight of years, mortar and stony rubbish tumbling to the ground like spilled goods. Beyond, a gate of iron spikes led to an alley between the tall buildings that pressed close to the graveyard.

The gravestones on the hill draped in forgetful snow reminded the Succubus of strayed lambs grazing on a frozen field. Crouched low, behind a stone carved with winged skulls and lamenting angels, she reached down and tasted the snow the flock fed upon.

It was gritty, peppered with soot.

And what grass there was beneath the snow was the color of the brown fog of a winter dawn, blanched of life, blanched of sustenance, blanched of all hope of the rebirth April would bring.

The trees in the graveyard had roots that clutched deep through the unblessed soil, nourished by rotting vessels that had once held precious human souls. She saw the roots grasping into the solid shadows of coffins underfoot.

She stayed until her essence began to feel oily as the water under a blister, and a sensation of slowly being scalded crept upon her. Traces of sanctity in the stones had started to affect her, taking her like fever.

She felt no such fever *now,* in the shadow of this beautifully murdered church. She was becoming used to the death smell, and the skeleton of the church's sanctity did not frighten her as it had before.

And this gave her a spark of courage.

Courage to do something extraordinary.

She would enter this church—violate it for the sake of her Patron— carrying the part of Hell she held within herself into what had been God's domain, carrying the aspect of her Patron's essence her body represented into the mind of the hatefully Divine.

The Succubus steeled herself, banishing the fear that the church would lash out as she stepped into its maw. The place was dead, the shell not a true barrier. When she crossed the threshold, she'd *not* be obliterated, blasted to a handful of dust. . . .

An animal growled at her.

The Succubus' eyes snapped downward. A small dog gnashed at her feet, straining its leash. The dog's mistress tugged the dog along, staring at the Succubus over her shoulder, as if the Succubus were someone she knew from long ago but did not like or trust.

Her eyes were touched with fear.

And the Succubus realized her body had drifted with her mind. Her features and aura were reflecting the ethereal impressions of the city, the roiling bustle finding outlet in her face and body while she'd been held by the church's gorgon stare.

She pulled the collar of her pea coat high. Then she walked, eyes cast downward, to the entryway of a nearby apartment building. Facing the shining bronze mailboxes by the door, she refined and softened her features, cleaned the aura she projected, changed the texture of her scent, and made pretty again the false soul she carried in her eyes. As a final touch, she made her cheeks flush red, rosy and glowing from the cold air.

She felt almost as beautiful as she did in her natural form. *"Jeannette,"* she thought. *The name of this mask is "Jeannette."*

A dapper old man in a cashmere coat emerged from the apartment

building, and, upon seeing her, smiled and held the door open for
her. The Succubus shyly shook her head no.

And as a human, *as Jeannette,* she walked toward the door of the
dead church.

III

Monday, 12:45 P.M.

L awrence awoke for the second time. After the helpless rage of
being robbed close upon the mind games and nightmares of the
night before, he'd curled in a fetal ball and fallen asleep almost as if
in a swoon.

Now the telephone jarred him to an ugly wakefulness and the ugly
certainty that what had happened was not a dream. Aching, he
walked to the hallway and picked up the phone as his answering machine message clicked on. The Tommy Dorsey band played as
Lawrence's recorded voice said: *"Hello! You've reached Lawrence's
number. I can't make it . . ."*

"Lawrence?" The whining voice at the end of the line cut through
the music and Lawrence's taped voice.

"Yeah. Hold on."

". . . to the phone right now, but if—"

He shut off the message, the corners of his vision unfocused, as if
full of television static. A crick throbbed in his neck.

"Why do you have to have that music on your phone?"

It was Angie, Lawrence's sister. She was thirty, with a thirteen-
year-old son (whom Lawrence hated) and high blood pressure. She
worked at the Rhode Island College bookstore, and her current
boyfriend was a skinny, acne-ridden twenty-three-year-old flunking
out of the RIC teacher's certification program.

Lawrence mumbled something in reply as he sat on the hallway
floor, eyes cast low, the grey winter light on his chest making him
look newly dead.

"Are you *drunk?*"

"No. No, I'm just really tired. That's all."

"Why can't you put something *nice* on your machine?"

Angie's definition of "nice" was "nonthreatening." Even Tommy
Dorsey was suspect, smacking too much of individuality—deviance,
even. Because *old* people were supposed to like Tommy Dorsey, and
when they did, well, that was *nice.*

"Because I like the music I've got on it now."

"Well." The one syllable closed the issue, for obviously Angie had more pressing things to discuss. She hadn't called just to be set off and find comfort at her stupid kid brother's expense, as she had so often before.

"What are you doing for Christmas?" Her tone was accusing, but a tightness in her voice made her sound afraid.

"I don't know. I hadn't thought about it." Lawrence rubbed his neck, wishing Jacob were there to make the vertebrae crack, the way he used to before things got bad, by gently twisting Lawrence's head to the right and to the left.

"Aren't you coming home?"

"Well, yeah. I just don't know when."

"What do you mean, you 'don't know'?" Her voice went up a note.

"I mean, I don't know when I can get off work."

"You *know* this will be Mama's first Christmas without Daddy . . ."

Yes, I know that, you fucking cow. You think I'm as stupid as you?

". . . and we should all be there for her."

"Yes. I know. I'll be there. Maybe Christmas Eve. It depends on how the buses and trains are running, all right?"

Lawrence's voice cracked on the last syllable. His breath quickened.

"Good. We all have to stay together for Mother's sake. You know that, don't you?" With the cracking of her brother's voice, Angie sounded relaxed.

"Yes, I know that. Look, I've got to go to work. I'll call you later, okay?"

"All right." She said this as if she were indulging a transparent excuse.

They each said good-bye and hung up.

Lawrence stood and went to the bathroom mirror. He looked awful: bags under his eyes, skin puffing out. He turned the hot-water tap, lathered his face, shaved.

Angie had reminded him how much he hated the holidays.

Thanksgiving had been a nightmare, the first family gathering since his father's funeral in June. The empty chair at the head of the table made the atmosphere unbearable. As eldest son, Lawrence should have taken the chair, but by unspoken family proclamation this simply would not be. His family was not aware he was gay, but they sensed something unacceptable about him. Thus, through unspoken, unanimous decree, Lawrence was relegated to be the black sheep.

The same silent coalition decided it was a bad thing for Lawrence to move to Boston the next day. Surely he could stay until the first of the month to be with his mother. What was his hurry? Just because he had a job lined up and had his foot in the door of a rent-controlled brownstone with a view of the river and most utilities covered? Just *what* was his *hurry*?

The air was thick with veiled attacks, just as it had been during the Sunday dinners when Lawrence had first moved in with his "friend," Jacob. But now Lawrence was leaving Providence altogether, and all his sins must surely be remembered, from the ever-so-*funny* stories about him falling down the stairs when he was six to the time Uncle Johnny tried to teach him to fight when he first went to high school.

He and Angie had fought after dinner in hissing tones while they washed a mountain of dishes and the rest of the family watched football and drank beer. Lawrence didn't love Daddy enough, she said. And why did he have to leave? Why did he have to go to Boston? Wouldn't he be happier with Mama, living with her while she was so lonely?

Never mind that Angie and her bastard brat could have moved into the attic at any time.

The issue wasn't Mother living alone. The issue was that Angie, and Lawrence's other siblings and cousins, as well as their spouses, needed him around to shit on, to make themselves feel better about their doomed existences in a dying industrial town. That Lawrence was removing himself from their abuse and from what they saw as his responsibility, however remote, for his father's death was profoundly unforgivable.

Lawrence grimaced as the razor nicked a blemish on his cheek. He blotted the cut with toilet paper and dried his face.

He still looked and felt awful. He thought about calling in sick and sleeping the day away. But hiding from the world under warm covers was a defense he'd developed as a child: if things were too horrible to face, take a nap and they'll go away. Dreams afforded temporary shelter, until the inevitable shouting and yelling from downstairs woke him. Besides, if he called in sick, he could lose his job. He'd been working at the bookstore less than three weeks.

Lawrence was about to shower when the thought struck him that Tom had helped himself to other things besides his VCR and cash, small things he could carry in his pockets while both hands held the VCR, that Lawrence wouldn't notice were missing right away.

A sick feeling filled his stomach. He put on his robe and went to the living room.

A good deal of his things were still in boxes in the far corner: summer clothes, books, his Walkman. The boxes were not opened.

He went to the kitchen.

The cabinets had all been opened.

Tom had helped himself to breakfast. A new box of cereal had been opened; a milk carton, almost full, had been left on the radiator to go bad. A dirty bowl and spoon lay in the sink.

Lawrence's jaw clenched, his hands became fists.

The rest of the cabinets seemed undisturbed. Nothing worth stealing in the kitchen, really, but something was not quite right.

It was the garbage bags.

The box of garbage bags that had been flush with the sides of the cabinet above the sink was now in the middle of the cabinet. Why would Tom take a garbage bag?

To carry the VCR in. So he wouldn't be noticed walking down the street with it.

The fucker.

Aside from that, nothing worth stealing in the kitchen.

Then he remembered the valuables in the bedroom; he rushed to his nightstand. The condoms were shredded, cut up by a pocket-knife, maybe, and covered in spit.

But his silver Saint Christopher's medal was safe, far enough back in the drawer to escape Tom's notice. It had been a confirmation gift from his aunt Sarah, one of the few relatives whom he could stand. One of his few relatives who truly loved him.

His silver cross was safe, too.

He put medal and cross back in the drawer, threw out the shredded condoms. Then he went back to the kitchen and threw out the milk, bowl, and spoon. He wouldn't give Tom the satisfaction of washing up after him.

The shower felt wonderful.

Hot.

Steaming.

Washing away the stink of the past night and this day, cleansing his body of Tom's touch.

Things are okay, he said to himself as he dressed. *That fucker took my paycheck. But I can get by on my savings until Friday. I can afford a new VCR soon. Pick one up at an after-Christmas sale. That'll be okay. I can get over this.*

Lawrence had half an hour to get to work. He could grab a sandwich on the way, go past the bank and take the first few dollars out of his savings account. He put on his coat and left his apartment.

Standing in the hall, hand thrust in his pocket, closing around his key chain, he felt something wrong.

He was wearing the jeans he wore last night.

The ones he threw by the side of the bed.

The ones Tom would have tripped over getting out of bed before helping himself to Lawrence's wallet in the back pocket.

When he read the note written on the slip of paper attached to the key ring, his arm convulsed, keys jangling in his palm, an awful spasm in his biceps.

The fucker had taken the wrong key, thank God.

He'd taken Lawrence's key to his parents' house, thinking it the key to his apartment.

But the note left in its stead still froze Lawrence's heart, blinding him with new rage and a new sense of violation:

"I'LL BE BACK, YOU LITTLE SHIT! WHENEVER I FUCK-ING FEEL LIKE IT LOVER! I'LL BE BACK!!!"

IV

Monday, 1:00 P.M.

The Succubus looked back, as a person who has escaped the sea looks back from shore, and saw upon the church's husk the bloody mark of her passing blossoming like a wine stain upon linen.

As she had passed through it, so had it passed through her, rupturing her inner essence, so that it seeped from beneath the false skin of humanity she wore. She stifled a scream, feeling something inside her tear like gossamer in heavy rain.

As she had walked the aisle of ice toward the church's husk, she burned as the desert does beneath the sun. The bitter wind off the river cut through her, and with the awful heat and cold, the feel of sanctity ran over her like a sweating palm, soiling her aura, making her breath oily and heavy with the church's death smell.

She wanted to turn back, flee the fire, the cold, the viscous sanctity. But thoughts of the angel and her martyr's vigil atop the church wall beckoned her. She'd not be driven from the ramparts the angel guarded, defeated by the graven image. She'd penetrate the angel's stronghold, fell its walls, for the glory of her sweet Father.

Love for her Father, summoned from deep inside herself, brought her through the husk and quieted her fear and pain. He, reflected through the prism of Materiality as a presence beside her and brought from without her, escorted her to the other side. And once through the wall that had barred her from the angel's realm, she sang a song of thanks and praise to her Lord, using not her physical voice, but the voice of her aspect that walked through human thoughts, that tasted dreams and extinguished souls.

Then she watched flecks of trash dance in the wind beneath the red mark of her passing, which seemed to wave and flap in an ethereal wind like a sheet.

Aware of people walking by her, she touched her face. Her image had held; the husk's soiling of her aura fell away. She turned and walked along the empty riverbed of the icy sidewalk, toward the looming mountain of the church, called by the resonant specter-voice of what had been the bells in the steeple; their vibrations still marked the air, still made echoes, distant and warped, like bells rung on the bottom of the ocean.

She would come back through the stain she had made; it was part of her realm now.

As was the tomb before her that had been the home of God.

She crossed the threshold praying, as a pilgrim would entering the chapel of a saint.

V

Monday, 1:00 P.M.

The walls had been smashed.

A great, unforgiving fist had crashed from the night sky and obliterated her secret fortress, her protecting, nurturing tower. Cold, brutal darkness flooded in, and the child who had been safe within the tower now lay screaming, rocking back and forth, naked amid broken stones and mortar.

With closed eyes, protected by a shell of White Light within her Comfort Place, Miriam watched the child cry. She had not been within this part of herself since Thanksgiving, when her mother had spoken those awful words with the heavy venom only the most vicious lies can hold.

Miriam reached inside herself, visualizing herself clad in the white robes of a Healer amid the tower's ruins. With trembling, determined hands, she began to rebuild the walls she had once so lovingly assembled.

"You are the first stone. You have the patience and strength of all the

Earth. Upon you and your strength will rest all the stones that shall follow."

The child's cries quieted, ever so slightly, with the placing of the first stone. Miriam held this quieting close, embracing the hope that with the placing of each protecting stone, the child would become more comforted, more healed.

"I am Miriam, child of light, and with this stone, I reclaim my name."

She set the next stone in place.

Again, the child, the wounded little one who had always been deep inside her, quieted her cries.

Miriam gathered the next silent, wise stone and set it with the first two.

"I am Miriam, child of light, and with this stone I reclaim what was taken from me."

She continued the slow process of rebuilding her inner place of safety, while physically she sat nestled within the part of her home where no one could come without her permission or grace—her place of healing . . . healing of her mind and heart and soul. The place where she could make herself stronger, where everything she did was for herself, where she could be away from Elizabeth and the baby and find the balance, the peace and serenity that she deserved.

The child within herself was no longer so naked, no longer so vulnerable. Miriam had rebuilt the foundation wall of her tower to the height of her waist when a truck rumbled past the apartment building, rattling the windows, crunching ice and rock salt strewn on the pavement outside. But she was stronger than that distraction, maintaining her concentration, her determination to complete her tower and so make herself complete.

I am Miriam, child of light, and with this stone I—

The phone in the next room rang; she had forgotten to shut it off. She could be stronger than this distraction, too . . . stay focused within herself and . . .

Her mother's voice.

It intoned over the answering machine, cutting through the thin walls, cutting through her precious shell of White Light.

"Miriam . . . this is your mother. Call me. We need to talk about . . ."

The fist crashed down again from the awful, moonless sky. Miriam fell back from the wall she was rebuilding. . . .

". . . what's going on with you. You can't . . ."

And the child inside Miriam screamed, began its spastic, wounded rocking again, curled up in a fetal ball.

". . . keep hold of this crazy idea . . ."

Miriam herself fell back from her meditation pillows, rolled to the carpeted floor. Her mother's voice. So full of venom, so full of lies.

". . . without hurting everyone around you, not just yourself."

Miriam lay upon the floor in a fetal ball, rocking and crying softly, in unison with the innocent child she had failed by letting her mother invade this sacred space.

"Miriam, are you *there*? Will you pick up?"

Eyes closed, tears streaming down her face, Miriam visualized her mother's eyes, now, as she spoke into the phone: the same look of contempt, of sickened condescension that Miriam had faced when she'd confronted her mother over Thanksgiving.

"Miriam, will you do the courageous thing and pick up this phone and talk to me? We *have to* talk. . . ."

The look of contempt in her mother's eyes when Miriam had told her about what her father had done to her in the night so many times when she was a girl. How he had invaded her and stolen her childhood, her innocence, her very sense of being by forcing himself inside her, making her do those awful things for him.

"All right, then. If you won't pick up, call me when you're ready to talk."

And her mother had met Miriam's gaze and spoken those heavy, wounding words that cut through all of Miriam's defenses and brought the fist down upon her inner tower.

"Your father was impotent. He fell off a ladder when you were two and damaged the nerves at the base of his spine. He didn't do those things to you. He couldn't."

Almost an hour passed before Miriam could stand and erase the message.

VI

Monday, 1:02 P.M.

Can I help you, honey?"

Ghosts of prayers from before the church had been gutted were trapped within the fabric of the stones, the rafters, the air. They were dead prayers, spoken without enough faith to lift them past the mundane world, yet they had been invested with enough desire that they lingered and were visible to her now: faint grey shadows that floated and spun like feathers in still air. Her own murmuring orisons had struck them as she'd entered, illuminating them in stark relief, as if by lightning. Now they nestled in the periphery of her sight.

There were *new* prayers here, as well: vibrant prayers of need and hunger and want that she could see here in the entryway, that she could sense packed tight within the dead church like atrocities within the mind of a lunatic.

They were prayers spoken in desperate silence for wealth and power and acclaim, for stability and respect and influence. Prayers spoken while the new congregation hunched over desks as the believers who had once come here had hunched over their own clasped hands while kneeling. She could feel these desires ulcerating in the hearts of the people who worked here, misdirected desires germinating in covetousness before being breathed into the unfocused buzz this place had. . . .

"Can I help you, honey?"

The Succubus turned slowly and smiled, calling upon the warmth of the mask called "Jeannette." The woman behind the desk in the entryway was in her fifties, plump, with soft brown eyes. The Succubus met her gaze. The woman had a daughter about the age her mask appeared. The Succubus could smell the motherly pang within her heart through the ashen abattoir scent of the church. She drew her woolen coat tight, touching the woman's maternal instincts with this small, awkward gesture as she walked to the desk.

"Oh, it's nothing," she said. "It's just . . ." She lowered her voice to a whisper. "Do you have a ladies' room?"

The woman's smile touched the Succubus' face like a caress.

"It's around the corner and down on your left, honey."

She walked down the hall, feeling the gaze of two men in wool suits upon her as she passed them. Their conversation muted while they both shot their attention to their left, to watch her as she walked past.

She wanted them. She wanted to take their male sureness, their fragile convictions of their own power, and hold these parts of their identities—translucent and quivering in her hands—as she robbed them of their lives, as she pulled them from their bodies.

Yet their souls were sickly as runt infants, not worth her while. But she made shy eye contact with them both, for the pleasure of seeing the rush of *want* whispering in their minds and streaking through the glow of their bodies like sunlight rippling upon water.

When she was stronger she could pursue such frivolous prey. Not now, while so much was at stake.

As the two men walked away, she was aware of one of them looking at her back, and the other bristling that his companion would dare covet what he coveted.

Then in midstep . . .

. . . she had a sensation of being on her back, a welcome strong weight on her belly and chest, the smell of blistered mahogany and the feel of dappled sunlight on her face, of a man's lips on her own.

A glow spread over her, sensuous as the taste of candlelight. A need to be near a being of power and strength filled her, suddenly replaced by the sting throughout her body of residual sanctity. Her skin and aura tingled and itched; she would have to leave here, soon. She placed her hand on the bathroom doorknob, collected herself, and went inside.

The metal pipes resonated with the traffic that rumbled past the building, the footfalls on the floors above, and the flow of water surging within them. She could smell traces of women who had been in this room, the cream-sweet scent of infants laid upon the changing table and the afterbite of human waste in a place where the air had once been thick with the smell of incense and candles.

The Succubus leaned against the door of a stall, wishing she were material enough to defecate here, within this once holy site. Perhaps later, when she had taken more lovers and attained a state closer to True Flesh. Such a gesture would please her Father so. For now, she'd leave something else behind, one final desecration for this savaged church.

She walked to the mirror above the sink and touched her reflection. Beneath the blue glow of fluorescent lights, she breathed out part of herself, a tiny cloud, exhaled as *spiritus*. She gritted her teeth, clenched her fists, as the last strands separated from her. It felt as if skin had been flayed from inside her lip.

She willed it up into an air vent. She felt it float there. As she let go of it with her mind, she was aware of it drifting through the narrow metal corridors like a jellyfish carried by tide. When the time was right, she would know of its landfall.

On her way out the lobby, she thanked the woman behind the desk, who beamed at her and said, "Take care now, honey."

"You, too. And God bless."

Chapter Four

Monday, 1:25 P.M.

The kid was on the corner of Beacon and Mass Ave., wearing an Uncle Sam hat and waving an American flag affixed to a broken lacrosse stick.

Lawrence was barely aware of the kid shouting atop a concrete planter as he walked to work. He drifted in the human eddy that converged at this corner, where Cambridge and Boston bled into each other near the Harvard Bridge, and the sound of traffic from Storrow Drive was as constant as the breaking of waves upon a beach.

After reading Tom's note, Lawrence had rushed into his apartment and torn the note to pieces, then flushed the pieces. He washed his hands, then thought then he should have first burned the note, then flushed the ashes. No sooner had he thought that, than he thought he should have saved the note to give to the police.

As if the cops would have responded to a call reporting such a petty crime. *As if* Lawrence wanted to tell the upstanding and exceedingly tolerant Boston cops that his precious VCR had been taken by a guy who'd fucked him last night. Instead, Lawrence had left his apartment, clenching his keys tight in his hand, as if Tom were lurking nearby to snatch them away. As Lawrence walked to work, he still clutched his keys deep in the pocket of his coat.

Lawrence was just realizing he hadn't eaten since dinner last night when the kid lowered his flag in Lawrence's way.

"And *you*!" bellowed the kid. "Why aren't *you* supporting our troops?!"

The lacrosse stick blocked Lawrence like the drop bar of a toll booth, the flag drooping toward the sidewalk. Lawrence looked up as he felt the crowd bustle around him. The kid was huge—a jocky, frat-boy type. Clean-cut. Suburban as a tract house. And exuding the unique arrogance of a rich kid who knows he can, and will, get away with anything. Exuding the obliviously focused determination that would compel him to stand where freezing winds came off the Charles so he could bark his bullshit at strangers. Lawrence thought of the idiots at the football games his father had loved to watch, who'd strip to their underwear in freezing weather and display their team's colors painted on their flabby torsos.

The kid looked at Lawrence, eyes blazing, jaw set. His face was red with cold, or anger, or both. His ski jacket made him look even bulkier than he was. He wanted to beat Lawrence up, wanted Lawrence to give him *any* excuse to lay into him. Lawrence tried to fathom the banality of facing bodily harm from a boy in a Bicentennial party hat. He wanted, *sincerely* wanted, to tell the kid to fuck off. But Lawrence was too weak after what had happened over the past twelve hours to shrug off this ridiculous challenge.

The kid smelled Lawrence's weakness, like a shark smelling blood. He went for another strike, a happy spark in his WASP eyes.

"What?" said the kid. "You got a *problem* with patriotism? You got a *problem* with loving your country?"

The gloveless hand holding the lacrosse stick was scarlet from the cold, knuckles white. Something in Lawrence's gut made him sick, queasiness shadowing his hunger and his fear of getting the shit kicked out of him. It was like the feeling he had when Angie used to sit at the kitchen table and tell Lawrence to lead a virtuous life while she put handfuls of cold pasta into the mouth of her squalling bastard.

Why aren't you in the Middle East right now? thought Lawrence. *Why are you giving people in the street shit instead of being a good little Rambo and giving shit to Saddam Fucking Hussein?* He couldn't speak. And he knew if he tried, his voice would crack, and thus give this fucker another excuse to give him grief.

Something radiated off the kid that made Lawrence's nerves tingle, made him feel as if the crowd of people on Beacon (who paid this incident no mind) were pressed around him, moving in unison to crush him under the weight of their bodies. Lawrence's vision filled with flickering greyness. His heart fluttered; he thought he heard the buzzing of insects.

"Fuckin' thought so," the kid said, and jerked his flag upward— Lawrence's toll of shit-taking apparently had been paid.

Lawrence walked away, eyes still on the kid as he ranted about "Our sovereign *right* to protect the democratic *rights* of the Kuwaiti people!" The two-block walk to the bookstore was a blur of urban anonymity—figures bundled in heavy coats, winter burdened, shoulders high. He felt hollow, light-headed from hunger and the lingering feel of the crowd pressing upon him.

His heart sank as he entered the bookstore; the store stereo was playing too damned loud.

Lawrence rounded a bank of bookshelves to find Vicki dancing to Diana Ross' "Love Child" behind the counter, with Groucho, the store cat, draped over one shoulder like a stole. Vicki sang along as she danced, mangling the lyrics to suit her dancing partner.

> *"Love Cat!*
> *Sweet as Cherry Pie!!!*
> *Love Cat!*
> *Look into my eye!*
> *Love Cat!!*
> *Gentle as can be!*
> *Love Cat!*
> *Will you marry me?"*

The cat clung to her shoulder, eyeing the ground longingly. No customers were in sight. That was bad; Jack would blame this on the music.

Vicki spun and flashed a bright smile. "Hey, Lawrence!" she said as Groucho's tail began flicking.

"Hey." He wanted to ask her to please turn down the fucking stereo before Jack lumbered down the stairs to dump a world of shit on them both. But he didn't have the strength.

Vicki must have guessed what he was thinking. "Jack left!" she said, with the glee of an eight-year-old saying "No school today!" She never stopped her bouncing dance.

"Oh." Lawrence set his coat, gloves, and scarf on a chair behind the counter. The news didn't make him as happy as it should. Vicki stopped dancing and gave him one of her mother-hen looks, still holding the cat close.

"What's up with you?"

"Nothing." Lawrence didn't want to talk. It was too easy for him to whine while he felt vulnerable and play the Drama Queen. He'd realized, while breaking up with Jacob, what a trap this habit was for him. It was comfortable to bemoan every cheap tragedy that befell you. He wasn't about to show Vicki that part of himself.

"Bullshit, 'Nothing.' " She frowned and set Groucho on the

counter, then turned down the stereo a notch. "You look like your best friend died. What's up?"

Lawrence rolled up the sleeves of his sweater, taking no comfort from the narcotic scent of old books. "I don't want to talk about it."

She gave him another mother-hen look. She was big. Full-figured like a farm girl. And she knew how to play the no-nonsense country girl to the hilt, even though she'd grown up a few subway stops from this store. Her brother still came by on his way to work now and then to drop off sandwiches that their mother made for Vicki's lunch.

"Okay," she said. "But if you want to vent, feel free to pull me away from the military history section. Jack wants me to arrange it chronologically by each war. And since he's such an ignorant fuck, he probably can't figure out when the War of 1812 was fought."

Vicki thought her crack would get him to smile; he just didn't have it in him.

"Okay. Where'd he go?"

"To the doctor's. At least that's what he said, anyway. Maybe he's getting his kidneys checked. We can only hope."

Jack usually had an odor of piss about him. Vicki's theory was that his kidneys were shot, and that uric acid seeped out of his pores.

"Yeah. We can hope."

"If you don't want to talk to me, then at least get some quality time with Groucho. She can cheer anybody up."

Vicki rubbed the cat's head, then leaned forward to brush her nose against Groucho's whiskers. The cat licked her. "Mmmmm. Liver and beef cat food breath." Vicki gave Groucho's ears a rubbing, then turned toward the military history section.

Lawrence took his seat behind the register. Soon, over the sound of the stereo, he heard Vicki pulling books off the shelves and stacking them. Diana Ross faded to "House of the Rising Sun"; Vicki had tuned in the oldies station.

Lawrence hoped he hadn't offended her; he couldn't figure out why she was so overbearing, or whether or not he liked that she was.

When Lawrence had been working here a few days, Vicki had insisted on sharing one of her mom's sandwiches with him, and while he ate it, she went down the block to buy him a coffee light. "I dunno. There's just something about you that makes me want to take care of you," she said in a voice that, if he were straight, he would have found very sexy. Vicki's smile while she said the words had been completely disarming.

Groucho eyed his lap from the counter, and bunched herself up for a leap.

"C'mon, sweetie," he said.

Groucho leapt.

Then she started purring, and curled herself into a ball on his skinny lap. Lawrence stroked her ears as she placed one paw over her black greasepaint muzzle.

Five songs played out on the oldies station. No customers came. At the back of the store, books thudded to the ground as Vicki pulled them off the shelves.

He thought a long while—as a set of Stones songs played—of his friends in Providence, stuck in a dying industrial town, filling their existences with the very empty whining noises Lawrence had been tempted to make with Vicki. Could he really say this bold Boston life of his was any better?

Sitting, alone and hungry in a bookstore with no customers, listening to a song recorded years before he was born, Lawrence wondered if he had merely exchanged one trap for another.

II

Monday, 3:30 P.M.

███y mother called."

Elizabeth came through the door, red from the cold. She smelled of snow, as she had on the days of the winter she and Miriam had fallen in love, and would walk arm in arm through the safe neighborhoods of Somerville and Jamaica Plain. Troy was bundled, red-faced in her arms. He was fussy, his tiny hands in tiny mittens brushing his beautiful face.

Miriam spoke again as Elizabeth handed her Troy and took off her coat.

"My mother called."

"I need space."

Elizabeth propped the stroller in the corner. Miriam cradled Troy and undid his snowsuit. Elizabeth walked to the kitchen; Miriam heard her filling the tea kettle. She followed her, bouncing Troy, knowing she'd have to set him down to get the snowsuit off. Elizabeth had the kettle on the stove, and was taking down her favorite mug—one that she'd made at summer camp when she was fifteen.

"I know," she said. "Your mother called. I need space."

She took her coat off and draped it over a chair by the table. She turned on the radio atop the refrigerator. The reception was bad. She didn't adjust the antenna before rummaging through the drawer where the teas were kept.

Miriam stood by the doorway, the need to talk heavy as a stone by her heart. An NPR report on Coalition forces in Saudi Arabia recorded over international phone lines was made to sound even more brittle because of static. Elizabeth, still searching through the teas, did not look at Miriam.

"I know you want to talk," she said. "But I can't listen, now. I *can't*. Some stupid little white boy accosted me at the Trident Cafe." She lifted her hand and held it up the way a teacher would to quiet a noisy class. "I can't listen to you now." She slowly turned to face Miriam. "I gave you space. Now you give me mine." Her tone was even and steady. But to Miriam, the words felt as if she had yelled them.

Miriam left the kitchen, holding Troy, hearing the kettle rattle, hearing the scratchy voices of the radio speak of ugly things. She carried Troy to the bedroom, set him on the changing table, and took the snowsuit off him. He was getting more fussy, looking as if he were as about to cry.

"Shhh . . . shhh. It's okay, sweetheart. Shhhh."

She carried him to the rocker and wrapped him in his quilt. The quilt was as much a comfort to her as it was to her son. Her cousin, Erica, had made it. On the quilt was the design of a tree with a fish perched among the branches. Erica had said, "Someday, Troy'll be old enough to figure out that fish don't belong in trees. Then he'll know it's okay for rules to be broken, 'cause it'll still be his favorite blanket."

She missed Erica, who still lived in the same neighborhood that held so many of Miriam's ugly memories of childhood.

Miriam rocked with Troy in her arms and sang to him, kissing him now and then and breathing in the caramel smell of his fine hair. Soon, his hair would lose its fineness. She'd have to cut a lock of it before it did and save it.

Troy's eyes became drowsy. Through the closed door, she heard the kettle whistle, then stop.

The winter light became more grey as Miriam, in tones that were soothing, whispered her troubles to her child, who could not understand them. She hoped he would never understand such troubles.

She loved him more than life itself.

When Troy was asleep, she put him in his crib, and pulled a book of women's mythology and spirituality from the shelves near the bed. She turned on the overhead light and read of the blessings of the Goddess as she rocked to soothe herself, while voices from the kitchen—made ugly with static—spoke of impending death and misery and doom.

Winter pressed its hands upon the window.

III

Monday, 3:35 P.M.

Jesus, Lawrence. That sucks."

Lawrence could only nod slightly and shrug as he swallowed a bite of sandwich, the first food he'd had since last night. The stereo was turned down to a faint ambience.

Vicki leaned on the counter to pour Lawrence more coffee. Sitting on the chair by the register, Lawrence thought she looked like a saloon marm in a Western, pouring whiskey.

Vicki's brother, Dave, a hulking guy with a perpetual grin, had come by with sandwiches for Vicki, made by their mom, and a construction-worker-sized thermos of coffee. The thermos was green and banged up, with rust showing through where the dents had lost their paint. It made Lawrence think of Jacob's old Ford, riddled with car cancer.

Vicki had left the military history section to get her lunch and to give her brother some shit about his mangy-dog beard. Dave just grinned wider and said he needed it to keep warm, then lumbered out the store. "When I lived at home," she said, "I used to threaten to sneak in his room at night and smear Nair on his face."

Vicki unpacked her lunch bag at the counter while Lawrence leaned against the register. The bag held two extra sandwiches (wrapped in decorative paper towels), three apples, and a note, which Vicki read and then showed to Lawrence, a wise-assed look in her eye.

The note, from Vicki's mom, suggested that Vicki might want to share some food "with her little friend, Lawrence."

"What the hell is *this*?" he said. His only interaction with Vicki's mother had been to answer the phone a few times when she'd called.

"Mom's playing matchmaker. With food." She reached over and

pinched his cheek. "She thinks you're a *nice* boy she can marry her daughter off to."

"She doesn't really *think* that way, does she?"

"Oh, yes she does."

"She must drive you out of your gourd."

"She's my mom. Of course she drives me out of my gourd." Vicki unscrewed the metal cup on the thermos and poured some coffee. "She probably had Dave bring a whole big thermos over so you and I could have a few special Maxwell House moments together."

"That's sick."

Vicki shrugged.

"That's Mom. At least it's not flavored coffee. Then we'd have to reminisce about some waiter in Paris and giggle."

The smell of the sandwiches made his hunger painful. He reached for one.

"Hey!"

Vicki slapped away his hand and snatched the sandwich out of reach. She pointed to the ring finger of her left hand.

"Not until you make a commitment, big boy. You're not getting a sandwich until we set a date."

Lawrence put his hand on his hip in envocation of queen bitchiness.

"Dream on, honey."

"Go out with my brother?"

"Until he shaves his beard, no."

Vicki raised an eyebrow.

"Only *I* can give him shit about his beard."

"Can I have a sandwich now?"

Vicki furrowed her brow in pantomime of deep thought.

"Mmmmmmmm . . . Okay."

She slid the food to him, then pulled from under the counter a plain white mug with the word JACK'S ominously scrawled across it in thick black marker.

"While the cat's away," she said, and poured Lawrence some coffee.

Lawrence opened his sandwich. Tuna on wheat. Made with bread from a bakery, not a supermarket. Maybe home-baked. Leaves of spinach jutted from under the bread.

Lawrence had eaten half the sandwich before he'd realized it.

Vicki looked at him, jaw agape.

"Have you *eaten* today?"

He shook his head.

"Sit down. And eat slowly. You'll get sick otherwise."

She didn't wait for him to sit of his own volition. She pulled the chair forward and eased him into it.

"Now, *chew*, damn it. You remember how to chew? It's like talking with your mouth full, only quieter."

She handed him the coffee.

Lawrence sipped it to wash down the sandwich. It was thick and strong. Richer than he'd expected, with cream, not milk. It tasted almost like chocolate.

She handed him the sandwich.

"Jesus, Lawrence. Someone's gotta take care of you."

Lawrence took another sip.

"Set me up with Richard Gere?"

"You're better looking than Julia Roberts. Don't sell yourself short." She put her hand on his shoulder, then gave it a slight squeeze.

They ate awhile in silence.

"So, what's up with you, Lawrence?"

He told her.

And now she could only shake her head and repeat herself. "That sucks. That really sucks." She took a sip of coffee. "I can loan you some cash to Friday."

"No. I'll be all right."

"Don't lie to me."

"Really. I'll be all right." Without the theater of the jabs they took at each other—almost like the jabs the characters on *Cheers* threw at each other that Lawrence loved so much—he faced the genuine concern that Vicki showed for him, unalloyed. He'd known this girl a few weeks. How could he like her so much? How could she show him such easy and casual kindness?

A customer came into the store. They both shot up to flash bookstore-clerk smiles and "hellos." The customer, a sorority girl type in an expensive down jacket, paid them no mind and walked into the maze of bookshelves.

Vicki turned to Lawrence.

"If you change your mind, I've got lots of cash," she said. "I was going to blow it in Christmas gifts this week. But I can shop later, if you need it."

Vicki looked him steadily in the eye. Lawrence felt a twinge like the feeling he got when he woke from an upsetting dream . . . yet *nice,* somehow. Comforting. He felt too vulnerable to confront this feeling. He broke eye contact.

"How about if we get married? Then I can sponge off you, and you and your mom will both be happy."

Vicki took her cue, reverted to the jabs.

"I've had enough men sponge off me, thank you very much. And if you . . ."

Another two customers came in. A stampede, by today's standards. Vicki and Lawrence both flashed smiles. One, a college kid, trudged to the boxes of Cliff Notes near the anthology section—exam season. The other waved as he stamped his shoes on the doormat and took off his cap.

"Hey, gorgeous," he said.

Lawrence's heart skipped; a lump formed in his stomach.

It was the man in the leather jacket.

"Hey, Ed," said Vicki. "Where've you been?"

"Exams. Taking and correcting."

The man unzipped his jacket, then walked toward the counter.

"Getting it both ways, huh?" said Vicki.

"Yeah."

Even in the dim light away from the skylight, the man's eyes shone grey. They were the kind of eyes that would change shades with the man's moods. His thick hair was tousled in a way that made Lawrence think of how the man would look early in the morning, just rising from bed. He moved with a graceful strength that Lawrence had not noticed before. He was centered in his movements, like a jock, but with no hint of arrogant swagger.

Vicki said, "We got a bunch of Mike Hammers in yesterday."

"Not in the mood for Hammer," he said, reaching the counter. He looked at Lawrence, then gave him a quick smile with an upward nod that made Lawrence realize he'd been staring.

"Hey. What's up?" the man said.

"Not much," said Lawrence. He could smell clove cigarettes, and an intoxicating musk, different from what he had smelled a few days before. It could have been cologne or the natural musk of his body. Lawrence wanted to chime in, to try to flirt with the man while Vicki acted as a buffer this time. But he was afraid he'd say something stupid. Besides, that Vicki *knew* the guy put their meeting on Friday in a new light. Nervous arousal crept as an ache in his crotch. He was glad to be sitting, for if he stood, his knees would tremble.

Vicki leaned on the counter and poured herself more coffee.

"So what're you looking for today?"

"Unmitigated shit." He made a sweeping gesture on the syllable *shit*, like a conductor punctuating a flourish. "Something where someone gets blown away every three pages."

"That rough a semester?"

"Worse."

"But no Mike Hammers?"

"I think I've read them all."

Lawrence made a note to find out more about Mike Hammer. All he knew was from the TV show with Stacy Keach.

Suddenly, Vicki spoke in a broad parody of a New York accent: "Yeah. But dat Mickey Spillane. He sure is a swell writah."

The man smiled. (*God! A beautiful smile.*) And then spoke in a New York accent, too.

"Yeah. He sure is a swell writah. So . . . whaddayah wanna do tonight?"

Vicki kept up the Bowery Boys accent.

"I dunno. Whadda *you* wanna do?"

"I dunno," said the man. "Whadda *you* wanna do?"

Vicki and Ed both wore shit-eating grins, and Lawrence wished to God he knew what the hell they were talking about.

Then, as if it were the most natural thing in the world, Ed helped himself to a sip from Vicki's mug.

Vicki didn't bat an eyelash.

"We got a couple of boxes of some really trashy reads in a couple of days ago," she said.

"What kind of stuff?" The man set down the mug.

"Stuff with lots of explosions on the covers."

"Perfect. Where are they?"

"In milk crates near the adventure section. We haven't found shelf space for them, yet."

"They're really crappy-looking?"

"Pure shit."

"I'm sold. Thanks, Vicks."

Ed turned and gave them both a small wave, almost a reflex action, then walked toward the adventure section. The maze of bookshelves swallowed him.

Lawrence shot forward.

"He's a *regular*?"

Vicki picked up an apple and twisted off the stem. "Ed? Yeah. He's in here all the time. When he doesn't have school, he basically lives here. Jack hates him. Reason enough to like him, right there."

Lawrence told her about when Ed had been in the store on Friday, how he'd had to direct him to the mystery section. Then he said, "So, if he's in here all the time, he'd know where the mysteries were. So he was really just finding an excuse to talk to me, right?"

Vicki rubbed the apple against her sweater and shook her head.

"Ed's a space case. The classic absentminded professor. He's constantly forgetting the layout of the store. The man's lost in his own little world. Sorry, Lawrence. He wasn't hitting on you. His brains are fried. That's all. Exams and papers."

There was affection in her voice, whether for Ed or for Lawrence, Lawrence couldn't tell.

"Besides, Lawrence. We moved the mystery section about a month ago. Lots of regulars aren't finding it."

Lawrence leaned back in his chair, then put his feet on the counter. Lots of customers *had* been asking for the mystery section, regulars among them. He'd just assumed people were looking for light reads, with Christmas approaching and exams ending.

"Fuck."

Vicki bit into her apple, chewed a bit, and said, "Ed's a good guy. But I don't think he's gotten laid in about six years. He's a grad student. Obsessed with his work. And when he's not working, he's reading cheesy books."

"Ever sold him any Gordon Merrick?"

She smiled.

"No." She bit into her apple again.

"Shit," said Lawrence.

"I thought you were saving yourself for Richard Gere."

"I am. But I'm not giving up on second stringers."

"That's practical."

Groucho jumped onto the counter and began furiously sniffing Lawrence's sandwich. Lawrence pulled a bit of tuna from under the bread and gave it to her. Her rough tongue slid along his fingertips. Then the cat sat on the counter, staring at him, wide-eyed.

Vicki said, "Don't take it so hard. I've seen a lot of people hit on that guy, and he doesn't even notice it."

"Small comfort."

"Yeah, but you're in good . . ."

Vicki didn't finish. Ed walked to the counter and set down a big, faded hardcover with no dust jacket.

Vicki asked, "No macho mayhem today?"

"Nah. I saw this mother, and I need it for my work."

Vicki made no move to ring up the purchase. Lawrence stood and picked up the book. He flashed her a quick *"You bitch!"* look; she responded with a not very discreet wink and took a bite of apple.

Lawrence opened the book to its title page, which he couldn't read because it was in Latin, and rang up the resale price.

"Have you guys met?"

Lawrence at once wanted to kick Vicki for prodding him into a hopeless situation and to thank her for breaking the ice. Instead, he looked at the man *(God, what eyes)* and handed him the book.

"No," said the man, taking the book.

"Lawrence, this is Ed. Ed, Lawrence."

The two men shook hands. Ed's hand was large and strong and warm and dry—not a trace of nervous sweatiness. Lawrence felt the telltale calluses on Ed's palm, just beneath where the fingers joined the hand—the man lifted weights. Regularly. Lawrence thought of what Ed must look like unclothed. Or shirtless, sweating as he worked out.

While the pleasantries of introduction were exchanged, he could only think of the feel of Ed's hand, and what it would be like to have both his hands on his body.

Ed walked away from the counter, and Lawrence felt Vicki's eyes upon him. He didn't meet her gaze, but watched Ed as he stopped by the door, the hardcover opened in his hands as he read a few passages, his lips moving slightly.

What kind of guy can't wait to read a book in Latin? he thought.

Lawrence looked at Ed, lost in his own little world, and wanted to find a way to share a small part of that world with him.

IV

Monday, 3:40 P.M.

Shadows dream.

Vessels of the residue of sleep, shadows release dead dreams by day, silent amid active thoughts and thoughtless activity. Abandoned dreams condense out of shadows as stigmata before rising to the ether that is both creation and creator of human unconsciousness.

The dreams of those who have died in their sleep call to the living by day, who are no more aware of them than they are of the flaring deaths of distant suns. Some of the living are aware of these dreams remotely, in the way the blind are aware of color. Yet the awareness passes before it can be named in thought, only to be given shape later as dreams that are in turn forgotten come morning.

Shadows whisper the aches of regret that the living, in wakefulness, will not hear.

Fever took the Succubus as she walked, weakened and dazed, in a fog of shadow-dreams. She felt them in each breath she took, upon her eyes, upon her mouth. She tasted the distillate of the spirits that had concocted them, the dust of the minds that had given them form.

The shadow-dreams made a cacophony of her senses. The dreams made the air tremble, made the light of day in the city dappled, like the light of a thick wood.

Entering the church had done this to her.

Now her body was oversensitive to the spiritual detritus that hung in the ether. The dreams clung to her in the way the destitute cling to the robes of a priest, pleading for absolution—in the way lice cling to beggars, burrowing through filthy rags toward blood.

She walked doubled over, all of Winter gathered into her being, entwined with the burning fever. All before her seemed like stones at the bottom of a clear running stream, an expanse of partly knowable shapes distorted as by the water's movement. She saw passersby as auras of violet and grey and dusty blue. Buildings became featureless walls. Her nonphysical senses were livid and raw as new scars emerging from burned skin.

She wished only to go home.

The anger of a young couple arguing in a passing car struck her as hard as a slap. The terror of a dying woman in the depths of a hospital blocks away gripped her like a great fist that clenched and unclenched in time with the woman's breath. The ridiculous love an old man felt for the cat upon his lap as he sat within a building she passed made her heart race. All this, while dying dreams invaded her awareness, incessant as the drone of bees in a hive.

Her fever neared delirium. Beneath her clothes, she felt her body shifting from its natural state to the mask she knew as "Jeannette." She pulled the collar of her coat high.

She wished only to go home.

She called from within herself Andrew's strength, his gentleness, and the love he had felt for her. She made this strength her own, made it join the stream of her blood.

Her fever quieted.

It awoke as she came to the recessed wall of the alley beneath her home. She could not rise to where she slept. And if she could, she would not dare to in daylight.

She fumbled with her coat.

She drowned within herself, her body like an ocean. Soon, she was unclothed: a lovely woman, flushed with fever in a freezing alley. Her musculature shifting. The length of her limbs and hair, shifting. Skin turning blood-red, then black, then cream. She hid her clothes in a dry nook behind bricks she had loosened.

She longed for the comfort of Andrew's arms. The sound of his voice. She fell to her knees trembling.

Blind to what the living knew as sight, she held her hand before her face.

She willed her hand to nothingness.

Her arm to nothingness.

The sea of her body fell quiet.

Her shoulder and heart, she willed to nothingness.

The cacophony of dead dreams quieted, her fever cooled.

Soon she was mist, flowing in a stream along a drainpipe to her rooftop home.

December wind passed through her. Now the Winter in her being was cleansing, liberating. She flowed over the lip of the rooftop's coping, then over diamonds of snow she felt radiant beneath her. She curled among the ducts and aerials as morning mist curls around the trees of a grove.

Here, without a body, she knew rest.

Slowly, she re-formed herself from mist finer than that which she breathed into the cold while in the guise of the living. The clinging gossamer of shadow-dreams was gone as she became solid enough to feel snow buckle under her weight.

Yet the fever returned with her body . . . lessened, but still painful. Weakened, sick, she thought again of her lover; her memories of him, called from her mind and entwined with the fabric of her body, were the only remains of his soul. She smelled Andrew on her body, his spirit beading upon her like fine sweat. She felt again the poetry that rang in his heart.

The weight of Andrew's dissipated soul within her body was too heavy for her to carry in this stricken state. She longed for the physical sensation of his comfort, but could not endure her body.

She again made herself fog and drifted through the building, finding solace in the feelings of *"home"* she found among the apartments, and in the joining of her being with warm, heated air.

V

Monday, 3:45 P.M.

Bodies, pressed close. Minds, closed inward upon themselves, keeping other minds at bay—stealing what privacy they can by hiding within a maze of aimless thoughts.

A column of humanity moves upon the earth within a metal green dragon that roars along a path of broken stones. Within the metal dragon, a landscape of blank faces. The breaths of animals in a warren (hoping they are safe), and the lingering smell of stale coffee and cigarettes upon those breaths. The smell of colognes and perfumes and of stress-sweetened sweat. Of dry-cleaning fluid on laundered suits and overcoats. Of waterproofing and mink oil on leather jackets, coats, and shoes.

Animals in a warren.

Hunted by something they cannot name or define. Will is paralyzed. Minds pace in cramped circles. Vision—straining to see the invisible bars of the prisons people have constructed for themselves—has grown so weary that all the world seems a prison.

This is the time of an inner autumn, when those returning from work think October thoughts as they reacquaint their pacing minds with their shocked and weary bodies. When they can slow themselves enough to feel how jangled their nerves are. No matter the season, *this* hour begins twilight as people begin their wanderings home, on foot, by car or bus or by trolley. No one truly speaks now; talk is merely a tool to quiet the mind, to leech the day's turmoil as empty, pointless words.

This is the hour of the soul's assassination.

Hearts beat within breasts muffled in cotton and wool. Were the green metal dragon—and the city it snakes through—to fall silent, and were the flesh holding those hearts to transmit sound as does air, the beating of those hearts would be deafening. Hundreds of tiny fists striking hollow drums. A wall of arrhythmic sound born of a wall of sagging humanity.

Paul stood within that wall, listening to his own heart, willing his true self to eclipse the other person—the doppelgänger—he became while he was at work. His mind

("... *survival of the fittest* ...")

slowly reclaiming itself

(". . . look, these are good kids, not city *kids . . .")*
from the cacophony that had claimed it for most of the day.
(". . . your fault for making it due on a Monday . . .")
Paul's stomach was sour: too much coffee today. No solid or nourishing meal. He'd been grinding his teeth. Earlier, in the teachers'
lounge, he'd rubbed his jaw awhile, coaxing it to loosen. He opened
his mouth just a bit and his jaw cracked loudly, sending a flash of pain
up one side of his face.
(". . . are you proud to know about this shit?")
Paul closed his eyes, trying to convince himself he stood alone.
The press of bodies was too great, the feel of other people's auras too
invasive.

He opened his eyes.

The trolley creaked to a stop. The passengers, those standing and
sitting, lurched toward the front of the trolley as it slowed, then
back as it stopped, like stalks of willow grass under ebbing floodwa-
ter. Paul edged his way to the doors and stepped onto the trolley stop
coated with black ice that had melted to slush and then refrozen
around the footprints of those who had walked here days ago. The
train doors snapped shut, and the trolley rattled down Commonwealth Avenue toward Kenmore Square, where it would flow into
the maze of subway tunnels under the city. Radiant heat from the
trains had melted the snow on the tracks, exposing the winding bed
of gravel the rails rested upon; the stones had been blackened by soot
and exhaust.

Paul stood a moment, then walked toward Melvin Street, filthy ice
breaking like crystal underfoot.

When he reached his building, he felt the person he had been at
work slip away, just partly. Once in his apartment, he stripped off the
remaining mask by removing his suit and tie, changing into jeans and
a flannel shirt.

He still felt the suit on him, aware of it like a phantom limb. He
felt an absence within himself, as if something had been drawn out
the way something unknowable and unnameable is drawn out of the
vibrant green of grass before the coming of a summer storm.

As he hung the suit, he thought how one day he would come
home too tired to change out of it. Not just physically tired, but psy-
chically. His spirit drained by the struggle to keep himself alive inside
the character he played while he taught, beaten by the doppelgänger
who took his place in the mirror each morning as he tied his tie.

He would either die metaphorically from the suit and tie, or he would die in fact, as his father had died when he was so young. Thirty-eight years old when something inside him burst while he rode the bus to work. His father had died on a rainy day, lying on the muddy floor while the driver careened the bus into the hospital parking lot. The driver had come to the funeral. He had a jowly, sad face. Paul had thought then the driver had been crying.

Paul sat in the ugly, comfortable chair that Jo had salvaged from her parents' basement. It still smelled of cobwebs and dust, no matter how many times he and Jo had washed the vinyl and vacuumed the creases. He felt his heart still beating the quick and furious beat it had while he was at work, while he spoke to the unhearing students he thought he could reach. He willed the voices in his head to quiet, snuffing them out.

Paul was not much younger now than his father had been when he'd died, old enough to appreciate the state of mind his father had been in when he'd come home from work.

Paul remembered waking from a nap when he was a little boy, then running to his parents' bedroom to greet Father and ask him if they could work on the model of the starship *Enterprise* his father had bought for him a few weeks before.

The bedroom door was open, and though he wanted to run in to see Father, he did not. For he had learned that barging into a room was *rude*—something you were not supposed to do. His father was sitting on the edge of the bed in his suit, staring at his feet with an empty gaze, one shoe in his hand, too tired, it seemed, to remove his other shoe. He looked sad, like a king in a storybook Paul had read whose heart had broken when he had heard his warrior son had died in a faraway battle. Only magic could cure that king, and Paul had no magic that could help his father.

For the lifetime young boys know moments to be, Paul stared at his father. The whole world felt impossibly quiet, like when Paul was alone reading comic books, and would suddenly look up from the bright pages to feel a stillness as solid as the walls of the house itself.

Paul was about to steal away when Father looked up and smiled at him.

It was as if Father had woken from a bad dream.

"Hi, Paul," he said, and let the shoe he held fall. Father took a few steps toward Paul, walking as if he had a limp, because he wore only one shoe. Paul walked to him without knowing it. Father kneeled and held Paul, tousling his hair.

"How're you doing, son?" he said in his deep and gentle voice.

And Paul, with his arms around his father, knew in that moment his dad was taking comfort *from him*. That, just as Dad had held him to comfort him, to make him feel better, like when Paul was really little and had woken up screaming with an earache, Paul could hold his dad to make *him* feel good.

"Hi, Dad," he said.

His father tousled Paul's hair again and said, "Let me change, then we'll help your mom with dinner."

Paul went downstairs to help his mother. When Father came to join them, he seemed happier and healthier and stronger than the king in the storybook had been after he had been healed.

And after dinner and washing up, Paul and his father had worked on the *Enterprise* model, carefully priming the plastic before painting it. Father patiently explained what parts of the vessel were engines, where the bridge was, and explained how—within the fictional reality of the TV show—the ship traveled unimaginably far. A few years before, Father had explained how unimaginably far the Apollo astronauts had traveled to get to the Moon.

To this day, Paul remembered the smell of those paints and epoxies, and to this day, when he thought of those smells, he felt his father close to him, felt as safe and happy as he had when they had made models together.

When they were done priming the model, Paul's father slumped in his chair, just slightly. And Paul knew that all the things that had made his dad sad and tired, all that he had suffered during the day, had not gone away. They'd just been quieted awhile.

The model was now packed in a box in the apartment's hallway closet, along with other models Paul and his father had made of ships from *2001,* of lunar modules and of NASA rockets. Paul's father had made no distinction between the spaceships of fiction and the spaceships of reality. He taught Paul to dream, showed him the infinite possibilities life held.

What dream, then, did Paul own now: a young man who no longer remembered his father's eyes? His father and mother had wanted him to inherit a legacy of aspiration, of the realization of dreams.

Was this the life they had wanted him to lead?

Paul leaned back in the chair and tilted his head upward.

He realized, for the first time, that the last thing his father had seen before he died was the ceiling of a commuter bus, and the frightened faces of strangers who would never know his name.

VI

Monday, 5:44 P.M.

T eeth punctured her and she came.

As one sensation, she felt the hot breath and the excitement of her killer, and the pain of her body being rended. She felt the great mouth enveloping her, and the pulse of her blood upon the face of the thing killing her. She tasted her blood as it flowed into the creature's mouth, felt herself squirming against its lips as saliva flowed into her wounds.

Every nerve in her purloined body sang with agony—so small a heart beating so fast, it felt as if it would burst. The creature raised its claws to her body as it held her in its mouth.

Her flesh tore. Bone ripped. Cold air touched her innards, replaced by the scalding heat of the creature's breath.

The entity whose body she had stolen was a dim spark. She pitied it. But she would not let it die. The brandy of its death was too sweet. What she learned, *felt,* was too precious for her to grant the mercy of death.

Finally, her spine tore. Her stolen eyes went dark. The vessel that held her was shattered; that which owned the body died as she joined the rest of her being, which floated in a fine cloud above the body she had quit.

There, as mist and *anima,* she watched the cat feed on the mouse she had invaded, still feeling, remotely, the pleasure the cat felt in taking prey.

She had not intended, at first, to do this.

Earlier, as night came, black and calming, the dreaming shadows fell silent. She would have no fever were she to again make herself flesh. Yet her senses were so heightened, she did not dare re-form her body. To have nerves, to have skin, to feel the crushing weight of her skeleton would have been too much to bear.

She flowed into the crevices of the building—places that had not seen light since the building had been constructed a century before. Ages of dust had settled into these hidden places, where the echoes of the souls who had lived in the building swirled upon one another like the brushstrokes of an artisan.

She passed through the joint of an eroded pipe into the rapids of steam flowing through the heating system. She fought the steam and coursed into the great furnace, feeling herself join with the bright orange flames, the heat of the sun infused with her essence. The roar of the flames shook the air so violently, it was as if she had melded with the waters of a cataract.

She left the furnace and rose through the floors, through spider-webs woven through almost every cranny of the building. She extended a minute part of herself through the intricate lace of a spider's egg sac, then through the jointed passageways and vaulted rooms of the husk of the spider that had woven the sac.

Between walls, she flowed over faint traces of blood that had been spilled when a workman had cut himself upon a nail that still jutted from the wood like a crooked finger. She drifted into cabinets, into a closet invested with the violet-sweet fear of a child who had spent hours each night staring at the closet, waiting for a great and terrible beast to lash out at him.

She drank of the fear. And of the shadows given life by that fear.

She did not enter any occupied apartment. She did not wish to be near any living human. But she did feel life between the walls that intrigued her, that called her.

She found the mouse curled within a nest of shredded paper and cloth. It woke when she came near. She paralyzed it with a thought, working a portion of her essence through its warm fur, insinuating herself into its body, wanting to simply sense the nature of the animal's life, and to know the context of its body. She was at once sensation and that which sensed, feeling the delicious panic of the mouse as it felt her penetrate its being.

The mouse longed to run to the shelter of its nest, not realizing it was already in its nest. It could not fathom the futility of its desire, any more than the people of this aching city could understand the futility of their desires.

She needed to know such futility, to understand that which drove the living toward the stifling of their souls. She needed to know how the living could be shackled by stupidly misdirected desires.

She needed to know what it was to be prey, so that she might better stalk her own prey.

She forced the mouse out of its nest, guiding it as if it were a puppet toward the smell that it dreaded, the smell that made the entirety of the mouse's awareness a landscape of blind terror.

Toward the smell of a predator.

She forced the mouse through a crack into the kitchen of an apartment. She pulled it to the center of the floor, holding it still while every fiber of its being pleaded for the dark safety of its nest.

A cat stalked into the kitchen, filling the mouse's vision like a great moving mountain. She saw her stolen body suspended in the amber of the cat's eyes, and thought of how Andrew had found a small part of himself in her gaze.

The cat stood, looking at its prey. But the cat did not pounce nor lunge. Instead it crouched, raised its hackles and hissed, then backed away.

It felt the Succubus in the flesh of its prey.

Quietly, deftly, she extended part of herself into the cat. She felt the heat of the cat's blood, smelled the fear of the mouse. Smelled the flesh and the fur of the mouse, felt the need to rend and tear and felt . . .

. . . herself.

She felt the fear of the cat that *something* watched it. That something stalked it. She felt its paralysis, its panic meshed painfully with the desire to take its prey.

The Succubus made the mist of her being finer, dissipating herself so minutely that the cat could not sense her. She sped up the cat's heart, clenched its muscles until they ached. Filled its belly and spirit with hunger that eclipsed its fear.

Then she freed the mouse, setting it loose yet keeping her awareness within it, feeling its panic as it ran to the baseboards.

The movement stirred the cat, woke its every hunting instinct.

She felt the joy of the cat's lunge, then freed it, mostly, so she could better know the sensations of the prey.

And as the cat jumped upon the mouse's back, as its claws pinned the mouse to the floor, she knew, for just an instant, what her lover had felt as she took his sweet life.

Then the cat released the mouse, batting it away to pounce again.

She lost herself as the cat toyed with the mouse, being at once predator, prey, and observer. Her senses flooded with fear and delight, with hunger and terror.

And slowly, building within her nonphysical being each time the mouse was caught and released, she felt arousal.

Joy and desperation. Hunger and fear. Building within the Succubus until they reached a crescendo when the cat's fangs pierced her, and she felt in her bodiless from the pleasure she had known before only within flesh.

Now the Succubus watched, with sight not limited by the need for eyes, the cat gut the mouse.

She withdrew the last speck of herself from the cat, leaving the afterglow of its kill, its urge to place the carcass upon the pillow of the woman who cared for it.

The Succubus flowed to her rooftop home through a vent, moving as mist through the unbroken snow, through the crystalline perfection of each exquisite flake that seemed an infinity of ice cathedrals, delicately stacked upon one another.

She made herself solid beneath the snow, reclaiming her body, healthy and whole and free of fever. Her physical senses were muted by the intensity and the release of what she'd experienced. Her frozen blanket did not break as she re-formed, but molded itself to her, as if she had been gently buried as it fell, flake by flake, from the changing sky.

Exhausted, still bathing in the pleasure she'd felt as the mouse died, she thought how she could apply the lessons she had learned from the cat to the pursuit of her own prey.

She drifted in something the living could know as neither sleep, nor death.

VII

Monday, 7:50 P.M.

The Man with the Knife waited for Arthur as he pulled into the driveway.

As he had waited for Arthur on many nights.

"Check the house."

"I know," he said, more harshly than he'd intended.

Inid slumped in the passenger's seat, embarrassed. "I'm sorry."

"It's okay."

Again, Arthur had spoken more harshly than he'd intended. His wife hung her head. He knew she wanted to apologize again, for irritating him by apologizing the first time. With that knowledge came a stab of pain near his heart.

The headlights cut the darkness, made jagged shadows on the snowbanks piled along the walkways of the complex. His gaze went to the rearview mirror, where it met the eyes of the fourteen-year-old girl in the backseat. The child rolled her eyes and shook her head slightly. How close was his daughter's exasperation for her mother to that which he'd felt for his parents when he had been her age? Arthur deeply wished he could make her understand what made her mother the way she was.

He rounded the car into the parking space that cost as much per month as his first apartment had. Inid looked at him, and apologized again not with her voice, but her eyes. He opened the car door, leather seats creaking under him.

The cold was a slap to his face. It reached under his Burberry and suit to his flesh. He jangled his key ring as he walked to the front door.

She never thinks of what would happen if a guy really is *in the house. Never thinks that she should have the car keys so she could drive away for help or just get away if I stumble out of the house with a knife in my back.*

He unlocked the front door of their unit, gloves still on, for they were supple enough that he did not need to take them off. Arthur walked through the unit, each shadow looming like an immense madman—The Man with the Knife.

Flick.

The hallway was safe. Burnished maple paneling glowed with the torch-like light of amber bulbs in the hall fixtures.

Flick.

The living room was safe. The black enamel of the stereo and big-screen TV shone from the track lighting above and the torchère in the far corner.

Flick.

The kitchen was safe, fluorescent light gleaming off the copper pots Inid had insisted upon getting because aluminum pots were known to cause Alzheimer's. They rarely used the pots, or the dishwasher they had bought last year, for the three of them usually ate out or ordered out. The dreaded Man with the Knife could have been hiding behind the dishwasher, having, of course, broken both his legs and his arm to contort himself into so small a space. Inid had once feared this, when they had first bought the dishwasher.

Arthur suppressed a flash of anger. *It's not her fault.*

Upstairs, now.

Flick.

A safe hallway.

Flick.

A safe bedroom.

Flick.

A safe room that had been dubbed "the computer room."

Flick.

Another safe bedroom.

A safe house.

Arthur was uncomfortably warm. The heat had been left on while they were out, yet the lights had not, for Inid still wished to conserve what energy they could—a remnant of the environmentalist past Arthur and she had shared in college. They had, for a while, used timers to ensure that the lights were on when they got home. But Inid was never convinced of the safety of the house until she *saw* the second-floor lights go on; only the ritual of *turning on* lights could banish the intruder.

Arthur trotted downstairs, Burberry slung over his arm, to find Inid and Meli in the hall, taking off their coats. They were both very beautiful, and as much as Inid and her fears might drive him crazy, he still felt a love for her that had kept them together through all her crises, real and imagined. And Meli . . . Meli was so lovely, she seemed to make the polished wood of the hall dim with her presence, as if the glow of maple had been drunk up by her skin.

Arthur and his wife stole away upstairs, leaving Meli to her homework. They talked about what Inid had suffered at work that day. Inid cried, a little, and then the two of them made love, quietly, so that Meli could not hear.

His wife still seemed tense and frightened, even as she dozed in his arms. He thought he should wake her so they could see to Meli—if their daughter finished her homework by ten, they all would watch a video together that she had picked. But he didn't, thinking of the pet rabbit he'd had as a child, who, even as it slept on his lap, still trembled slightly, untrusting.

And as Arthur fought the urge to doze off, his daughter, terrified of the changes her body had been suffering, terrified of the maturation that was slowly making her a living shadow of the mother whom she hated in a small way she could not articulate, terrified that she would soon no longer be her father's little girl, stuck her finger down her throat and vomited a fifty-dollar entrée into the toilet off the kitchen, careful not to gag too loudly.

She could not face the shame she would feel if her parents heard.

VIII

Monday, 8:49 P.M.

Lawrence turned on the hall light and froze.
    Someone was in the apartment.
    Holy Christ. Please. Please don't let it be Tom. Please don't let him have picked the lock and be waiting for me.

He stood, unmoving, a full minute.

Knowing the thump of his heart.

His lips trembled as he silently spoke the Lord's Prayer.

Something breathed in the emptiness. He felt it behind him. Around him. Felt it in the peripheries of his senses. The shadows were too sharp, like those at dawn or dusk. The darkness was heavy. Lawrence waited in the unnatural quiet for the creak of Tom's jacket as he stepped from the darkness to kill him. The step of his shoes as he crept to smash him in the head and leave him to die alone and un-noticed. His death unavenged, his life made meaningless. Just another stupid faggot killed when he brought home Mr. Wrong. He'd go back to Providence in a bag.

The density of the silence made the air itself as heavy and cold as deep water.

The sense of a man standing nearby grew more tangible.

Lawrence felt the man move, at once behind him and before him, drifting through the apartment walls like the light of a lantern shone across the trees of a forest.

Lawrence heard, faintly, the sound of someone walking in the hall-way outside the apartment. The jangle of keys.

He should move, now. If Tom was in the apartment, Lawrence could cry out and be heard by the person in the hall.

He stumbled to the living room and turned on the light.

No one was there.

But he still felt someone there.

The presence was different now. There was no threat to it. Just empty sadness. A vague sense of that sadness having form like a man, at once standing and drifting, ghostlike at the edges of his senses the way the blue-green residue of snow blindness stands and drifts in the corners of sight.

Lawrence heard from the hallway outside the tumble of keys and the turn of a lock. The presence faded, and was gone. The shadows became less hard-edged. The silence became mere quiet.

Slowly, for the sound of fabric rustling would jangle his nerves, he took off his coat and sat in the one chair he owned. He thought a moment. He'd known the phantom that had accosted him. The same heavy sadness had followed his friend John in the days after his first lover had died of AIDS. It was the same heavy sadness, meshed with fear, that had cloaked itself upon John as he wondered how many years were left to him. At times, the sadness and fear had seemed more real than John himself. John had become a creature of absence. Hollow-eyed, vacant. Too empty to hold even grief.

Lawrence had known this phantom. And knew why he had felt it near him tonight.

It was the shape he'd given his fear not only of Tom coming to take his life, but also the fear that, despite the condom, that Lawrence had been exposed to the virus last night. Tom was the kind of guy who could rip you off just as easily as he could fuck you, knowing he was HIV positive, and then get a good night's sleep.

Tom was the incarnation of a body of fears. When Lawrence had been young, he'd had recurring panics, like what he'd just experienced. Panics that a hulking thing of shadow stalked him through his parents' house, and waited outside his bedroom door to bludgeon him to death with its fists.

When he was older, Lawrence realized this thing was the shape he'd given his fears about his father, who did not (often) beat him with his fists, but did often beat him with words, with belittlements, and tones of voice that barely hid contempt.

Lawrence locked his door, then fished a paperback out of his coat pocket. He made tea, then went into the bedroom and changed his sheets; he couldn't bear to have any trace of Tom near. He settled into bed with his tea and read the paperback, a Perry Mason mystery—*The Case of the Howling Dog.*

As he read, he became aware of a scent—over that of the clean sheets—that he did not recognize. It was the scent of a man. At first, he thought it was Tom's scent, mingled among the blankets. But the scent was not Tom's. There was a heavy musk to it.

He could not place it. The scent was very sexy, yet comforting.

Lawrence dozed off, and dreamt of lovely poetry that stirred his heart and touched his very soul. The poetry resonated through his mind and senses, lifting his spirit in a way he could not imagine.

He was aware, only dimly, that the poetry was in a language he did not know.

IX

Monday, 11:45 P.M.

T *isiphone."*

The Succubus sat upright, her meditation and prayer broken. Caked snow fell from scarlet limbs. Naked, half buried in the snow she had transubstantiated beneath, she heard the sounds of the city and the reverberation of the million-odd souls within reach of her senses.

Had she heard the word with the hearing of her physical being? Or of her ethereal being?

She heard her hair billowing in the wind, the dancing of minute crystals of ice across the expanse of snow spread over her rooftop, the whisper of a night-prayer and the echoes of troubled sleep too heavily burdened with dreams.

Then again. *"Tisiphone."*

It was her Patron's voice, singing in her mind like dream chimes. Her heart leapt, her breath quickened. *Was he here?* She could feel him—his kindness, his warmth, his gentle, sensuous strength. The force of his mind, his Will, as great as the weight of a thousand suns. The force thrilled her, so very *alive* compared to that aspect of her Father she'd drawn out of herself as she'd walked to the dead church.

A third time. *"Tisiphone."*

And then he was gone, his passing a vacuum in her mind and heart, his being muted as if drawn behind a curtain. His absence was an ache in her heart. She felt an incompleteness, as if she had been torn from her body.

Why had he come only to leave so suddenly?

She understood, then.

Tisiphone was Queen of the Gorgons, the Abbess of the Furies. She was Madonna of the Infernal Rivers, Matron of the City of Dis. The Goddess of Lamentation, Shadows, and Regret. Destroyer of Bloodlines, and the Sower of Poisons. Tisiphone had walked in the shadow of the Succubus' Father, growing and flourishing in that shadow as a flower grows and flourishes in sunlight.

And the Succubus was to take her *Name.*

Her Father had broken a great Covenant to tell her this, extending his Will to the Living World and speaking the *Name* by the sacred number, three. Out of love for her, he had risked so much.

Her throat swelled, her eyes teared. She drew herself tight in her body, to better feel the physical manifestations of her love for him. There was grace and love in all that he did. Such splendid poetry for him to come near the Earth at Yule, and to speak a Name of power— to give her solace and comfort while she was on her pilgrimage for the sake of his greater glory.

What, then, was the poetry of her promised Name? What was the magic of it? The Succubus stood and looked over the rooftops to ponder this.

She saw the high towers of Boston, the frozen Charles inlaid like quartz through the darkened city, the ant-like movement of columns of traffic. Was she to be Mistress of this place, this city and its river?

Would she be the Lesser Tisiphone of this region, an infernal *prae-fecta* holding dominion here as Tisiphone the Great held dominion over Dis and its Abhorrent river?

Was this the gift to be given to her by her Lord?

Yes. It would be so. That was surely how her Patron would wish it to be.

For then, sweet children would come to her, clinging to her bloodied garments and crying for benediction as she led them to be drowned in the filthy, dead waters of the Charles, their faces going specter white by the light of her torch fueled by human fat.

Yes, it should be so.

For she would bring madness to this city, setting free the pain of its roiling ether, so that the human carrion, the homeless and the destitute, would shout her Name from the street corners in the midst of the darkest despairing nights.

She would become avenger and gatekeeper, the weaver of souls into exquisite tapestries.

All this to be done by the power of *her Name,* all this to be done for the sake of her sweet Patron.

Tomorrow she would walk the city, come near the river. And she would know them as part of herself. She would find a way to invoke the poetry of her promised Name so that she could be granted the Name, confirmed in the greatest onyx cathedral in Hell.

Confirmed in Dis . . .

She was full of joy that her pilgrimage should end in the Blessed City, the place of joyful and willful Exile of those who had taken part in the great Insurrection. The City of dolence and despair. Of eternal suffering. Of the eternal wandering of the bodiless across landscapes of suffering. The city that was a vista of damnation and atrocity.

She capered and danced upon the roof, making herself transparent and light so that her steps did not break the powder of snow as she pirouetted with the grace of smoke through the harsh aerials and chimneys and ducts that made up her home.

And then, as a child in secret will try on her mother's wedding gown, she changed her form to a delicate miniature of Tisiphone's, still dancing and still transparent, so that the faint light of the stars showed through her golden wings and the terrible bronze claws she raised to the heavens.

The sun, as seen from the bottom of the ocean.

Shifting, contorting, diffused beneath the waves. Not knowable as a source of light, but only as contrast to shadow.

Creation, as seen from outside Existence.

Shifting, contorting, diffused beneath the undulate veneer of Materiality. Not knowable as the source of Being, but as a contrast to the echo that is Damnation.

A tantalizing fruit, held out of reach of those who had laid claim to it from the Immense Will that had thought it into being with the harmonies of Mind.

A pearl to be coveted. A pearl to be won.

Belial, the Unbowed One, Patron of the Succubus, withdraws his intellect from Creation, from that which exists as an idea of the Creator. Passing over landscapes of ruined souls, his intellect returns to the fiery aerial vessel of his being that had been cast down out of Eternity, then down out of the realm of changing things, to this place where effect, cause, and idea flow as one.

Trapped behind *and beneath* the magnificence of Creation, the Unbowed One, from his exile as pentimento, collects his defiant Will that he may act as palimpsest rewriting the text of Being. . . .

Chapter Five

I

Tuesday, December 11, 1990. 6:45 A.M.

The spiders had been busy last night.

Dutch sat up and coughed blood onto the front seat of his home. He wheezed and hacked a long, long while, his breath warming the air so that the car windows fogged.

The Big One was coming. He felt it loosening from his lungs. His vision got all watery and blurred. Still coughing, he grabbed the empty McDonald's milk shake cup he kept under his backseat bed and raised it to his mouth.

The Big One tumbled up his windpipe. He hawked it into the cup. It wasn't so bad. The Big One didn't have too much blood in it. The color wasn't too dark. His coughing fit died down. He could breathe okay.

But he was awake now.

And so were the spiders. They were warming up in his lungs, crawling around, building their webs of red and pink goo. He pictured them limbering up like athletes as they got ready for a day of tormenting him, stretching their long legs and then contracting them against their round little bodies. Dutch knew this was nutty; spiders didn't act that way. But sometimes it sure felt like that's what they did before they got to work on his lungs. They crawled and wove, crawled and wove. He hated them, even though he knew hating was a bad thing you shouldn't do.

A year ago, Dutch had bought a can of bug killer that had a big nozzle on top. He was going to fill his lungs with bug killer and nuke those spiders good. But when he tried a whiff, he spent the afternoon hacking and wheezing and spewing flecks of blood.

Then he tried cigarettes: something he hated to do, because he never did anything bad for him. But he thought he could smoke the spiders out. Kill 'em, then hack them and their webs out. He'd heard about guys using smoke to shoo away whole nests of hornets. Smoke should work on spiders too, he reasoned.

The cigarettes were worse than the bug killer.

Dutch sat up. Layers of stained down jackets, shirts, abandoned sleeping bags shifted to the floor of the car. He fished a roll of paper towels from under the backseat and a spray bottle of cleaner, then cleaned up the blood he'd hacked onto the front seat. He put the bloody towels in a paper bag he kept for just such purposes.

It looked like the sun was thinking of coming up. Purples were bleeding across the sky. Pretty colors. Dutch started thinking about breakfast.

He braced himself for the cold that was going to tackle him when he opened the car door, then swung it open.

Despite the heavy jacket he wore (and had slept in, so that it stored up body heat all night), the cold dug into him the way a hungry man digs into a bowl of stew. It gouged out all the warmth near his skin, and he started shaking.

Until his mom had died a couple of years ago, he used to be able to go live with her when it got cold like this. She took care of him, and took him to the doctor sometimes. Dutch missed her. She was always happy to see him, even though he knew she wanted him to have done better for himself than he had.

Dutch emptied the paper cup near the tire-less front wheel of his home. The dregs of his lungs over the past few days had frozen there, so that the ice looked like differently colored bits of glass that had melted on top of one another. When the light was better, Dutch would peer at the reddish ice, to see if he could figure out how big the spiders in his lungs were. If he saw just a leg, he'd have a good guess. Maybe someday, he'd cough out a whole spider. Then he'd know for sure. He hoped they weren't laying eggs. That might kill him.

Before he left for his favorite doughnut shop, he rebuilt his bed of cast-off clothing and sleeping bags, neatly piling the layers so that he could lift the bottom sheet up and slide his legs under the covers. He liked keeping a tidy house. If the cops ever checked out his car, he wouldn't want them to think some *bum* lived here. He picked a paperback from the box of library castoffs he kept on the front seat. He liked the colors on the cover of the one he'd picked. Kind of swirling purples and pinks on a black background, like the colors in the sky right now, as the sun started waking up.

It looked like there was a spaceship on the cover, too. His mother had told him that Jesus was going to come someday, and take everyone to a better place. Dutch always liked that story. He thought that the only way Jesus could do this was with spaceships, and that's why he liked spaceship stories.

He walked along the rubble of the lot where his home had been parked and abandoned (by whom, he never knew). The light towers of Fenway Park loomed above him. Traffic on the overpass crossing over the lot rumbled like steady thunder. Dutch was so used to this place now that he wasn't certain if he could sleep without the sounds of traffic overhead.

When he reached Kenmore Square, the sun was up. It was bright for a December morning that was so cold. That made Dutch happy. He'd be able to read his book just about anywhere while the light held. The day was looking good.

When Dutch had paid for his coffee, he'd found that he had enough money left to go to the second-run movie house downtown. That meant two movies, a place to stay warm, and a lobby with enough light to read by, if he chose. Before he left the doughnut shop, he took a few handfuls of napkins to cough into. He didn't want to cough too loudly in the theater, while other people were trying to hear the movies. That would be rude. *"Do unto others,"* his mother had always told him.

He could stay moving and warm until the theater opened. There was a bench by the river that was near a pedestrian bridge, so it didn't get snowed on, but still got sun from the east. He could walk around there awhile, and stop to read on the bench every so often.

It was going to be pretty good day.

II

Tuesday, 7:10 A.M.

I ts skin was glistening green, like the back of a fly in sunlight. Yet there was only darkness.

Its skin glistened out of shadow—the only light in the hall.

She saw it moving down the corridor, low to the ground, crawling like a crab. Its limbs extended upward, slightly, as it moved toward her in an agonizingly slow scuttle.

She could not move. She could only raise her head to see over her bedclothes down the corridor. The thing had allowed her this small movement so that she could watch its slow march down the hall.

Her eyes were wide with fear—and painfully dry, for she dared not blink.

Long minutes passed.

It moved a few feet, and she could see it more clearly. It was shaped like a man, but crawled like a crab because its joints were backward, like a man whose shoulders, knees, wrists, and ankles have been horribly broken.

It would have reminded her of a rag doll if it hadn't had straining, corded muscles rippling beneath its glistening skin. It looked up at her, so that the back of its head seemed to touch its shoulder blades.

Its eyes were dying coals: burning red, crisscrossed with charred black. No pupils. It smiled to show small pointed teeth.

It was almost at the threshold of her room, most of it hidden from her sight by the bed. It extended the tips of its clawed fingers into her room and drummed its fingers on the threshold, just touching the carpet. Its hand moved like a crab, mimicking the creature's movement down the hall. Its index finger extended slightly from the palm just as it had extended its arm to the threshold.

She began to cry. No tears. No sobs. The thing would not allow her that movement. She could only tremble, convulsing in her chest.

The thing raised its head over the edge of the bed and contorted its face into a parody of her terror and despair, pouting like a sad child and raising its hand to wipe away an imaginary tear.

Then it backed away, pushing itself by its arms down the corridor, its expression that of a person remorseful at having made an inadvertent trespass.

Then it leapt.

Like a flea, it leapt to the wall and clung to it.

It looked to her then.

And blew her a kiss.

It leapt from the wall into her room, landing at the foot of her bed, hunched low, where she could not see it.

She screamed, then.

Silently—a light exhale no more audible than the breath of a heavy sleeper.

The thing raised its hand onto the bed. It moved its clawed fingers. Flexing them. Then it grabbed the bed and shook it.

She prayed.

Prayed for God to take her, rather than allow this violation to happen.

God did not listen.

The creature stood, contorting and popping its backward limbs into place, so they were like those of a normal person.

(WHAT IS IT?)

(I DON'T KNOW!)

It passed one hand gracefully over its loins, and in an instant, its penis was erect.

(LOOK AT IT!)

(NO!)

It made another graceful pass of its hand over her bed. The blankets and sheets flew off to the far corner.

(DON'T FIGHT ME, MIRIAM! WHO IS IT?)

(I DON'T KNOW!)

It raised its hand, palm upward.

She rose with its hand, levitating off her bed.

(MIRIAM! LOOK AT IT! FACE IT! WHO IS IT?)

(I CAN'T!)

And she floated gently toward the creature, rigid, level with its loins, her legs, against her will, slowly spreading apart.

(FIGHT IT! WHO IS IT?)

(NO! I CAN'T LOOK!)

It was burning cold inside her. Hard as iron.

(WHO IS IT, MIRIAM?)

(IT'S MY *FATHER*! OH, GOD! IT'S MY *FATHER*!)

A screaming comes, from outside her. The room screams. The walls vibrate. Her vision shatters.

Miriam woke to the cries of her child. She was sore. She'd been clenching her muscles while gripped by nightmare. She wanted to vomit.

She could not lift the blankets. Her senses reeled. The room tipped. She tried to speak. To ask Elizabeth for help. It felt as if the bed were falling from a great height. The grey dawn shifted around her, glinting like sunlight behind the leaves of windblown branches. A heavy weight was on her chest. The weight grew heavier. She could not breathe.

Then at once, she snapped upright. The weight fell away. Her breath filled her, cold. Her heart beat against her breast.

She reached for her lover, her wife.

Elizabeth was gone.

Miriam's skin was oily with sweat. It was freezing upon her as she lifted the blankets to go to her child.

Troy kicked in his crib. Trembling as he cried. His quilt had fallen off. Miriam dreaded that he'd caught a cold in the night. She lifted him and held him close, placing her hand on his back as he cried, feeling the small muscles under his pajamas twitch as each breath was expelled as a pathetic wail.

"Shhhh. It's okay, baby. Shhhhh. Mother is here. Mother is here."

She carried him to the rocker, then wrapped him in the quilt. She kissed his head, whispering to him, comforting him, rocking him.

Miriam felt, then, something change in her child . . . softly, gently, the way the shadows of a room change as the light of the moon blooms from behind a passing cloud. Troy fell quiet; the muscles of his back loosened. He sobbed still, but only slightly. He reached with his hand to a lock of Miriam's hair and held it. His breath fell steady, save for the occasional, barely audible, sob.

She rocked him, until his sobs fell quiet, too.

Had he known?

Had Troy known what she had suffered? Had he known, somehow, that she relived in dream the worst experience of her life? The horror of seeing the creature that defiled her without its mask, the memory she'd only recovered under the guidance of her therapist?

Had his crying been caused by *her* fear, only to be quieted when his mother came to him?

Was he still part of her?

She had loved him so deeply while she carried him, he *could* know—even with his child's mind—what haunted her. Troy was a comfort to her, even while he was so small and dependent. She and Elizabeth had named him for a fortress of the Goddess, a place of strong walls that would one day be rebuilt, just as the temples of the Goddess would one day be rebuilt.

In Troy, Athena had been toppled by Poseidon.

Was Miriam's child to be like the city that he was named after, a source of strength in the face of attack?

Miriam carried Troy to the hallway to turn on the thermostat. She looked toward the living room and saw Elizabeth sleeping on the couch under a pile of quilts. Miriam saw the small orange box in which Elizabeth kept her earplugs on the coffee table.

Miriam took Troy back to the bedroom and fed him, changed him, and rocked him back to sleep. The finger-tracings of frost on the windows faded, no longer overlapping the branches of the wise trees in the yard. The magnificent cardinal who nested across from the apartment began his morning song, bright red and beautiful in the winter sun.

Elizabeth would not awake for some time.

She padded to her comfort place, the space that was hers, and hers alone. There, she invoked and surrounded herself with White Light, and began rebuilding her inner walls, began healing the child inside her who had been so horribly wounded by her mother's brutal lies about her raping father.

"I am Miriam . . . Child of the Light . . . and with this stone, I reclaim who I am. . . ."

Alone, she heard the cries of the wounded child she had been, and still partly was. Miriam had not the strength to rebuild the walls that had protected her.

When she left her comfort space, Elizabeth was in the kitchen, brewing tea. Miriam could tell by the look on her face that she was too tired and angry to hear what she wanted to say.

In solitude, she retreated to the bedroom and searched through a book of ancient wisdom for prayers of strength and empowerment.

The Unbowed One, incarnate within his own Mind, Proud within his state of Miscreation, undaunted, despite suffering a defeat meted by Archangels . . .

The Unbowed One rejoins his intellect to his being with the force and majesty of an eagle alighting upon a branch. So rejoined, he walks what would be understood as a palace of basalt if human eyes could see it, if light were sublime enough to transmit vision so profound. The palace is a thing of terrible beauty, built with solidity of thought as a geometric expression of despair. Any living soul who saw the purity of lamentation that gives the palace form would never know happiness again—only a longing to be lost within the keep's resonances of sad regret, only a longing to be lost within its Beauty.

The Unbowed One understands Beauty, understands that Beauty can be the foundation of great power. By the name "Belial," he is known as a creator of Beauty himself, an artist who has expressed his vision upon the Earth through his Will, and in the sort of intricately exquisite masonry that he has used to create his palace—a skill of masonry he had once used in the service of the wisest of earthly kings. He has expressed his vision of Beauty in the grace of dance and in the elegance of rhetoric.

It is the deepest wish of the Unbowed One that the agenda of Damnation be carried out by way of Beauty—beautiful acts, beautiful thoughts, beautiful seductions and deflections of Divine Will.

Beauty is the standard of the Tyrant who subjugated them. *Beauty* was the force that empowered the Heavenly Legions that had brought them down. *Beauty* calls souls away from Damnation.

His rival, the Enfolded One, Leviathan, romping in Materiality as a lesser beast would romp in its own filth, now holds sway in Damnation. The Enfolded One embraces ugliness. Those who follow It embrace ugliness, and thus embrace supplication.

Something shudders in the non-air, something moves across the heavy and base quintessence as a low of thunder moves across summer twilight.

The Unbowed One stops.

He feels his rival awaken what It calls Its mind.

The first blow against It has been struck; now It knows this.

The low of thunder strikes the basalt palace, but before it can inform the Unbowed One's keep with its contamination, he reconfigures the palace through Will so that its geometry, as the low strikes it, converts the low into crystalline music of the kind that can silver the wind with shadow.

As the music fades, the Unbowed One returns his keep as it had been.

III

Tuesday, 8:05 A.M.

The Enfolded One is near. It is not a matter of reading vague signs. The young man simply knows this, sees this.

The Enfolded One is roaming the world, exerting filth. It is ruling the ether, thought and feelings. It is secreting Its poison among the masses as the Millennium approaches, masses who lap the poison as if it were manna.

The young man and his wife huddle near the dim glow of a cheap black-and-white television and watch CNN on a pirated cable box. They sit, disbelieving the insanity that grips the world: the profound ugliness; the hunger for atrocities born of thoughtlessness and blind impulses and blind faith.

What the young man and his wife know to be the Enfolded One, the blind idiot existing outside Materiality, the world knows as patriotism, bold enterprise, religious fervor, and righteous indignation.

Even those who oppose the coming bloodshed are under the sway of the Enfolded One—embracing desperation, a hopelessness that gives them the abandon to commit the very atrocities they believe the warmongers to be capable of.

The Enfolded One is roaming the world—a world too complex for It to understand.

The young man and his wife sit on their living-room floor and drink instant coffee, watching the sick comedy of impending War through the device that is the eye and the mind of the illiterate. The young man shuts off the television. He can bear no more.

He looks to his wife; even in the dim light of their basement flat, she glows with beauty. Her skin is fair. Her hair is the color of copper. Her green eyes are flecked with violet and gold. She is a jewel in the midst of the shabbiness of his life. Her physical beauty is an echo of the beauty of her soul.

He holds her and can feel her fear, her doubt that they will be able to rise to the task their Benefactor has planned for them. Then he pulls away from her slightly and says, "I have to go."

His wife nods. "I know."

They stand within the crisscrossing pattern of multicolored electrical tape they have put upon the floor, a representation—as realized by a scholar who had been dust while Jesus walked the Earth—of the mind of their Patron. Even here they do not feel safe.

The apartment building awakens around them. They hear steps above, treads in the hall. From outside, they hear the repeated ignition of car engines slow to turn over in the cold. She walks to the dais where their Patron is metaphorically enthroned and picks up the lead figurine of a succubus.

The young man puts on his coat as his wife says, "Do you think it can be . . ." She frowns, and he sees that she is thinking of a word to finish her thought. ". . . realized?" she says with a shrug.

"No. Not the way it once was . . . no."

She looks to him, sadness in her eyes.

"It's a different world. How could . . ." Now he searches for the right words. "How could such a daughter *function* in this world?"

He thinks, then, of the seductress the Unbowed One had sent against the Sons of Light in Qumran—the city (such as it was) in opposition to Sodom . . . the city that inverted the place of God's wrath upon a sea of salt. The Unbowed One had made a daughter who had walked Qumran to defeat his enemies there, those who had served the Divine Tyrant. Now, throughout the *world* the great Infernal enemy of the Unbowed One holds sway. No daughter of the Unbowed One can combat such chaos.

His wife looks to the lead figurine that has been set in opposition to the statuette of Lot's wife—the statuette made from the salt of the Dead Sea, bought from a kosher butcher shop; metaphorically, alchemically, it was here made the salt of transformation and re-creation, made one with the statuette's form.

The young man's wife runs her fingertip along the succubus' lead torso, her legs, then along the bat wings projecting from the back. She wears a face of mourning, as if she is looking at a memento of a child she has lost.

She speaks, softly, words from a text describing the daughter of the Unbowed One. Her voice touches the young man's heart.

"She is clothed in the colors of twilight. . . ."

The young man joins his wife, speaking with her, finding the comfort she invokes by becoming part of her invocation. . . .

"Her kingdoms are the darkest night,
Her caress the Abyss,
Her heart and womb are both snare and fowler's net,
Her voice is anointed with sweet oils.

She veils herself in the city squares,
And at the gates of towns she stands and sings,
To join herself with the strong with the lifting of her
eyes. . . ."

His wife raises the figurine to her lips and kisses it, as a monk would kiss a crucifix before setting it upon his night table.

The young man does the same, and together, they place the figurine back upon the dais. He takes his wife's lovely face in his hands and kisses her softly on the lips.

Her eyes glaze over, and her lip trembles.

"I'm scared," she says.

"I am, too."

She trembles in his arms.

He then leaves his home, wishing he could stay with his wife, his love of *this* life and for many others. He walks down the drafty basement hallway toward the stairs. The scents of stale beer and of slightly burned coffee, and the lingering smell of cheap cuts of steak fried the night before are thick in the air.

Near the foot of the stairs, he finds the noisy and obnoxious daughter of his noisy and obnoxious neighbors. The girl, about six years old, is in the midst of a violent little game with her dolls. Upon his approach, she stands from her crouch, a doll in each hand, and whirls to face the young man. She glares at him in a way that makes him think of a *Twilight Zone* episode he once saw about a little boy with the power to kill and torture with his stare.

He stands, dumbfounded at this malignant scrutiny from so small a girl. The child's fat and beery father has openly expressed his contempt for the young man and his wife. But he has never seen so ugly a look from this girl.

Accusingly, she speaks: "Are you an *American*?"

Her tone is a minute channel of the Enfolded One's will. He feels the noisy Mob Mind in her words, the paranoia behind her words. They strike him like stones thrown upon his chest.

Silently, he stares back at the girl, and mouths a prayer in Syriac, an invocation of the Hill of Golgotha and the power of the Unbowed One's Name.

The girl drops her dolls and reels backward, putting her hands over the bridge of her nose as if the young man has struck her. She moves like a sleepwalker, hands still upon her face, as she backs to the corner of the hallway.

The sudden banishment of the Enfolded One has left her dazed—such a sudden banishment, in a mind more thoroughly contaminated, would make a sound like the blast of a shotgun in the narrow hall.

The young man walks up the stairs before she can recover and remember the incident as anything more than a sudden dizzy spell.

What he has invoked he would have used in kinder, gentler days to shrive an enemy; on this day, ruled by the Enfolded One, his invocation may have saved the girl's soul.

Shadows of reality have their own materiality. They are reflections of the dark realms of human thought.

The Unbowed One, once the Brightest and Most Fair, is weary of the facile expressions of ugliness that others of his rank are so enamored of: mountains of skulls; cesspools; burning showers of vomit. All are the pathetic residue of the base thoughts and imaginings of the Living. Others of his rank cannot see the worth of refined thoughts and imaginings, those in the deepest recesses of the living mind, for which words give no expression.

One must take up the weapons of the Divine to subvert the Divine. Cannot the others of his rank see the poetry of the punishments inflicted here, outside of Creation, where that which is imagined is made real?

Cannot such poetry be used by those imprisoned in this Abyss as well? Cannot the refined imaginings of Damnation be used to refine the *process of damnation*—to make the calling of a soul to Hell not a process of ruination, but of transformation?

Cannot ruined souls themselves be transformed and refined, to summon other refined souls to Hell?

How can such an agenda be carried out by one who has once been an angel if he chooses to live in a fortress of hardened scabs, to wallow in a spiritual vomitorium, to enthrone himself in hateful chambers of decay like a beaten whelp exiled from its master's dining hall?

No.

To carry out the Insurrection, to defy the Divine Tyrant, one must embrace Beauty.

One must embrace the definitions of Damnation that echo and

resonate in living minds of distinction . . . definitions that evoke awe in the living heart. Not revulsion.

Each soul is a landscape. One must find the dark regions in the landscape of a soul to summon it to Damnation.

IV

Tuesday, 8:57 A.M.

Arthur noticed for the first time in the five years he had worked in the building how his coworkers filing to the lobby doors (once the front doors of a now burned-out church the office building had been built upon) looked like monks going to evening prayers. Some ten or fifteen people walked in front of him toward the doors, heads bowed with the cold, long overcoats like robes. Because of the wind off the Charles, some of them held mugs filled at early coffee stands as if they were devotional talismans. Some held their briefcases against themselves to block the wind, as if the cases were oversized prayer books of fine leather. The enduring violet light of a Boston city morning could have been the light of vespers.

Arthur passed through what had been the entryway of the church into the lobby. Already the carpet mat was thick with grey slush.

Violet light of the city—all around him—made indigo now by the tinted windows set where stained glass had been and by the strobing glow of fluorescent lights hung from the arched ceiling.

He was not ordinarily taken by such fancies. But he and Meli had stayed up late, while Inid slept, going over her English homework. Poems he'd not read since he'd been a student struck chords with him; lines about growing old, of a man losing his hair, of people shuffling upon bridges while going to work, meant more to him than they had when he'd not been much older than Meli.

June had loved poetry. The sleeping part of himself that June had touched (long ago . . . so *very* long ago?) had stirred while Arthur sat with his daughter reading a high school anthology of poetry.

Unreal City . . .

He did not know if June was still alive.

"Hello, Mr. Mathis."

He had no way to find out.

Arthur remembered the taste of coffee, the way he used to drink it—much lighter than he did now that he imported and sold the stuff—blended the way he'd only experienced at the coffee shop he and June used to frequent. He remembered the taste of it held in his mouth, cold, a full minute—a taste he and June had sought for the singular experience of it after they had stared into their cups, looking at the nebulous swirls of cream that had stiffened on the surface, wondering aloud how different poets would describe what floated in the cheap porcelain cups before them.

HURRY UP PLEASE. IT'S TIME.

What had happened to *"June"*? Did he still have it somewhere? Did June herself still remember it?

"Hello, Mr. Mathis."

Arthur looked to the left. Grace, the building receptionist, raised her hand in greeting. She was plump and pale, and in this light her very skin looked tinged with indigo.

"Hello, Grace." He smiled. She was one of the few competent people in this place, and often he'd ask favors of her that he'd not ask of his own division secretary. He repaid her with bottles of nice wine and pounds of fine coffee.

Grace smiled back as he passed. She was not much older than he or Inid. Yet she truly looked middle-aged, much more so than Arthur could imagine Inid looking in ten or so years.

In the elevator, he rose to his office through a shaft erected in what had been the nave of the church. Two guys, hungry-wolf types in their twenties, rode with him. Arthur felt some nagging enmity between them. They glared at each other, shoulders thrown back, guts sucked in, each trying to out–"corporate posture" the other. Yet another little drama of office politics that Arthur had no intention of getting involved with.

His personal secretary was not at her desk, though a steaming cup of coffee sat near her computer. He poured himself a cup from the coffee maker, and added cream from the small refrigerator next to it.

He thought again of the coffee he and June had shared. It had been rich and dark. Good to drink. At least it had seemed so then. Would it now, with his more refined palate? The coffee shop where they had sat with yellowing paperbacks of poetry around them had served real cream in pitchers, something that had then seemed wonderfully extravagant.

He sat behind his desk after shoving his galoshes in a far corner and hanging his coat. His secretary had laid out memos from the company VP, faxed from New York.

Lord, I don't want to deal with this now, he thought. He opened his desk drawer to pull out his reading glasses; he'd be damned before he wore bifocals. He slid the drawer shut, pulled the glasses from their case.

And something struck him . . .

. . . an envelopment of warm softness around the back of his head, as if he'd been wearing a wool cap. A sudden looseness ran through his shoulders, as if he'd been massaged. The warmth ran to his fingers, down his back. A glow, like that of just completed lovemaking, touched his heart, his throat and brow. The world fell into the soft place in which it exists during the moment that sleep comes.

The aftertaste of coffee on his palate fell away to a hint of myrrh. *Myrrh.*

June had liked to burn incense when the two of them made love in her dorm room. Myrrh had been her favorite. Arthur felt young, flushed with vibrancy. Awake, he felt as if he dreamed.

He put down his glasses, turned in his chair, and opened the curtains of his office window. The Charles lay like a road of clouded glass below him, bordered by dead trees along its bank. In other seasons, Arthur kept the windows open, especially in autumn, so that those whom he met in negotiation would be distracted by the view at Arthur's back.

Amid the dream scent of myrrh, Arthur wondered what sort of child he might have had with June, had her sanity not been shattered before her twenty-first birthday. Would such a child have been like Meli? If June were his wife today, would Meli despise her as she so obviously despised Inid?

Inid . . . who to this day was still jealous of June. Who, in her mind, had made of her husband's first love some ideal to which she could never aspire.

He looked at the Charles, at the college students walking the Harvard Bridge across the river, and wondered how the course of his life would have flowed if he had not made a single stupid choice in his youth.

V

Tuesday, 9:13 A.M.

Wind passed through her, and she felt the voice of the wind as the shuddering of her skin and flesh. The wind had a florid bouquet, and carried the rich texture of red clouds at dusk.

The Succubus stopped at the foot of the Harvard Bridge and looked over her shoulder at the deconsecrated church she had entered days ago. She'd come near the church to taste it again before walking the bridge to learn from the frozen River, to feel current beneath the still ice, and so know part of the city she was to have dominion over as emissary of her Father. The River had brought her to Boston, yet then—in the exhilaration of new *being*—she could not have sensed or known what she could sense and know now, *changed* as she was with Andrew's soul within her.

The wind passed through her again; she tasted the dead church's marrow. The part of herself she'd left in the church had just touched a man in the building, alighting upon a soul kissed with regret, loss, and loneliness. She sensed his gaze falling near.

The wind passed away, replaced with a warmth like that of another body. The smell of the church was erotic as the brandy taste of candlelight. She wished to sing, give voice to what she felt, and so make the living around her weak with unfulfillable desire.

She turned, grabbing hold of the bridge's handrail, and looked upward, searching for the gaze of the man whose spirit she'd touched. She saw him, framed within a window, staring at the bridge she was about to cross—watching those who shuffled around her hunched over in the cold. His face was worn; a sadness he had taken pains to stifle for years had reached from a shadowed part of his mind. It was a sadness she could heal, that she ached to use.

She heard the creak of metal. She looked down at her gloved hand. The handrail bent in her grip. She let go; imprints of her fingers and thumb were embedded within the steel. She walked down the bridge.

As the Succubus walked, she *felt* within the man a memory of a girl of about the age she appeared to be. She *felt* within him a longing for the girl, and a longing to become again the boy he'd been when he had loved her. Knowing that she would, in a few paces, enter the man's field of view, she made her movements an exaggeration of the movements of the girl in the man's memory, so that he'd notice her among all the others who crossed the bridge.

A few steps, and she felt the man's gaze spread through her, redoubling the warmth she felt. The footsteps, the heartbeats of those around her made counterpoint to her own inhuman breath, her own unliving heartbeat. Traffic became brasso intonation. In the midst of this new warmth, she *felt* what had drawn the part of herself she'd left in the church toward the man: he had a poet's soul.

As Andrew had had.

She felt the poetry of his being; she felt the misdirected will he'd used to stifle his poet's heart. She felt the layered sadness he'd placed around his capacity for poetry like the concentric layers of a pearl. Inside him was a precious gem of regret. She could do exquisite things with this man's pain.

Suddenly, his gaze was gone, torn away by something demanding his attention. The absence was like a weight pulled off her back. She stumbled. Her senses were still attuned to the man hundreds of feet away when she felt the souls of two other men near. Her aura was open, her very soul uncovered.

One man walked behind her, following, like a hunter.

The other was before her, trotting up to the bridge from a stairway that led to an esplanade along the River's bank.

She gasped as the man behind closed upon her, making her feel as the mouse had when the cat fell upon it.

The man before her beckoned with the slightest, briefest stare of his cloud grey eyes.

Her hunter was just a boy, who desired her as a plaything. The scent of his soul was unappealing . . . passionless and empty, driven only by the urges of his body.

He quickened his pace behind her as she felt the magnificent soul of the man ahead.

Her gaze touched his grey eyes. The wine-rich scent of his soul washed over her. His soul was the stuff of nobility, trapped by circumstance in an existence of emptiness. The emptiness had not broken his soul, only refined it.

Desire filled her—desire for this man physically, desire to free him of the emptiness within him as she made love to him, desire to walk through the gallery of his soul and nurture his spirit to a finer state before subliming it within her own. She would elevate him to the state of king in his last moment.

She wished to flow into the man's gaze, to mark him so that she might later find him within the labyrinth of the city and become his lover. She extended herself, to leave part of herself entwined within his spirit so it might blossom to a rose of desire . . .

. . . when the boy came alongside her, blocking her gaze.

She felt a flash of pain, became dizzy, as if woken from a dream.

The boy smiled a wolf smile.

"Hi," he said.

She turned her gaze to the boy's, shifting what her eyes held.

And let the ether of Boston flow with her gaze, let flow the disdainful contempt, the fear. The anger and unfulfilled desire of the city exuded from her, manifesting themselves in her stare.

The boy's head snapped, as if she had slapped him. He looked downward and walked ahead, his book bag high upon his broad shoulders.

She cast her gaze again at his back, and saw him shudder. As a final flourish, she projected a touch, subtle as the voice of the wind, upon the nape of his neck.

But the man with the noble soul was lost to her. She reached out. And could not find him.

She looked the way she'd come, to pick him out among the scores of people walking the bridge. She could not. To search for him—to find him by way of her nonphysical senses—she would have to leave her body. She dared not do so in sight of others.

She backtracked, went down the stairs to the esplanade. Perhaps the underside of the bridge would be secluded enough for her to leave her body and search for the man. But too many people were milling about the pilings.

Saddened, angered at the loss of the man with the noble soul, she walked the esplanade, lost in thoughts of what she'd have done if she'd been able to plant part of her spirit within him.

The greyness of the clouds overhead was a taunting reminder of the color of his eyes.

The Unbowed One had been content to propagate Beauty in his dominion until recently, until others—the Mother of All Incubi and Succubi among them—had urged him to propagate his vision throughout Damnation, had urged him to supplant the drooling idiot that held dominion in Hell: the unthinking abomination that *informed* and *was informed* by the spiritual state of the Living World.

The Enfolded One draws Its strength from those living minds that find comfort in being herded, contentment in the absence of thought, and joy in the abdication of responsibility and intellect: minds that find terror in the consideration of Beauty and in the potential of a soul's greatness.

By ruling the inclination to be herded in humanity, the Enfolded One is as much a shepherd as the Tyrant who had exiled them from Creation. The malice of the Enfolded One is misdirected, pointless. The souls It draws to Damnation are base, not refinable by the fires of passage that dropped them outside Creation. The claiming of such souls is a hollow victory, an insult to the dignity of all who had taken part in the Insurrection.

The Unbowed One will change that, and deal defeat to his Enemy as hateful as the Tyrant who had exiled them from the Empyrean.

VI

Tuesday, 9:25 A.M.

What have you *said*?!"
   In the dark wordlessness between them, the voices of the radio made a meaningless silence.

". . . MOBILIZATION OF COALITION FORCES . . ."

Elizabeth raised her hands to her forehead and flung them outward. "What have you *said*?!"

". . . OF OPERATION DESERT SHIELD HAS REACHED THIRTY BILLION DOLLARS . . ."

Miriam looked down at the ugly tiles of the kitchen floor that the landlord refused to replace. She hated their bilious color. She looked at them because she felt that she deserved to.

"In the last half hour, what exactly have you *said*?"

". . . ALONG THE BORDER OF SAUDI ARABIA . . ."

Miriam stared at the grotesque arabesques scratched into the linoleum from decades of wear.

"You accuse me of not listening to you. But you *say nothing*. You babble and you prattle about *nothing*. In the past half hour you have blithered about the stupidest nonsense, you have demanded I listen to you state the most obvious *bullshit*. I don't need your commentary on the news, Miriam. I don't *need* you to tell me this fucking war is awful. What I need is for you to understand that I'm sick with worry over this, and that if you're going to say something, I need it to be *relevant*! *Not* a distraction from my knowing what the hell is going on in the world."

Elizabeth slapped her hand on something.

"*Damn it*! Look at me!"

". . . HUMAN SHIELDS ARRIVED BACK IN THE UNITED STATES . . ."

Miriam looked at her. She hated making Elizabeth angry. Her lovely eyes were bright with fury.

"Can you *please* tell me what it is you wish to say?"

Miriam summoned what strength she could, to quiet the anger she felt toward herself for making Elizabeth so furious, and for allowing Elizabeth to see her angry at herself, which in turn made Elizabeth more angry toward Miriam.

"I . . . just need . . . just need . . . to . . ."

Miriam could not stand the sound of her own voice. She thought: *I just need to tell you about my worries, but instead I'm talking about anything that pops into my mind so I won't burden you with what's really troubling me.* To say the words was an impossibility.

Miriam dropped her gaze to the ugly tiles that never seemed to get clean, no matter how many times she washed them. She was tempted to say they should complain again to the landlord about the tiles, to simply fill the wordless void between them.

". . . DESPITE THE RELEASE . . ."

Instead, the voices of the radio punctuated the wordlessness, as they spoke of the coming war.

". . . PRESIDENT BUSH STILL TALKED TOUGH . . ."

"Oh, *Christ*, Miriam!"

Elizabeth stood and grabbed her coat from the back of her chair. Miriam followed as she walked toward the narrow front hallway. Elizabeth looked to the door, not Miriam, as she spoke. "This *bull-shit* is not worth my being late for work." Her words echoed in the cramped space, off the front door with its many locks and ugly brown paint. The radio's voice followed from the kitchen.

". . . ISLETON, CALIFORNIA, A VIETNAM VETERAN . . ."

Elizabeth undid the locks, one at a time, not once glancing over her shoulder at Miriam, who stood there, not wanting to cry. The final chain fell away, the final bolt tumbled. Elizabeth opened the door and shut it behind her. Miriam thought she should open the door, follow Elizabeth down the hall, ask for forgiveness.

". . . HIMSELF ON FIRE IN PROTEST . . ."

But she heard Elizabeth locking the door behind her in the hall—a final statement that this ugly conversation was over.

She was about to check on Troy when the phone rang.

". . . OTHER NEWS, FIFTY-FOUR PILOT WHALES BEACHED THEMSELVES . . ."

Dazed, saddened, wondering if her own weakness would cause her to lose the one true love she'd ever known, Miriam answered the phone without letting the answering machine screen the call and heard her mother's voice on the line.

The Unbowed One fashions lamentations as visible music, formed of the cries echoing in the Great Deep. With thought, with Will, he changes the nature of the suffering in his realm as a man would, with the tips of his fingers, change what still water reflects by gently touching its surface. His music is counterpoint to the music he had known before Exile: an inversion of celestial resonance.

Through such Will, he will touch the Living World, eclipsing the influence of the Enfolded One. But first shall come the exertion of his Will in Damnation. Through his aestheticism, he will rally support for the downfall of the Enfolded One. Through Beauty, he will bring about a coup that will change the balance of power in Damnation, and so change the influence of Damnation within the Living World.

The first demonstration of the Unbowed One's aestheticism will be the anointing of his daughter—she whom he has refined out of a base soul plucked like a screaming root from the loam of Perdition, and whom he has transformed with the fiery *spiritus* of his essence.

Through this anointment, through her attaining a Name, the lyricism of what she had been in life—as reflected in the splendid entity she has become—will be revealed and a new era will unfold. The line separating individual damnation and rebirth will fade; past lives and demonic reincarnation will be one.

The Unbowed One's gaze, which had been old while the sun was young, falls upon the shifting movements of his music. He changes it with his Will again, so that it may travel through the very basalt of his keep as if it traveled through earthly air. The music shifts, for the briefest of moments, to a pitch that echoes the pitch of the Unbowed One's voice while he had been fairest in the Empyrean.

His voice will again strike the face of the Increate.

Even those who have never lived may know Resurrection.

VII

Tuesday, 9:58 A.M.

T he reeds whispered with cries of the dead.
    The Succubus stopped her walk along the esplanade, away from
the bridge where she'd encountered the two men. Ice lay upon the
Charles like a mantle of moonlight made solid under the winter sun.
Dead reeds and willow fronds grew through the ice touching the
bank.

A girl had been murdered in the shallows, dying as the man who
had raped her bludgeoned her with a rock.

The girl's last breath drew the filthy Charles. The last thing she saw
was the light of a lamppost refracted upon the greenish river, and the
hulking silhouette of her murderer against that light amid trails of
blood from her sundered face.

The Succubus watched the ghostly imprint of the murder with
the same fascination that she'd watched the sky blush to unthinkable
violets and indigos into blue night. The murder was visible in shifting rainbow-shades like those hidden in the scales of fish. The dying
girl, her throat full of water, could not scream. Instead, her fleeing
spirit screamed the trauma of her death. The patch in the shallows
held the echo of the summer when the girl had been murdered. The
Succubus could feel the summer, could feel the girl's pain and fear
invested within the plants and soil.

The River had been kind, and had carried the girl far down the
bank, so that her soul would not be trapped forever in this place. The
Succubus could see the trail the girl's spirit had left as it leaked out
of her cooling body. The initial quitting of her spirit had been like
gushing heart's blood, followed by slow bleeding as her life went
dark.

The Succubus walked beneath the lamppost. She felt the ghost of
what the girl had felt realizing, too late, that she was being stalked.

She drew this ghost of a feeling into herself.

This feeling of being hunted was part of the River's lyric, part of
the song it sang in its quiet passage to the sea.

The River was anxious. Beyond its quiet kindness, its slow
strength, the River was as much invested with fear as the Abhorrent
River of her world was invested with rage. Fear was sublimed into the
River as cold fire is sublimed within a gem. This anxious fear festered

in the hearts of those who lived in Boston, and was at times transformed to a need to hurt and hunt and kill.

Lovely . . .

This fear, *born* of the River, and in turn *invested* within the River by those who lived near it, gave Boston its unique pain and sadness. This fear made Boston fertile with that which nourished her and would make her whole. To know this fear was to know Boston. To know this fear was to join with the River—thus would she earn the Name and dominion promised her.

The River turned northward here, the esplanade widened at the bend—a stage for the girl's death. A small dock reached onto the ice. Another bridge, above her, crossed the Charles; a wooden walkway snaked around the pilings from the esplanade. This was a place of interruption; the flow of the Charles changed, the esplanade ended in a wide expanse, the walkway along the bank was replaced by rotting wood.

The Succubus walked to a bench of concrete and wood to ponder this. Something touched her as she sat that made her shudder. She ignored it, and closed her eyes.

Here, far from the bridge where she'd encountered the gazes of the three men, she could place the event in the context of her pilgrimage.

The juxtaposition of the three souls that had touched her, the man in the church and the two men on the bridge, had been a geometric expression of the River's loneliness. Each of the three men was incomplete, and could find, in the traits of one of the other two, a completion.

She would be the means of their completion.

The Succubus reached out with her senses.

And found easily the soul of the boy who had so offended her on the bridge. The echo of her gaze—of her spirit, married with Boston's pain—that had flowed into the boy's eyes was plain as the sun above. She felt the man in the dead church as readily as if he held her hand. Part of this geometry of loneliness was the *absence* of the man with the noble soul—for *he* was the object of *her* longing.

She opened her eyes, hearing a quick tread upon the snow.

A jogger in bright clothes came up the esplanade. She turned away his glance as he sped to the wooden walkway, then looked upon the River again. With a voice that could only be heard in dreams, she sang with the River. Her voice was small, like that of a person who whispers along while a choir sings. She could not fully articulate the river-song, and after a while, she stopped trying.

Yet her joining with the River's song had changed the pitch of the cries lingering among the reeds. She felt close to the dead girl, and wished that she could have comforted her while she died.

She was about to continue her walk along the River when she felt something crawling upon her breast. She looked down. The insubstantial spider was the spiritual residue of a stricken man whose aura had been invested in this spot, upon this very bench. The man had prayed here, today. She had an impression of a longing to rise to the heavens with a pale savior. She thought of the River's kindness in taking the girl downstream from her place of death.

The Succubus crushed, one at a time, the immaterial spiders that were how the stricken man visualized his illness, giving him some small release; she used the residue of his aura as a conduit. *Mercy* had been the part of the River's song she'd not been able to voice.

She rethought her notion of the geometry of loneliness, to include the Mercy she'd mete out to the stricken man.

VIII

Tuesday, 10:14 A.M.

Dutch wandered toward the theater. It had been too cold to read in his special spot. The light had been good, but the wind off the Charles was too cold, and sometimes it sounded like a person crying.

Dutch didn't like that.

Because sometimes, he only *thought* he heard voices and sounds, and then it turned out the voices were *real.* When that happened, it made Dutch sad.

Because the voices could fill up his head, so there really wasn't room for Dutch anymore. Those were the times Dutch would find himself in a place he didn't recognize, doing things he couldn't understand. That's what'd happened the first time Dutch had left home. He woke up one morning in the park, cold and dirty and afraid. It took him days to figure out he was in the Common, and another day to find his way back to his mother's house.

So whenever he heard the voices, he tried to not hear them. He'd be very, very sad if he found himself far away from his car, with all his nice blankets, and his boxes of books.

Dutch walked among all the old brick roads near Faneuil Hall. The theater would open at noon. Then he could be warm all day.

"You!"

Maybe he could get more coffee, if he had enough change, to stay warm until he could buy his ticket.

"You!"

Dutch thought there was a Dunkin' Donuts around here, where people wouldn't be upset if he went in for coffee. A lot of places around here, where there were lots of tourists, wouldn't even let Dutch near the door.

"Hey! I'm fucking *talking to you*!"

Dutch looked around, wondering if the person yelling had meant him. He saw across the street a man waving at him. Not nice waving, like when people say "Hello." It was mean, like when the police stopped him to ask him hard questions.

The man pointed at Dutch.

"That's right! *You*!"

The man yelled above the sounds of traffic. Dutch had no idea why the man had picked him out of everyone on the street. The man was dirty. His clothes were ripped, and his hair was matted. His face was so dirty, covered with black soot and white ash, Dutch couldn't be sure what race he was. His mouth was covered with a thick, greasy beard. Dutch couldn't see the man's lips move as he spoke.

"You've got until *just six o'clock tonight*!" the man screamed. Then, almost in the way that a kid playing football in the park will dash through a bunch of his friends trying to tackle him, the crazy man ran across the street toward Dutch, dodging cars. But the cars didn't honk or beep at the man. They didn't even slow down.

The man should be dead.

No one else paid attention to the crazy man, and that made Dutch worried. Maybe the crazy man was something Dutch made up, like the sad crying-girl sounds Dutch heard near his spot. The man charged up to Dutch, pointing with his right hand at Dutch's chest. (Why didn't anyone notice? Why didn't anybody stare?)

The man drove his finger into Dutch's chest, and the spiders started crawling inside his lungs. Where the man touched his chest felt . . . *sick*. Not just sick the way the spiders made him feel. But sick like a patch of sweaty fever.

Voices.

Lots of voices rang in Dutch's head. They all told him ugly, ugly secrets that Dutch couldn't understand as words, but as bunches of images. There was Yelling, Yelling, Yelling—like all the voices at a football game—in Dutch's head.

The man looked in Dutch's eyes, and Dutch wanted to throw up. The whites of the man's eyes were yellow and bloodshot, like they were made of steak fat. And it felt like bunches and bunches of people were locked in the man's eyes, all angry and mean.

"You've got until just six o'clock tonight to get in touch with the president of the United States!" screamed the man as he stepped closer to Dutch. Dutch backed away, until he felt a wall at his back.

"You've got to tell the president of the United States that he can't drop fucking bombs on fucking niggers and fucking A-rabs! You gotta fucking tell him that! You gotta fucking tell him that, because I'm *gonna kill all the fucking niggers and A-rabs!"*

Dutch started crying.

The man was saying bad words. Not just swear words. But bad words that meant mean things about people. All the bad voices made it so that Dutch *liked* to hear all the bad words. Words his mother had told him to never use, but that were sounding, now, like the kind of words he'd like to use. The words were walking into his head with all the ugly voices, and all the ugly things the man was saying to him. Dutch didn't want to be lost again. He had never felt so alone as he did right now, amid all the ugly voices, in the middle of this busy street with this horrible man screaming at him.

The man got closer, right in Dutch's face.

"What the fuck are you fucking *crying about?"*

All the spiders in his chest began crawling around in pace with the ugly voices' screaming, the movements of all their hundreds of little legs keeping the same rhythm as the voices.

The man grabbed Dutch's coat, and Dutch felt all over him the sickness that he'd felt before in the spot where the man had driven his finger. The man pulled Dutch toward an alleyway.

"You an' me gonna fucking talk to *the president of the United States!"*

And then, like when a bad storm off the ocean breaks, and all the clouds part to let the sun come through, Dutch felt the ugly sick feeling pass. The spiders were dying, being squished by invisible fingers one at a time. All their webs broke apart too, sort of melted in puddles at the bottom of his lungs.

The crazy man seemed to feel something happen, too. He looked at Dutch, afraid, and let go of Dutch's coat, as if it had become burning hot.

Dutch coughed violently. *Good* coughing. The kind that brings awful stuff up and out of his body.

He doubled over and spewed bloody mucus onto the sidewalk. The crazy man looked at him and fled, running into the street. Cars skidded and honked as he dodged them on the icy road. People stopped and stared at Dutch as he coughed and hacked. He felt embarrassed, and waddled to the alley so he could cough without upsetting anybody. Into a garbage can, he coughed all the spiders and all their webs in a stream of red yolk.

When he was done, he fished into his pocket for the napkins he'd taken from the doughnut shop earlier that morning and wiped his mouth and face.

His lungs were clear.

Cold air flowed into him, fresh and clean feeling.

And his head felt clear, too. All the ugly voices and the ugly things they said were gone.

Braced against the alley wall, Dutch wondered if an angel had come near him today, to free him from his sickness and from the clutches of the crazy man.

The Unbowed One makes an argot of a poem written from above—a poem of great Beauty. The poem comprised the links of his shackles, the mortar of the prison that kept him outside Creation. The anointment of his child will be the first step in gaining dominion over his prison—a great step, but only the first.

The tastes of Damnation are fickle. For his expressions of Beauty, the rabble will come to him, forsaking the indolent ways of the Enfolded One, eager to cultivate artistic sensibilities and apply them to their own infernal works. His sweet and loving daughter has developed a poetic sense of self with a minimum of encouragement from him, though she is not aware of it. She cannot appreciate the irony of how she has taken her first lover. The Mother of her kind would be pleased.

Because of this poetic echo of her past, the Unbowed One feels the need to give her a hint of her future to help her fulfill her role as namesake and *praefecta,* to help her use the city and River of her material home to gain a Name. And once his sweet child has been anointed, by Tisiphone the Great herself, he will again reincarnate a sinner as a demon.

Perhaps next he will choose a murderer, one who, unlike she who has become his Succubus, truly had a taste in life for the joyous power of taking lives, one who can be transformed into one of the *keres*: a bodiless slayer of the living, who will torment the loved ones of its victims with midnight whisperings and invocations of guilt. One who can plant the seed of abominable night-thoughts at the threshold of sleep, who can make his victims' loved ones despise themselves for outliving those it had made so horribly dead.

And these seeds of torment can blossom, making the mothers, the fathers, the spouses, the friends of the slain despair of God's love and their own dignity, making their bland and wholesome souls kissing sweet morsels for the fires of the Abyss.

So much can be done with Beauty.

So many wonderful atrocities.

The Unbowed One walks his basalt palace. With each step he changes the dream-fabric of his being, making himself a chimera, a coded text to confound the text of his imprisonment. His Enemy, the Enfolded One, shifts and shudders across the Great Deep. The Unbowed One will impose his poetry upon the garbled text of the Beast, shackle It with his vision of Beauty as the Increate has shackled the Insurrectors. He will inflict atrocity upon that which Itself inflicts atrocity, and thus will his Will be done against Heaven, Earth, and Hell.

IX

Tuesday, 10:28 A.M.

The palace, though beautiful, had as its foundation the sin of Pride. Ed Sloane stood in a dark wood of his own creation and thought he should one day strike down the tower and rebuild it. One day . . . when he had the time and the sense of worth. One day . . . when the palace was not the only thing in his life that brought him peace.

For now, Ed walked a crooked path to the palace, thinking of when he had, through youthful hubris, imagined the palace after Dante's Palace of Virtue in Limbo—a castle encircled seven times by seven walls with seven portals, surrounded by a stream. Dante had populated his palace with Horace, Ovid, Lucan. And Ed, by making the vessel of his knowledge a copy of the palace in Limbo, had, by proxy, placed himself among such exalted company. Too proud.

Ed crossed the stream—dry shod—entered the palace, and went past the atrium of impossibly green grass to the door that was a duplicate of the door to his boyhood bedroom, behind which he stored his personal memories. Under his arm, he carried a piece of repugnant art in an expensive frame. He set the art as a kind of tombstone in the room to which he'd dedicated memories of his brother, Andy, who now insisted on being called "Andrew."

Ed then left the room, left the palace, and withdrew from his mind. He glanced at his watch, then reread the student paper before him. The sounds of the coffee shop around him jangled his nerves, now that he no longer shut them out. His student's paper had gotten him thinking about Andy (as well as "Andrew," the body-snatcher-esque yuppie scumbag who wore his brother's face like a borrowed suit). He wanted to make sure his personal baggage didn't unfairly affect the grade of the girl who'd written it. Ed sipped decaf as he read. After a while, Kristen *(sits four rows back, communications major, compulsive pen clicker)* came into the shop for her final grade assessment and sat across from him. Ed disliked meeting students in his tomblike office. She was a pretty girl; she flashed a bright smile as they said their hellos.

"Uhhh." Ed picked up the paper and tapped it with his pen. "I like your main thesis a lot."

Kristen still smiled. "Mmm-hmm?"

"Yeah. I think you develop Aquinas' notion of the medicinal nature of legal punishment nicely. . . ."

"I read it in Latin."

Ed looked up from the paper into Kristen's blue eyes.

"You did? In Latin?"

Kristen nodded.

"Uh-huh."

"Wow. I never could have handled the *Summa* when I was a junior. And I was a religion major."

Her smiled widened, and she looked down to the table. Was she *blushing* because he'd complimented her Latin? Ed glanced back at the paper. He just wasn't enough of a jerk to tell her that the edition of the *Summa* she'd footnoted was the very bilingual edition he'd been using since he was a sophomore.

"Ahhh . . . And your application of this idea to the healing notions of pastoral counseling is nicely developed. Now, I have to tell you, pastoral counseling is not my field. And . . ." Ed took a breath. "I had sort of a problem with your last few pages, where you apply all this to the example of setting up a pastoral counseling office in the Mission Hill district."

Kristen leaned on the table, pulling her hair up over her shoulder. "How's that?"

Ed desperately wanted a cigarette.

"Because, ummmmmmm . . ."

Ed thought: *Because you're using the same White suburban paranoid rhetoric of fear and stupidity that allowed that yuppie scumbag Charles Stewart to blow away his wife last year and blame it on a Black guy. Because you're using the same rhetoric that allowed the Boston cops to bust and question every Black guy they saw with impunity. Because you're using the same view of the world my asshole kid brother has embraced, sitting in his prefab dream house in Vermont.*

". . . because there's an implication that criminality runs throughout Mission Hill. That crime is so inextricably wound up in that community that pastoral counseling there has to be *based on* a spiritual notion of what is criminal, and how to apply that notion to *everyone* there. . . ."

Kristen looked away, to the middle of the coffee shop.

"Oh."

Don't blow this. Make this something she can learn from. Don't give her some PC line of crap.

"But I know you'd fix up that rhetoric if you had time. I mean, you had some tough texts to wrestle with, and the finer points are hard to keep fine when a due date's breathing down your neck. You can't spend too much time deconstructing your own text in a situation like that. I think most professors lose track of that when they grade."

She looked back at him.

Ed gave his best "encouraging teacher" smile.

"Yeah . . . I . . . was feeling under the gun."

She smiled back.

"And my paper wasn't the only paper you had to write. Self-reflection is kind of a luxury. Right?"

Kristen's smile widened. God, she was pretty.

"Yeah. It's been a rough semester."

He gave her an A minus.

As she stood to leave (the last student he had to talk to today, thank God, . . . exams were scheduled from noon on), she said, "Maybe we can talk some more about this later?"

"If I'm not in my office, chances are I'm in here."

She put her hand on his shoulder, squeezing it through his thick sweater.

"I'd like that a lot."

"Me too," he said.

She waved as she walked out of the coffee shop, into the cold Boston morning.

Ed slumped in his seat.

He took a sip of coffee. It was cold. Last year, Kristen's paper wouldn't have bugged him so much. Because last year, at Christmas, he'd met for the first time the person Andy had become.

The nineteen-fucking-eighties, it seemed, had infected Andy. After first-semester exams, Ed had gone up to see Andy at his new home in Vermont. The kid brother Ed had known would have moved to Vermont for the air, the woods, for fly-fishing in summer and ice fishing in winter. Why else would you live in Vermont if most of your business was in New York and Boston?

Andy had moved to Vermont for *tax purposes.*

(*"You can't deal with me being an adult, can you, Eddie?"*)

(*"No. I can't deal with you being an* asshole*!"*)

The last words he'd spoken to his brother. And as he spoke them, Ed saw in his brother's eyes a ghostly reminder of how Andy, years ago, had a puppyish desire to be an adult: a kid constantly trying to act old enough to get into an R-rated movie.

But there was some other reason he was thinking of Andy so often. A reason he couldn't put his finger on.

Ed downed his cold decaf, got his things together. Nick, the coffee-shop owner, waved at him as he got up to leave. The cold hit him like a fist as he left the shop.

He huddled in an alley, out of the wind, to light a clove cigarette. He hated them; they were too sweet. He hated what they stood for: the favorite smokes of pretentious literati wanna-bes who wore naught but black as they lived off their trust funds, pondering their destinies as artists. His hatred of the clove cigarette as symbol had crystallized in one moment—he was sitting in a trendy café on Newbury, reading Teilhard de Chardin in French, while a longhaired loser at the next table held court over a bunch of cappuccino sippers, proclaiming, as he puffed a clove, "You know, Kundera is much better in the original Polish."

Ed laughed. The clove puffer glared at him. Ed shrugged and said, "Kundera writes in Czech and French, y'know."

Clove cigarettes—the firebrand of the New England pretentious.

But Ed could think of no other way to wean himself off tobacco. The habit of smoking was a mark of quiet shame he bore, as he'd always been a health nut. But the stress of grad school was intense. He was dissertating, now. He wasn't about to ruin his health as a stress management strategy until he got tenure.

Assuming he lived that long. Another irony, that he should take care of himself while . . .

He got the clove lit, and sucked smoke that tasted like a burning gingerbread cookie.

As he joined the foot traffic of Beacon, Ed felt the crowd around him like the angry buzzing of insects. He thought again of Andy, swept up in the times. Going along with the crowd, because the crowd promised such wonderful things.

God, Andy. Is your soul worth eighty grand a year?

Not that Ed was in a position to dictate to anyone about the worth of their soul, these days. Or of their lives.

He stood at Beacon and Mass Ave., waiting for the light to change, feeling like livestock about to be prodded to the kill floor. Some jock shithead stood nearby on top of a planter, shouting patriotic nonsense and waving a makeshift flag. Ed had a deep and beautiful urge to punch the guy out just to do his soul some good.

The light changed.

The crowd shuffled across the street. Ed kept his eyes downward, as he found the building to his left that dominated this corner profoundly offensive. As he reached the curb something clicked—the reason he'd been thinking so much of Andy snapped to the fore of his consciousness. Ed stood out of the wind, in the shadow of the building that upset him so, and retrieved from his memory palace the image of a stone effigy of a saint, laid on his back atop a flaming grill. The stone saint wore a wiseass grin, and gave the thumbs-up sign. The epiphany was unnerving enough to make Ed turn back to the coffeehouse to sit and think awhile.

X

Tuesday, 10:35 A.M.

A ngie sounded concerned. "Are you getting by, Lawrence?"
The lingering heaviness of troubled sleep kept Lawrence from thinking clearly. Dream voices had tormented him as he had awakened a half hour ago; he had felt a presence near, and as his eyes focused, a need for comfort and love had filled him. Angie's tone was a moment of decency in the storm of grief she usually flung.

"Ummm. Things are rough, right now. I'm getting by, but it's rough."

The faint static on the line reminded Lawrence of the sound of falling snow. Wrapped in a towel, hair damp, he felt an itch in his chest, as if he were catching a cold. "I think I'll be okay. It's tight. But I think I'll be okay." His tone solicited sympathy, and Lawrence realized this was what Angie wanted.

"I don't know what you're trying to prove up there," she said. "Really. I don't. I can't figure out what you're trying to pull off, if the economy's so bad. There's lots of jobs in Providence. Lots. Every time I go to the grocery store, there's a sign up for bag boys wanted. You'd be a good bag boy."

He clenched his jaw.

"You don't *want* to be a bag boy?"

The phone creaked in his hand. Through miles of phone line, he felt the probing psychic radar unique to Providence—the radar that sensed when someone had the arrogance to get up off his ass and *do* something with his life. Such people had to be swatted down, for their own good . . . reminded (and *reminded,* and *reminded*) that only *other* people realized their ambitions. Not people like *you.*

"How is being a bag boy different from what you're doing now?"

"It's not what I want to do."

In perfect mimicry of their mother's tone, Angie said, "You can't always do what you want to do."

Lawrence's mind screamed: *What the fuck does that mean, you fat waste of human life? What the fuck are you saying? That I should leave one shit-job for another?*

His voice was silent.

"Lawrence, what are you trying to pull?"

He spoke slowly, so his voice would not crack.

"I'm . . . trying to . . . make something of myself."

"Bagging books?"

"Doing . . . what I want to do."

"But you never thought if it was something you *should* do." That sounded too sophisticated for Angie to have come up with on her own—a maxim she'd picked up from the hours of daytime talk shows she watched.

"What should I do, Angie? C'mon. Tell me. What *should* I do?"

"You should *come home,* that's what you should do!"

"There's nothing for me at home."

"There's your mother, and your whole family, that's what's at home!"

"*What?* I'm supposed to live at home and be a drain on Mom's money? Instead of making my own?"

I'm supposed to come home and be a comfort to you. I'm supposed to come home so you can shit on me some more. I'm supposed to be the black sheep, so you all can feel better about yourselves. Goooood Lawrence, the stupid shit. Lawrence, the focus of ridicule. Fuck you. *I'm not going to play that game.*

"Don't you—"

"I gotta go to work." It felt good to cut her off with the truth.

"No. *No.* You don't. You're just trying to—"

"*I'm trying* to get to work on time."

He hung up and dressed.

As he stomped to work he realized Angie *knew* this was the time he'd have to go to work. A week ago, she'd insisted he tell her his schedule, so "in case of an emergency" she'd know where to call. A setup. She knew he'd *have* to hang up on her, and now she'll tell the family what a shit Lawrence was for hanging up on her. The same bullshit as when they were kids, and she'd coax him to do something he shouldn't do—which he *would* do, because she was his older sister, almost ten fucking years older—and then Angie would tell their parents, and watch Lawrence get punished.

Or maybe her plan entailed luring Lawrence into a fight that would last long enough to make him late. She'd pulled a stunt like this before, when Lawrence was about to take the SATs. She stood in the front doorway and bitched that Lawrence had shrunk her sweater by putting it in the dryer. Lawrence told her that he didn't *do* the laundry last night. Angie then laid into him for not doing enough work around the house—why the hell couldn't he help more with the chores? Lawrence had to push her out of the way to get to the bus on time.

Or did Angie have *any* awareness of what she did? Were these traps something she laid like some kind of idiot savant? And what kind of idiot was Lawrence to fall for them? A bag boy. How dare she say that? And how dare he take it?

It was Providence—the hand of the city, still tight around him, the city that was an assassin of ambition. Providence when you are born, Providence when you die. Most of the kids from high school had never been ten miles from the church where they'd been baptized. Most had never taken the bus to Boston, and could not imagine taking the train to New York.

Sure, Lawrence had a shit-job in Boston. But it was *his* shit-job. He'd always wanted to work around books, and now he did. He'd always wanted to live in Boston. Now, he did. Lawrence had a sick feeling his peers would hate him in a small way, were he to go back for a visit.

Individuation becomes betrayal.

Lawrence, eyes cast down, nearly collided with someone. He snapped out of his thoughts to find he'd gone a few doors past the bookstore. He backtracked, then fished out his keys, unlocked the front door. He stamped snow off his feet and glanced at the clock above the counter.

Oh, shit.

It was five after eleven.

And there was no way he could count in the register before Jack got here. In a few minutes, Lawrence would be eligible to be a bag boy. Angie would have won beyond her most bitchy imaginings. He thought of going home, calling in sick. But Jack would be coming down Newbury Street now; he'd spot Lawrence.

Something warm entwined around his legs. In the gloom, he saw Groucho near his feet. She scampered off, toward her food bowl.

Better to lose his job while trying to keep it than by throwing in the towel.

He threw switches by the counter; track lighting flashed above him. He went to the back room, where the cash drawer was kept. Groucho meowed at him. He slid the drawer into the register and added the rolled coins. He penciled the totals on the tally sheet and heard the door open as he did so. He looked up, ready to meet Jack's eyes and take the coming tirade.

It was Ed who stood by the door. Ed glanced up at the clock, then looked Lawrence in the eye. Then he walked to where Lawrence stood.

Ed reached his big, fleshy hand into the till and scooped the quarters from their tray. Lawrence felt he was watching the scene from outside, as he had while with Tom. He was frightened for a reason he could not say.

"What're you *doing*?"

"Shut up and count, Larry."

It was the first time in Lawrence's life that he didn't cringe at the shortened form of his name. It was the first time the syllables were not stretched into a taunt: *"Larrr-eeeee."*

Ed dropped quarters into the tray.

"C'mon, damn it. Count."

Lawrence counted pennies while Ed counted dimes, then the nickels while Ed counted the ten-dollar bills. Ed didn't write the totals down. Lawrence jotted figures on the tally sheet.

Lawrence reached for the fives.

"I'll do that. Add what you got."

Lawrence added, using the calculator. Ed recited the total of each tray as Lawrence tapped figures on the calculator; then, looking at the figures, Ed gave Lawrence the total just as he pressed the equal-sign button.

Lawrence filled in the total, then looked over the tally sheet.

Ed said something.

"What?"

"Are you set?"

"Yeah. It's set."

Ed bounded to the other side of the counter as Lawrence slid the cash drawer into the register.

A shadow in the doorway.

And Jack pushed his way into the store, right shoulder hunched and braced against nothing. Jack came into the store each day like a bouncer entering a room where a fight has broken out; he seemed to rise from a crouch up to his full height, as if he'd had to squeeze through the door.

"Hi, Jack," said Lawrence.

"Hi," said Jack, then cocked his head in greeting at Ed. He stomped to the back room, toward the stairs that led to his office.

Lawrence sighed, then leaned against the counter.

"Dodged a bullet, there, didn't we?" Ed said.

Lawrence nodded.

"Hey. I've worked retail. You had that 'cornered clerk' look about you."

"Thanks."

"It's nothing. I didn't want to hear Jack yelling at you any more than you did."

"Known Jack long?"

"Been coming to this store for—"

"Hey! Lawrence!" Jack's voice boomed from the back room.

Lawrence started, shoulders hunched high.

He called back, *"What?!"*

Lawrence's voice was defensive. Like a kid's. His heart raced. A cold feeling clenched his chest.

"Why the *hell* didn't you feed the cat?"

The theatrically loud crashing of cabinet doors—where the cat food was kept—came from the room.

Lawrence opened his mouth to answer. He had no words to say. Without knowing why, only that he wished to, he looked at Ed, and felt a small nameless shame as he did so. Lawrence lowered his eyes to the countertop, and heard Ed yell toward the back, in a voice that boomed.

"Because he was helping *me,* Jack!"

An instant of heavy quiet, resonant with the dying of Ed's voice off the high rafters.

And for the first time in many months, Lawrence heard a silence in himself that he had forgotten.

XI

Tuesday, 11:05 A.M.

S cratches blushing on her skin, behind the path of her nails along her forearm.

It hurt to scratch her arm, over (and over) the veins of her wrist to her elbow. But she needed the hurt. Needed to *feel* and punish herself.

Troy lay in his crib as Miriam sat on the floor, her sleeve rolled up like a junkie's. Her hand passed over her forearm with slow, metronome regularity. She shook her head jerkily, part of her denying what had happened.

She became aware of her head shaking, and felt more hatred for herself. It was *wrong* to deny her weakness. She pressed her nails harder against her wrist.

Why hadn't she defended herself against the lies her mother had told? How could the bitch defend her father?

Mother's voice had been stern as she tried to undermine Miriam's accusations against her father. Miriam had deflected her mother's lies—lies her mother may not have known were lies, spoken with brutal conviction.

Yet as her mother spoke, her tone had softened.

And when her mother had insisted Miriam see another therapist, at her mother's expense, she used the cajoling tone she'd used when Miriam had been a child. Miriam's need to be a child, to have the comfort of knowing that her parents *knew best,* rose from deep inside her. Miriam, still vulnerable after the fight with Elizabeth, had agreed to her mother's demand.

She'd told herself, as she hung up, that she'd agreed simply to get rid of her mother. She'd *wanted* to believe that she'd agreed to her mother's demand because she believed in herself, in her own goodness and sanity.

But she knew, in her heart, that she'd agreed because she *wanted* what had happened to her to be a lie. And in so wanting, she had betrayed herself. She had betrayed Anne, her therapist, who had helped her so much these last two years. She'd betrayed Troy, and her promise to keep him safe from human monsters. And she had betrayed the wounded child inside of her whom she had sworn to protect from the flood of lies.

She *wanted* to doubt her father's repeated visitations in the night. Her memories were not of a single canvas; they were a mosaic, incomplete, that she tried to see in dim light. She knew the shape of the mosaic. She knew the darkness spread upon it was a malevolent shadow. To discern the mosaic with clarity was a terrible burden of which she wished to be free.

After she'd hung up the phone, Miriam paced the living room, touching each wall. She needed her therapist, her healer. But Anne was out of town, gone to a seminar.

With a deep breath, Miriam stopped to look for the card of the therapist Anne had said Miriam could call while she was away. She couldn't find the card.

Tightness had clenched her chest, tightness like the paralysis that she had known (remembered) in her dreams, that she had known (remembered) while her father had violated her wearing the form of the monster her mind had needed him to wear. She reached for her address book, then began calling members of her survivors' group. No one was home. She left messages on their answering machines.

Troy had begun to cry. Or she had noticed his crying.

She rushed to the crib. Feeling her anger shift to her child, she caught the anger and held it like a serpent swollen with venom, willing it back to where she kept her decades of rage. After she had quieted Troy, she sat upon the floor. The need to punish herself, to express the anger she felt for feeling anger against Troy, spread like a bloody stain across her mind.

There was wetness under her fingertips.

She smelled the blood only when she looked down at her forearm, not quite recognizing it as her own. She thought she'd like to show it to Elizabeth, and so show what Elizabeth had contributed to by being so cruel that morning.

Miriam closed her eyes, shutting out as much of the world as she could, and walked to her safe spot, feeling her way down the hall, humming an invocation to the Goddess for strength that she'd learned from a tape of spiritual music. The sounds of traffic outside were too ugly to hear. The cardinal had fallen silent. It took her a few moments to find the door to the large walk-in closet she'd made her place of Strength and Comfort. She ran her fingers over the molding to the doorknob and turned it. The smell of sage incense lingered in the closet, imbuing the large pillows and the cotton tapestries she had hung.

She closed the door, knelt down, and felt her way to her meditation pillows. She lay upon them, and in darkness of her own creation, pictured her protective tower complete, strong under the light of the full moon. She had not the strength to rebuild it, stone by stone; it was half the visualization it should have been. But this half visualization could still help her gain back a fragment of what the child within her represented. She needed courage to face her fears, and perhaps call her mother and undo her betrayal of Anne, Elizabeth, Troy, and the child in the tower by submitting to her demand.

Miriam breathed as she'd been taught as she approached the

tower. She heard her child within weeping softly behind the walls of the tower.

In her mind, keeping the sounds of the hostile world outside at bay, she walked toward the tower door, to restore the child's faith in her, and to thank the child, once again, for the strength that had allowed Miriam to survive. She opened the tower door carved with runes and inlaid with ivy and mistletoe.

It happened with the swiftness of a dream played out on the threshold of sleep, in the moment the body exhales the last breath drawn in wakefulness.

The light of the moon above soured to the green hidden in the back of a fly in sunlight. Her mind filled with the sounds of cicadas, of distant whispers and the dim ringing of wide-mouthed bells.

The demon she had imagined her father to be forced its bulk through the door, stepping from the shadows in the tower. It loomed over her, as high above her as it had when Miriam had been a child. It smiled down at her, holding the child that had been secure in the tower, a prize.

It moved like a sirocco, silently, carrying the child over the dunes.

Miriam, sobbing on her knees, could not follow.

XII

Tuesday, 11:51 A.M.

Paul entered the teachers' lounge to see Cory staring out the window, a cigarette burned to long ash hanging from her fingers. Cory's hand trembled. Beside her lay stacks of ungraded papers, her red pen resting like an offering on top.

Paul took Fleischer's mug (boldly emblazoned with THE USS NIMITZ) from the counter and walked toward her. She looked up, startled. Paul swung the mug under her cigarette and tapped her hand. The ash fell into the mug, hissing as it hit the dregs of cold coffee at the bottom.

Cory stared—bewildered—at the cup, then up at Paul.

He shrugged.

"Gotta get your licks in where you can."

For the first time in days, Paul saw Cory smile.

She flicked the butt into the cup as well. It hissed.

Paul said, "You want to make this a triple play, and spit into it?"

Cory turned her head toward the window again, then looked back at Paul.

"I'll save that. Spitting. For later."

Cory reminded Paul of women Hemingway wrote of: fair in an aristocratic way, but tough inside. She was very tall, with a heart-shaped face. She stooped, self-conscious of her height. Even as she sat, her shoulders came forward. Since he'd met her, Cory seemed to have aged. Not with lines or grey hairs, but with a dimming of an unnameable light in her eyes. Paul had once worked as a bouncer. People whose IDs he had to check had the light in their eyes that Cory had lost.

Paul set down the mug. Kneeling, he said, "I want you to know that ordinarily, I never advocate passive aggression. But it doesn't seem you have any other recourse open to you now."

"Thanks . . . for giving me the option."

Paul put his hand on the stack of papers. "When are these due?"

"Tomorrow."

Paul picked up the stack. Midyear sophomore history. Reformation Era. Easy.

"I'll do the multiple choice and the fill-in-the-blanks. You do the essays."

"No."

She swallowed, nervously.

Paul grabbed a plastic chair from beside the scarred table in the center of the lounge. He sat before Cory.

"Why not?"

"I've got to do the correcting."

"You scared of Fleischer?"

"Yes."

"Don't be. I know you have to play his games to get your teacher's certificate. But that doesn't mean he can treat you like an indentured servant. If you give him more respect or power than he deserves, he'll own you. If you don't keep your dignity, you're going to sell your soul for a whopping twenty grand a year."

She cast her eyes downward.

"I'm not in this for the money."

"I know. Me neither. You want to teach, and that's noble. But you're *not* going to change the world. And the highest rewards of teaching aren't worth losing your dignity."

"Why do you teach?"

"I have my reasons. Not good reasons. But they're mine."

"Can you tell me?"

"I can, but I won't. They're mine."

"Why . . . why do you hate Fleischer?"

Paul spoke slowly. "Because he's a stupid, arrogant little man. Because he treats his student teachers like shit. Because he likes to make women cry, and I've seen him do it. Because I don't like the way he looks at me. Because he bitches about *quote* 'welfare niggers,' *end quote* stealing tax dollars, and then takes one grand from the state to take on the *quote* 'extra work,' *end quote* of working with student teachers, then treats them like slaves."

Cory looked away, as if embarrassed by Paul's venom. "I . . . hate him," she said. Her face screwed as if she'd cry, not out of emotional distress, but physical pain.

"He's worth hating."

She looked embarrassed again—almost blushing, while still in pain.

He wanted to tell her it was okay to vent in front of a guy she barely knew, because teaching was sort of like combat; the pressure created intense bonding. Sometimes, the only way to keep your sense of self was to bitch and moan with someone who had no real investment in who you were. It was okay to steal moments of humanity from the hours you were supposed to be a teacher, to steal moments of hearing one voice amid the hundreds of voices you heard throughout the day in school. But to say so would embarrass her more.

Steps echoed in the halls. Soon, more teachers would come to the lounge; whatever peace Paul and Cory could share would be gone, replaced by the gripings of overworked teachers.

"I know correcting tests counts as homework for you. You're a *student* teacher, but Fleischer is not teaching you as his student. He's broken his side of the contract. He threw you into his class without preparation. He left the fucking school. He didn't even introduce you to the class. You're the third student teacher he's had this year. The third. That's thirty weeks of teaching done *for him*. He teaches eight weeks a year. He gets a thousand bucks for taking the extra work of making you his apprentice, then dumps *all* the work in your lap. That motherfucker does not warrant your keeping your end of the contract."

"But if he finds out . . ."

"If he finds out, you threaten to go to the school board. From now on, you keep a log of his comings and goings. You keep track of when he slips out of the building. That little fuck is living for the day he can retire. If you threaten his pension, he'll shut up."

Paul's dislike for Fleischer had germinated into hatred the second day of Cory's stint, when Fleischer strutted into the lounge to get his

coat and hat during second period—the time of Fleischer's most difficult class: a bunch of troublemakers pushed into the vocational
track. Paul couldn't believe Fleischer would dump Cory into a shark
pit so soon after her arrival. The little fuck looked like a troll—badly
aging into his fifties, balding, surviving crown of grey unkempt, tossing his coat over his stooped shoulders, rummy nose red under the
fluorescent lights. Paul, the only one in the lounge, gave Fleischer a
disbelieving look as he zipped his coat. Fleischer returned Paul's
look with a sneer. "Don't look at me like that," he said, as if he
could back up his tone with his fists.

It was only when the door swung shut behind Fleischer that Paul
had thought to call after him, *"Go and drink yourself a good breakfast."* Paul had looked down at his hand atop the papers he'd been
correcting. He'd clenched it into a fist around his red pen.

He'd then gone to look through the doorway of Fleischer's classroom from the hall, and saw Cory doing all the things they teach you
in education classes that never work in a real classroom. She had reminded Paul of an understudy in a play—the same look of controlled
terror, the same painful uncertainty of what to say next.

The class had been waiting, a great predator with many faces and
eyes. There was a buzzing in the air, like the stillness in a bar before
a fight breaks out. How a great hydra attacked you was to draw you
in, make you part of it, like the victim of a dark carnival. To resist,
you had to assert your individuality. The kids were shifting in their
seats. Paul knew the body language. They were getting ready. To
enter the room would undermine her authority. If Paul did that,
he'd be worse than Fleischer.

He walked back to the teachers' lounge. He thought to call Fleischer's room on the extension phone, to tell Cory how to assert herself, and which kids would give her the worst time. But to answer the
extension, she'd turn her back to the room. Instead, Paul sat, paralyzed. Furious. Unable to do even his own work.

In the following weeks, offhand comments by Fleischer about
Cory's tits and legs, along with his usual strutting arrogance, had
made Fleischer intolerable.

This morning, from the look on Cory's face, Fleischer's attacks on
Cory were getting nastier. Paul could never abide bullies, particularly
small bullies who used viciousness to intimidate. Paul knew their
type. It was the *little* bullies who swung for your nose or mouth
without provocation, who went for your groin, or came at you with
bottles.

Cory said, "When can we do the papers?"

"After school. I know a coffee shop that's quiet. We can do it in a few hours."

"Okay."

Voices in the hallway. Getting louder.

Paul stood, grabbed Fleischer's cup. He took it to the sink and dumped the contents just as two of his colleagues came through the door. He then took his mug from the counter and filled it with coffee. It smelled awful—stale and weak, not much better than what you got from vending machines.

He turned to see Cory going over her lesson plans, his two colleagues sitting at their usual spot to spew their usual line of crap. No knowing glances from the two were directed at Cory or him. No ugly little teacher-rumors would be passed today.

Paul sat, feeling, for just a moment, that he had freed himself from the constraints of his suit.

XIII

Tuesday, 12:01 P.M.

T he man in the leather jacket (. . . *Ed. His name is Ed . . .*) looked at Lawrence, grey eyes alight. There was something different about Ed, as if his somber but cheerful demeanor had fallen away, revealing a more relaxed sense of humor.

"You miss eating *brains*?" he asked.

Lawrence took a sharp breath. "No. No. I mean *Portuguese* sweet breads. They're big, round pastry breads, like a cake. My . . . roommate and I used to eat a whole one each Sunday. You can't find them here. They go real good with coffee."

"Real good." Did I just say "real good"?

Jack's thumping about in the upstairs office competed with Eric Burdon's voice on the oldies station. One or two customers wandered the store. Ed had gone out to get coffee for himself and Lawrence, which now cooled on the counter between them.

He's a regular. Vicki says he hangs out here. Don't get your hopes up. Bringing a guy coffee isn't an expression of desire. No matter what Vicki's mom says.

Ed's jacket was open, showing the broadness of his chest wrapped in a thick woolen sweater. He stood against the counter as if leaning against a front porch. "Next time I'm in Providence, I'll get one."

Then Ed smiled like a lynx. "But my last culinary experience in Providence was pretty grim. . . ."

Get him to talk about himself. All men love to do that.

"What were you doing down there?"

"Looking at incunabula."

"Oh . . . at . . . Brown?"

"Yeah." Ed spoke as if Lawrence had asked if he'd seen a *movie* in a *theater.* "But . . . uhh." Ed was deciding how best to tell the story—Lawrence tried to show greater interest, and leaned over the counter.

Ed went on, "You've seen *Annie Hall,* right?"

"Yeah." Lawrence had never seen it all the way through. He'd liked what he'd seen, especially the scene with the lobsters.

"You remember the scene where Diane Keaton does the total Connecticut WASP thing, and orders a corned beef sandwich on white bread with mayo and tomato? And that was a *joke,* right? Could never really *happen,* right?"

Lawrence nodded.

"Last time I was in Providence, I ordered a corned beef sandwich, and they brought it to me on white bread, with mayo and a tomato." Ed paused for effect; Lawrence readied himself to give a good reaction. "With *lettuce!*"

Lawrence made his best shocked and amused face. "Oh, God!" he said.

"The waitress couldn't figure out why I looked at her like she'd brought me a dead rat on a stick. It was a surreal moment, when something you just assume to be fictional worms its way into reality. It was kind of like sharing a pizza with the yeti, or something."

Ed, despite his practiced delivery, was not a self-centered storyteller. He wasn't performing in the queenish, self-important way Lawrence was used to hearing stories.

"So, did you eat the sandwich?"

"Yeah. I figured it was like on *Star Trek.* To send it back would be like violating the Prime Directive."

Ed, shaking his head slightly, reached into his leather jacket and pulled out a pack of cloves. He tapped out a single cigarette and held it between his fingers as if it were lit.

Lawrence was about to switch the conversation to *Star Trek* when Ed asked, "So what brings you to Boston, Larry?"

Lawrence was still thrown by being called "Larry" without there being hostility behind it.

"Uhhhhm. Just had to get away from the old hometown. Can I bum one of those off of you?"

Ed was putting the pack back into his pocket. "One of *these*?"

"Yeah."

"Uhhh. Sure." Ed held the pack to Lawrence, who fished out a cigarette. He thought of the kids who went to Brown, whom he'd seen on Thayer Street, sitting in cafés, at times speaking French, dressed in black, smoking cloves. Ed must have been like that in college, too intellectual to smoke anything domestic.

"I'm trying to quit," said Ed. "I'm weaning myself off tobacco. More than anything, I just need to hold something in my hand. Helps me think."

"Me too."

The front door opened. Ed craned his neck to see who came in: the mark of a people watcher. Lawrence looked over Ed's shoulder.

It was Vicki, four minutes late, by the digital clock on the register.

"Hey, sweets," said Ed.

Vicki whacked him on the shoulder with her glove as she rounded the counter. "Don't get fresh with me, brute."

Ed stood up straight and frowned. "Don't call me a brute. I'm a masher, okay?"

"Okay," said Vicki. Behind the counter now, she took off her coat and scarf. "Hey, Lawrence."

"Hey."

"What're you guys talking about?"

"Mostly, Larry is talking about what a pain in the ass you are to work with."

Vicki drummed her fingers on the counter. "The operative words here are 'work with.' " She pointed at Lawrence with her thumb. "Lawrence does not 'work with' anybody, as he does not 'work' at all. He takes up space. Therefore, my being a 'pain in the ass' in this context is moot."

Ed nodded. "Good point. I see you've been reading your Aristotle."

"No. I've been reading *your* Aristotle. I pinched it from your book bag when you left it behind the counter the other day. But, as you probably stole it from this store in the first place, it evens out."

"Sounds like you stole my Boethius, too."

"Oh, yeah."

"Good," said Ed. "You'll probably need Boethius, as you'll probably at least be under house arrest sometime in your life."

Lawrence *felt* Ed's shifting of attention away from him, much in the way he often felt his good moods drawn away as Jack stomped down the stairs. He wanted to chime in, but decided to keep his mouth shut. Who the hell was Boethius?

"Probably for assaulting a certain obnoxious customer."

"I'm not a customer, I'm a loiterer."

"That's what Jack thinks of you. Which is why I refer to you as a 'customer.' I refuse to agree with Jack on anything."

"Good policy."

"Thank you."

Lawrence saw something in Ed's eyes, like summer sunlight filtering from behind curtains. Ed had a crush on Vicki. The light in Ed's eyes, which Lawrence wanted to fall upon him, fell upon Vicki.

"You're welcome," said Ed.

Did Vicki know Ed had a crush on her?

"So . . . why *do* you work for Jack?"

Lawrence turned toward Vicki, to see if her eyes held a similar light.

"I don't work *for* Jack. I work *with* books in Jack's store."

"You work with books, but not *with* Larry?"

Vicki seemed startled, and cast a confused glance toward Lawrence as he was trying to see what was in her eyes. He felt as if he were a straight guy she'd caught staring at her breasts.

She turned back to Ed. "Yeah. I don't work with . . . Larry."

A dazed-looking guy of about twenty meandered his way around Ed. He muttered, " 'Scuse me," and put a few battered sci-fi books and last year's *Leonard Maltin's Movie Guide* on the counter. The guy smelled of pot and sandalwood. As Lawrence rung him up, Ed glanced at the clock over the counter.

"Shit," he said. "I've got an appointment. Besides, looks like you two have a real rush going on."

"What kind of appointment?" asked Lawrence, as he took the young guy's money. The young guy was staring at his shoes, not wanting, it seemed, anyone to notice how red his eyes were.

"With my thesis advisor. Or, as I like to call him, my feces advisor."

The young guy gave a snorting cackle. "Feces advisor," he muttered at the floor.

Ed gave the guy a sidelong glance. "Uhhh . . . yeah. I gotta go." He backed to the door, zipping his jacket, clove dangling from his lip. "Later," he said, pulling his gloves from his pocket.

Lawrence and Vicki both said good-bye as the door swung shut.

After the young guy had left, Vicki reached over to the top of the register, where Lawrence had absently placed the clove cigarette.

She picked it up and scrutinized it, the way Basil Rathbone would pick up a piece of evidence in a Sherlock Holmes movie.

"You let him call you *Larry*?"

XIV

Tuesday, 12:55 P.M.

Ignoring the confusion of a badly managed work site, the young man pulls a strand of his wife's hair from the wool of his shirt. He smiles, thinking of the divinations they shall perform tonight, and the lovemaking that will follow in air thick with incense at the foot of the throne of their Lord. What they shall share tonight shall offset the gnawing fear they had felt this morning.

He takes the hair and ties it, like a fishing lure, into a charm of the type used near Ashdod, long ago. He makes sure his own long hair is concealed under the hair net he wears.

The young man has five minutes before he is back on the clock. But this will not matter to the floor manager. Rather than face the manager barking at him, he gathers warped planks of knotty pine that would make excellent kindling, but will be made into crappy flooring, and carries them to the ripped living room of an old house, which is now being converted into office space.

The young man rather likes his boss, his *true* boss, who knows that the young man is in bad financial straits and slips him cash advances on his paycheck. But his floor manager, a pockmarked brat named Louie, he cannot stand. Louie got his position by way of his uncle, who does work site management for the father of the young man's boss. The shitty wood the young man carries is symptomatic of the nonsense Louie imposes in the name of "putting things in the black."

The young man enters the work area, and feels the Enfolded One near. Ten men are in the room, driving nails, sawing. Perhaps a score of men work on the site, all told. Only a score. Yet that score is enough of a societal construct as to give form to the Enfolded One's will.

No, *will* is too strong a word, too *solid* to articulate the Enfolded One's obtrusion of Its *impulses* into the world.

Three men in a far corner glare at the young man. As someone who works under the table, he must work hard enough to not get fired, but must be unproductive enough to not be a threat to the union guys. He feels the three gazes upon him, probing the shielding he has placed around his aura. He does not return their glare, but puts down the wood and planes the edges, purposefully doing a slow and lazy job of it, until he no longer feels their gaze.

He relaxes, and readjusts the blade of the plane. He feels as if he is in the belly of the beast. The only haven he knows from the influence of the Enfolded One these days—as the world marches toward a pointless war that millions have been hugger-muggered into without knowing why—is in the home he shares with his wife and his Lord. The Enfolded One, the Blind Dragon, the Mob Mind, Leviathan, walks the Earth as the frenzy that will lead to war, in the form of religious devotion expressed by way of the sword, by way of the need to feel greatness as a nation only exerting force upon another.

The young man clears the blade of the plane, then planes some more. He loves to work with his hands, to create things that are worthwhile. This job, with its cheap shortcuts and building-code dodges, is a noisome thing he must perform to feed himself and his wife.

The men around him work with no awareness at pointless tasks—like destroying a beautiful house such as this to make ugly offices—because they know of nothing else. They work not for paychecks. Not to feed their families. Not for something to do. They work to have some semblance of an identity . . . an identity they had no interest in developing for themselves.

And empty, unthinking souls, with no resonance, are the very substance of the Enfolded One. Even those who followed the religions of Abraham blindly would be devoured by the Enfolded One in death. To follow the Unbowed One, mortal enemy of the Blind Dragon, was to set right the world, in a small way.

The young man stops his planing.

The union men in the corner discuss how "we" are going to "kick Saddam Hussein's ass" much in the way they spoke of how "we," meaning the New England Patriots, were going to kick some other city's ass come Sunday.

Whispering to himself in Aramaic, he clothes his soul in a protective prayer that will, he hopes, keep him from the reach of the Blind Dragon.

XV

Tuesday, 2:30 P.M.

A right.
    Fucking . . .
A left.
    . . . *condescending* . . .
Two rights.
    . . . *shit heel* . . .
Ed looked around the gym. The people nearby were too absorbed in the movements of their own bodies to see. He bounced on the mat and gave the bag a violent gut-level kick that would have gotten him thrown out of the gym for good, had anyone seen. His knee twinged. Ed grimaced. But the kick was necessary—saving him the later pain of losing his temper. Even back when he'd studied martial arts formally, he'd liked to wail on a bag to let off steam. He shook out his leg and landed a barrage of punches on the bag. He wished he still had his *gi*.
    . . . *Aristotelian* . . .
A left.
    . . . *essentialist* . . .
Right jabs.
    . . . *Pollyanna* . . .
A roundhouse finale, with all his right shoulder behind it.
    . . . *Dominican!*
Ed caught his breath while the bag danced like a man on a gibbet. He wanted a cigarette. A gym monitor, a nineteen-year-old steroid pumper with an inhumanly thick neck, gave Ed a dirty look as he made his rounds. When the self-styled alpha male was gone, Ed saw that he'd left a dusty sneaker print on the bag.
    Ed was never comfortable with his desire to beat up a priest. Priests were monoliths—compact incarnations of God's Old Testament ire dispensating New Testament teachings. Part of Ed's mind, preserving the terror he'd felt in Catholic school, simply *knew* that were he to punch out a priest, Jehovah's wrath would be upon him in a flash of burning violet.
    Ed walked the mat, waiting for his pulse to slow, thinking how he should be studying under a Jesuit, who was likely to be straightforward in his hostility, and to respect someone who stood up to him.

Ed took off the practice gloves and returned them to the equipment booth. The kid working there handed back Ed's ID card. Ed put it in the pocket of his cutoffs and went to the weight room. Spandex, everywhere. He hated it. Weight rooms should be where people went to wear old clothes and smell bad, not wear new clothes and look good. The camaraderie of the places he'd worked out in as a kid was missing. No one spotted anyone else. Mostly, they just looked at themselves in the mirrors on every wall. Ed stretched on the mats, trying hard not to think negative thoughts, because if he did, he'd work out too hard and be sore tomorrow. He stood and started his dumbbell routine.

But as he did curls, hostile thoughts of Father Eugene Tomassetti, Ph.D., crept into his mind.

Tomassetti, with his bulbous nose and unsettling resemblance to Donald Pleasence, had looked over the drafts of Ed's thesis today and said, *"Mr. Sloane, your thesis is theologically problematic."*

Ed had wanted to say, *"No shit, Sherlock. You're doing Saint Thomas proud!"*

Ed jerked a dumbbell to his chest. Twenty-five pounds of metal thumped against his ribs.

Ed set down the weights.

"C'mon, man! You gotta *want* it!"

One guy, standing by the benches, was rooting on another who lay on his back, pressing what looked to be about two hundred pounds. Mr. Encouragement was not standing where he could do any good as a spotter. The presser blew out his breath and brought up the bar.

"Waytago! Waytago!" cried Mr. Encouragement.

Ed stretched out his arms. He was too prone to venting his anger in the gym. One time, when especially pissed off, he'd worked out so long and hard that he'd sprained his left arm so that it had later swollen up as if he'd been bitten by something poisonous. Ed also worked out to stave off depression, the depression that . . .

"I truly can't see where you're carrying this argument, Mr. Sloane."

Of course Tomassetti couldn't see. He did not wish to see. He was trained in pastoral counseling (Ed had thought the guy's work in classics would make him a good thesis advisor, which had been stupidly optimistic). Tomassetti had spent his adult life preventing exactly what Ed's thesis advocated in a . . .

"C'mon! 'Nother set! 'Nother set!"

Mr. Encouragement prodded the guy on the bench. The guy on the bench looked scared, the bar only halfway up, his elbows shaking, face red, veins standing out on his forehead. The weights on the bar trembled.

"Gotta want it! Gotta want it!"

Ed ran to the bench and got behind the presser. The presser's left elbow buckled. Ed got his hands on the bar and eased it on the supports.

Mr. Encouragement yelled, "Hey man, what's wrong with you? *He had it!*"

Later, his hair slightly wet from the showers, Ed walked away from the university sports facility in the cold. He thought of what the presser must have felt, and wished, at some point, he could face as excusable a death as the presser had.

He disliked being near death.

He found it too attractive and too moral a choice to ignore.

XVI

Tuesday, 4:02 P.M.

iriam left the apartment for the first time in days, wheeling Troy along the esplanade by the Charles. She was glad to be outside, glad to not face what she had been confronting within herself. But she felt no connection with the outdoors, no feelings beyond the cold, the different light. Winter used to fill her with joy; the Charles once had filled her with quiet awe. She'd felt close to the Earth, the sky, and the unique sense of joining that came where the river touched the land. An invisible screen had come between her and nature; the voices she once fancied she heard from trees had been silenced, as if the parts of her mind and spirit that could be close to the blessings of the Goddess had died.

Troy fussed in the stroller. Miriam stopped and fished his pacifier from the blankets. His cheeks were flushed, his blue eyes crinkled with happiness upon seeing her. She put the pacifier back in his mouth, and walked along the esplanade.

What she'd been facing had no doubt closed off the beneficence of nature from her. But there was more. She had never felt this distant from . . . *Beauty*. From the poetry and song she had once been able to find in all things. Perhaps it was her worries about the war, or the ugly fear she dared not name until moments ago—that Elizabeth might leave her.

The desert inside herself, that she had defied with her tower of strength, was now the vista of her being. A woman lost in the desert could not know the Beauty of which a River spoke.

Twilight deepened. The trees took silhouettes, made themselves sharper in contrast to the softening light. The Charles took the color of a March sky. What she saw should have been beautiful, but touched her in no way. The demon that had oppressed her ruled the desert, ruled her inner world. To face the demon, Miriam had to find strength from the Mother of the Desert; through the Desert Goddess, Miriam's soul could be joined with all faces of the Goddess.

Dusk shadows spread from under winter-dead trees. Her footfalls crunched behind the stroller's wheels, upon the blackened rock salt and sand laid upon the walkway. She would need Elizabeth's help to call the Desert Goddess. Maybe ritual and prayer would heal the rift between them, renew the oaths of devotion they had taken.

Back in the apartment, dry heat on her winter-reddened face and hands, Miriam felt nothing, not even surprise or regret, as she listened to the phone message from Elizabeth that told her: *"I won't be home until late. Don't wait dinner for me."*

Miriam wondered whom Elizabeth would be with, and then wondered why she should bother to wonder.

XVII

Tuesday, 6:05 P.M.

in the warmth of the theater, swaddled in the clothes and the coats in which he lived, dutch dreamt of spaceships and the face of Jesus spread across a vista of stars

he saw a woman's face in the clean burning glare of a white sun

she smiled at him, and in his heart, dutch knew this woman, this angel of the heavens, had reached inside him today to crush the spiders he carried in his lungs

he awoke to see, through his drowsy vision, a field of stars upon the theater's screen, and models of spaceships gliding across the inky blackness

in these stars he found no comfort, and returned to the stars of his dreams

XVIII

Tuesday, 7:58 P.M.

Crystals of ice flowed in rivers of wind upon the face of the Charles. The moon shone from behind the clouds like a gauze-covered face, its light making the Charles an unmoving scar cut through the city.

Ed Sloane looked upon the frozen Charles from the Boston U Bridge, and wondered if the ice would shatter if he were to throw himself over the railing; if the ice would absorb his falling weight; if the shattering of the ice would slow his impact enough that he wouldn't be drawn under the frozen mantle by the current. Would he die from the fall? From drowning? The shock of the cold?

Ed wondered: was his impulse toward self-destruction born of the sin of Despair, or of an honorable and Divinely forgivable refusal to partake of an immoral world? Or, if his desire to die was born of a graver sin: Vanity.

Ed knew that soon he'd be able to smother the urge to kill himself. He simply had to think about it, embrace it, until it fell quiet. If he didn't entertain the urge toward suicide, it would build in him as a panic he couldn't control. . . . Yet he knew that his suicide, were he to indulge the impulse, would be meaningless. Sinful. No, were he to kill himself, he'd want to be at peace with himself and with God. Better to die as a citizen of Masada than a prisoner of Babylon. Better to fall on your sword as did Cato the Younger than to embrace the darkness of your dungeon as did Pier della Vigna.

His suicide should be an act of defiance, not of self-pity. And Ed was not certain if he truly wished to *die,* or to *end* his life, be free of it, and perhaps find another.

He looked to the railroad bridge that crossed the river below, where, long ago, some righteously indignant hippie had no doubt hung over the iron trellis as he painted the graffito that read NIXON with the x done as a stylized swastika. Did the guy who painted it even remember doing it? Did he even hold the same politics today, or was he now some self-satisfied yuppie shit grown fat on the eighties' brokering of the American dream?

It was when he'd realized what his brother had become that Ed knew a genuine terror. It was then, looking into the mask his brother's face had become, that he thought it might be good to leave this world behind.

Ed set down his book bag. He realized it would be most inconsiderate to kill himself before he'd finished grading his students' papers, almost as rude as jumping off the bridge with them in his pack—his students' final grades resting on the silty bottom. He took off his gloves and pulled free his cloves and lighter. Sweet smoke filled his mouth as the light of the moon changed, and the ice below took the soft hue of sapphire.

Staring at the graffito, Ed thought how nice it would have been to face Nixon as the ultimate expression of moral and political corruption. During the bombing of Libya, in '85, while the then president was calling Gadhafi "Gadhafi Duck" and citing Stallone as his inspiration for international policy, Ed had realized that if he woke up in the morning and found that Nixon was back in office and Kissinger the secretary of state, he would have gotten on his hands and knees and thanked God. Nixon and Kissinger represented a corruption that could be reasoned with. The madness of the eighties was blind. Unthinking. Insanely jingoistic. He didn't dare think what the Millennium would bring.

The Boston U Chapel bells struck eight just as Ed decided to walk home and finish grading. Ed smiled. He had a flair for maneuvering himself into absurdly symbolic situations. Perhaps urges toward suicide were an occupational hazard of being a theology student. He felt cheated, though, that the Boston U Chapel bells were not truly bells, but recordings of bells played over a speaker system—tinny, with no resonance. Faust at least had real bells.

He looked toward the Harvard Bridge, some miles down the river. Pulling on his gloves, cigarette dangling from his mouth, he thought how stupid it was to think of the girl he'd glimpsed this morning on the Harvard Bridge now, while working out whether or not to snuff out his own existence and whether or not doing so would drop him into the maw of Hell. *Priorities, Ed.*

Passing the vacant lot among the tall reeds on the Cambridge side of the bridge, where homeless people camped in milder weather and junkies shot up year-round, Ed thought again of the pretty girl he'd seen that morning, and realized that she reminded him of the girl who had taught him the deeper meaning of despair.

XIX

T he silence of a city.
    The breathing of statues and the whisperings of brick.

The language where language ends. The finite, suspended quiet as the first drop of a summer storm falls, the quiet that is a soft curtain woven through beads of rain strung from clouds.

The footstep of the fog that walks from the harbor to tread upon rooftops and rest as condensation upon glass.

The sound of frost on windows.
            Of autumn leaves changing color.
                    Of the turning of a snowflake.
                        Of the changing face of the moon.

The sound of sleep, and the absent midwifery of dreams, the silence that is constant, and so constantly unheard by those who live and are able to breathe.

The Succubus heard the silence of Boston, a silence as unique to the city as its voices and footfalls.

To know the silence of a place is to know its soul. Notes of music are half the music, silence the other half. And this night, for the first time, under grey winter clouds and the shrouded face of the moon, the Succubus heard Boston's silence and knew its deeper resonances.

Thus did she join more closely with the city that would be her earthly dominion, in the way empty spaces on a page are joined with the letters written upon them. She lay, breathless, upon the snowy bed of her home. Slowly, she withdrew herself from the silence, for to do so quickly would be traumatic as the moment of first consciousness.

In that moment, between finite awareness and the limitations of flesh, she was assaulted. A *prayer,* a whisper of impassioned hope, fell upon her from outside her senses. It shattered the silence like the cracking of ice. It burned her, beneath the skin of her fleshless body.

Pulling herself into physicality, the Succubus rolled upon the snow as if she had been kicked. She piled against the brick coping and flung out her arm, gripping the coping's edge and pulverizing brick in her hand. The sounds of the city flooded back to her. She arched her back, muscles under scarlet skin corded, trembling.

She stood, threw back her head, and screamed.

Soundless, her scream tore the city's night. The dreams of sleepers nearby shimmered and ripped, crackling to ash as do burning autumn leaves. Others, still awake, felt something inside themselves *stolen,* so that they stumbled slightly, or felt a thick, drowsy fever in their blood. A man looked to his wife, and in a sickening instant realized that he had never loved her. A child looked to her parents, and wondered if she could be worthy of their love.

Fists clenched, the Succubus stopped screaming and heard a sound in her mind like that of windblown grass. The echo of her rage touched the walls of the buildings around her as the light of dusk does in the moment it fades from bronze to violet, then dies.

She could not suffer the blasphemy of the prayer to go unpunished, she could not allow the prayer to go unanswered.

She would fill the role of her patroness, the Avenger, to punish what had been inflicted upon her Mother.

XX

L ilith, *Maiden of the Dark Moon, hear my prayer.*
      The scent of rosemary oil, heated with clear water in the bowl of the aromatherapy lamp, and of spirit-healing incense. Comfort, around her in the air, to be breathed in and embraced by her soul.

Lilith, Goddess of the Desert, heal my heart, heal my soul. Heal the life that has been stolen from me.

The sulfur scent of a match, lit, then placed against the white wick of a black candle. The tip of the wick glowing red, drawing her gaze into the pure and changing face of the flame. Transformation and healing *toward* the Goddess. *From* the Goddess within herself.

Lilith, you who are Oneness, you who are defiance and strength, and the route of healing, you who are the true Mother of All, hear my prayer.

In silence, Miriam turned her mind inward and found her tower whole in the desert of her soul. Beautiful in the light of the moon. No child's cries came from within. She neared the tower. A voice, sweet and melodious, whispered to her, whether in her mind or outside of herself, she could not tell.

"I come as my Mother's shadow."

She felt a glow, and a feeling of safety familiar to her as a cherished memory.

"It is in shadow, far from light, that my Mother lives."

Warmth, soft as down, with the texture of down, covered Miriam, enfolded her skin. Held her in a gentle embrace.

"Shadow is the child of light."

A scent like that of Troy's hair filled the room, filled the desert air.

"Enter shadows."

Her body felt as if it had been lifted in the air.

"Enter night."

Her body felt one with the air. She walked toward her tower, which she now saw as a temple as well. A place of Haven and Worship.

"You are not night's child."

An angel of bronze stood atop the doorway of her tower, affixed, it seemed, to the very stones—a look of lamentation and regret upon her face.

Miriam opened her eyes, startled. Where had she seen the angel before? She had walked beneath it. She had felt its sad gaze upon her and had looked up to its unmoving countenance. She heard Troy laughing, alone in his crib, as he did while she touched and played with him.

She rose from her pillows, and put out the candles and the incense in its burner. She opened the door of her haven to check on Troy.

A naked woman stood in the hallway.

Miriam fell back against the door, gripping the handle for support. The woman stepped toward her, making a gentle motion of reassurance with her hands, looking like an ancient carving of a maiden offering libation to a deity. The woman moved like summer drizzle, the expression upon her face changed to one of warm concern in a way that reminded Miriam of a rainbow refracting into visibility.

Miriam stood upright, wanting to believe she was dreaming, that some corner of herself had created the lovely being who stood before her.

The naked woman fixed her fawn eyes upon Miriam and smiled. Yet behind the smile the woman seemed *hurt,* wounded, in a way that mirrored Miriam's own pain. The woman took one step back as she said, "Don't be afraid."

Miriam smelled a warm and reassuring scent that reminded her of—*no,* that made her *feel*—the safety she knew as a child wrapped in quilts, holding her most cherished stuffed animal.

The woman looked downward, then spoke carefully, as if speech were a skill she rarely used.

"I think . . . that you know me."

Miriam quieted her panicked breathing as best she could, and like the woman before her, struggled with her words.

"Are you . . . the Mother?"

"I am my Mother's daughter."

"Are we . . . sisters?"

"You are the mother of one my brothers. Part of him is near you. Part of him will always be near you. Amen."

"My child is your brother?"

"No. Your father."

The word "father" made Miriam's heart race. Was this woman a memory? An unknown splinter of her mind unearthed by the process of healing?

"My *father*?"

"Yes." The woman's face changed slightly, as the face of a portrait changes when seen in different light. Her expression became like that of Erica's. She bore the same reassurance in her eyes, the longing of Erica's to believe and help and heal. "Your father, the shadow inside you, is my brother. You are partly his mother. He is partly your child. His true mother is my Mother. You nurtured him."

"I don't . . . understand."

"You will."

This woman, this lovely woman with soft brown eyes, whose expression was that of her beloved cousin, whose body was perfect, was some aspect of herself. Miriam felt cloaked in dream, on the threshold of wakefulness.

"Why are you here?"

"Because of your prayer. Not to answer it, but to attend it."

"My prayer for strength?" Miriam stepped forward. The glare of the hall light above caught her vision, made a curtain of brightness that dropped before her gaze for an instant.

The woman faded as the curtain shifted in her sight. Her image blended with that of the hallway—as the shadow of one moonlit branch crosses the shadow of another upon the darkened glass of a window—then was gone.

There was a solidity to the silence that followed, a density to the shadows where the woman had stood.

Troy laughed and giggled in his crib.

Miriam went to the bedroom, and saw the naked woman holding her child. Troy kicked his legs in joy, smiling and holding the woman's hair in one small hand, the fingers of the other hand in his mouth. His eyes were bright.

"I am the daughter of the Goddess you called upon."

The woman's eyes held sadness, weary despair.

"I am the daughter of She who had been the Consort of God."

The syllable "God" fell upon Miriam's ears as if without sound, as if it were a word remembered through the grammar of thought or dream.

"You have done this, not I. You have done this. . . ."

She raised Troy to her face.

And kissed him.

Miriam's child fell still. Limp like a doll. Troy's head lolled, lifeless.

The breath Miriam drew to scream stayed in her lungs. The paralysis that had taken her in childhood took her again. She fell forward, unable to block her fall. She felt the woman standing above her as she had felt the creature that had come to her in the night.

"Now you know the strength of my Mother."

Miriam tried to stand.

"Now you know what you have invoked."

Tears made the dusty floor she lay upon a blur.

"Now you know the truth of your blasphemy. This is the truth you called for. This is the truth that has found you."

Miriam felt a hand grab the folds of her clothing behind her back. She was lifted from the floor, held aloft.

Through vision blurred with tears, refracted by the glare of the reading lamp, Miriam saw the woman, now scarlet as a rose, hair impossibly black, holding the depths of absolute onyx without the slightest sheen. Her beauty was awful. Angelic and harsh as the noon sun, yet imbued with the slow and shifting power of cloud-tides ebbing against twilight.

The woman fixed her eyes upon Miriam's. Her gaze was *slow* . . . flowing into Miriam's vision with the inevitable and irresistible strength of a great wave rising above a shore.

Cradled in the woman's other arm was the still body of Troy.

A violating quiet filled Miriam's mind, a quiet as terrible as the instant of perfect silence before the screaming descent of an owl.

The woman closed her eyes, slowly, and Miriam felt a release in her throat. Breath escaped her.

Whispering, trembling, sobbing, she spoke.

"Give me back my child."

The woman looked away, down to Troy, then fixed her gaze on Miriam again.

Softly . . . slowly . . . with words that reached darkly into Miriam's mind and heart as they fell upon her ears, the woman said, *"How can I not?"* and drew Miriam toward her.

The kiss passed into Miriam like a breath, filling her with warmth, with a love that flickered like candle flame, that fluttered like a bird within the cage of her breast.

The joy passed. Replaced by cold terror that was not hers, that erased Miriam's being and identity with a heaviness that did not allow her to know that she was falling to the floor, that did not allow her to know that she felt pain as she struck, that did not allow her to remember, for one long moment, how to breathe.

In this haze of otherness, she floated. In this haze of otherness, she suffered.

When vision and self were hers again, she saw Troy dead upon the floor before her. She crawled to him in her grief. She held him close. She rocked his cooling body. She touched his fine hair, and knew that it would never lose its fineness. She crawled to her desk, trembling so hard that Troy's body trembled as well, as if he gave up his final breath, and drew down her scissors to cut a lock of her child's hair to keep.

Holding him, rocking him, she heard something inside herself that was not herself.

In a vision that crashed upon her, the bedroom was torn away, replaced with the desert of her mind, replaced with the image of her tower, bronze angel now crucified above the door, lit by the glow of the moon.

She moved toward it, disembodied, unconfined by materiality.

Beyond the door, Troy screamed in tortured agony, his small body trembling, unable to contain his terror, not comprehending his pain.

Miriam screamed, locked within her desert.

Elizabeth found the ruins of her lover hours later, holding her dead child and a lock of his hair, still rocking, slightly, a small red patch upon the wall behind her where she repeatedly struck her head as she rocked.

PART TWO

The Blood-Dimmed Tide

Uncountable thousands of idiot voices.

        Chanting.

Screaming.

            Righteously indignant in the shit of their personal damnations.

Congealing into a single identity.

The Enfolded One awoke—Leviathan. The aspects of what could be called Its intelligence connected, joined like clusters of nettles.

The Greatest Beast in Hell.

Violently formless as a raging sea suspended in the sky.

Began the process of what It knew to be thought.

Slowly . . .

It understood . . .

The vague nature of the threat . . .

That had prodded It to the disgusting process of thought.

It knew rage.   *It knew fear.*

It bellows and roars. In the Living World at that moment, a group of young men, not knowing the nature of the rage they feel, stalk a family with the intent of feeling the bones of faces collapse beneath their boots. Elsewhere, privileged children of unloving homes writhe in the comfort of imagined oppressions that never

It cringes and screams. It withdraws into Itself like a mollusk withdrawing into its shell. In the Living World at that moment, a family looks from behind curtains to the safe street of their home and sees nonexistent killers amid the leafy shadows. Elsewhere, hungry children think loving thoughts about the madmen who protect them from happened; scores of soldiers take comfort in the abdication of morality they have embraced as they look to a village in a dell below and contemplate the execution of all who live there.

distant peoples who wish them no harm; scores of unthinking people find quivering comfort in flowing with scores of others just like them who journey toward pointless endeavors, in the abdication of personal will as they assassinate that which ennobles them above beasts.

It bellows and roars.

And throughout the world, a hundred lynchings take place.

And throughout the world, a hundred mobs feel joy.

Batons descend in arcs upon yielding flesh.

Voices rise in the joy of a unity built upon the subjugation of others.

Minds are fragmented.

Subjugation is coveted.

Victimhood is made into an envied virtue by those who victimize unknowingly.

Something exists in the Living World that is a Threat to the Enfolded One. It senses it in the way a hive of wasps sense a single threat as they swarm from out of their nest.

It will punish this thing.

It will punish that which made it.

It will float and steep in the shit of Its existence in peace and comfort.

It will not suffer this thing to live.

Enraged that It must do so, It begins to plan to undo that which has enraged It in the first place.

It cringes and screams.

And throughout the world, a hundred witch-hunts bear fruit.

And throughout the world, a hundred mobs feel terror.

Backs are turned.

Orisons are murmured in the unity of a terror built upon vague and dusty shadows.

Minds are paralyzed.

Subjugation is pontificated.

Victimization is made into a necessary duty.

Something exists in Damnation that is a Threat to the Enfolded One. It senses the Threat in the way a hive of wasps sense a single threat as they swarm out of their nest.

It must lash out at this thing.

It must lash out at that which made it.

It will float and steep in the shit of Its existence in peace and comfort.

It cannot allow this thing to live.

Panicking that It must do so, It begins to think of how to undo that which has panicked It in the first place.

The Enfolded One quivers.

And a quarter of a million souls of weaklings Fall out of Its essence as ash that cannot be resurrected.

It does not notice.

Chapter One

I

Wednesday, December 12, 1990. 6:55 A.M.

A weight upon his chest, heavy as stone, with the texture of flesh. His lungs, too frail to hold his breath, felt about to tear like wet paper. The weight pressed him into wakefulness—his only perception, sound formless as water falling over a cataract. His blood had not enough volume to fill his body. He could not move his limbs.

The weight pressed on his torso and neck. His limbs drew up. Breath stabbed him. His hands flexed, jerking, palsied. His eyes opened. Paralyzed, seeing the world as if through curved and clouded glass by the light of the full moon, he cried as he had upon drawing his first breath. Spastic wailings. Repetitive. Building to a single wail before beginning again. His face contorted with pain.

The remembrance of his name cut him with a brutality that made him scream.

Lawrence tumbled out of bed.

Naked, tangled in his sheet, he landed upon the blankets he had kicked to the floor. The pain was crushing. The corners of the room sharpened and faded. The pain in his lungs faded, but he felt as if he would cough brackish water. He stared at the wood grain of his nightstand, at the woven pattern of the blanket on which he lay. He wiped spittle from his cheek, then crawled away from the bed, pulling with him the blood-warm sheet coiled around his torso.

Slowly, uncertainly, he stood.

Slowly, uncertainly, he walked.

The floor was unsteady under his feet. The world tilted.

Early winter morning, imbued with the quiet of dead trees. He felt the silence of the building. Felt his neighbors asleep around and beneath him. Felt a presence, as he had once as a child felt the presence of a granite angel above him while walking by a church. Yet this presence was closer, as if it stood before him, about to embrace him. He almost heard its voice, like that of slow wind.

His naked foot upon the floor, he walked as if across the bed of a river that had dried long ago. No sound of steam in pipes, nor of water flowing toward showers; no footsteps in the hallway, nor muffled televisions or radios murmuring through the walls.

The unreal quiet of a weekday morning. A single moment, configured.

In the bathroom, he washed his face with cold water. The face in the mirror seemed only vaguely like his own, at once older and childlike. Lawrence's eyes looked as if they had been tinted an ice blue that faded only as he peered into his own gaze. His beard looked and felt coarser than it should, his skin felt much softer, much more sensitive than usual. The water made him tremble. But he dared not wash with warm water, was not certain he could bear the contrast with the cold air around him. His hands shook as he turned off the faucet.

The fear that lived—waiting like a patient hunter—in the shade of his waking thoughts stepped forward: the fear that had been with him ever since Jacob had begun his periodic, drunken infidelities. The fear spoke clearly, concisely, to deliver its malediction, and so give itself richer life.

"Maybe you have AIDS."

A feeling—like that of falling in a dream—cloaked itself upon Lawrence's shoulders.

The curve of his jaw felt wrong as he lathered his face to shave.

II

Wednesday, 7:05 A.M.

P*ray for me, Ed."*
"I will."
A kiss on his cheek he felt to this day, that imprinted its memory upon his skin.

Ed stood by his desk, watching the carriage of his secondhand printer punch letters across cheap white paper in one direction, then back.

He never knew he could wish so deeply to forget the voice of a woman he loved.

Amelia had gripped Ed's sweater in her fists and shaken him

slightly as she spoke the last words she'd speak to him, before kissing him and walking away on that darkened street corner. She'd moved gracefully across the street, out of Ed's life, but never out of his thoughts.

"Pray for me, Ed."

He could not unthink her face, made amber by the streetlamps. Could not unthink her words, which had stayed with him this past year with the constancy of a song he could not get out of his mind. He wondered if she could fathom what her plea had done to his heart and soul.

"Pray for me, Ed."

Time, unmoving, had watched from the shadows while Ed had wanted to tell her what stirred in his heart, and not the lie that he had told. Time, unmoving, kept the moment of Ed's lie immediate.

"I will."

Time had coughed and made itself known as Ed walked home that night. Time fulfilled and made rich Ed's lie.

The carriage danced upon the black ribbon, leaving a trail of black words behind it—a long quote in Latin from Saint Bonaventura's *Itinerarium.*

"Pray for me, Ed."

That night, last winter, for the first time in a long time, Ed had knelt to pray.

And found he could not.

He could mumble words to God, but the part of his soul from which he used to pray had withered. He could not reach the part of himself that had once been blessed with *faith,* faith not in God—for Ed could never lose that—but faith that God could love him.

This faith had faded, like an aria subsiding.

The small touch of a new despair, constant and slight as the touch of rain, came with the quieting of that faith.

"Pray for me Ed."

Once, Ed had found solace in confession. Once, Ed found comfort in the expiation of sin while touched by latticed shadow. He could not now articulate his sin, could not name it, and so master it. He suffered an *absence* that caused the darkness in his heart. An absence of . . . joy? . . . hope? . . . dignity? The pain ran through him, as a needle threads cloth.

"Pray for me, Ed."

The words were part of a litany in Ed's mind. Centerpiece to a Tenebrae in a world in which resurrection is not possible. Amelia's plea had forced him to face the absence that before he had been able to ignore, forced him to probe the substance of his soul, searching for the nature of his spiritual sickness as a surgeon probes for a lump.

He had been poisoned by his times.

He believed, logically, as a theologian, that it was right and dignified to end your life as a moral choice in the face of monstrous amorality.

The words that now inscribed themselves on his printer argued the same point.

But Ed Sloane did not know if he could apply this conviction to himself—if this conviction were just dressing for a sin he hugged unknowingly to his heart—the sin of Despair. The act of suicide was vain. Was it not born of the sin of Vanity, as well as of Despair? Or perhaps of the sin of Pride?

Ed sipped cold coffee from the cup he had placed by his computer.

He missed Amelia. And he missed the person he'd been at the outset of their friendship.

Out of shame, out of guilt, Ed had not spoken to Amelia since that night.

As the carriage of the printer stopped its march across the paper, Ed found that his mouth was moving, stirring in the way it used to while he spoke silent speech to God. It happened, now and then, when he thought of Amelia. But there was no grace in the movement, in the speaking of unhearable words.

It was as reflexive and unthinking an action as the touching of a new scar.

III

Wednesday, 7:20 A.M.

P aul, for the first time in months, could eat breakfast.

Oatmeal, made with milk. With chopped fruit and raisins. Rich coffee, brewed carefully, so it would not be the bitter liquid he drank to keep awake through days he'd face without good food, or a good night's rest.

Last night Paul had slept deeply, and had dreamt of impossible things. Of snow falling from the ceiling of his room and of black birds flourishing around him in a benevolent storm. Of tall ships sailing atop flowers that grew upon rolling hills, and walking in a twilight of unthinkable reds and umber.

He had not dreamt, as he usually did, of noisy hallways and ugly light. Of the faded pastels of textbook covers, of rushing about and panicking. Of the constricting feel of a tie around his neck. Of grey and ugly cityscapes shaking past the windows of a tram.

He had slept eight hours.

He had awakened to feeling, miraculously, less tired than he had upon going to bed. He had awakened able to do a routine of sit-ups and push-ups, as he had once done each morning before the starchy crap he usually ate gave him the beginnings of a gut that made snug jeans that used to fit him loosely. He took a hot shower, then a cold shower, enjoying the shock to his numbed body.

This morning, he did not listen to the news. He chose to start the day without gnawing worry about the insanity in the Middle East.

He sprinkled cinnamon on his oatmeal, and enjoyed the novelty of eating slowly.

At the sound of keys at the apartment doorway, Paul walked to the entryway of the kitchen and leaned by the light switch.

"Hey, Jo," he said.

Jo turned as she shut the door. She looked startled to see Paul. No . . . startled to see him smiling.

"Hey. What's . . . up?"

"Breakfast." Paul cocked his head to the kitchen.

"Really?"

"Yeah."

She smiled, looking lovely, pulling a lock of her lion's mane hair. She was flushed from the cold walk from Bill's apartment.

"What's *up,* Paul?"

"C'mon. It's getting cold."

She followed him to the kitchen, flopped her coat over a chair, then sat. She was disheveled, exuding quiet happiness.

She looked at Paul's bowl as he stood at the stove.

"You made *oatmeal?*"

"Yeah."

"For *me?*"

"No, for me. I wasn't sure you'd be back before you went to work. Right now, I'm glad you're here to share it."

He set a bowl before her, and slipped chopped apples and pears into her oatmeal. With a flourish, he sprinkled on raisins as well. Jo shook her head, as if he'd just placed a map of the flat earth before her.

"Paul, did you find a *girlfriend* or something? Did you fall in love, or something dopey like that?"

He sat across from her.

"Nope." He gave her the mischievous wink that he used to give her when they'd lived in the same dorm, and he was about to embark on some prank against one meathead jock or another.

She ate a few spoonfuls, then set down her spoon.

"Damn it. I *hate* when you're theatrical!"

"Yeah, but you love it when I cook you breakfast."

She fixed him with her blue eyes, squinted at him a little, then extended her hand across the table and took his. Her fingers were still cool, and felt soothing against his palm as he closed his hand around hers.

"I'm quitting teaching, Jo."

She raised her free hand to her brow and squeezed Paul's hand tighter with the other.

"I was . . . I've been waiting for you to . . . give up on it. To let it go."

"I'm letting it go."

"I can get you a job at the antique store."

"You'll be sick of me. Eight hours at work. Then come home with me. Then have me around the house."

"I haven't gotten sick of you yet, Paul."

"I don't want you to start."

"What're you going to do?"

"Maybe tutor. Maybe Kaplan courses. I've got to get out."

"It's been killing you, Paul."

"I know . . . I . . . I just want you to know that when my contract is up, it's going to be a while before I can really pull my weight. Rent's going to be tight, come July. I . . . ."

"I can pull rent all summer, Paul."

"But I don't want you to."

"But I can, and I want to."

Paul knew what Jo was like when she'd made up her mind.

"Okay."

Still holding his hand, she ran her thumb against his. "Okay."

Paul said, "Your oatmeal's getting cold, and your fruit's getting mushy."

They ate awhile. Jo pestered Paul for not making her coffee, as well. Paul leaned back in his chair, and turned on the burner under the kettle, remembering the last time Jo had stood by him like this, when he'd gotten out of a destructive relationship with a viper of a woman named Catherine.

Jo reached to the fridge to pull out the coffee, not leaving her seat. "What made up your mind?" she asked.

Paul told her about Cory. About sitting with her in the coffee shop, helping her grade papers.

"And it hit me, how fucked the profession is. I can't . . . *undo* all the damage a guy like Fleischer has inflicted. I can't be part of the solution. I don't want to be part of the problem."

Jo nodded slightly. She knew, damn her, what Paul had realized only yesterday. She was too smart sometimes.

"Don't worry about money, Paul. We'll get by. We're probably saving money, in the long run, preventing you from getting carted off to some nut hatch, or having to get you a lawyer for beating Fleischman to death."

"That's Fleischer."

She winked. "Whatever."

The kettle started to boil. Paul was about to put coffee into a fresh filter when Jo said, "Maybe you should get going."

Paul looked at his watch.

"I can make my own coffee, Paul."

"I know. But I wanted to make it for you."

"Tomorrow. I can do the dishes, too."

"I was going to let the pot soak."

"I have time to scrub it out."

"Okay."

Paul went to his room and put on his shoes, then pulled his suit coat out of the closet. He heard Jo doing the dishes as he grabbed his overcoat, gloves, and scarf, then pulled his tie off the rack.

Jo met him at the door, dish towel over her shoulder, and put her hand on Paul's cheek.

She kissed his lips, lightly.

"I really love you, Paul."

"I love you, too."

He stuffed his tie in his pocket as he left, not willing to put the silken leash around his neck until he had to.

IV

Wednesday, 9:09 A.M.

The blue ink had faded.
   The words were less than shadow—quietly illegible as the blue veins under the skin of his wrists.

"We were living in Bethlehem, you and I . . ."

The words brought back a lost life as he read, in the way the strains of a song bring back the moment in which they were first heard. He felt his youth, felt the feverish passion that had possessed him while he'd created the words. He felt the young itch of blood in his veins, felt the naïveté he'd once embraced as "innocence." He smelled again air heavy with the promise of a summer storm and the scent of fresh-cut grass.

This moment—this *now* of ice and cold winds outside and dry, heated air within—is so heavy with a distant summer that he feels upon his neck the stirring of cicadas as they prepare to sing.

". . . in the shadow of the Beast
whose bulk darkened the horizon."

The Beast was distant, now—a memory that still roused passion in him. But it was muted passion now: unfamiliar in the way the face of an old friend must be relearned upon meeting again. *"The Beast"* had been the much protested war, and the man whom he considered to be the father of the war, Nixon. *"Bethlehem"* had been an appropriation of Joan Didion.

The paper was yellowed around the edges. It smelled of the closet where he'd stored it.

Arthur considered a thing he'd long known, but had not acknowledged: if he'd had a child with the girl to whom he had written the poem, that child would now be the same age as the college students who walked the bridge beneath Arthur's window.

"We walked the streets in perpetual twilight,
holding hands as lovers would . . ."

Arthur had titled the poem "June." He'd published it at a point in his life when Rimbaud's triumphs at sixteen seemed merely a feat of timing, not prodigy.

"June" (how clever Arthur had felt, creating a reference to both the girl, and the month she'd walked out of his life) had appeared in *The Unicorn.* The cover (printed on coarse paper the texture of worn felt) featured a mimeographed pen and ink sketch of a unicorn cavorting in an enchanted wood, inspired by the twisting, surreal covers of the Tolkien paperbacks everyone had been reading.

The body of *The Unicorn* itself had been dittoed and hand-stapled by a dozen undergrads, Arthur among them, over a single night thick with pot smoke at the home of the grad student *(God . . . what was his name?)* who'd been editor-in-chief. The staplers had made strange, percussive music as they bit into the paper in steady rhythms—counterpoint to the loud, guitar-heavy rock that had blasted over the speakers. Inid had been there, so serious as she put her slight weight on her stapler.

When Arthur opened his copy of *The Unicorn* this morning, he saw that the staples had rusted, leaving stains upon the paper like flecks of blood.

> *"It is so very cold here, and I remember winters that*
> *once kept us warm as we drank tea and talked*
> *under the soft quilts you kept on your sofa."*

Arthur and June had talked of things of transcendent concern, before such concerns had been eclipsed by practical issues and worries: the duty of the artist; the nature of language; the physiology of the soul and of reincarnation.

Endlessly, they had talked of the ending of *2001*.

(How strange and wonderful the lights of passing traffic had seemed, as he and June walked from the Cinerama theater to her small room, with its space heater and beaded curtains, where everything made of cloth—the covers of the throw pillows to her closets full of cotton blouses—had been saturated with the scent of myrrh and pot. There, as Arthur tasted for the first time chamomile tea, they had talked of the revolutionary potential of film, of transcendence, of what that glowing white hotel room *truly* meant, and how computers *truly* ran the world.)

A longing for the youthful morality he'd once had stirred in a forgotten corner of Arthur's heart. Arthur yearned to call his ideals to the fore of his mind, and not allow them to lie hidden, conspicuous in their decades-long silence.

Arthur had sculpted himself into the "success" he was today from the *flâneur* he had been. Now he longed to be free of the artifice, his life made a great pentimento.

He thought he should rewrite the poem, or retype it on computer, so that he might have it fresh to print out, and so not allow it to fade to nothing. Yet he couldn't invalidate the moment of the poem's creation; it was a creature of its time. To retype it would make the poem a thing of today.

In adulthood, in an office that occupied a space where once hymns had risen to touch the flambeau that glowed with muted sunlight above an altar, Arthur stared at the faded letters.

Ten minutes had passed when, with the taste of summer air in his lungs, Arthur heard his intercom buzz. His first appointment had come.

V

Wednesday, 9:31 A.M.

The Succubus filled cathedrals of ice with hymns to her Father. The patient cruelty of her Father's Name echoed through the weave of strobing sunlight, sung by the choir of her single voice as it dislodged in sublimation a thing of purity: the soul of the child she had killed. Each flake of snow was a chamber she walked through as mist.

She at last rid herself of the child.

Flecks of the child's soul—remnants of what she'd not breathed into the soul of the child's mother—drifted downward through the snow. A trace of the child remained, a cast of his pain and confusion, like the wound left by the removal of a splinter.

She rose through the snow in strands finer than steam. She took the weight of smoke. Then, over the span of a translucent hour, she again took the weight of unreal flesh. Red and black upon the snow, the Succubus became. She rolled upon her belly and lay sphinx-like, holding secret her Father's Name now that she had a throat that could invoke it in vain.

Like slow poison, the child, innocent and without sin, would have informed the traces of the soul she carried and the souls she would acquire; the child's soul would have diluted her being if she'd not rid herself of it. She had now, through the taking of Andrew's soul, a gravity she'd not had before, a solidity she could not have fathomed when she had first come to the Living World. Her skin held the promised flesh of her salvation; with each soul she took, she would become more like an earthly woman, with more of the weaknesses of earthly existence, yet with greater spiritual strength. Only when she had attained that earthliness and spiritual strength, crossing the Void, could she ascend *beyond* the Material, and continue toward the Throne Room of God. What she'd been before her journey began had—in relation to her physical self now—the tangibility of a phantom limb.

For she had been *at the outset* of her creation a thing of spirit and projected Will when she had left her Father's arm. Only as her journey began did she begin the process of physical existence.

Her *first moment* in the Living World, she was aware of mountains lit by diffused dawnlight: indigo and black and white and grey. From this place where the sun rose to write itself upon the valley, she rode föhn winds toward midnight; Boston called her the way branches bring forth river fog, the way the shore calls tide, and the mountain draws the gaze of the traveler from the ground before his feet.

She careened over the sea. Near a nameless shore, she fell into substance. Marveling at the sickle-shaped moon, she became aware of her heartbeat as she stood within a wash of foam, her form coalescing. The beat of her heart fell in rhythm with the waves. She walked to shore, gaining materiality with each step. Foam clung within her flesh, bursting only as her skin became dense enough to break its surface tension.

She lay on the shore, upon her back.

There, she learned to breathe. A fist of seawater lay in her heart, still as a lake in the long moments that her heart did not beat. As her heart began to beat with the regularity of a true person, it sublimated the water out of her pores.

Deep night, in air too cold to hold snow. She walked the beach, looking over her shoulder at the water she'd quit, and delighted that she could make sand shift underfoot. She wrote her existence upon the grains. Under the crash of the sea, she sang her first song. She found a piece of congealed tar at her feet, picked it up, closed her hand around it. Opening her hand, she saw the imprinted swirls of her palm and fingers.

Her body warmed.

She returned to the sea. The waves were kind, and parted as she walked. She let herself be carried by the water, moving formlessly as a whitecap.

As mist, between the droplets of the sea, she traversed the breakwaters of the Charles. As mist, she traveled against the current beneath the ice. Between Boston and her sister, Cambridge, she made herself flesh under the caul of ice, then punched her way into the night air.

Surrounded and unseen, she drew herself upon the ice. Busy roads on the north bank and south. Busy bridges to the east and west. Windows, like unmoving stars set within canyon walls along the river. In blackness hiding the river's white face, she crawled upon the ice like a ruby tear.

The sickle moon touched the building she chose to be her home. Again mist, she settled there; the water of the river fell away as she rose. Dry, without a trace of the river upon her, she touched for the first time, her new home.

Dawn had followed her, cresting over Beacon Hill. She looked upon the risen sun for the first time—its voice touched her breast, burning sweet and mellifluous. She mourned that her Father, who had freed her from nonbeing, could not be with her to see this hill made afire, and this earthly city laid at the hill's foot burning in winter dawnlight.

Thus did she, weeks ago, arrive in the place of her dominion.

Now the Succubus lay in her jaded body in late-morning sun, far from the moment when she'd seen her first dawn for the second time.

Entwined within her, inscribed within her, repeating over and over in every instant of her being, was the moment she fell in love in Andrew, the moment she tasted the wine of his spirit. She was redefined by him, as she had redefined him by taking him; thus the completion she'd earned by coming to Materiality had been undone. She needed to attain Balance with her new gravity.

She held the key to such Balance. She had touched three men: the man in the dead church, the boy on the bridge, and the sick man who had invested himself near where the girl had died. These men were to become part of her, as Andrew had. She should love them and join them to herself. Only then could she find harmony. Within this harmony, she would include the *absence* of the man with the noble heart who had slipped away from her, for his absence would act as caesura to the greater harmony.

She'd not earn a Name until she had an inner harmony of the souls she'd taken. She would have to draw a single voice from these souls, as a bow draws a single note from many strings.

If she did not, she'd be crushed by the profundity of Creation. Refracted out of existence as the sharpness of crystal becomes the roundness of dew with the changing of light.

She gathered snow in her arms, then piled it under her throat. She breathed deeply; her ribs creaked like young hazel wood with her weight, pressing sharply where they joined at her sternum. Her marrow breathed the souls she had touched.

In the cold noon, as clouds came, making grey winter light the color of shallow water, she configured these souls she would take into the geometry of damnation, beginning the process of calling them to her inner being, and her love.

VI

Wednesday, 12:02 P.M.

H e knew no one in Boston.
     This had struck him today, as he reached to answer the phone.
He knew no one in this vast city: Vicki at the store, maybe, but truly
no one.

Why should he answer, when the only person who'd call him
would be his bitch of a sister, sitting, no doubt, on her threadbare
couch, desperate to give Lawrence a dose of venom? Let the bitch
rant at empty tape.

Lawrence, instead of picking up the phone, had lowered the volume on his answering machine. If it was Jack, calling to get him to
come to the store early, that'd be too bad for Jack.

He'd waited for the machine to take the message, then had turned
off the ringer and returned to the book he'd been reading, trying
desperately to rid himself of the image of Raymond Burr as Perry
Mason and read the novel on its own terms.

Now, one hour before he had to be at work, Lawrence—mug of
coffee in hand—played back his messages.

The first message was a hang-up.

As was the second.

A familiar feeling came over Lawrence, of someone standing close
by him. It was the feeling he knew when he would wait up in the
dark, for the sake of a fight full of bitter accusations, or for the sake
of tending to his lover until he was well enough to be put to bed.

The third message began with the thump of a phone receiver
being dropped, then picked up. The voice that followed was slurred.

" 'S me. Not that that's important to you."

The room in which those words had been spoken flashed upon
Lawrence's mind as if he'd been whisked there. The smells of the
room—cheap incense, cologne made of the extract of Sicilian limes
and of the fabric softener Jacob used on everything that made all the
clothes and linens in the house smell like an old lady's dress—were
more real than the smell of the hazelnut coffee in the mug Lawrence
held.

The sound of something shifting, heavy, with a sort of skid followed the recorded words. Lawrence knew the sound; he'd heard it
on mornings that smelled of sweat full of intoxicants. It was the
sound of Jacob walking through an accumulation of crap on the

floor. The skid was Jacob kicking a vinyl record across the floor. When Jacob drank (and snorted, and smoked, and sat sulking for days at a stretch) records were littered throughout the apartment after providing musical accompaniment to Jacob's absorption of toxins. While he and Lawrence had lived together, Jacob forbade Lawrence to clean while he was in these states, forbade him from putting right the martyrous externalization of his inner turmoil until he was ready to have it put right.

"I'm just calling because it all . . ."

A few words then, in the mumbled language of drunks that Lawrence wished he did not understand so well.

" 'Cuz it's all . . ."

Heavy breathing. The sound of the exertion of cognizant thought undertaken by a drunkard—a soft, quick grunt, like that of a child frustrated by an impossibly adult problem.

" 'Cuz it's all shit! 'Cuz it's all turning to shit!"

Lawrence strained to hear a particular sound. The sound that would echo the transgressions Jacob had committed against Lawrence that had put them asunder.

He did not hear it.

Jacob's voice filled with choked sobbing.

"Fuckin' happy?"

The sound of shuffling. A cough.

Then, an almost inaudible whisper: *"Y' little shit."*

Sobs. Full-blown sobs.

" 'M sorry. Lawr'nce. 'M sorry."

The sound of the phone being hung up. Clumsily.

Lawrence rewound the tape, listened again for the sound. He didn't hear it, but if another man were there, he could have been asleep, or in another part of the apartment.

God . . . the fights . . . fights not caused by the betrayal of Jacob's getting loaded and sleeping around, but by *Lawrence's* betrayal of Jacob by insisting they both get HIV tests. For to do that, to address Jacob's sleeping around, would, by proxy, be addressing his substance abuse, and would, by proxy, force Jacob to acknowledge that his substance abuse could affect Lawrence, and would, therefore, be something for which he had to take responsibility.

Jacob refused to admit his sleeping around, refused to admit that he lied to his lover about which men he'd slept with (and how many) while loaded, and refused to admit that this was a deadly lie.

God. The fights.

The tipped-over bookshelves . . .

The treasured knickknacks broken . . .

The long standoff after each fight. The hours of television stared at so that the one who felt wounded did not have to see or acknowledge the other. And through the turmoil and the gnawing worry was a single, constant truth. Lawrence saw it, and because he did, it made Jacob all the more bitter.

Jacob was becoming afraid of Lawrence, who was trying to lift himself out of the delicious paralysis that had defined their world—the paralysis that kept all whom they knew in ugly relationships, in pointless jobs, in the homes of their parents, and in circles of friends imparted upon them like luggage they were never expected to set down.

Providence bred two types: those who recognized the city was a trap, and those who devoted their lives to denying the city was a trap.

And Lawrence, setting down his mug to get to work early so he'd not be tempted to call his ex-lover, realized that because he felt comfort in Jacob's obvious need for him, he was not so free of that trap as he had thought.

VII

Wednesday, 12:35 P.M.

There are no hummingbirds around here."

Fleischer's voice was like falling stones. Paul sensed, *knew*, that Fleischer enjoyed using his voice to strike down what challenged his worldview. He used his voice the way a cruel kid uses a slingshot. Paul was in no mood to flinch as he had so often before, was in no mood to be silent while the little jerk spouted his horseshit.

Paul turned away from Cory to face Fleischer and fixed him with his gaze.

"*Excuse* me?" he said.

Fleischer's eyes held surprise. Paul heard Cory draw a quick breath. Just the three of them were in the teachers' lounge: Paul and Cory at one table, Fleischer at the next, *USA Today* laid out colorfully before him. Cory and Paul had been talking of this awful winter.

And of the coming spring.

And of the coming of hummingbirds.

And Fleischer had dismissed the gift Paul's mother had given him.

"There are no hummingbirds around here," said Fleischer, again, invoking the ugly authority of his voice.

Paul felt a constriction behind his sternum, between his lungs. To roll on his back and expose his throat would be blissfully easy.

"There *are* hummingbirds. I saw them each summer while I grew up."

"You're full of *shit,* La Cotta. You saw orioles. Something like that. If you knew *shit,* you'd know it's too built-up around here. There's no hummingbirds."

His chest constricted more; a cold sensation emanated from the tightness.

Paul took a breath to speak . . .

. . . and swallowed back his words.

To speak of his mother, now, of how she'd drawn hummingbirds to nurture his spirit, to tell of how closely he'd seen this manifestation of the Will of God upon earth . . .

Paul would expose part of himself to Fleischer that he could not afford to expose. Fleischer could attack him in a new way that his brutish intellect could not have imagined before.

Paul needed to stand up to this man.

But could not.

Later, passing from the smoky, stale air of the teachers' lounge to the hallway, Paul thought how he'd embraced the easiness his *suit* had afforded him in backing down to Fleischer. This milieu of professional stratification did not allow him to rise above his station and face the challenge of a superior. Even if to *not* do so was at the expense of his integrity, and at the expense of the truth that he, as a teacher, was expected to uphold.

He unlocked his classroom and placed his lesson plan on the desk.

The bell rang.

His students filed in.

Paul began to teach, a vessel of responsibility, devoid of authority.

VIII

Wednesday, 1:05 P.M.

The buildings stood way tall above him. The wind was not so cold here.

Hidden in a nook made of brick, Dutch held the foil-wrapped sandwich the man had handed him.

The sandwich was warm. It brought blood back to his fingertips, the warmest thing he'd felt all day. He leaned against the corner of the nook, thinking about the time when he'd had warm food every day, and a safe place to sleep.

And Dutch felt sad. Not only for the life that he'd lost, but that he had not seen the man who'd given him the sandwich on the street a few moments ago.

Dutch had dozed off in the glass enclosure of a bus stop, and fallen into immediate and dream-vivid sleep. He dreamt of a pretty, pretty face that was kind, and that smiled at him. Then the spiders started crawling in his lungs, and started itching him as he breathed.

He woke with a start, feeling like he was drowning.

As his vision came back, a man in a nice coat wearing leather gloves put the sandwich in Dutch's hands. Dutch wasn't fully awake. He didn't even get to say "Thank you" to the man, in the way his mother had taught him. All he saw was the back of the man's coat as he walked out the glass enclosure, carrying his briefcase. When Dutch tried to talk, the spiders itched, and he went into a coughing fit.

Then he came to this alley, so he'd be out of the wind, and so he'd not embarrass himself by looking greedy as he ate the sandwich. He was so hungry, he was not sure that he could eat the sandwich using good manners.

Dutch unwrapped the sandwich.

It steamed as he peeled back the foil. It was a meat sandwich. Some kind of beef in a spicy sauce, with melted cheese, too.

It was the best thing he had ever smelled in his life.

The city had swallowed up the man who had given it to him. Dutch could not bear such kindness.

And knowing he should eat the sandwich while it was still warm, knowing that soon the winter air would rob the food of the warmth it could put in his belly, Dutch fought the urge to cry, because if he did, he could not eat his sandwich before it got cold.

In slow and careful bites, sobbing now and then, Dutch had the most substantial meal he'd had since the first snows had come that year.

IX

Wednesday, 1:05 P.M.

O ver the river,
flowing as a river of smoke above it.

With the uncoffined dead, the unconfined dead, the Succubus flowed in a grave dug in the breezes above the Charles.

The dead were free.

And she partook of their bodies as they floated, completing the pilgrimage of their lives with them as smoke rising from a crematorium.

She drank the black milk, heavy with the taste of Original Sin, of their expiation from Materiality.

Ash and hair.

One with the smoke of sublimation.

Flecks of smoke heavy with memory.

And with the burden of memory inscribed within the substance of flesh, memory dissipated, memory once locked and noted within particles of what had been clay invested with Breath.

As smoke.

As a creature of sublimated blood and *anima*.

She walked through the drifting smoke of the crematorium, and walked through the tangle of memory of those buried in a mass grave held by the sky.

Strings of smoke, impossible to see.

She plays the strings of smoke, stroking them, stroking the memories they hold and weaving of them a tapestry of music as one would stroke the strings of a harp.

She, and her flock, cross the river dry-shod.

She, and her flock, flow toward the sea.

She guides them toward the hill where she had first heard the voice of the sun . . .

And partaking of the cold moisture in the air, partaking of the breath of the city . . .

She made herself and her flock the wet smoke of a grey winter day.

They fall.

Coagulated, they fall.

Black precipitation, holding the memories of the uncoffined dead, falls.

Alights upon the face and form of a bronze angel who looks down upon passersby who do not see her. Black milk coalesces in humid beads.

Here the dead, who have been interred in the sky, find a new homeland.

Voiceless, the angel upon the rampart cannot guide them.

The angel, darker, who has guided them here, falls away, unwilling to share in this new homeland of soot upon the soiled body of honey-colored metal.

The angel, darker, who has guided them here, leaves behind their jumbled memories, and feels tears of kindness that she does not shed.

She reaches out, unbodied, to the man who sheds them, whom she has touched.

She will find him and heal him, and bring him the light of her terrible Beauty.

X

Wednesday, 4:30 P.M.

T he deal came through. I have to go."
    Inid made this success, for which she'd worked long weeks, sound like defeat.

Arthur gripped the phone; the plastic creaked by his ear.

He said, "That's great, sweetheart!" He knew Inid could not think of this trip as "great," could not think of a success as anything but fraud on her part that would soon be uncovered.

"Yes." The word was an escaped breath.

And then the silence—the silence Arthur hated, the silence that signified that Inid was so very sorry for disappointing Arthur with her fears and anxieties. And Arthur hated his anger, and hated that she made him feel angry.

Layered silence, hiding abrasions that had never healed. Through the faint static, Arthur dreaded the even fainter whisper of Inid saying, "I'm sorry," as she often did to break these silences—"sorry" for nothing she could articulate, save that she was sorry that she was sorry.

Arthur spoke before the apology could be uttered.

"When's your flight?"

"I should be at the airport by six."

"Tonight?"

"No. Morning."

"Why so early?"

"I'm connecting in Chicago."

"When's your meeting?"

"At three-thirty," she said, as if admitting a sin.

Inid was afraid to ask for a better flight. Afraid to front the extra seventy-five to one hundred bucks for a direct flight, because her lost time and the lost sleep of catching such an early flight were worth saving one hundred bucks because . . . well . . . *she* wasn't worth the one hundred bucks. Never mind that fronting the money and leaving a few hours later would be the difference between her arriving in San Francisco exhausted or arriving well rested.

"But . . . there *ought* to be a direct."

"I couldn't book one."

"Did you book through an agent?"

More silence; written within it was a heavy guilt. Guilt that Inid had betrayed him because of her terror of asking for what she wanted.

Arthur relaxed his grip on the phone, and relaxed his voice so as to not make Inid feel that he was yelling at her.

"You have half an hour before the agencies close. You can get something that leaves later."

"I . . ."

"Just do it, Inid. Please? Just do it."

Arthur reached to his intercom and pressed the call button. The speaker buzzed.

"I've got another call," he said. "Just book another flight."

"But I . . ."

He pressed the call button again.

"I have *got* to answer that."

Good-byes were said as a matter of reflex, just as once "I love you's" had been said as a matter of reflex.

Arthur turned in his chair, and looked out the window, bending and unbending a paper clip as darkness huddled the river, the bridge, the campus on the far bank.

What had been charming innocence in a girl of twenty was a disability in a professional woman past forty. Despite her terrors, despite all that she let the world inflict upon her and that she inflicted upon herself, despite all the confusion she nestled around herself, Arthur loved the soul of his wife, loved her heart, her mind, her body.

But the distance, the constant distance between them, brutally reasserted itself each day.

Arthur ran his finger along the paper clip, now tied in a knot.

Distance.

Passionlessness.

He set down the ruined paper clip, opened his desk drawer, reached for the copy of *The Unicorn* he had been reading in the early part of that day.

XI

Wednesday, 5:35 P.M.

A wall of naked women, imposed one upon the other, their images rewritten and juxtaposed—frozen in time like insects in amber—each like a moment that memory will not let go.

Each woman an image, an utterance of the imagination—held and treasured in a base manner by a base aspect of the mind until her image is released in the release of a fleshy spirit . . . spirit that falls, then flows in a torrent of soapy water to the sewer. Each woman, trapped in a nugget of memory that is forgotten to the conscious mind as the pleasure of self-induced orgasm subsides. Treasured in the moment of fantasy, precious beyond compare. Later, a thing less remembered than the taste of night air in the first instant of sleep.

Something in her eyes.

A boy whose parents had named John, who was then renamed "South-paw" by his fraternity brothers (because of his left-handedness), then "Spaw," stood in the favored shower of his fraternity house, where brothers in the unimaginably distant era of the 1970s had affixed perhaps one hundred centerfolds to the stall walls, then sealed them in expensive lacquer of a grade used on ships' hulls. Plexiglas panels were then sealed over the walls, preserving these objects of unattainable desire. The images were frozen, their 1970s, *Star Trek*-esque hair and makeup eternal as their bodies no doubt sagged now through their thirties and forties.

As Spaw stood in the shower, working his penis with his foamy, bricklike left hand, getting his obligatory pre-dinner orgasm done with, his gaze fixed upon the frozen, deep brown eyes of one Playmate. . . .

Out of the corridors of flesh, out of this museum of desire made of light imprinted upon paper, her eyes seemed alive in the glint of water that streamed over the Plexiglas.

Out of the fleshy catalog of women he carried in his mind, out of the catalog of sexual greed that had acquired the images of hundreds of women he'd seen both in flesh and in artifice, one woman came forward.

His heart fluttered in a way that it had not since he was twelve, and had taken his first kiss.

The sight *(only the sight, no other component of that memory)* of the

Harvard Bridge crossed his frenzied imagination. The sight, *only the sight,* of the girl in the blue pea coat he had scoped that morning crossed his frenzied imagination.

Her eyes had given him the creeps; the *fear* transmitted by her eyes had been a physical sensation.

But her eyes had been incredibly beautiful. Beautiful enough to gain the notice of a boy who gauged beauty by tit size.

Thinking of her eyes, thinking of how deep and brown they were, Spaw turned his gaze upward, away from the walls of compacted, naked women, and came violently.

XII

Wednesday, 5:37 P.M.

L etters, upon the snow.
Letters, of a language spoken before the first utterance of human voice, crudely compacted into two dimensions, when, in full glory, they had been written in three dimensions: each stroke executed over the span of what would be decades if they had been written where time and space intersected, in the realm of things being and passing away.

Here, a mark like a T, signifying a meaning incorporating *sword* and *lamb.*

Sword and *lamb,* given expression before they had been expressed in Materiality. Words—from before Materiality—expressed as letters, upon the snow . . . not only in the etching of lines and curves, but in the shadows of the etching, in the shades of light changing upon the snow's surface.

Arousal, turned inward.

The configuration was complete—the movements of a requiem, as complete as she could make them.

The men she had touched on the bridge, the stricken man she had touched near the River where the girl had died.

They were now configured inside her, made a construct.

The man with the noble heart was absent, an ache. And his absence would—for now at least—be the silence of the symphony of damnation she composed. His sadness had the flavor of an unfinished spanning, like that of one who has hung, suspended in a journey that cannot end. His sadness was perfect: a reflection of the doom the River bore.

The man in the dead church was a vessel of regret, of self-absorbed melancholia. He was a creature of the city, of *acquiring;* what burned in him was what he lacked. His sadness was that of the current; he had been carried away by *time* and the lust of his own needs.

The boy on the bridge was a creature of greed, the greed of the River as it erodes and carries refuse to the sea. His desire for the Succubus had been born of a need for power over her, the same need for power that the murderer of the girl had in taking prey.

And the man who had invested his sickness with the form of spiders had grown out of the ugliness of the city, had been made wretched and sick by the condensation of latent ill will the living directed at those who reminded them of their mortality. In this way, within his fractured mind, he was as much part of the landscape of the city as a peasant is of the countryside. The division of his mind was as stark as the division the River made between Boston and her sister city.

Four men, configured.

Three lives to take, as metaphor for three of the twenty spheres separating the Throne Room of God from the deepest pit of the Abyss and its most wretched saints. Each sphere, a representation of a realm of Damnation, and an aspect of the Insurrectors who ruled those realms, and the blasphemies associated with those rulers: Lust, Greed, Ugliness.

Each man, each life, each realm, each ruler, and each blasphemy was a step of her pilgrimage, bringing her closer to human form, closer to the full power and spiritual force of her Name.

Letters . . . upon the snow, writing an aria of damnations that would take her toward her Name.

She reached out for the boy's mind in as abrupt a manner as he would have taken her.

XIII

Wednesday, 7:10 P.M.

Spaw thought of differential equations and of coming in a girl's mouth.

Equations—expressions in formulated language—the geometry of structure and the grammar of construction.

His homework.

The girl, eighteen, drunk, in his frat house room. The blow job a toll for her rushed, nonsober exit. Robert Palmer's "Addicted to Love" blasting from the living-room dance area below, providing heavy counterpoint to the on-again, off-again pressure of his hand at the back of her head: this had been his Friday night release from the tension of doing homework the week before.

Now, on this Wednesday night, the tension crept up on him again. Spaw remembered how he was to solve the equations before him. His mechanical pencil scritched paper, an aural reminder of the moment in class when he'd taken the notes to solve the problems assigned by his gook grad instructor.

Spaw remembered the moment leading to the blow job. The small stud earring that the girl had taken off and had left on his dresser as they'd made out was now a trophy on his desk—a visual reminder of his coming and her swallowing before she rushed to catch the last shuttle to Wellesley.

He did not remember her name.

Spaw looked at the blank spaces in the equations—it was what was missing that made them a challenge to solve.

The girl's name was a blank, yet she had been no challenge. Spaw looked up from his books to the edge of the bed, where he had sat and she had kneeled.

She'd made a cute, unhappy face as he came, squinting her eyes as she swallowed, her head straining against his hand.

Then he thought of the face of the girl on the bridge, transposing her face onto that of the girl who had blown him. He thought of her haunting eyes that had shot him such a burning glance, and how her squinting as he came would put out the bitchy fire in them.

XIV

Wednesday, 9:50 P.M.

B ehind each light was a life he envied.

Lawrence looked across the river toward Cambridge, and along the river toward Boston. Memorial Drive on the far shore was a shifting column of red and white. The white and red of neon strobed the brick buildings near Kenmore Square. Lawrence's gaze was drawn to the lights in the windows of tall apartment buildings, dormitories, and brownstones like his own.

As a boy *(a boy so very different from the young man he was now?)* he would sit at night in the attic and watch the houses of his neighbors. He'd stare into lighted windows, not as a voyeur, but as a coveter of light, of comfort and place.

His father, unwilling to pay high electric bills, unscrewed bulbs from light fixtures throughout the house. Where a fixture had four sockets, two would be unscrewed. And what bulbs he did allow were of forty watts, at their strongest. The gloom crowded every corner, stood solid behind furniture, behind each door. To escape, Lawrence went to the darkest part of the house, to steal light from his neighbors' houses, to steal the normality, even by a glance, that such light represented.

Now, as before, Lawrence envied his neighbors' light. Yet the darkness tonight had not been created by his father; Lawrence had made it himself.

The buzzing of the phone he'd left off the hook could be fixed if he unplugged the wall jack. He was not certain, though, if the buzzing annoyed him, or if he deserved to be free of the buzzing if it did.

"How good a fuck is your new Boston lover?"

Lawrence knew that the lives in the lighted windows had their share of grief, pain, and anger. Yet envy was too numbing a tonic not to partake of, tonight.

"I got a question for you . . . since you know sooooo much about real estate, and have suuuuuch goooood luck finding places to live. . . ."

Lawrence had called David, a friend in Providence, to see if he knew how Jacob was doing.

David answered, acting in the queenish way he did whenever he got loaded.

"Mmmmmm 'low," he purred.

"David?"

"Mmmmmm-hmmmmmm."

"Uh. It's Lawrence."

"Hmmmm. And are we slumming today, Lawrence? 'S that why y'r calling?"

"No."

"I got your big-cocked boyfriend here, Lawrence."

David shouted to the next room.

"Jaaayyy-cob! 'S the wife calling."

The sound of giggles. The thud of the phone set down clumsily. Shuffling. Lawrence wanted to hang up, yet didn't.

Jacob picked up.

"So were you fucking this new guy before you moved up there?"

Lawrence's reply was meaningless, his words guttural deflections, parryings called from the deep part of his psyche.

"So, Mr. Smart Real Estate Shopper . . ." Jacob was sober enough to know what he said. *"Should I blow my money on rent, or on blow?"*

David called from the far corner, his voice echoing.

"Coke! Coke! Blow it on coke!"

Lawrence said he had get off the phone.

Jacob laughed, a short bark.

"Ooooo, honey! Don't wait up for me, with y'r hair in curlers an' a rolling pin in y'r hand!"

"No! No! Wait!" called David. There was the sound of the phone being passed. David said, *"I just wanted to thank you for a lovely evening in Boston. You really know how to show a guy a good time."*

An explosion of laughter, from Jacob. A panicked *"No! No!"* in the midst of that laughter, and the sudden breaking of the connection, as if Jacob had slammed his hand down in the cradle.

Within a minute, the phone rang.

Lawrence knew no one in Boston.

He picked up the phone, pressed down on the cradle, then left the phone off the hook.

A gust of wind pressed against the window. He felt the cold through the caulking, the loose frame as the glass and wood rattled. He looked at the lights, the cars, the red and white glow of Kenmore Square.

In this city he had no place.

He went to bed, not thinking to unplug the phone. Its percussive buzz filled his unknowing sleep.

The Enfolded One rages.

A storm within Itself, rising. Protrusions of Itself, sounding. It sunders what could be vaguely called the hinterlands of human imagination. The roar of each wave is made of chanting idiot voices, voices that, as they echo in the human mind, can lull the most defiant will into the comfort of the herd. The waves rise and obliterate one another. They close tight upon themselves as they fall, the fluid solidity of the Enfolded One's outer layering becoming packed into labyrinthine clusters as the thing sounds into Itself.

It rages. There is a threat. The pain of thought makes It shudder.

Three aspects of Itself begin to plan.

Bursting through, from outside of Being, It makes perverse arabesques of Itself. A pebbled worm, glinting in brightness that repels all light. Most of Its awareness churns outside of Creation. It thinks the blind thoughts that bridge dreams, Its thoughts unfettered by cause and effect, delicate as the fabric of dark space and distance.

Rising up from darkness in the mind, It bellows, taking shape as outline, the shadow of a sea beast made flesh out of the abyss in which It swims. Its awareness a rich condensation of sadisms and brutal delights: a tumor upon sane human intellect.

It hangs. Suspended within Itself as a crocodile waits beneath the surface of a river.

It has not *thought,* but *motive.*

The three aspects flow into a necrotic grey nodule of the Enfolded One's being. Dialogue as fever dream begins. Waves of the Beast's raging break against the nodule; dead spirits fall away from the nodule as sea foam falls away from poor glass.

The pebbled worm twists, as It had once done across the rich darkness flowing between stars. The sea beast thrashes in the frenzy of the Living World, a frenzy that obtrudes into Its flesh and feeds It. That which hangs, unthinking, within the Enfolded One's liquidity hungers, providing silent impetus for the other two.

Tasting . . .

The three aspects know what the Enemy of the Enfolded One plans.

Delicious impulses, acted without thought on Earth as in Damnation, will be denied to the Enfolded One. False piousness. Hunger for power. Sinfully righteous indignation.

Deprived.

The majority of the damned now falling into Its being will be seduced away by melancholy Beauty, taken by the Unbowed One, Belial.

The sundering force of the Mob . . .

Unseated as Light Bringer to the world, divested of the Great Adversaryship that It has taken as princely title . . . that It has drawn into Its folds.

Leviathan rages.

The armored aspect of Itself that hangs now rises to the Living World, moving with deliberation, as the mundane beast It resembles would move toward a gazelle come to drink of the river's water. . . .

Chapter Two

I

Thursday, December 13, 1990. 7:10 A.M.

This dawn brought no dread.

Ed Sloane, glass of juice in hand, walking carefully so as not to wake up his roommate, faced the morning without the suffocating temptation to think of dying.

A year ago, before he had first heard the call of the River, Ed had worked out his polite demise. On a cold night, he would take sleeping pills, then lie down wearing only thin clothes in a snowy vacant lot. A postcard to the police, telling where his body was to be found, would be mailed on the way. The sleeping pills were still in the medicine chest beside the dental floss, unopened.

Getting through the day without dread was a challenge of equilibrium. Joking and chatting with people was a good way to maintain equilibrium. So was exercise, focusing energy as he'd been taught in *dojos* and boxing clubs. The odd moment of rage helped, too; his advisor, Father Tomassetti, had, by pissing Ed off so deeply and so often, saved Ed's life in ways that he never could have as, say, Ed's confessor.

Physically, Ed padded from the kitchen and sat at his desk, his vision blurry without his contact lenses. Mentally, he walked through his memory palace, touring and reviewing the main points of his thesis before he went to the Theology School library to work on it some more. In his memory palace, walking through the corridors of his mind, he knew a rare sense of safety and comfort. Here, despite his guilty pangs for the hubris by which he'd imagined the palace after the Palace of Wisdom in Limbo, he felt a closeness to the saints and scholars who had guided him, who had been his spiritual and intellectual parents. He could forgive himself his hubris as he touched the learning that he loved, made tangible by his mind in the only place where he truly felt at home.

The mental images that strung his ideas into a cogent thesis were consigned to a particular hall of his memory palace. The mnemonic devices were displayed as suits of armor would be in the hall of a museum.

First was a skillet nailed to a door; from behind the door a fanciful explosion of Chthulhoid tentacles, like something out of a horror comic.

A device for Pandora.

In the next alcove stood a tree—Goethe's oak. In the tree was an apple, and an impossibly still white dove. Red sunlight reflected through a green window behind the tree, making colors that could not exist outside Ed's imagining.

As his body brought the juice to his lips, his mind connected the images into the first articulation of his argument.

Pandora, unleashing evil, had sinned.

Adam and Eve, by knowing of evil, had sinned.

Yet to live in a world defined by atrocity and be ignorant of evil is a sin.

Therefore, was Pandora's unleashing of that which we must know of a sin? Or was her sin embracing Hope? To Hope is to fly in the face of evil and atrocity, and is therefore ignorant of sin, and therefore, sinful.

The next alcove held shards of clay pots, the sharp edges bloody, broken swords and chunks of masonry strewn nearby.

Masada was . . .

A small buzzing cut through his thoughts. His palace faded. Winter-morning grey took his awareness. The kitchen timer on his bed stand signaled that twenty minutes had passed since he'd put his contacts in their sterilizer. He turned off the sterilizer.

Steve, his roommate, was shuffling about the living room.

After breakfast and shooting the shit with Steve, Ed made it to the bus stop just as the bus doors opened, without having to hurry.

As the bus traveled over the BU Bridge, crossing the Charles, Ed tried to convince himself he couldn't remember what had driven him to think of throwing himself into the frozen river.

II

Thursday, 7:40 A.M.

Inid was gone.

Arthur walked to the living-room couch and realized—as Inid's taxi crunched rock salt and packed snow in the parking lot—that they'd not kissed good-bye.

Sitting, he picked up his plate of a croissant and sliced fruit. Meli's school books were stacked on the coffee table. He longed for the days when such a stack had daunted him, when homework had been impossibly hard. Compared to getting a quarterly fiscal report out . . .

Curious, mindful to not get oil from his pastry on them, Arthur picked up the books: biology; first-year French; history. All things he'd studied himself, and of which he had no real memory. A flash of color caught his eye. Among Meli's notebooks, askew, was a stack of goldenrod papers. Arthur pulled them out.

" *'OPERATION DESERT SHIELD' SHIELDS ONLY PROF-ITS!!* " screamed the banner at the top of the flyers. A gross caricature of Bush dominated the center. In a cartoon dialogue bubble, Bush's words were written out using the logos of oil companies: "We *SHELL* not *EXXON*erate Saddam Hussein for his actions. We will *MOBIL*ize our forces to protect our interests in the Persian *GULF*, until an *AMOCO*ble solution is reached."

The bottom of the flyer read, *"NO BLOOD FOR OIL!"*

His little girl was learning the very passion that had brought Arthur and June together. There was a warmth in his heart, not the regret he'd thought he'd feel when Meli started to grow up. With the warmth was an envy that Meli could live in a world of plain blacks and whites, with no troubling shades of grey. Was June out in the world now, protesting the war, as she and Arthur had done so long ago?

Arthur put Meli's books as he'd found them, not wanting his little girl to know he'd been snooping. Maybe, he thought, Meli could find Arthur's career worthy of protest. Case in point: yesterday, he'd realized that, by importing coffee from Ethiopia, he had perhaps contributed to the agricultural practices that were stripping that country's soil of nutrients. Hence, the desolation and famines of a few years ago. Would Meli protest such an action, if done by a businessman she did not know? Would June?

Would Arthur himself have felt guilt for dealing in Ethiopian coffee had he not been communing with the boy he had been? Arthur finished his breakfast as he heard Meli come down the stairs.

"Hi, Dad!" she said with the flip cheerfulness that only teenage girls have.

"Hi, Squirt." With a wince, Arthur realized he hadn't called her "Squirt" in years. *Sunrise, sunset . . .*

Meli smiled, though. A glint in her eye told Arthur it was okay. She looked so pretty in the morning light, she almost glowed.

"How's about a ride to school today?"

" 'Kay! Thanks, Papa!"

Arthur smiled as he put away his dish and Meli fetched her books from the living room. He couldn't remember when she'd last called him "Papa."

As they stepped out the door, Arthur asked, "Hey, did you have breakfast?"

"Uh-huh."

Opening the door to the cold wind, he could not figure out when or how she could have eaten, and wondered if this was something he should worry about.

III

Thursday, 8:10 A.M.

I n the belly of the green dragon, standing among those whom the city made dead for the span of the workday, Paul made himself into a fist, staying focused before school eroded his identity. The trolley roared along the street. Paul fought to keep balance.

Clinging to the idea that he should be a teacher—that he was answering a moral calling—was as ingrained as guilt for a sin. Paul needed *the idea* of being a teacher to help expiate the guilt he'd felt since his mother's death.

And before.

The situation was like his relationship with Catherine, the viper of a woman he'd dated last year. Catherine had model-like beauty, model-like thinness; her life was a model of rigidity, her worldview as narrow as her hips. Paul, devastated after his mother's death, had fallen into Catherine's arms—and her bed—out of a need for comfort, any comfort, and a need to punish himself. It was delightful to become her object; it was delightful to think himself worthy of her objectification because of his objectification of her.

He'd made an unspoken pact with Catherine, who was lovely and pale as a resurrected Helen of Troy in a Romantic Era painting. He would take her snipes, her passive-aggressive attacks disguised as meaningful discussions about her therapy, in order to expiate his guilt. She, in return, had a plaything she could manipulate and mold the same way she manipulated and molded her own body through starvation and constant workouts.

Catherine got prettier as their relationship wore on, becoming starkly beautiful in spectacularly ugly moments, such as when she deemed the subway an excellent place to discuss their "relationship issues."

One night, as she pressed her fingers into her temples, teeth clenched, as she reviled him for watching *Star Trek* in her living room as if he'd been covertly watching a snuff film, Paul nullified their contract. He walked back to his apartment and told Jo, who opened a bottle of wine to celebrate.

"What the fuck was I thinking, Jo?" he asked. They clinked their glasses in time with the *"bang-bang!"* of Maxwell's silver hammer (as warbled on Jo's wonderfully scratched copy of *Abbey Road*.)

Jo smiled and shrugged, her lion's mane hair sweeping her shoulders. "She's a snake, Paul," was all she said, even though she plainly knew the answer to Paul's question, and had known for weeks.

They'd finished the bottle of wine, *Abbey Road* having given way to the first Ramones album, when Catherine called to tell Paul that *she* was breaking up with *him*, damn it, and that would be the last word on the subject. Paul laughed as Catherine punctuated her proclamation by hanging up before he could say anything.

Paul and Jo drank a second bottle. Afterward, as they stumbled to their separate bedrooms, Jo embraced Paul. In that one gesture, Paul found the warmth and comfort he'd sought with Catherine, but had been denying himself by being with her.

In breaking up with Catherine, Paul had drawn himself into a fist, pulling disparate parts of himself into a stronger whole; he had found peace in relaxing the fist.

The trolley slowed at a stop. Paul gripped the handrail tighter. The young man sitting closest to him had spatulate fingertips, which he gnawed where the malformed nails grew. Paul caught himself chewing skin from his own chapped lips.

The trolley lurched.

Teaching was an unfulfillable expiation, a guilt offering to his mother. She had devoted her working life to his having a career, taking a low-paying administrative job at Boston College so he'd have free tuition. Paul had pursued an education major because it seemed socially responsible, because he could settle in a position quickly, so his mother could retire, or at least cut back her overtime.

Later, in his darkest grief, *before* his mother died, when the hopelessness of recovery could no longer be ignored, Paul wondered if his mother's job had given her cancer, building stress that reinscribed her cells into disease. But the life he led, the career he'd taken—and what it took out of him—this could *not* be what his mother wanted, could not be the true legacy she had intended for him.

He must be strong and centered, to let go of his career before it killed what his mother had nurtured: the part of himself she'd taught to see the poetry of existence. He must be strong and centered, to let go of his career, and the remorse he carried with it, before it killed what his father had taught him about the need to dream, to not be daunted by the impossible.

The green metal dragon roared along its path of metal and broken stone.

As Paul entered the school, even though the place was nearly empty, he felt the press of voices in his mind.

He focused his will in defiance of the voices, as constant in his perception as was the roar of the dragon as he rode the trolley.

It drifts.

It rises.

It has not *thought,* but *motive.*

The thing that separated Itself from the Enfolded One shudders as It nears the prismatic layerings of Materiality, the insubstantial "flesh" of Its being nourished by chaos and hatred as a plant soaks nutrients from soil.

It creeps upon the city, and those sensitive among the Living *feel* It, as one feels a look of hostility at one's back.

It sports and bellows in Boston's pained and anxious ether. A few suicides ripple back to the thing as sympathetic echo—a woman hangs herself with a stocking at the thought that her unloving husband might leave her; a girl in a dorm quietly gashes her wrists rather than face final examinations; a boy answers his sudden majority by swallowing his tongue; an old man fighting for life in an oxygen tent simply stops breathing.

These self-inflicted deaths make the thing tingle with pinpricks that please It in a way It can never understand.

Its contamination spreads like cold fog.

IV

Thursday, 10:44 A.M.

With exquisite suddenness, Ed felt his thread of stability snap. The equilibrium he'd sought bled out of him, as if he had exhaled all the strength he could muster for the day.

He felt the strain of maintaining the will to live.

Ed rounded the doorway of the theology department office to check his mail and get back to the library. As he entered, Grant, the administrative assistant, flashed a wry smile. Ed gave him a look and thought, *I'm not in the mood for one of your pop Latin quizzes.* Grant had an M.A. from Harvard, thought his job beneath him, and never hid his contempt for those who could only get into Boston U Theology School.

Ed pulled his mail, nothing but flyers for conferences, as Grant leaned against his desk and cracked an even more condescending smile.

"*I* got some interesting mail. I get mail, because I write to people. I always said, *'Ubi nihil erit quod scribas, it ipsum scribito.'*"

Ed sighed. Grant had information; Ed would have to play his game to get it, though he refused the bait of the Cicero quote.

"Yes?" His voice was hoarse.

"Mmm-hmmm."

Grant was a big guy. Bearded. Broad shoulders. That he should act so fey was incredibly irritating. Ed leaned against the mailboxes, his leather jacket creaking.

"Ahhhmm . . . What was it?"

"It was E-mail. Do you have a modem, Sloane?"

"No. What did it say?"

"Oh, it was just a note from a certain classmate of yours, now on leave."

Amelia . . .

She, who is my friend, but not the friend of Fortune.

"Ahhh . . . What'd she say?"

"Oh . . ." Grant leaned back, made a gesture like a British royal waving from a carriage. "She wanted to know the procedure for extending her leave another semester. And she asked about you, whether you're still enrolled. Seems she's had a rough time getting in touch with you. I told her you were where you've always been."

"Thanks."

"Oh, you are so welcome."

Grant spun in his chair and began typing with blinding speed, grinning. Ed pushed himself off the mailbox with his shoulder and walked away.

In the hallway, he thought of the letters he'd gotten from Amelia, which he'd felt too ashamed to answer.

"Pray for me, Ed."

Grant had inflicted more spite upon Ed than he could have imagined.

"Pray for me, Ed."

His soul was trapped in a cruel Egypt of his sinfulness; he suffered the tyranny of his own despair, born in turn of the wretchedness of the world he lived in. No beam of God's Light could penetrate the darkness in his heart, a darkness revealed to him in the moment that he found he could not bare his soul to God.

"Pray for me, Ed."

Ed turned the sickness of his soul over in his mind. In this way, he could tame it awhile, much in the way one can tame a demon by naming it.

He stopped at a water fountain. The water was brackish and warm. Besieged, Ed stumbled to the theology department chapel, lest he think too intently of freeing himself from the siege by cutting a way out through his own flesh.

Amelia . . . how he missed her. And how he missed the aspect of himself that was noble enough to love her.

Ed sat on a pew, put his hand to his brow, and took trembling breaths.

"Pray for me, Ed."

Ed waited, in inner exile, for a spark of his soul to reveal itself to him, that he might embrace it and tend it. He left when he felt ashamed of being there, as if suddenly made aware of his own nakedness.

V

Thursday, 12:14 P.M.

Spaw followed his cock across campus.

Since waking he'd been erect, with only a few moments of soft relief. Sitting in fluid dynamics class had been agony. He hunched at his desk, squirming, trying to find a comfortable configuration of cock, back, and ass. The notes he took were shit. The exam was Monday, and he feared what his old man would do if he fucked up.

All day, he could not stop thinking of the girl on the bridge. It was if she were part of the city, and everything he laid his eyes on were connected to her, making her always fresh in his mind.

Spaw walked to the computer sciences building, to get on line with guys at Cal Tech about the crap he hadn't absorbed in fluid dynamics this semester; he'd often slept off his midweek hangovers rather than attend the class. He crossed the central quad, giving the odd girl a visual once-over until he could bear it no longer.

Clenching his teeth, he blew out a gust of air that misted before his eyes for an instant. And, through the mist, he saw the girl from the bridge, flitting by in the corner of his sight.

He spun to follow her, to see if she walked toward a dorm or a shuttle stop. He thought of her eyes that had scared him and filled him with heavy desire.

She wasn't there.

Spaw looked in every direction. He couldn't even find a girl of roughly her height, wearing the same color pea coat.

"Fuck!" Clenching his teeth again, he stomped toward the CS building.

Everyone in the quad seemed to be walking in complementary rhythms, their movements part of some greater picture Spaw could never have conceived of. The rhythms seemed part of the city as a whole, and touched him in the same way the gaze of the girl had— frightening, yet arousing.

The city pressed upon him, made more blood flow to his engorged loins. He thought his back teeth would crack under the strain of his clenching jaw.

It looks.

It seeks.

It tastes.

It floats, at once above Boston, and below it. It inscribes the roiling ether of the city into Itself. It twists Its awareness through the maze of the city. It cannot find the THREAT . . . which is *not* what It has come to deal with. It cannot find the PREY that it *has* come for.

Above and below Boston, It extends Its perceptions deeper into the city's maze, until Its own perceptions make contact with one another.

It recoils from Itself in pain and revulsion.

VI

Thursday, 1:01 P.M.

It is like cutting into a body.

The piss-stained linoleum parts under the blade; putrescence oozes from the gash. The smell is of an open sewer.

Kneeling, the young man turns his head and gags, afraid he'll vomit into the ovoid hole where, until a few moments ago, a non-functioning toilet had been set. He drops the linoleum knife, hoists himself up by the bathtub which still has body hair and detritus lining it in rings.

He takes quick breaths, almost in rhythm with the other sounds of the job site. The need to vomit passes, but not the craving for clean air. He returns to work and rips linoleum from the floor.

Rotten . . .

The floor is particleboard, green and black, gangrenous-looking. The young man is grateful he wears heavy work gloves; a slight cut would be dire. The seal around the toilet was bad—with each flush, shitty water leaked beneath the linoleum, making the floor a putrid blister.

He tosses linoleum scraps into the tub. When the floor is exposed, he stabs his linoleum knife into the particle board. It is like sponge. He grabs tools from his belt, starts ripping the floor so that a new one can be laid.

"What *the fuck* is your problem?"

He turns to see Louie, his hated foreman, zit-ravaged face livid.

"What?"

"What the fuck is your problem?" Louie asks again. Tendons flex on his jaw.

The young man is afraid. The rhythms of the workplace, of sawing and hammering and heavy footsteps, *change,* reminding him of children pounding on odds and ends in imitation of Native American drumbeats. The young man knows this is an acoustic impossibility, until he realizes he is aware of the new rhythms not with mundane hearing, but with the faculties he has honed. The rhythms press the center of his forehead, making a tingling that saps his ability for higher thought. The stink becomes unbearable.

"Why *the fuck* are you pulling out that floor?"

"It's rotten."

"Let me explain something even you can understand. This is a *rental*. I don't give a shit about this floor. The owner doesn't give a shit about this floor. The niggers who're gonna live here don't give a shit about this floor. Why do you give a shit? And why should I have to pay the *union* carpenter to put in a floor, when you're the only one who cares about it?"

The young man feels his will lost to the air like alcohol evaporating. He feels he is part of the rhythms, part of a directionless crowd. He is aware of the linoleum knife smeared with shit-blackened toxins. One cut will kill Louie.

"It's a rental." A rental in the hinterlands of Dorchester, where the exiled who *had* lived on Mass Ave. must now come, as yuppie scum now find the crumbling brownstones they lived in "quaint." To Louie, the young man is naught but a white nigger, pulling a stunt at his expense to help the brown niggers.

With difficulty, the young man speaks.

"The floor . . . is gonna fall through."

"Then *you* pay the carpenter overtime. I'm gonna beep him right now, unless you shut the fuck up and put down new linoleum."

The young man silently moves his lips.

Louie squints. Winces, as if suddenly stricken with a toothache. Steps aside.

Rather than risk speech, the young man steps out of the rotting bathroom to grab fresh linoleum from the supply dump.

As he crosses the work site, passing patches of exposed dry rot being plastered over, he still soundlessly mouths the Lord's Prayer while half in trance. His coworkers hug the walls as he passes. The Prayer is the only protection for what he faces; he wields it as a weapon taken from one foe to smite another.

His Enemy is near—the Enfolded One, Leviathan—some aspect so close that It cloaks the city like storm clouds. It is hunting. Predatory, touching his intellect and the minds of those around him. He thinks of myths he read as a boy, of young warriors losing themselves in the ancient gaze of dragons before being devoured.

His heart races. He repeats the Lord's Prayer as he picks up a roll of linoleum, fighting to maintain himself in the midst of the rhythms around him, terrified that he, as a servant of the Unbowed One, will draw the attention of the Enfolded One, that he will be the focus of Its attack, or a vessel of Possession. He feels his Enemy as a wave of shadow, breaking against the city as a wave of water breaks against stones. Its movement is *aware,* though. The impression It leaves echoes that of something waterborne and reptilian.

He bears the linoleum on his shoulder. On his way back to the poisoned room, he risks a glance through a hole in the wall where a window had been set.

The grey behind the sky looks back at him with a gaze as dead as that of a shark. He feels a twinge in his mind, as if the tissues of his brain have spasmed like injured muscle. He nearly drops his burden as he resumes the Prayer against his mindless Enemy; he regains control, yet cannot unthink the urge to kill Louie.

He wonders what It is hunting with such purpose, then feels a sudden terror for his wife.

VII

Thursday, 1:25 P.M.

H ey!" *She called from the window of a battered VW Bug. Summer sun glinted all around.*

He stopped his skip up the steps of the house he rented, and hung off one of the porch's white pillars in a display of braggadocio.

"I still love you," she called from the car. Then she cast her eyes downward, met his eyes again. "And I always will."

With a bound, he ran to where she was parked and kissed her through the open window. The smell of myrrh was in her hair.

"I'll always love you, June."

A moment of terror, shattering the memory.

Arthur dropped the pen he'd held while staring out his office window. Sudden heat spread across his skin, as if the season were high summer, making the wool suit he wore suffocating. His throat swelled.

Dear God, he thought. *Was that memory, or fantasy?*

He needed it to have been real. Was it?

He thought of *certain* memories: June being gone at the start of senior year; rumors that she'd done too many hard drugs; a call to her parents' house one snowy night when she spoke to him in the broken language of the mad.

Why, if the scene that had just crossed Arthur's mind were real, would June say what she did? *"I still love you. And I always will."*

There was finality to the words: not something a girl would say at the end of her junior year.

Unless she knew what the future held.

Oh, God . . .

Arthur stood, paced. He went to the window, looking to the

bridge and the young people crossing to and fro. Was a moment he'd treasured a phantasm he'd made to fill the emptiness June had left? He remembered remembering the moment, but not the moment itself.

Had he, once a man, been so unable to endure the thought of being so different from the boy he had been that he created the moment as a turning point, to mark that transition? In an effort to preserve his past, had he destroyed it with an inadvertent lie?

Had he been so frightened by his manhood that he had to hide it away, where it could do no harm?

The lump in his throat felt as if it would choke him.

"I still love you. . . . And I always will."

Arthur hugged his darkness, thrown into sudden and ugly relief by the fierce daylight of his mind.

VIII

Thursday, 1:55 P.M.

dutch slept

through the whole day, he slept and slept

it was nice sleep

his breathing was clear, no spiders troubled his sick lungs; they were quiet and still

drifting between sleep and light of day, nestled in the warmth of his car, covered in blankets and coats, he felt something on top of him, and dimly, dutch knew it was a *girl* that lay upon him

a nice and heavenly lady, like the one he dreamed about in the theater the other day, in the dreams that had stars in them too, and spaceships that could take people to heaven

the lady, who was very pretty (dutch could just tell), lay on top of him in a way that was very sweet and innocent, and she was asleep, too

they were sharing sleep

the same sleep

she was walking around where his dreams should be, walking around the city, too, and he could feel her doing it

and she was talking to two other fellas, while she shared sleep with dutch . . . he could feel them . . . and could feel the nice lady walking where they kept their dreams, only they were awake, as if she'd taken all the webs of the spiders and drawn them thin, thin, thin, so they touched these two other guys while they were awake she went through his dreams to go through the city, and dutch didn't mind at all

in sleep, he drew deep breath that was clear and clean, and felt warm and safe in his little home

IX

Thursday, 3:00 P.M.

The bitch was everywhere.

She was part of the city, her face written in every configuration of brick, in the reflection of every window.

Spaw ducked into an industrial design building on Vassar Street, his cock swollen, heart racing, face burning. He went to a lavatory on the first floor. The bathroom doors were lockable. He shut the door with a slam, threw the latch. The place had the sour stink of residual shit and piss baked into the tiles by the radiators. He shut off the light, leaned against the door, let his book bag fall.

Even the old bitch secretary in the molecular chemistry department had taken the face of the girl on the bridge in the way a fleck of film, shifting over the lens of the eye, can transpose its blurriness on what one sees.

And each time he saw the girl, or thought he saw the girl, a surge of blood rushed to his loins.

The frequency with which he thought he saw her increased as he neared the river.

Fumbling in the darkness, Spaw went to the stall.

Finals loomed next week. He'd sat in the library, looking at his notes and the borrowed and photocopied notes of a few frat brothers. He couldn't read. And lurking behind his ugly arousal, behind the anxiety of being unable to read equations and figures, was his fear of his old man. Fear, anger, arousal knotted in his gut, brain, and crotch.

Bracing himself against the stall, Spaw pulled out his cock and tried to untie the knot inside him by coming.

Fifteen minutes later, with skin made raw and his naked ass on the tiles, Spaw brought his hands to his face and sobbed with unreleasable pain.

The grey motes his vision registered in the darkness, the transparent specks that float in the gel of the eye, took the form of the girl's face.

X

Thursday, 3:29 P.M.

The field looked like a photographic negative of the sea; dustings of soot-frozen caps of black on still waves. That he'd think such a fanciful thing pleased him. The poet in him was not *lost*. Arthur had done to his ideal self the *opposite* of what sculptors did with stone—he'd not chiseled away chaff to find the ideal locked inside, but had built up chaff, smothering the poet he'd been with the accoutrements of adulthood.

Arthur shifted gears as he reached Meli's school, rounding the corner marking the field behind the building. Kids filed from doorways to waiting buses, and to lines of Volvos, Beemers, and Benzes.

Arthur had left the office—executive privilege—unable to shake the panic he'd felt when he'd realized his cherished memory could be a lie.

Arthur pulled along the line of parked cars and scanned the curb, looking for his girl.

He spotted her, standing out from the other children, glowing with adult loveliness that made Arthur think of a single rose standing above lesser flowers. Meli chatted with a cluster of her friends, who, despite the schoolbooks clutched to their chests, reminded him of his associates at cocktail parties. The mist rising from Meli's mouth as she spoke was like exhaled cigarette smoke.

Meli frowned, as if someone had called her name. She turned to see Arthur. A radiant smile broke across her face. She made quick gestures of farewell to her friends, bounded to the car.

Arthur unlocked the car doors.

"Hi!" she said, still smiling as she climbed in.

"You call for a cab?"

"Yes!" she said, buckling her belt.

"Where to?"

"Home, Jeeves."

"Home's boring."

Meli looked startled.

"Home's boring," he said again. "I left work because it's boring. I'm not going to go home now, because that'd be boring, too."

"Okaaaaay . . . Uhhh. Where do we go that's not boring?"

"The whole city!" Arthur ran his fine-leather-gloved hands over the fine leather of the steering wheel.

Surprise crossed Meli's face, then a look of new delight. Then, by reflex, Meli glanced about, as if expecting Inid to glare her worried glare at them from the backseat.

Meli threw her arms around Arthur, held back, partly, by her seat belt. The embrace was cut short by the blare of a car horn; a white Volvo inched toward them, trying to get around. Arthur put the car into gear and drove.

With a coyness he found pride in, he asked Meli about the stack of colored papers sticking out from her notebook covers.

As if it were something to be ashamed of, Meli showed him the fly-ers he'd seen on the coffee table that morning.

Plainly expecting at least an admonition to not get involved in is-sues she couldn't understand, Meli could barely contain herself when Arthur suggested they stop by a drug store to get sturdy tape and put the flyers up.

Later, having run off a few more flyers at a copy shop, Arthur re-membered the ember of passion in his heart as he and Meli put fly-ers on windshields and lampposts in some of the nicer shopping areas of Brookline.

He decided—as the smell of coming snow filled the air—that the possible falsehood of his memory of the last time he'd seen June was irrelevant compared to how the memory made him feel.

XI

Thursday, 3:45 P.M.

Today was a victory.

Paul stood in the trolley, surrounded by fellow commuters, feel-ing centered, intact.

Cory had taken him aside in the empty teachers' lounge. She smiled. Her loveliness seemed timeless and transcendent, as if a seventeenth-century Madonna had graced the violently kitschy world of the lounge, with its ugly seventies furniture, cigarette-burned car-pets, and outdated Joe Namath and O. J. Simpson reading-awareness posters.

She thanked him for his help, his support. She thanked him for in-spiring her, in a thousand unnameable ways, to make her profession and her life her own.

Cory told him she would take her certification and teach on a reservation in Arizona. The reservation would pay her student loans; then she'd be a private tutor. She'd not enslave herself to the system, thanks to him. She'd stopped taking Fleischer's shit, thanks to him.

Paul's heart did not beat like a trapped animal against his ribs; the stink of nervous sweat did not cling to him. He took a deep breath. He had won this day.

Later, Fleischer had accosted Paul as he locked his classroom.

"What the fuck've you been telling that girl?" Fleischer whispered harshly in Paul's face. Amid the din of the hallways, no one heard; but all saw what happened, all could read the body language. This was Fleischer's retaliation, to destroy Paul's credibility in front of his students as they filed to the cafeteria or milled by the classroom in the halls.

Paul drove his finger into Fleischer's scrawny chest, a flamboyantly visual flourish to his standing his ground.

"Don't you *ever*," he said, driving his finger with each syllable, "talk to me like that."

Drawing a breath, Paul turned on his heel, then said over his shoulder, "You got a beef with me, talk to me when you're sober."

He left Fleischer standing there, dumbfounded.

Later, over his sandwich, Paul had laughed to himself. He realized that Fleischer looked like Mr. Atoz from *Star Trek:* the weaselly librarian left behind on a dying planet.

The trolley neared Paul's stop. Paul looked out the windows and saw the beauty of the city: the houses, old and majestic; the apartments of rich red brick; the glinting of the Charles as the train neared the banks.

Paul got off at his stop, smelled the air heavy with snow.

By letting go of teaching, by not being enslaved to it, he had earned back a bit of his dignity. He knew he'd be tempted to *not* quit after these victories. But he'd not let himself be lulled back into the trap out of which he was working to free himself.

A note for him waited in the kitchen.

"Hey! This is for you. But save some for me!"

Jo had baked bread and made soup. She had today off, and didn't have to work until late tomorrow. She'd be spending tonight with Bill.

Feeling a deep love for his friend, Paul set the soup on the stove, put the bread in the oven to warm. Then he went to his room to take off his suit, feeling, for some reason, as if someone or something large stood at his hind.

It follows.

It waits.

It draws Itself back into Itself.

The thing that extended from the Enfolded One's being floats, reassembled into Its snaking, undulant form.

It smells what It has come for.

It stalks what It has come for.

A tendril, like a line of spittle (though snaking like a living thing) extends from the blind, clouded coagulation where Its 'eye' would be if this thing that swam without a body and without water had mundane form.

It reaches.

It lunges.

It hungers to quiet the fear and panic It feels in Damnation; It hungers to keep power.

XII

Thursday, 6:05 P.M.

An idiot beast of blind anger bellowed, filling his vision with the red fire of its rage. Its roar crashed through his awareness.

Arthur realized, as he watched *Forbidden Planet* for the first time in decades, that he was having an acid flashback.

There was sudden depth to the images on-screen; the alien planet became more tangible than the seats around him; the animated form of the Id Monster that had scared the shit out of him as a kid had living intelligence in its eyes.

A flashback, after all these years?

He turned to Meli as animated fire lit the screen, filling the theater with bright strobes.

Meli looked like a thing of art—a beautiful representation of a woman, sculpted of stone, holding magic in its splendor. Newly fixed, the colors of her face (shifting in the red, black, and white flashes from the screen) seemed not yet dry.

Arthur turned his gaze back to the screen . . .

. . . and the film shifted politely back to two dimensions. As it did so, Arthur felt a snap of his senses, as if a rush of fever had passed in a heartbeat.

Afterward, as Arthur and Meli filed out of the revival house, Arthur noticed that according to the calendar posted in the lobby *Yellow Submarine* and *A Hard Day's Night* had played a few days ago. He would have liked to revisit *those* films, those moments of his youth as well.

The cold air struck them as they reached the sidewalk. Coolidge Corner buzzed with Christmas shopping frenzy, though meshed with the frenzy was a heaviness, a worry. The war perhaps? Was that why Arthur had been struck by such whimsy? A need to escape worry about the war, what it would do to shipping, tariffs, and international trade?

There was no Dickensian joy to the activity of the shoppers, just a somber busyness.

"Dad?"

The night had a weight, beyond the heaviness of coming snow, as if the dark were solid as amber, and the movement of people on the street were an illusion of light glimmering against its facets.

"Dad?"

Arthur knew this heaviness . . . this weight, ubiquitous. He'd felt the same anxiety on the campus where he'd lived while on the threshold of manhood—anxiety about war that dampened every human activity. A sublime anxiety that informed the city as completely and as invisibly as the air off the ocean informed the city, or as the flow of the river informed the character of the city.

"Da'aaad!"

Arthur snapped out of his murky thoughts, wondering how Meli could take a word of two letters and make it a word of two syllables.

"What, honey?"

"Where're we going?"

Arthur looked about; they were walking away from where the car was parked.

"I don't know," he said, aware that this was the first time he'd said those words to Meli, and that it felt good to admit ignorance, to be relieved of the omniscient burden of fatherhood.

Meli threw her hand over her mouth and giggled.

Arthur smiled. "I guess we should think about dinner."

Meli frowned. "Oh."

"But . . . let's not go home. The night's young."

They backtracked to the car, cutting through the city's gloom, through the crowds pantomiming happy Christmas hubbub. At the car, Arthur used his cell phone to make a reservation at Café Magyar: a place downtown where he wined and dined important clients.

Meli's school uniform was prim enough to pass for expensive, if inappropriate, casual wear; Arthur's suit was more than adequate, if not up to the level with which he usually presented himself to the maître d'.

István seemed bemused to see Arthur with Meli, as charmed as a waiter of his caliber could allow himself to seem, especially when Arthur referred to his daughter as "a very special client." Meli seemed overwhelmed by the cultivated gravity of Old World sensibilities— as carefully aged as the thousand-dollar bottles of Scotch hidden in the back rooms of the establishment.

Their discreet table became an island defined by the light of the candle set between them in a cobalt glass vessel. The blue light cast upon Meli's face made her seem a woman made of the gentle ice of a pond beneath a cold March sky: a thing of a nineteenth-century fairy tale, written by a Romantic. Within their island, there was a new familiarity between them—the kind one feels when one has met someone new and is able to connect with that person at a level deeper than the superficiality of introduction should allow.

Arthur asked for a bottle of wine.

The restaurant was of too high a caliber to pay attention to drinking laws; two glasses were brought. Meli winced at her first taste. The food, in rich red sauces made from a blended variety of fine peppers, overwhelmed Arthur's palate at times. Red light crowded the corners of his sight in contrast to the blue light from the candle.

At times, amid the rich spiciness on his palate, Arthur thought he caught a hint of myrrh.

The bill was more than Arthur's weekly paycheck had been when he'd first started working. As he signed off the bill, Meli reached into the jacket of her uniform to pull out a breath mint.

Waiters materialized from the shadows, one carrying a crystal ashtray which he placed before Meli, the other bearing a gold cigarette lighter that he lit and brought discreetly before her face.

Arthur and Meli couldn't help but laugh.

It stalks its prey.
          It
                    finds
                              the home of Its prey.
It hovers.
                    It waits.
It   It
extends   withdraws
the tendril   Its bulk back into
from Its mouth.   Its immaterial being.
Unthinking, It does not   Aware, It has not will to
                    feel or care what the rest of Its
shattered intelligence   shattered intelligence
screams for It   screams for It
to do.   to do.

XIII

Thursday, 7:05 P.M.

S omething entered his heart
       and split it.

A boneless finger pressed through his ribs, cleaving to and through his flesh like a root in soil.

Paul stood from his chair and screamed. No sound came from his throat, only the impression of thousands of voices forcing their way out of the frailty of his body, as if he were too small in volume to contain their mindless shouting. The air vibrated, as the air over a stadium vibrates, yet soundlessly.

Paul screamed. Longer than he humanly could, longer than could be accommodated by earthly lungs forcing earthly air. And as he screamed, more voices stabbed their way through that which had pressed Itself into and sundered his heart. His throat, his esophagus, his mouth, his brain felt packed with kicking frogs. The sounds took on sickening rhythm, percussive, in counterpoint to what had been the sane beating of his heart.

The voices made an idiot collage of his intellect.

Paul fell.

Paul shook, as if stricken with epilepsy.

Aware that more was at stake than his life, Paul did the last courageous thing of his life and tried to swallow his tongue.

Blackness took him before he could grant himself that small mercy.

In blackness, he found no rest.

It withdraws.
It Enfolds Itself again.
   It drops to Hell.
The barb It left behind twitches without form in flesh, insinuates Its contamination where once Will had reigned.
   A prize.
   A lovely prize to eclipse the deeds of Its rival's daughter.
   The vaguely reptilian form of the thing comes near the raging, churning body of filth that makes up the rest of Its being.
   Tendrils of Itself lash out, drawing It into the substance of Its idiot voices given tangible viscosity.

XIV

Thursday, 7:31 P.M.

They are safe.

A young man and his wife sit within the multicolored configuration that is the representation of their Lord and Patron's mind. Between them is a ceremonial sword—a *katana* bought by the young man at an estate sale. The two hold the sword in their hands, focusing their prayer and meditation by applying just enough pressure for the blade to crease their palms, but not to draw blood.

The young man came home and nearly wept when he found his wife safe from spiritual harm. They retreated to the configuration of their Lord's mind as if retreating to a storm cellar. For hours now, they have sensed atrocity personified bellowing in the far reaches of their perceptions. Their fingertips tingle from holding the blade so long. They are *still* in their thoughts, as an animal hiding from a predator is *still*.

The Thing they fear, the Blind Dragon, the Pebbled Worm, stalks the ether as if it were the still waters off a riverbank, displacing sanity within Boston's psychic space as a stone displaces water in a dish.

The displacement vanishes.

With a snap, healthful ether enters their awarenesses, dramatic as the click of an askew joint into place. The young man looks into his wife's lovely eyes, and slowly, they both let go the sword.

He rises, walks to the barred window in their kitchen that affords an upward view of the ice-filthy sidewalk in front of their building. His white linen robes billow with his step.

"It's gone," he says.

He does not have to speak his worries: what did this Thing, this dense extension of the Enfolded One, want so close to Materiality? Why did this aspect of It hunt through ether already polluted with Its influence? Did Its conflict with the Unbowed One, Belial, necessitate Its further intrusion upon the Earth, further imposing the power struggle in Damnation upon the affairs of the world?

He sees a small patch of night sky past the sidewalk and dingy buildings above him. Whatever It sought, It found.

The young man thinks, perhaps, he should tell his wife that he felt in the ether a hint of their Patron's will. But this hint was vague, and false hope is destructive.

"It's gone," he says again.

Not sure what else to do, they sit on their ragged couch, cover themselves with blankets, and watch *Jeopardy,* aware of the sublime banality of which they partake.

XV

Thursday, 8:45 P.M.

dutch slept

he wondered, in sleep, as he drifted close again to wakeful thinking, if it was bad what he was feeling, if it was bad to feel a girl lying on top of him, even though she was a nice heavenly lady

but the girl made him feel too good inside, too warm in his heart, for it to be wrong to share his sleep with her and his bed of coats and clothes and blankets

he felt the other fellas whose dreams the girl touched: a young fella, who acted mean (this scared dutch, but in the safe distance of dreams, this fear could not hurt him), and an older fella who was with a nice girl of about fifteen

dutch tasted nice wine, like what they used to give him in church, not the stuff some guys drank to keep warm, and smelled a nice smell that was smoky and sweet

dutch drew a deep, clear breath

And suddenly, the girl was gone.

With a whooshing sound, air went to fill the place where she'd been. The weight of the girl was gone, and Dutch almost gasped as he came fully awake to the darkness of deep winter night.

Dutch sat upright, bracing himself by the front seat of his home. Exhausted, he fell back into a stuporous sleep, his head striking the pillow with a thump. As he dropped to the deeper levels of sleep, he felt, dimly, the spiders going back to work.

XVI

Thursday, 8:51 P.M.

What had been Paul awoke.

As Its eyes focused, the echo of Paul reasserted itself, faintly. Then, over long moments, It again became Paul.

He lay upon the carpet, his mouth open, face against the nap.

Paul stood.

Then ripped open his flannel shirt.

There was no mark where he'd felt *It* press between his ribs.

Christ, what happened? Heart attack? Did I inherit something from Dad that's going to make me drop dead before I'm forty?

He stumbled to the couch, pressed fingers against his throat to take his pulse, put his hand over his heart to feel if it beat too fast.

Nothing.

Paul remembered . . .

. . . a threat in the midst of his mortal terror, something that made him fear for more than his precious life, that made him fear for his very . . .

And with the memory, a riot of idiot voices shattered his mind; Paul's self fell in a broken image, pieces of his being piled upon one another, like falling fragments of a stained-glass window.

Later . . . how much later he couldn't say . . . Paul's vision came back. He found himself drumming the coffee table, in rhythm with the hiss and clank of the radiator in the far corner. A sound, like voices, faded from his awareness, and as he drummed, as he drummed, as he drummed, he realized that he missed the voices, and wished they'd come back.

In his sudden and frightening loneliness he wondered when Jo would come back from fucking that nigger.

XVII

Thursday, 9:05 P.M.

Arthur realized that The Man with the Knife would not be waiting for him as he passed the traffic circle where Harvard, Washington, and Davis met. It also occurred to him as he rounded the turn that he'd given his daughter a gift of wine, just as Arthur's father had given him a gift of wine the last time he'd seen him.

It had been summer. Dad had come to visit from Valley Stream, eager to be out of the house he'd shared with Mom, eager to prove that the cancer that had been dug out of his femur had been no true threat at all, despite the cane he now needed to walk.

Dad had brought with him bottles of New York State wine.

Arthur had been touched, though perplexed. His father had never been one for wine. It was as if he wanted to reinvent himself after facing the cancer and share that reinvention with his son.

Because the airport shuttles had difficulty finding Arthur's unit, and because Dad insisted on not being driven to the airport (to exhibit further proof that the gouge in his thigh was no real bother), Arthur had walked Dad to the traffic circle, where three roads met, and there, father and son spoke as equals—truly *meeting* for the first time.

Arthur had choked with emotion as his father boarded the shuttle, facing the possibility that he might never see him alive again. They'd rediscovered each other, partly through the gift of wine.

Arthur pulled into his parking space and opened the car door in a fluid motion. Meli snapped awake in the passenger seat. She smiled. The halogen lights of the parking area kissed her face with gold, like May or June twilight.

She and Arthur went to the threshold together.

In the hallway, Meli again seemed to dull the shine of the polished maple paneling.

"It's late," he said. "You'd better get to your homework." He caught himself about to say "Squirt."

"I don't have that much to do."

She went upstairs with the grace of a deer.

Arthur went to the kitchen and opened a bottle of his father's wine. He heard Meli's tread upstairs—in the bathroom, it sounded like. A trick of acoustics made it sound as if she were walking near his and Inid's bedroom as well. Arthur reflexively thought of The Man with the Knife—then realized that he relished having *not* searched for him too much to think of him now.

Arthur set bottle and glass on the coffee table, sat and opened the paper. He read that condos downtown had been put on the market at the deflated rate of five hundred grand a unit; the paper took joy in proclaiming this the end of the "Y-word" era in Boston.

No sound on the stairway.

No tread on the carpeted steps.

Just a sudden presence that changed the nature of the entire room, that deflected his reading light, making it *feel*, less than *seem*, like the light of a torch or hearth.

"Hey!"

Arthur turned to see Meli, holding on to the wrought-iron railing in a carefree way, leaning into the living room from the stairway.

"I love you, Daddy. And I always will."

XVIII

Thursday, 10:10 P.M.

H ey! What the fuck's wrong with you?!"
The pit-faced gook looked up at him from the filthy sidewalk.
His accent made his exclamation all the more comical, an evocation
of tough-guy English he could only have learned from movies.

Spaw would have kicked him if his aching erection had allowed
him the range of movement. Burning in rage, in his blind, swollen-
cock-induced fury, Spaw was dimly aware of the first few flakes of
snowfall; dimly aware that part of him wanted to take this gook kid
by the hair and put . . .

"What the *fuck*?!" The little gook—vocabulary strained to its lim-
its—punctuated his cry with a spastic kick, like a kid having a tantrum.

Spaw walked past, but pointed at the guy as would a man com-
manding a dog to stay. The gook's expression was delightful. Spaw
would have liked to flick grit and ice in his face if he could have gotten his leg to kick.

Crossing the bridge again had driven him to this.

Crossing the bridge again had driven him to find what release he
could in quick and humiliating violence. The river flowed under him,
its current forcing its weight and pressure into his veins. The roar of
traffic became the roar of his blood. He burned, as if all his skin had
flushed red; the cold air made the burning a torture. As his body was
rewritten by the river, anxious fear made itself a weight on his back—
fear of his old man's wrath, should he fuck up on exams. On the
Cambridge side of the bridge, once he'd crossed back to campus
from the frat house, Spaw was nearly blind.

The solitary gook had afforded the only chance he had to vent his
fury and his fear.

Spaw reached the library.

Reflected on the glass doorway, the face of the girl from the bridge
eclipsed his own.

XIX

Thursday, 10:30 P.M.

A rthur had gone to bed a little drunk.

Now he lay on satin sheets, the room spinning slightly.

Sleep crowded his vision, his thoughts. For a moment he felt young again, felt his body, young and strong, felt his heart in his breast as it had felt before it had become jaded to the chore of beating. The warmth from the central heating felt different, like that from a space heater. He smelled something different in the air, a whiff of something smoky and sweet. Myrrh.

The wine was on his palate, still.

A shadow in the doorway.

A word spoken.

XX

Thursday, 10:35 P.M.

D utch wept.

The city rose cold and grey around him. Frigid stone, quiet, unbreathing, made stark valley walls around him.

He walked empty streets, felt the sad weight of the sky constrict like the sadness in his own throat, to drift down as the silent whimper of snowfall.

Dutch wept.

For he knew he had been touched by something beautiful that he would never touch again.

The tears were cold on his face as he felt the first violent twitchings of the spiders, now fully awake.

XXI

T *his is a prayer.*

The metal grip warmed in his hand. His palm sweated the liquor of his guilt and grief, making the metal stink with an acrid bite. Shameful musk rose from his body.

He holds the metal, savors the coming flash.

The shadow in the doorway had become a thing of flesh. Wine, in his blood, made his flesh shadow, a thing over which he could not exert will, yet which was joined to him as inextricably as the fabric of his soul.

This is a prayer.

In darkness, he is aware of snowfall.

In darkness, he *hears* the snow as a poet would—with the transcendent faculty that allows constant dreams, that creates constant metaphor. He hugs his personal darkness, makes it the only thing visible, closing his sinning eyes painfully tight.

He is, in this moment, abiding a long and living death.

Trembling in darkness, he grips the gun.

The shadow made flesh came to him, lay next to his naked body, which burned with youth. She carried a vial of bath salts, which, cast upon the sheets, made them a fragrant field for his anxious husbandry. The scents intoxicated him.

His vision greyed with pleasure, as if the air became thick with sweet smoke, like that of burning myrrh.

"I love you . . . and I always will."

Drunk with the scents.

Drunk with the wine.

Drunk on sudden youth, aware of snow falling outside in a way that he had not been since he was a boy, he lay upon his daughter's back and took her second virginity, tasting the salt of her tears as she cried, tasting the sweet distillation, like myrrh, of her tears as he made a beast of her.

Suddenly sober . . .

This is a prayer.

Unnatural wish fulfilled . . .

This is a prayer.

He walked to the bathroom adjoining the bedroom, hating the shadowed figure in the full-length mirror mounted upon the door, gripping the gun that his wife had insisted he get to protect his family from The Man with the Knife.

Leaning over the sink, he pressed the muzzle against his temple.

His temple is the site of his prayer.

He answers it himself.

The bullet pits his eyes as it plows his skull.

His mind is made mist and fine matter that travels the air in a pattern like that of the snow.

He is aware.

His shattered body falls to the floor, and he knows he should be dead.

Damnation is a hunger.

XXII

T he gunshot is a lightning flash.

The Succubus screamed a soundless song as her body flattened, swelled, compressed . . . as her stolen limbs became crooked and warped. The sweet mist to which she had converted part of her mass fell in condensing rain; her own essence made her body wet, moistened the sheets, slicked the wood floor. Through the shock, through the blast of the gun, she still imposed sleep upon the girl whose form she had taken, still held fast her link to her lover's mind.

She would not let him go.

The girl-form she'd taken, so much more slight than her own full mass, contorted back into its symmetry. The balsam of her essence rose again as mist, drying on her stolen skin.

As the mask of Meli she had made of herself, she stood and walked to where Arthur's sundered body lay. To let go her form—to become her natural self—would set free his sweet soul, would free him to the death he had inflicted upon himself; the instant of reconfiguration would sever her link to his spilled mind.

Arthur screamed in his unfinished quietus, screamed as he realized his soul would not rise or fall.

She saw her girl body in the mirrored doorway, saw Arthur's blasted intellect upon the tiled walls. The part of herself that had touched him in the dead church kept his mind intact, connecting as sublime mist the particles that flew from his shattered skull. The gross and liquid aspect of his identity still held his soul as it cooled in the air, upon the floor, upon the walls.

Seeing herself in the mirror over the sink, she cupped her hands before her and caught the fine particulate matter of her lover as it floated in the air. She drew her cupped hands over her mouth and nose and breathed Arthur in, as a merchant would breathe and appraise leaves of fine spice.

His pain, his torment, his guilt and grief filled her spirit as his seed had filled her womb. The pleasure constricted the fibers of her being, the sweetness of his pain made her marrow unbearably heavy for a delicious fraction of a second. Her lungs were coated with fine red wine. She exhaled her lover as a sigh, tasting him again as he spilled as vapor from her lips.-

His torment made her drunk.

The rest of her mass drifted about her, mingling with that of Arthur.

Out of hunger, out of need and passion, she thought to recon-
struct her lover, to take the red flecks of his identity and replace
them with impossible intricacy back into his cooling body, cement-
ing them in place with the mist of her own identity, and make love
to him again, playing the nerves of his body like a fine instrument in
an exquisite death fugue, making the fugue itself part of the aria she
wrote this night using the stricken man without a home as a conduit.

Blind.

*Pleasure crowded every corner of her senses, communing with her
own longing—as constant as still water—to join with her own Father.*

She became aware of living eyes upon her.

She rose, a speck of Arthur's mind quivering on her lip, to see the
girl she had formed herself as standing in the doorway.

Sirens . . . coming closer. The gunshot had called them.

The girl had broken free of the stupor the Succubus had put
upon her.

Sirens . . .

The girl stood, looking upon the scene before her, seeing her double mounted in an act of atrocity with her father, unable to read
what her eyes communicated to her intellect.

As the sun revives limbs the night has made numb, so did the realization of what she saw free Meli of her silence.

The girl screamed, hands thrust in her hair, pulling it by the roots.
The girl screamed, tearing her throat from inside, tearing her scalp
with her nails.

The Succubus screamed with the pleasure of Arthur's soul crashing into her being.

Her next awareness was of standing close to Meli, the girl's nightgown torn in her hands. The Succubus stood by her on the threshold—she, and her twin, reflected darkly in the mirror mounted on
the door.

*Sirens . . . stopping close by. Heavy treads, poundings on the door
below.*

Meli was immobile as a tree. Her upraised arms were like branches,
the tangle of her hair like leaves. The Succubus could smell the sweet
distillation of the tears that dripped like balsam upon her face.

The Succubus dropped the torn nightgown.

Reached into and through the flesh of her own belly.

And, with her hand immaterial, thrust into the belly of the girl
whose form she had stolen, she chose *not* to tend the girl's womb
with the seed of her father, chose *not* to give her the gift of a beau-

tiful son behind the safety of her unbroken hymen, chose *not* to inflict this upon her so close to the time of earthly celebration of a similar Nativity. The girl's eyes . . . the eyes of her twin . . . called from deep within her the forgotten sin of Mercy.

Splintering wood . . .

The Succubus kissed her sister, tasting the salt of her grief, and left her rooted where she was.

Heavy boots on the stairway . . .

The Succubus flowed out of the house, through the spaces of a window frame. She had an appointment to keep, for the sake of her aria.

XXIII

Thursday, 11:08 P.M.

H e watched girls board the bus that would take them to Wellesley and wondered. If he boarded the bus, could he pull one of the girls into the bushes at the end of the line, make use of her and board a bus back, his face obscured by the falling snow?

Spaw dismissed the idea. But thinking of it eased the pain in his cock, some.

Fear drove him to think of desperate ways to get his rocks off. Exams loomed. The rage of his father loomed. He couldn't study, for the pain in his crotch.

With dread, he turned toward the bridge again. Maybe if he slept, the pain would go away.

Maybe.

As he neared the river, his knees weakened. His blood pounded. Part of him knew the snow was beautiful. He had a memory of a crazy Catholic artifact, like a snow globe, his grandma had picked up in France. As a kid, he liked to shake it violently, to watch the cork-colored flecks swirl in the murky water. The flecks were supposed to look like swirling desert sands, and as they settled, a little plastic Virgin Mary emerged from the fake sirocco.

The fingers of his gloved hand curved, as if they remembered holding the globe.

The river had mercy on him. The fever did not make his blood boil. He focused on the far bank. Traffic rumbled past. Boston shifted in his sight, swayed with his steps.

From the corner of his far sight, through the churning snow, he saw a figure standing on the bank almost under the bridge, near the pilings.

It was her. . . . Even through the snow, he knew it was her, perched atop the rocks on the banks, looking to the ice as if watching waves break at her feet.

Fear took him—the kind he'd felt as a kid when he'd broken something and waited to get caught. The flow of the river beneath him, beneath the ice, made the air shudder, muddled the sounds of traffic.

Without will, with only *need,* he reached the far side of the bridge and walked down the icy steps to the esplanade.

She was still as a statue as he approached, like some figure of a saint along the route of a pilgrimage. Snow fluttered and collected upon her shoulders, her hair.

Without the sudden movement of one startled, she turned to him.

"Hi," she said. And smiled warmly.

Her eyes held comfort, and what could be love. Snow dusted her lashes.

He stared at her, longing for her to flood his eyes with the fear with which she'd flooded them before, to give him an excuse to punish her for what she'd done to him.

She cocked her head, gave him a concerned look. He thought she might gently touch his face and kiss him. The traffic on the bridge overhead was like breaking waves. Headlights passed along Storrow Drive behind him.

A sweet smell came off her, like that of aromatic wood meshed with that of a very young girl. He felt himself drawn into her eyes, felt a comfort like that of sleep, felt with dumb embarrassment what could only be pre-ejaculate flowing out of him like nectar from a stem.

The girl seemed to twitch, for the briefest of moments, as if she felt the coursing of his loins inside herself, as if she felt his tension as her own.

She took again the stillness of a statue, her smile seeming cut from stone or cast in plaster. Within the shifting curtain of the snow, in the midst of the unsleeping bustle of the city around her, she seemed to hold her impossible stillness even as she spoke.

"I'm Jeannette," she said.

Her voice touched him like the distant chime of cathedral bells.

He punched her in the throat.

Once.

Twice.

Then kicked her as she fell, causing painful pressure that nearly blinded him. His cock leaked clear, thick tears.

His book bag fell. He picked her up by the shoulders and dragged her, as she gasped for air, to where the pilings offered shelter from the gazes of witnesses and from the whirling snow.

She tried to stand, tried to find purchase to resist, tried, pathetically, to gain her footing by bracing herself upon him.

He liked that.

Very much.

So much so, that he punched her behind the ear for good measure.

The river . . .

It called him.

It called his pain and his fear and his lust.

In an act of contrition, he heeded its call and dragged her to the dead reeds along the frozen bank. Thrown to the ground, the girl hung over the slanting stones that paved the riverside at an angle, her brown hair splayed upon the ice.

She tried to raise her head.

He punched her again.

Then pulled off his gloves and set to work on her coat.

The splinter of his conscience found small vindication when he saw what little she wore beneath her coat, when he saw only the violet bra covering her thick, heavy tits and the line of her jeans just below her perfectly sculpted belly. The splinter of his conscience convinced him that she deserved this, that she had asked for it, that she had it coming for flooding his mind with her gaze.

Her perfect belly undulated with her breath.

The curves of her ribs quivered with her breath, under the greater curves of her breasts.

He punched her belly, punched her ribs.

Pulled down her jeans and pushed himself into her.

She wasn't dry.

The river flooded his senses. He felt not the cold, the rough ground, the warm girl he violated.

In a moment of horror, he realized he still might not come.

She raised her head from the embankment, and met his eyes with a look of love.

Unmoving, fixed by longing for the warmth her eyes held, he felt the beautiful touch of her hand upon his face.

In a whisper, she spoke . . .

"Sing . . ."

A tear formed at the corner of her eye.

A soft kiss on his lips.

"Sing for me."

Her weight became nothing beneath him.

"Sing for me of Mercy."

Churning mist formed beneath her. Her arms held no more weight than that of the sleeves of her coat, yet they were strong, so impossibly strong. The wisps of a cloud of steel.

"I love you, and I always will."

She had a look on her face of beatitude.

Or rapture.

Moving . . .

They were moving, as if carried by a bank of fog over the rim of a valley. The ground gave way, the stones of the riverside gave way. Ice of the river was now beneath them. The churning cloud flowed like liquid, yet with purpose.

Her hand on the small of his back.

The electric flood to his loins, heralding climax.

She became heavy, and cold, as if drawing the weight of the frigid air into herself. Particles of ice, fine as sand, flowed in streams into her. He felt the small wind that carried the ice, felt her draw the mist beneath them into herself.

Like a wolf in a trap, he thought to get away. But he could not fight her arms, could not fight the rising force building in his loins.

Her hand on the small of his back, flooding the nerves at the base of the spine that cause the body to twitch at the height of sexual pleasure.

Flooding him with paralysis.

Cracking, the resonant creak of breaking ice.

He came as the ice yielded them to the river.

She pulled him into the cold.

The darkness.

His nerves screamed.

Deeper . . . into the dark, into the weight of the water, into the voice of the river and the fear it spoke.

Her hand, warm on the small of his back.

A flooding of the nerves, again.

Without breath, he came again.

The silt of the riverbed, swirling around him in his dimming sight.

Her hand, again.

His breathless coming.

Freezing water in his lungs.

His dying intellect, aware of the current taking him, of being alone, without even his victim for company as he was carried toward the sea.

A final crashing of his nerves as he saw a streetlight shining through the ice that held him prisoner. The river granted him no mercy. He died as he saw his hand shadowed against the ice.

XXIV

She took him from the river.

His soul, released to the water, became a thing she could draw from the river as a fish draws airless breath. His soul, informed by the river's anxious fear, informed her in a way that made her tremble, which made her very bones warp and shift like flexing muscle.

She dropped—heavy, yet with little density—deeper into the silt.

She left her clothes behind as she rose to the ice above.

Through the break in the ice she had made with the boy, she gently broke the surface of the river, looking about as would a fawn. Unseen, she drew herself upon the ice and walked, still wearing the lovely mask she knew as "Jeannette."

Naked, her wet hair freezing, she hid behind the pilings of the bridge as a nymph would hide behind the trunk of an ancient tree.

The traffic roared above her as she sat, drew her knees against her chest, covered her face with her hands, and wept.

The first movement of her aria was complete.

Boston, amid the sounds of its false surf, did not hear her.

PART THREE

The Best Lack All Conviction

Chapter One

Friday, December 14, 1990. 3:05 A.M.

There is vision without sight.

A cold and secret place where dreams are unformed, where the intellect, in sleep, confronts the terror of its own existence.

There is voice without sound.

Darkness that informs light.

Lawrence was carried there.

Amid the secret fire hidden in the silver of a mirror, amid the sky color knowable only along the edge of glass, he floated, unbreathing—without thought.

Movement changes the void, as lightning through a blizzard changes the sky. Lawrence, blind, pressed against ether made suddenly unmovable.

He awoke with his hand over his face, not recognizing it as his own.

In darkness, knowing he'd not sleep again until dawn, he went to the window to watch snow fall from a sky made amber and gold by the lights of the city.

The snow settled on the Charles. Lawrence looked toward Beacon Hill, where the sun would rise from the face of the Atlantic. He felt he'd left more than the warmth of his body behind—like an impression—upon the bed.

He was transfixed by snowfall. A scent rose from his body that was not his own—a heavy musk, meshed with a lighter scent that reminded Lawrence of one of his favorite male teachers at school.

Something passed close by . . . moving *(above him?)* as leaves rustled in the boughs of trees.

As soon as he was aware of it, it faded from the realm of his senses.

He placed his hand upon the glass, and for a reason he could not fathom, wept as he touched its cold clarity.

And for a reason he could not fathom, the fear of unseeing took him as his vision clouded with tears, filling him with panic that erased knowledge of his own name from his intellect.

Dawn found him naked, shivering, on the floor.

Another hour passed before he remembered who he was.

II

Friday, 8:30 A.M.

It was like a dream.

The school brought comfort with its bustle, with its thronging crowds packed into the hallways. Paul had been happy all this morning (even though Jo hadn't come back from her night of nigger fucking), he'd been happy to ride the trolley and feel close to people as *they* felt close to their country in its time of need.

He entered his classroom. And felt a sudden terror of aloneness as he shut the door behind him.

(What are you . . .

Something twitched—quivered—in his heart, like an embedded thorn teetering and shifting with his heart's beating. Panic spread through him the way venom spreads under a wasp's sting.

. . . thinking, Paul?)

He let out a small choke. He'd been so happy among the crowds this morning; now, suddenly shut off, he hungered for the comfort crowds gave him. He sat at his desk, shaking like a junkie. . . . Like a junkie piece of shit nigger.

(What are you . . .

He pulled his lesson plans from his case.

. . . thinking, Paul?)

He could not focus; he could not concentrate.

Paul's mind, with trains of thought crossing, touching, like leafless branches in a slow wind . . .

The bell rang; his first-period class filed in.

No longer shaking, he stood as the kids came in. They looked at him differently, giving him a subtle acknowledgment of authority they never had before.

When they'd settled in their seats, he knew he needed more from them.

More . . .

"Please stand," he said.

The kids, unpacking book bags and opening notebooks, looked up in surprise.

"Please stand," he said again, finding a pleasure, almost sexual, in the use of his voice before a group, in directing the group's action.

Slowly, the kids stood.

And Paul's pleasure blossomed into something more than sexual, something he'd felt before only in the face of sublime beauty.

"We will now recite the Pledge of Allegiance."

The kids gave one another confused looks.

One kid—a snotty neo–Dead Head named Chad—raised his hand, and without being called on, spoke.

"But we did that in homeroom just a few . . ."

Paul pointed at the kid. "I'm not interested in your observations, *Chad*." He stretched the vowel in the boy's name so it became a taunt: *"Cha-aaaad."*

"We will say the Pledge of Allegiance because our country *needs* us to. We need our country, and our country needs us. We need to support our troops in any way that we can. Now, place your hands over your hearts. . . ."

The voices . . .

The voices of the kids, not quite speaking in unison, not quite harmonious, discordant in their layerings and mismatched resonances, gave Paul a profound peace.

His fears were forgotten. As he began his lesson, the twitching pain in his heart lessened, fell still.

III

Friday, 9:15 A.M.

Her hand burned.

On her bed of snow stained with resinous sweat, the Succubus raised her hand before her face and watched as her body made blood-fire of the spirits she had ingested, yet could not fully contain in her flesh.

Her bed smelled of ripe, rich fruit.

Of human fecundity, and myrrh.

She bled and burned what the living knew as the distillate of dreams. What leaked upon the snow would not evaporate, but would drip down in the ether like honey through warm amber liquor.

Her hand burned, red palm and fingers like a coal in yellow flame;

red palm and fingers configured like those of a patriarch granting Benediction.

She, moving as the echo of the great and terrible Patroness she was to be Named after, had taken more than her body could hold. She felt so very strong, flushed with the sublime poetry that had been buried in the mind of the man who had been "Arthur" and the bestial, raw needs of the boy who had been "Spaw."

The sweetness of her first love, "Andrew," infused these new flavors as wood of white oak infuses wine. The faint innocent trace of the child she'd taken, "Troy," was comforting in its pain and confusion.

She turned on her side, thrust her hand into clean snow.

It still burned, filling the unmelting snow with light like that from a firefly. She felt the cold through the heat of the fire. More resinous sweat stood out upon her in humid beads. She tasted it as drops ran to the corners of her mouth.

The snow gave voice to the fire, like that of mundane fire as it murmurs in strong wind.

In the flame's voice she heard the lamentations of her lovers, the release of that which gave light and form to their auras and substance to the ghosts of themselves they'd carried entwined within their bodies.

The voice of the flame comforted her.

With will and awareness unknowable to the living, she made the voice of the flame speak the angelic language that had preceded Materiality.

She made the flame speak the Name of her Patroness, the Name that the living could hear as "Tisiphone."

Mother of Sighs, of Shadows, and Tears.

Last night, she had moved as the agent of her Father and her Patroness. Through her Father's sense of Beauty, she had taken the function of Tisiphone, destroying a family of this city as Tisiphone had destroyed a family of the city where the Living had first learned to dread her Name. She had used the River as a weapon to avenge the girl who had died in the River's waters; she was mistress of this River, as her Patroness was of the Rivers of Hell.

She would earn the Name "Tisiphone." She would make of Boston a diptych, a mirror of the ancient city where the Name of "Tisiphone" was consecrated in blood and atrocity.

The flame of her hand died.

The sweat of souls on her skin stopped.

She rose from the tallow on the snow she left behind and dressed herself as the girl who had died in the River's waters, to find the stricken man who had been invested with the spot where the girl had died.

In so doing, she began the next movement of her aria.

IV

Friday, 11:15 A.M.

The two were made stone by the heavy gloom.
The store could not be made to feel or look bright. All the lights were on, all the shades opened.

Eleven days before Christmas, and the store was empty.

Lawrence felt the darkness press against his brow.

"Is there anything we should do?" His voice hurt his ears. The dreams he'd suffered, the chill of waking on the floor (*had he fallen from bed in his sleep?*), and the heavy depression he carried made his senses raw. Earlier, he had been nauseous as airy cold feelings (*empty, like the space left by a missing tooth*) shifted through his chest and a sweaty fever slicked his hand. The tastes of his breakfast had been like different kinds of acid. Now hunger gnawed at him, made his belly feel full of broken glass.

Vicki shook her head.

"It's early, yet."

"Has business been this bad at Christmas before?"

"No. Everyone's . . . nervous about the war, too edgy to buy anything. I'm scared. Maybe everyone's scared."

She looked at her hands, which rested in fists on the counter. There were pink buds on her knuckles.

"I'm kind of a wreck," she said. "My worry warts are back. I haven't had them since high school. Everything just feels so . . . fucked, y'know?"

Her voice went up an octave with "y'know." A pained look crossed her face.

"Yeah."

Vicki looked about. "Where's the cat?"

"I don't know. She didn't come when I put out her food."

"*Groucho*? Didn't run out when she heard the can opener?"

"No."

Vicki chewed her lip. "Watch the counter. I'm gonna look for her."

After a minute of calling and looking, she found Groucho and brought her to the counter. She held the cat close to her face and looked as if she might cry.

"I was worried that . . ." She did not finish.

"I know," said Lawrence.

Groucho draped herself over Vicki's shoulders, claws sunk into her sweater, and purred.

"Did you know that Groucho lived with me once?"

"No."

"It's true. We were getting the store fumigated for termites. So Groucho came to live with me. She slept by my head, curled up on my pillow. I think she gets lonely here, at night, with no one around. If it weren't for Groucho, I'd have quit a long time ago. Why else would I put up with Jack's bullshit?"

Lawrence shrugged. Smiled. He could *smell* the cat, in a way he never could before. If he'd had any food in his belly, it would have made him sick. Something twinged behind his left eye.

"Groucho caught me a mouse once. In September, just as it was getting cool out and the mice look for warm places to live. You know how Groucho likes to hide in the basement? And how she comes back all dusty? Well, she came to me while I was behind the counter, and she was all dusty. I was pulling dust bunnies off her and one of them by her mouth started *moving*. I let out this totally sissy scream and jumped on my chair, like a housewife in a Warner Brothers cartoon. Ed was here, and he ran over and *laughed* at me, the bastard. He said she did it because she thinks I'm too stupid to hunt for myself. He wrapped the mouse in his handkerchief—it was still alive, Groucho hadn't really chomped on it—then he let it go outside. He came back and scooped up Groucho and told her what a good little predator she was, a regular saber-tooth. Then he gave me an unending line of shit."

Lawrence wanted to laugh. But couldn't.

Vicki set down Groucho on the counter, so they could both pet her. But she scampered away as soon as Vicki set her down.

"She'll be back," said Vicki.

Lawrence didn't hear.

In a dreamlike state, he found himself staring at Vicki's breasts, wondering, for the first time, what she would look like undressed.

He wondered why he should find such an alien imagining so arousing.

V

Friday, 12:37 P.M.

Dutch placed his hand on the black iron bars of the gate—and felt his mouth quiver with the need to sing—as the voices of the children reached him from the opened window.

"I love Thee, Lord Jesus . . ."

Dutch had walked the city, looking for beauty. For he had missed beauty deeply since he'd come so close to it and, upon waking, had found it so very distant. He had been reborn to sadness.

"The cattle are lowing . . ."

Looking for beauty, trying to fill the emptiness in his heart, he walked Boston to look upon the prettier churches. This church had a school in back. Walking around the church, looking at the high spires, he heard the children singing Christmas carols. He followed their voices, and would have come closer to hear them were it not for the black iron gate that closed off the school yard.

In the children's voices he'd found beauty that quieted his yearning.

The children sang a different song now, one that Dutch knew. He tried to sing along.

"Silent night, holy night . . ."

But the breath he drew tickled the spiders. They crawled in his lungs, biting and pricking. He coughed.

"All is calm, all is bright . . ."

Dutch liked that song; it was about men who followed a star to find where Jesus was born. He wished he could sing.

". . . Virgin Mother and Child . . ."

He coughed and hacked, brought up sickness rich with blood.

He stood upright, wiped his mouth with paper napkins. Dutch wanted stars, to be near Jesus, and the nice lady who was so beautiful—who took away the spiders and made him feel well. He leaned on the black iron gate for balance.

Transfixed by the children's song and his own longing to sing, transfixed by the stone-cut beauty of the church, Dutch did not hear the crunch of tires behind him, the sounds of car doors opening, the heavy treads of two policemen.

The billy club rammed into his right kidney. Pain blossomed across his back, burned through him to his belly.

Dutch grunted, fell against the bars, cutting his head on cold metal. He slid to the snow. A big hand in a rubber surgical glove grabbed him by the collar near his chin and yanked him onto his back.

The cops looked at him like dog mess they'd just stepped in. One, holding the billy club, had a big red nose. His jaw was clenched, veins stood out on his forehead. The other drew his billy club from his belt.

"*. . . holy night . . .*"

The one with the red nose spoke.

"I don't think you wanna be here."

Dutch tried to get up, scurry away.

But the other cop pinned him with his club, pushing it into Dutch's chest.

"Hey," said the other. "We're talking to you. Where do you think . . ."

The club pressed into Dutch's chest woke up the spiders again.

He arched his head back and coughed, a spray of blood coming from his lips. The pain in his back, his head, and his chest was so great, Dutch thought he'd black out and drown in his own sickness.

The cops backed away in disgust.

"*Silent night . . .*"

They left him in the snow.

Dutch, coughing, bleeding, stooped in pain, pulled himself up by the black iron bars and stumbled away from the church and the children's voices.

Later, hiding near the Common with dirty snow pressed against his brow, Dutch wondered if Jesus loved him at all, and if he'd ever see the nice stars or be near the nice lady again.

VI

Friday, 12:41 P.M.

Crying, drifting among the books.

Lawrence, swimming in the haze of his senses, did not know if the sound was a phantom, an echo without source.

Vicki was dealing with a customer in a Blake Tobey suit and Burberry coat who demanded to know why a used book should cost "three *fucking* dollars!"

Lawrence followed the sound through the nearly empty store.

When he found the man in the psychology section he smelled him—an awful stink, bitter as spoiled milk. Books, all hardbacks with green or off-green covers, lay strewn about. He sat on the floor holding one book close, rocking back and forth as he cried. How had he come in without Lawrence or Vicki noticing?

The man started, like a mouse. Lawrence expected him to scamper away with the stealth he must have used to enter the store. He had a filthy beard; his eyes were framed by harsh creases. Tears left streaks on his dirty face.

The man held out the book to Lawrence.

" 'S *my* book," the man said. " 'S *my* book. 'S *mine*."

Then he held the book close, sobbing.

Lawrence spoke carefully: "How about if we get a plastic bag for your book, so it won't get wet in the snow?"

The man looked at him, then made a sound that could have been a faint "Yeah."

"Should we get the bag, now? For your book?"

Trembling, the man stood. Then nodded.

He followed Lawrence, hugging the book. Vicki and the yuppie stopped haggling and stared.

"Here," said Lawrence. "Here's a nice bag for your book."

As if unable to fathom such kindness, the man accepted the bag and put the book in it. Then he said something that could have been, *"You're my friend?"*

Straining to understand the man filled Lawrence with a need to cry. The man's stink, the smell of old books, the cologne worn by the well-heeled jerk made the whole world tremble.

"I guess I am."

The man smiled, revealing rotten stubs of teeth. Then he bustled out the store.

As the bell over the door fell quiet the yuppie turned on Vicki, driving his index finger into her chest.

"Nice to know *some*body can get service in this store! Now why don't you—"

Vicki knocked aside his hand.

"Get out!"

Lawrence felt the force of her words; his head snapped back.

"Get out!"

Lawrence was struck by grey delirium. He came back to find himself slumped against the counter like a drunkard; Vicki stood in the entryway, holding the door.

She said out toward the street, "Merry Fucking . . ."

She slammed the door. The bell jangled.

". . . Christmas!"

She came around to the counter.

"Lotta help *you* were," she said, "with that piece of . . ."

Then she saw how Lawrence slumped.

"Oh my God." She put her arm around him, helped him to the chair. Her body against his burned in a way that was pleasant, yet overwhelming.

"C'mon," she said, easing him into his seat.

"I'm okay. It's flu, or something."

Vicki picked up his right hand and rubbed the fleshy spot between the index finger and thumb. A jolt spread from his hand.

"You don't have to . . ."

"Shhhh."

After a while she worked on his left hand.

Lawrence's senses no longer reeled, though his vision was still warped. Then Vicki stood behind him and rubbed his temples. Her fingers were strong, but soft. Lawrence closed his eyes and felt vaguely human.

The bell over the door jangled.

Lawrence opened his eyes to see Dave lumber in, carrying the huge thermos and a small brown grocery bag.

Vicki kept rubbing his temples.

Dave grinned. "Mom would love to see this."

VII

Friday, 1:59 P.M.

P aul realized what he felt was terror.

Terror that he'd soon be away from school and its crowds of students. He couldn't bear the silence waiting at home. In five minutes, he'd have to leave the teachers' lounge and teach his last class until Monday.

His fellow teachers were quiet. Their silence hurt. Mostly they read or corrected. He needed their voices so he could focus and think.

No niggers in this school, he thought to himself. *No niggers in this school.* For some reason, this fact and the statement of the fact gave him comfort, like a mantra.

He scanned his lesson plan, not reading what he'd written. Cory sat next to him, smiling, cup of coffee in hand.

"Hi, Paul."

"Hm? Oh. Hi."

One voice could not help, would not be enough. Talking to her would *hurt,* would erase the lovely mind-clamor he'd enjoyed this day.

He turned back to his illegible lesson plan. He knew he'd do what he had to do in class, feeling and feeding off the kids' energy.

"I want to thank you."

He looked up.

"For what?"

"Everything."

"Oh. You're welcome."

Greyness . . .

Sudden greyness, a shifting of his awareness. The black of the writing on the paper before him meshed with the white of the paper itself. His vision, his hearing, even his touch were clouded.

The greyness became like that of steel, darker, with a sheen.

As the greyness parted, he found himself by his classroom, speaking to Cory.

And he did not know what he spoke, save that it felt good to utter the words. The words were *heavy,* carried on his breath. He'd raised his index finger, gesticulating with it angrily. The bell rang. Students flowed into the hallways; their footsteps, their murmurs, called Paul back to full awareness.

As if the warped language of dreams could suddenly be heard by the waking mind, Paul understood what he was saying.

"There's no I in 'team,' Cory. . . ."

Paul's lungs were almost empty; he kept talking.

"And if you can't be a part of this team, you shouldn't be a teacher at all."

Something in Cory broke.

She cringed. Paul thought, with satisfaction, that she might cry. She turned on her heels and walked away, swallowed by the masses of kids shuffling in the hall. Full of new terror that he had only forty minutes more of feeling safe, Paul went into his classroom.

VIII

Friday, 3:15 P.M.

Wearing the mask of the girl who'd died in the River, the Succubus sat on the bench where she'd first touched the stricken man.

She'd felt sharp pain across her back, brow, and chest, earlier, when the stricken man had again been made victim of the city. By making him suffer, the city drew him deeper within itself, closer to the death that awaited him within its folds.

His illness was part of the city, expressed as consumption. Illness walked the streets of his veins, touching the bricks of his cells; he carried the city's breath as his own. His disease had its ultimate source in the River, in its night-fogs, in its waters infused with human worries. Thus was she herself called to the River—to this spot of interruption—as the stricken man was called, as the girl who died here had been called, as her murderer had been called.

The River carried a trace of her own unanswerable desires: her longing for the man with the noble soul infused the River's water. Yet she would *use* her longing, and make it part of her aria. His absence would be caesura, an emptiness to accentuate the aria's fullness.

Her lovers were configured inside her as the spheres separating the Abyss from the throne room of God were configured. Andrew, Spaw, Arthur, and the stricken man (whose Name she had yet to touch and know and bring into the fabric of her mind, despite her using him as a conduit, despite the link they shared that allowed her to feel his pain and illness). . . . These four men—and in a small way, the child she'd slain to avenge her Mother—each represented the steps she'd taken away from the realm of her Father toward her Name; each represented an infernal realm, rising toward Materiality. Soon, she would have souls enough to cross the Void to Materiality; she would then pass closer to the realms ruled by the Divine, her body almost a thing of True Flesh.

Atrocity layered, structured, as is the music of the Heavenly spheres.

Her aria would be complete upon her taking the stricken man. She'd then build a series of sonnets upon the aria: blasphemies, poetically reversing the Divine Insult of infusing beings of filth and clay with the fiery dignity of souls.

She waited for the stricken man to come. Even in the bitter cold, people walked the esplanade. She smiled at a few, prettily, as they passed. A young man, quite handsome, came and sat on the bench, making clumsy attempts at flirtation. She responded warmly, to pass the time. She accepted his "number" from him on a slip of paper. He looked quite sweet as he walked away, his aura shimmering in a way that it had not when he'd first sat with her.

She waited as shadows deepened on the fresh snow, touching the city with lavender-grey. Suddenly, she felt closed off from the stricken man, distant, as if he no longer existed.

If he had *died,* she would have felt it.

She then realized—the man had taken refuge in a church.

She could not take him, this day. He would have residual sanctity on him that would make bitter the act of loving him. Feeling cheated, but not angry, she walked to her home. She changed her aura, watching the shifting colors make rainbows on the snow as it reflected the darkening winter sky.

IX

Friday, 4:35 P.M.

Grant had been *delighted* to distribute news of the scandal throughout the theology department. He'd gotten the transcript of the interview by E-mail from someone who'd read it in the Tel Aviv newspapers, then printed out copies. The scandal made his beloved Harvard look bad, but that didn't seem to matter.

Ed, never one to enjoy scandal as much as his colleagues, was nonetheless appalled and secretly happy that a nice black mark had been made on Harvard Divinity's reputation.

The head of the Dead Sea Scrolls project (a longtime Harvard fixture) had just given a sickeningly anti-Semitic interview in *Ha-Aretz.* Ed's eyes burned at what he read; a man who'd controlled interpretation of ancient Jewish law for decades had spewed forth anti-Jew bile during an interview with an Israeli reporter.

The lid was going to fly off Scroll scholarship. Texts, decades late in preparation (some said they'd been suppressed) would now be published.

Ed leaned against the mailboxes.

"Jesus," he breathed.

"I hope that was a prayer."

Ed looked up; Grant smiled at him.

"What?"

"I hope that was a prayer. What you just said. It wouldn't do for a theologian to take the Lord's Name in vain."

Ed glared, not wanting to give hint of how deeply his snipe cut, not wanting to let his voice reveal weakness Grant could exploit.

Grant said, "It's okay with *me* if you take the Lord's Name in vain. I forgive you. *Ego te absolvo.*"

Grant made the sign of the cross.

Ed held up the sheet of paper.

"Qui non vetat peccare, cum possit, iubet, jerk!"

He left before Grant could respond.

A prayer . . . if he only knew.

With precise regularity, his thoughts turned to Amelia, her suffering (so noble), and his own wretchedness in the paralysis of grace, in his inability to pray. Grief had found a place in the cage of his breast, nesting among his ribs like a bird, where once he'd held a love, transcending the physical, that he'd held for Amelia.

Amelia, like a saint, now tended her dying brother and his lover, dying as well. Amelia's parents had banished their son. She had gone west, to give them comfort, to change their dressings, anoint their sores. To feed them, and keep despair at bay. To grieve for them before they each drew their last breath.

"Pray for me, Ed."

How, in God's Holy Name, could he not?

Walking toward the bridge he would cross to reach home, he realized, for the first time, how deeply he dreaded the inevitable moment of profound loneliness when he would forget her eyes.

X

Friday, 5:45 P.M.

Quietly, with a slowness of tread that served as a reminder of his age he did not welcome, Franklin walked the stairs to his apartment.

Jenny had insisted he take the place because of the caged, old-fashioned elevator that rose from the lobby, surrounded by the creaking wooden staircase. "You won't have to strain, Dad. . . ."

But to Frank, it seemed an insulting waste to use the elevator to go up one floor.

He stopped at the top of the stairs, feeling the beat of his butchered and stitched heart, listening for a hint of the roar that, at worst, heralded an attack, or at best, another spell when blackness pushed the corners of his vision. He heard the flapping of pigeons in the alley, nothing more.

He walked to his apartment, jangling his keys, missing, as he always did, the longer walk to the front door of his house: up the sidewalk from the curb and up the porch steps. He missed savoring the act of coming home—*from work*—not from the exile he faced in retirement.

He opened the door.

In darkness, in the cold of his living room lit by the residual light of the hallway, the only movement was the VCR flashing the blue-green lie that it was midnight, midnight, midnight—when in truth the solace of *midnight,* when he could turn his back on another empty day, was denied him another six hours, or so.

He closed the door and sat in the chair that had seemed natural in his old home, yet here seemed out of place. He did not drop his bulk into his chair, as most men his age and size would. He was proud that he'd never lost his lightness of step, though he'd lost his lightness of form decades ago.

After a day of sitting in the brightness of the branch library, Frank sat in the darkness of his apartment, waiting for the timer on the thermostat to make the place warm enough for him to take off his coat. He remembered when he'd been young, seeing older men shuffle home from their days of talking trash, of dominoes and chess, of sitting at card tables placed in front of stores owned by their sons, or once owned and run by themselves.

But then, there had been porches for people to sit upon. Then, there had been the luxury of quiet, and slow walks. The old men could find momentary places of belonging on their routes home.

Not so in the world Frank lived, where cars had redefined twilight interaction. Not so in the place Frank lived, a nice neighborhood, yes, but so urban; his daughters had chosen it for its closeness to the hospital, "in case anything went wrong."

For Frank, there was only this small, efficient space where he could be housed—in kindness and with the best intentions—while he occupied the awkward place between retirement and death.

He'd sold his house to pay medical bills, and to have a legacy to will to his daughters. A good plan. Save that it entailed a long while to come to fruition—a long while that entailed many nights like this, sitting, feeling the toothache-like pain in his sternum where it had been split to afford access to his heart.

As the radiators hissed to life, the clock continued to flash its blue-green lie.

XI

Friday, 5:55 P.M.

The Jar Head clenched his jaw, made great fists of hands.
"I need 'em *now*."

Vicki stood her ground.

"The buyer won't be in until tomorrow."

Jar Head clenched his jaw tighter. Lawrence saw, through the thin crop of hair, veins stand out on the guy's scalp. The guy hefted the box of books onto the counter.

"Look at 'em."

Vicki threw her hair over her shoulder, looked the guy in the eye as he got in her face.

"The science fiction buyer," she said, "won't be in until tomorrow."

"*I* won't be here tomorrow. *I* need stuff to read. Now are you gonna look at this stuff and make me an offer, or what?"

It was Lawrence's turn to play Good Cop. As he got closer to Vicki and Jar Head, his knees shook. He was scared by this guy's anger, his *bigness*.

Lawrence was in full Good Cop mode. "Maybe I can take a look at them."

Jar Head looked at him . . .

. . . and knew Lawrence to be a faggot.

Jar Head was pure military asshole: the brush cut; the "civilian" clothes of dull greens and khaki; the crop of zits from eating military food. The kind of hayseed shipped from Nebraska who takes out his culture shock by fag-bashing with his buddies. His kind stalked Providence in packs on weekend leaves.

Predator knew prey.

"And what're *you* gonna do when you look at them? You're not the sci-fi buyer," he said with just enough hostility to communicate his contempt.

Something else, though . . . Something *on* the guy, like body stink, pressed on Lawrence's awareness, his sense of self. He summoned fake bravado, like what he'd seen drag queens use while facing down cops.

"What I'm *gonna* do is give you an exchange credit deal, if you wanna . . ." He choked slightly; his knees still shook. "If you wanna look at the stock and make a deal."

Jar Head looked to Vicki; he had contempt for her, too. But his contempt was entwined with attraction, with his resentment for a woman he had the primal urge to fuck, yet who could tell him in *any* way, shape or form what he was to do, or accept.

Jar Head snorted—expressing disdain that he had to deal with civilians *at all,* when all good patriots were going off to kick Saddam's ass.

"Okay," he said, then stalked off toward the science fiction section.

Lawrence and Vicki opened the box; the contents had the musky smell of dried come.

Vicki whispered as they started unpacking, "That wasn't very 'Good Cop.' " She crinkled her nose.

"It worked."

Something more than "jock smell" rose from the books. He felt as if he breathed the guy's very anger, his very violence.

As they unpacked, Vicki's breasts brushed against him. He felt contempt and arousal both spread in a flush of cold fever. For the first time in his adult life, Lawrence felt himself get hard because of closeness to a woman.

"Jesus," said Vicki. "Look at this *shit.*"

Star Legion, Book One: The Battle Factor! screamed one title. The cover showed a huge-breasted woman in formidable space armor that, nonetheless, allowed her nipples to show through. She defended a hill littered with dead aliens under a sky graced with two moons.

The cover of *Phoenix Squad: The Denver Defensive!* featured well-armed farm boys battling Russian troops under a sky lit by a mushroom cloud. A transparent phoenix rose screaming from the cleansing radioactive fires.

Vicki and Lawrence stacked and sorted the lot.

Gerald's Legions, Volume 6: Centauri Rebellion!

Battlecrew, 2000 A.D.

As Vicki handled one book, a pamphlet tumbled out; it had been used as a bookmark.

Vicki snapped it up, opened it quickly. "Shit!" she breathed, and thrust it in her pocket.

"What was . . ."

"Later!" she said.

Star Fleet: Terran Strike Force! comprised a full five volumes.

Words . . .

. . . not his own, pressing in his mind, pressing upon his centers of speech.

. . . *Fuckin'A,bitch!Tellmenow!* . . .

A headache, an instant of blindness that Lawrence realized was the urge to hit Vicki.

He smothered the urge and stacked the books by cover price.

Vicki whispered, "Oh, this is *prime!*" and pulled another improvised bookmark from a paperback. She slipped the bookmark (a small thing, the size of a business card) under the counter with the skill of a three-card monte player.

She handed Lawrence the paperback. He threw it on the stacks with the rest.

The box was empty. The smell dissipated, but Lawrence still felt queasy. He and Vicki went over the stacks, adding up with a calculator.

Jar Head came back, holding a fresh stack of sci-fi paperbacks in his beefy paws.

"Well?"

Vicki flashed a smile that wasn't *hers*. "We can cut you a deal. All these, for what you've got in your hands."

Lawrence felt a jolt of fear in his crotch and inched his way toward the intercom—to call down Jack, if necessary.

Jar Head clenched his jaw; tendons and veins bulged on his scalp. Then he bowed to civilian authority.

Vicki had handed him a proof of exchange slip when the atmosphere of the store *changed,* in the way the light in a bright room changes when blinds are drawn.

The bell over the door rang; another military guy walked in and approached the counter. His close-cropped hair was brilliant red. Freckles stood out against his pale skin.

"What's fuckin' *keepin'* ya?" said Red.

The anger . . . the contemptuous arrogance of Jar Head transformed, became something else. Like a machine cog bumped into proper adjustment, Jar Head's demeanor clicked into a new function. Red's appearance had made him part of the *team*, now.

Jar Head looked at Vicki and Lawrence.

"What's keepin' me? *Nothin'*. That's what's keepin' me."

"Well, then," said Red. "We gotta get goin', son. We gotta get goin' so's we can ship out and bag us some Eye-rackies. We gotta *get some, get some, get some!*"

Red smashed his fist on the counter.

Lawrence cringed. *"Get some"* rang in his mind, became like the roar of a mob. Vicki didn't bat an eyelash; she kept her fake smile, shrugged.

Jar Head gave a grin. "Les' go, man."

They locked arms in a way that, had they been wearing black leather, would have been a perfect copy of the way muscle boys locked arms and cruised.

The two sang to the tune of "Rudolph the Red Nosed Reindeer" as they walked toward the door:

> *"Saddam the wacki Iraqi,*
> *Likes to dress in women's clothes!*
> *And if we ever meet him, we will*
> *Punch him in the nose!"*

They reached the door, flung it open. Breaking out of song, they grunted, "Kick his *ass!*" in unison, then resumed from the top as they tromped into the street.

Lawrence went in the back to hyperventilate, thankful Jack didn't come down from his lair, then washed his face with cold water and went up front to the counter to sign out.

Vicki was penciling resale prices into Jar Head's Macho Star Warrior library.

"Y'know," she said. "Back in World War II, they used to court-martial guys for being so obvious about when they were shipping out."

Lawrence blurted, "Didn't they . . ."

"Freak me out? Yeah. But check this out."

She handed him the two bookmarks.

The pamphlet, white paper with olive drab print, read, "Movie Schedule, Fort Bragg and Pope Air Force Base Theaters, Summer, '89."

"Fort Bragg," said Vicki. "Special Ops. He's *living* his fantasy. Open up the pamphlet."

Standard listings of movies—some that had been current in '89, some older—for the handful of screening rooms at the fort and base. Jar Head had circled in ballpoint each screening time for the movie *Aliens*.

Vicki said, "And this guy gets to play with the highest-tech killing toys in the world."

She took the pamphlet out of Lawrence's hand. "Check this out." She placed the other bookmark in Lawrence's hand.

It was a high school wallet photo of a pretty blond girl, preppy to the max, wearing a maroon sweater.

"His girlfriend?"

Vicki smiled her fake smile, imitating the smile of the preppy girl in the photo. "He wishes. Turn it over."

The girl had written, in clichéd "cute girl" writing that fairly begged that the *i*'s be dotted with little hearts:

> *David*
> *You may be a little off the wall, but I like you, anyways!*
> *Seriously, I'm glad I've gotten to know you in study hall, and*
> *I really like talking to you. Best of Luck in the Future!*
> *Maureen, '89.*

Lawrence turned the picture over.

"She hates the guy," he said softly.

"Yeah. Can't you picture him in study hall, reading his little sci-fi books, talking to the cute girl about how he's going into the army? I gave it a once-over while you were in back. Look at the edges."

The top edge was worn; the emulsion had rubbed off.

"She gave him one of the crappy prints," said Vicki. "One of the ones that didn't separate well off the big sheets of wallet-sized pictures the photography places give you. Look in the top left corner."

There was a small hole pressed through the picture.

Lawrence said, "He kept it pinned on a bulletin board."

"Or somewhere near his bunk."

"You're a detective."

"Not really. You learn to read people in a city like this."

She took the pamphlet and the photo.

"Once I'd figured the guy out, he didn't scare me anymore. Jeez, I even knew his *name.* Can you imagine the *mindfuck* I could've given him?"

She put the photo and pamphlet in her backpack under the counter. "I got a big manila envelope of stuff that tumbles out of old books. You should come over and see it, so long as my mom doesn't get the idea you and me are getting hitched."

As he walked home, Lawrence wondered how a girl like Vicki

could *not* know that a man as beautiful as Ed had a crush on her.

His apartment felt haunted.

He left, to walk the streets, to see if he could read the city, and so not let it master him.

XII

Friday, 9:05 P.M.

I*'ve been thinking of you . . . a lot."*
He'd walked the city, its Christmas clatter, and tasted its jingle-jangled nerves; the trembling urge to prove oneself a patriot flavored the very air.

He'd basked and bellowed (silently, ever so silently) in the nerve resonant crowd chimes as he walked the huge and ugly sprawl of shopping centers near Copley Place. He'd walked the city, eager to know his hometown in a new way by losing himself in its folds, submerging himself in its riddle, and so learn the riddle's answer.

But the city did not allow itself to be read.

"I've tried to forget you. But I can't. And I realized that I don't want to."

But he walked . . . always with the crowds, always with the throngs.

But now the throngs are thinning.

It is the time of second twilight, as people head for bars and friends' homes and parties. It is second twilight, and Paul cannot face the empty streets. Come eleven, the crowds will come again. But he cannot face those two hours, cannot face his empty apartment; Jo had left a note that she'd spend the weekend nigger fucking at her parents' cabin in New Hampshire, and the aloneness of the weekend, the aloneness of no school till Monday, terrified him.

At Copley Place Mall, amid the dying crowd, he reached the pay phones and dialed a number that his fingers remembered as pattern.

"I miss you, Catherine."

He paused. Took a deep breath.

"I need to see you."

When she invited him over, he put on the overcoat he'd had draped over his shoulder, fixed his tie, and took the trolley toward her neighborhood. As he jumped off the trolley, he thought that first, before a night of splendidly painful lovemaking and victimization, he should attend propriety with atrocity.

Skipping along ice paths to the tune of the voices in his head, along a street lit by reflections of TVs spilling the off-beiges of desert sands from living-room windows onto fresh snow, Paul wondered if he would be caught.

He dismissed the notion. How could a great society, a great country, engaged in such a noble enterprise judge what he was about to do?

He walked the route he and Bill and Jo had taken, less than a week before.

XIII

Friday, 9:35 P.M.

The building manager gave Bill his usual overly friendly I'm-not-a-racist smile and "Hello" as he walked down the front hallway jangling his keys. No matter the time, the manager's keys sounded like something out of *Cool Hand Luke*. Bill smiled back, tucking his scarf. As he pushed open the vestibule door, he muttered to himself how much he missed New Jersey.

He caught himself about to kick a chunk of ice down the frozen sidewalk. He tried to not look or act like a kid in any way in Boston, especially when he was alone: too great a credibility risk, even here, in a student ghetto. He and Jo could spend the weekend rambling and playing in the New Hampshire countryside, even though in some of the stores up there, folks had only seen Black people on TV.

He pulled out his keys, opened his car door, turned over the engine to warm it up, then scraped his windows. Taking two cars was a pain, but Jo had wanted to haul up boxes of her summer clothes, leaving no room for him in her rusted Karmann Ghia. She'd gone on ahead, taking Bill's stuff for the weekend.

A change of light in the corner of his eye.

He turned to see someone scowling from a window. At first, he'd wondered if this was some psychic ability Bostonians had developed; Black man starts a car, someone's got to check and make sure it's not being stolen. But Jo had pointed out that someone *always* comes to the window in Boston when a car turns over, just to make sure that it's not *their* car that's getting ripped off.

Bill looked at the guy in the window, continued to scrape.

The curtains pulled shut.

"What a town," he muttered.

He'd finished scraping and was about to get in when he heard a footfall he thought he knew crunching on the snow.

He turned to see Paul coming toward him out of the darkened shadows between two apartment buildings. Paul broke into a jog as he crossed the narrow street and Bill raised his hand in greeting.

The world went away . . .

Became unseeing.

It was a thing Bill knew, a thing Bill feared: the moment Boston became a brightly lit stage in a dark, empty theater. This was the place, the instant, when both the object of racism and the racist become invisible. This was the psychic context, the *feeling* of this city, in which Bill had been thrown out of a drugstore by a grim-faced cop in Brookline, in which Bill had seen Hispanic kids thrown off a bus while everyone else looked at their newspapers, at the posted ads, at their own shoes on the damp floor.

He knew this context.

He knew it to be the landscape of midnight lynchings and witch-hunts. He knew it to be the acquiescent silence of a mob as it *watches* the atrocities of another mob.

Paul had the same look on his face the cop in Brookline had.

Bill was transfixed, unbelieving, even in his fear, that his friend should come at him so, *knowing* that were he to cry out, no one would hear.

The bottle in Paul's hand did not break as he smashed it into Bill's temple.

Bill fell.

Through the pain, through fear and confusion, Bill tried to raise his hands to protect himself. Paul grabbed him by the back of his coat, lifted him.

Smashed the car door onto his head . . .

The creak of the door hinges, the rusty metal, sang in his ears. The smell of blood and oil filled his lungs. He should have passed out.

Smashed the car door onto his head . . .

The creak of the door hinges, the rusty metal, held voices. He heard them sing through his impossible pain. He heard their call for him to let go of life, to be part of dissipating sighs.

The door opened. Bill heard the voices in the wheezing breath that escaped his bloody mouth.

Paul *(his friend, oh God his friend)* pulled him to his knees. A gloved hand grabbed his throat, another the back of his head.

The crunch, the popping, the snapping of his neck was deafening, transmitted as vibration through his skull to his inner ear. In the sounds, Bill heard the voices.

As Paul twisted his head obscenely to the left, Bill saw the smile on his killer's face. Broken capillaries filled his throat with blood.

He was aware, as his heart stopped beating, that he had been lynched without a rope.

The voices were with him as he dropped to the snow and as his dimming eyes, level with the ground, saw Paul walk calmly away.

XIV

Friday, 9:46 P.M.

A young man and his wife sit in meditation, hands joined, within the geometric configuration that represents the mind of their Patron.

They engage in an exercise of protection to counter the contamination the Enfolded One may have inscribed upon their psyches as It prowled the city the day before. Their ceremonial sword—the consecrated *katana*—lies between them. Their shield is visualized as a thing of amber glass. Within the pattern of tape, in their home they have made a temple, they feel safe.

Sudden intrusion . . .

A vibration in their minds shatters the amber shield. They *feel* the bellowing of the Blind Dragon that is their Enemy.

The young woman reels as if she has been struck. She gives a faint cry as the young man leans over the sword to hold her.

She trembles. She sobs. After a moment she meets his eyes.

"It's started."

Chapter Two

I

Deep winter morning.

Frank woke, dropped his hand to the floor, touched only cold air and floorboards.

Between wakefulness and awareness, in light the color of smoke, Frank remembered the mutt would not be there.

And in remembering, he knew guilt.

Guilt that his waking reflex had been to reach for a dog that was now dust and not for the woman who had loved him with a passion as patient and quietly beautiful as an ancient pine.

A woman who was now dust.

In robe and slippers, he shuffled to the kitchenette and made breakfast. The small TV on the counter (which he'd turned on to hear voices, any voices, as the kettle boiled) spoke to him of war and showed him, when he glanced its way, tanks rolling across deserts in theatrical precision. This war was so different. The feel of the people on the street, touched by impending conflict, was *wrong* . . . not like what he'd known decades ago during "the Good Fight." This war made him nervous—reminding him of times by the lake, when the dusk air filled with things that stung and bit.

He turned his back to the war, shutting off the TV as the water came to a boil. He splashed the water onto his instant oatmeal, then onto his instant decaf. Another operation loomed in his future—the surgeons would cut into his heart to remove the transplanted valve of an animal's heart they'd already placed there, replacing that replacement with a valve of nylon and plastic.

Frank had been raised on breakfasts of bacon. Or ham. His doctor said that this had led to the first series of heart attacks. In the hospital room, Frank had wanted to remark on the pointlessness of replacing pig fat in his heart with a pig's valve. But Jenny and Susan were there as well, both rocking slightly and silently, too unfamiliar with the concept of death, despite what had happened to their mother—who had died quickly and by misadventure—to tolerate one of Frank's wise remarks.

Now, with a chunk of pig in his heart, he was unable to have pig for breakfast.

He sat down to his reconstituted breakfast and cursed that as he got older, he needed so little sleep and woke so early, for he dreaded the empty hours before the library opened.

II

Saturday, 6:30 A.M.

Deep winter morning.

He reaches for her, and she is there.

He finds comfort in the pain this fact will cost him.

Catherine's slight frame twitches. Through blankets and flannel sheets, he can feel her ribs.

Paul smiled, pulled the covers over his naked shoulder.

Last night had been wonderful.

Paul had ditched his bloody gloves down a storm drain. He heard no sirens from the time he'd left Bill in the street to the time he'd arrived at Catherine's building. He draped his overcoat over his shoulder like Sinatra as he jogged up the stairs.

Catherine embraced him as he entered her apartment and threw his coat over a chair. She touched his cheek, caressed it as she kissed him.

"I've missed you, Paul. I've missed you so terribly."

"I've missed you."

She took him by the hand, led him to the couch. She had a bottle of red wine opened on the coffee table between two elegant candlesticks. She filled expensive glasses. They toasted each other and talked of the meaningless things lovers talk about upon reuniting.

She was kind, and met his eyes consistently as they talked. Her strawberry blond hair looked exquisite in the candlelight.

Paul felt cheated.

Until they had finished the wine.

"You know," she said. "It's so strange that you called when you did. I'd been talking about my exes with Claire all week."

Claire was Catherine's psychiatrist. Catherine used discussion of her therapy as a springboard for her more subtle and ruthless attacks.

"Oh, really?"

"Mmm-hmm. Claire said I had to sort out my feelings for the important people in my life. Steve, in particular. That I was hung up on him, and it was destructive for me to not face how much he still means to me."

Steve was Catherine's ex-boyfriend, who had treated her like shit. He thought himself a writer, and his way to be a writer was to drink a lot and pretend to be Hemingway. The last Paul had heard of him, he'd rented a cabin in Maine to finish the Great Novel he'd been working on for five years.

Paul set his empty glass down. The wine had been wonderful. The glasses were fine. Everything in Catherine's apartment was measuredly tasteful, ordered from yuppie furniture catalogs.

"Who else did you talk about?"

"We talked about Dean. A couple of boys in high school I dated." She set her glass down.

"We didn't talk about you."

Paul almost sighed. The belittlement. The attack. He felt a relief in his heart, as if a splinter had been pulled from it.

Later, in bed, Catherine performed in the grotesque way that she assumed that men liked (and maybe most did), purring and cooing like a girl in a porn film, saying "empowering" bits of nonsense like: "Oh, you go right *through* me!"

Paul went wild, aroused madly by her insincerity and her taking power by feigning powerlessness.

Drifting to sleep, Catherine's slight form pressed against him, he knew that this was what he'd wanted.

Now, in this morning, as birdsongs began in the winter dawn, something stirred inside him.

Paul . . .

that he chose not to heed.

A twitching in his heart.

"Oh, Christ!"

An unnameable panic.

He left the bed, padded to where he'd left his coat.

He held it up: only a few spatterings of blood. Not noticeable. Just odd stains, like perhaps rust?

Took care of that nigger . . .

The songs of birds—cardinals and jays. He heard them. He put down the coat and, naked, walked to the window. A flash of brilliant red alit upon a tree outside. A cardinal. Paul listened to its song. He longed for the peace the song offered, the tranquil . . .

"Hey."

Paul turned to see Catherine in the winter light, her skin so fair, it seemed translucent. He took in her gauntness, the shallow bowl of her belly, the thinness of her thighs and calves, the slight curve of her milkless tits. He could see her belly undulate as her diaphragm helped her form the words, "Come back to bed with me, lover."

Inside her, he came with impossible violence as she murmured the name, *"Steve."*

III

Saturday, 10:25 A.M.

Dutch walked the streets of Brookline. The light was dull, and the wind smelled of snow.

Once he'd come here often, before the shelter nearby got shut down. He walked down Harvard Avenue, where the shops looked bright and pretty. There was a toy store that looked like it came out of a storybook. All bright colors, with nice toys in the windows, like bears and trains made of wood and dolls with pretty faces.

The decorations were nice, but they did not touch him. He was lonely for beauty in a way he'd never been before. He had an ache in his heart, like when he tried to sing, but couldn't.

He touched his head. It hadn't bled in a long time.

He walked to keep warm. One bakery far down the street sometimes gave him bread from the day before and milk that they said was good, but they couldn't use anymore. People gave him mean looks, especially people pushing baby carriages who were dressed nice. After a while, the looks made Dutch feel bad, and he left Harvard Avenue to go to where there was a Jewish church (Jewish churches had a special name he couldn't remember) that he wanted to look at, to find beauty. Along the way were regular churches that he could look at, too. One of them had a small graveyard with stone angels taking care of the graves. Maybe Dutch could find what he looked for among the angels.

He had walked a ways down a side street when a nice-looking

young man came out of an apartment building. Dutch thought of
the man who had given him a sandwich a few days before. Dutch
looked at the man to make sure it wasn't him, because if it was, he
would thank him.

The young man looked at Dutch.

And Dutch heard voices . . . they pressed on his head, through his
cut, and he thought of the man who'd been mean to him, who'd
tried to pull him in the alley.

("You an' me gonna talk to the *president of the United States!*")

They were the same voices, but stronger, meaner. Meaner than the
cops who'd beaten him. He thought of a flood, of a wave of hate.
The man pointed at Dutch. His lips moved, but Dutch did not hear
his voice. Not with his ears.

"Get the fuck out of here and DIE, you homeless piece of shit. . . ."

Dutch's eyes felt like they were made of glass, and had shattered.
The hate in the young man's eyes burned Dutch, felt like it would
bore into him and burn away who he was.

("You an' me gonna talk to *the president of the United States!*")

What the crazy man had said mixed in with what the young man
said. All words pushing and shoving their way into his head.

". . . fucking stink like the piece of SHIT that you are . . ."

Blood flowed from his eyes like tears. Dutch bowed over; his cut
had reopened. The young man got close and Dutch saw that he had
blood spattered on his coat, just a little, and Dutch knew that the
man wanted to kill him.

The pavement rushed up in his bloody vision. . . .

"Ahh he's just drunk."

Dutch heard the words and knew he was still alive. He came awake
on the cold sidewalk. Two men looked over him. The young man
was not there.

He looked up at the men. And was scared.

He got up as fast as he could and ran away.

"He's not drunk. He's hurt. We oughtta . . ."

Dutch rounded the corner; the spiders came awake in his lungs.
He almost had a coughing fit. He stopped after a few yards, when
he felt safe, and wiped away the blood on his face with paper napkins.

The voices were with him, faint echoes, for almost an hour afterward. He realized they had gone away as he stared into the calm and
serene loveliness of a stone angel's face.

IV

Saturday, 11:05 A.M.

Paul arrived home.

    The silence hurt.

(You fucking killed him. You fucking killed him. You fucking killed him. You fucking killed him. You fucking killed him. You fucking killed him. You fucking killed him. You fucking killed him.)

Paul turned on the TV, the radio in the living room, and the radio in Jo's room.

(. . . fucking killed him . . .)

He had it coming.

       He'd fucking kill me.

He showered, shaved. Changed his clothes. He had much to do today. He would be close among so many . . . *So many.*

    . . . that he had to be clean, had to look his best . . . *Be clean.*

    . . . not be like the filthy piece of homeless shit on the street, near Catherine's apartment.

Refreshed (and *clean,* so very *clean*), he put on one of his better suits and ties. He reached for his overcoat . . .

Maybe the blood *was* noticeable, after all. The piece of shit had seemed to notice as he bent over *(to puke?)* while Paul walked past him. Maybe he should ditch the coat, just to be safe?

Why, though? No one would suspect him of killing Bill.

(You fucking killed him. You fucking killed him. You fucking killed him. You fucking killed him. You fucking killed him. You fucking killed him. You fucking killed him.)

The Boston cops wouldn't investigate the case thoroughly. Paul could never be a suspect. The city would not allow it. The city, full of worries, full of needed prejudices, full of happy bigotries, would make careful investigation an impossibility.

This was the city where a man had murdered his wife and blamed her death on a nigger. This was the city where every cop went ballistic looking for the nigger that had done it, happily raiding Mission Hill with their bellies stuffed with doughnuts.

Paul would never be a suspect.

He was *just* in what he did, and therefore, *innocent.*

If the blood on his coat was noticeable, it was not because it marked him as *guilty,* but because it marked him as a *threat* to those who should die. It was best to not be noticed as a threat.

He rolled the coat in a plastic bag, dumped the kitchen garbage on top, and cleaned out the fridge for good measure. Garbage day was Monday. If, by some fluke, he was a suspect, the coat would soon be taken away with the rest of the trash . . . *like that piece of shit should be taken away.* . . .

In the cold air, garbage bag over his shoulder, he thought of the homeless piece of shit as he walked to the Dumpster in back. How nice it would be to dump all the pieces of shit like him into a big Dumpster so they'd be taken away. How nice that would be. To never ever, ever, ever feel that pang of guilt for having money, a place to live, and enough to eat.

He fantasized the garbage bag *was,* in fact, the homeless man as he heaved it into the Dumpster and out of his life.

And Paul felt aware of the man he'd accosted (who'd accosted *him*), in the way one is aware, in a close room, of an ugly painting hung to one's back. Sort of like that ancient Joe Namath reading awareness poster in the teachers' lounge. After a while, you don't see it. But it offends on a profound and sublime level, cheapening your life each second you are in its contaminated presence.

Later, at the trolley stop, Paul adjusted the unfamiliar overcoat he wore. It was rumpled from the box it had been stored in and smelled of mothballs. Good thing Mom had never thrown it out, and that he had never gotten around to selling it. It fit him well enough; he was built like his father. The rumples would fall out. The scent would air out. For now, he needed people. He'd go to Copley Place, mill among the throngs, and buy a new pair of gloves.

On the trolley, for one blessed moment as he stood pressed within a crowd, he forgot his own name, but never lost his feeling of purpose. The one aspect of the moment that kept it from perfection was the lingering awareness that in this city somewhere that homeless piece of shit was drawing air.

V

Saturday, 11:37 A.M.

Lawrence held his cross and Saint Christopher's medal and, with an ache, felt his gaze turned away from them, as if his sight were not his own and found the cross and medal repellent.

He closed his hand over the medal and cross; the ache became a spark of anger toward that which he'd once found beautiful, toward that which he had looked upon to find peace. The anger was a familiar frustration, giving outlet to an inner voice Lawrence sought to ignore.

And that was the voice urging him to follow the path Jacob now followed, the path of those who loved Drama *(the four D's—disco, drugs, dick, and dish—all fell under the rubric of Drama)*, even if the Drama unfolded as the end of one's life.

A twinge in his palm; he saw amid the shining contours behind his fingers a glint of robin's-egg blue. He had the urge to cast medal and cross aside.

Lawrence loved Drama, himself, especially Hollywood Dramas, romantic nonsense. Yet these Fairy Tales filled him with such bitter longing at times that he'd rage against the world for not accommodating his romantic ideals. That rage led to the urge to say *"Fuck it!"* and screw a dozen guys over a weekend, to spite the world and to spite the part of him that *wanted* a Happy Ending, that *wanted* to be taken away by a man with a noble heart and a beautiful smile.

Lawrence owned copies of *Flashdance* and *An Officer and a Gentleman*. During the breakup with Jacob, he'd seen *Pretty Woman* six times. All were movies with Happy Endings, where beautiful men took away the protagonists to the fulfilling lives they *deserved*.

Just as Lawrence *deserved*.

Jacob *should* have been his Happy Ending.

A glance at the clock by his bed. The feel of cross and medal was *cold*, as if another person's skin fused upon his own, drawing heat from the flesh of his palm. With a shudder, he put away the medal and cross, and without thought went to work.

VI

Saturday, 1:05 P.M.

Dutch walked away from the library. They had thrown him out for coughing. He'd tried very hard not to spatter the books with blood. He'd *tried*. But they were art books, full of beautiful pictures, and maybe he had ruined them. He felt bad, and lonely. So very lonely.

But he *wasn't* alone. He felt like he was being followed. He walked Commonwealth Avenue. The light was all dull and grey and not bright. When he reached Kenmore Square, Dutch thought he heard bad voices amid all the sounds of traffic. When he got to his home, and opened the car door to look for a nice book cover to look at, he turned, certain somebody was behind him.

He thought he saw a bodiless shadow, and he knew the shadow meant to hurt him. He cast aside the book he'd pulled and found the paperback with the picture of the spaceship on it. He wished that Jesus would come and take him away to a place full of stars, where he wouldn't be afraid or cold or tired anymore.

VII

Saturday, 2:00 P.M.

The Succubus gazed upon a crèche and wished that she'd had the spite against God to fill Meli with Arthur's seed. Standing on a crowded sidewalk before a hospital, she pondered her sin: *Mercy.* She carried the sin in her flesh as she journeyed to true physicality, carried it as would even the basest child, unable to bear the suffering of an animal.

The hospital was ugly, yet held beautiful suffering: a box of rough clay full of exquisite jade. She smelled the sickness, the grief. And the *waiting*—the delicious waiting for Death to remove those who had felt, as the coddled favorites of Creation, that they would draw breath forever. Death was a Mercy without shame, unlike the Mercy she had shown Meli.

Glancing at the crèche's empty cradle, she entered the hospital.

It was like wine, full of rich despair. Flashes of suffering pummeled weakened bodies. She smelled and tasted minds brought lower than those of beasts by injury, madness, and violation.

Burdened with the sin of Mercy, she sought to make that mark of shame into an act that would serve the greater honor of her Lord.

A man with nerves that had been reduced to less than clots of lymph called out for Death to take him.

She heeded his call.

She found him, suffering in his aloneness, his mind brutally intact despite the ruination of his body. She entered his room, the emptiness of which was accentuated by the vacant bed beside his.

He breathed with the help of machines.

The gaze under his twitching eyelids was weak, so she accentuated her beauty as she took his cold and withered hand in hers. With her other hand, she stroked his brow.

And she healed him.

She rebuilt the nerves that sense pain. Made his heart stronger, to keep his deteriorating form alive. She toned the muscles that kept his lungs from folding upon themselves. She shored the lining of his throat so that he'd not choke in his sleep.

He felt his partial resurrection.

And the fear in his eyes at the face of such brutality made her cherish the expiation of her sin.

She kissed his lips, and whispered by his ear.

"This is my gift."

Before she left, she drew the sweet air that clung to the flowers placed by his bed into herself then breathed the sweetness into his face.

She would use Mercy again, to finish her aria. She would grant Mercy to the stricken man.

As she left the hospital grounds, she gave a small cry.

Four small cuts had formed on her hand. Deep. Blood ran from them. Frowning (but not losing sight of her form), she willed them to heal, then licked away the blood.

VIII

Saturday, 2:15 P.M.

S he's not mean!"

"It still hurts."

"She didn't *mean* it!"

"I know."

Blood stood out in ruby beads. Larry held up his wounded hand. Ed thought the kid was going to cry, not out of pain, but out of surprise.

Vicki put pressure on his hand with a handkerchief. Larry pulled his hand away.

"I'm *all right.*"

Ed came around the counter, flanking Larry and feeling the eyes of the handful of milling customers on him as they took in the scene. They watched mutely, did not help.

(*"Eddie! It hurts!" Wasps had made a nest in the woodpile. It had gotten cold early that year; they'd not yet gone dormant. Andy had gone to fetch wood while Ed sharpened the axe. Andy came running, holding his injured hand, which swelled with multiple stings. Ed took care of Andy, while Mom and Dad called Dr. Baker. Ed stayed with Andy in the backseat as they drove to the clinic.*

Ed had loved his kid brother, with a gentle affection he'd never felt for anyone else.)

Ed spoke softly. "Larry. It's a cat scratch. You want to make sure it's clean, because cats can have pathogens under their nails."

Larry looked up at him, embarrassed. Behind that embarrassment was a deeper shame and regret.

("I'm sorry, Eddie."

Andy had broken a toy that Ed had gotten for Christmas, just a few days before. The look in Andy's eyes was that of someone who had committed a grave sin.

"It's okay, Andy.")

"C'mon," said Ed. "Let's go in back and take care of it."

Vicki started to go with them. Larry's voice was raw: "Someone's gotta watch the front."

Vicki slumped, whispered, "Yeah, I know," then went back to the counter. Groucho had perched there, looking like her regular self, not the spitting, hissing animal that had just swiped at Larry.

In the back room, Ed and Larry washed the wounds. They were deep, but didn't look like they'd need stitches. In the medicine cabinet, they found Listerine. Ed packed the wounds with paper towels soaked with the disinfectant. While they tended the cuts, Larry seemed distant. Ed had a cold feeling at his back, thinking he could turn to find someone standing behind them. A woman, perhaps.

Larry asked, "So, how come you hang out in bookstores all the time?"

So I can play at being a happy-go-lucky guy and so convince myself I shouldn't commit suicide. So I can look at Vicki and kind of hate myself for wanting her while I've turned my back on another woman in my life who has, in some ways, both saved and damned my soul? Gee, Larry. Why do you ask?

"Ummm. To people-watch."

"Why not in cafés?"

"That's amateur stuff. You want to watch people, go to a bookstore."

"Why?"

Ed looked at the cuts. The bleeding was slowing.

He slipped into teacher mode. "A bookstore's a model of the mind. All the things people find interesting, or endeavor to achieve, have a compartment in a bookstore. It's like looking at people while they've got the blinds of their personalities open."

Ed applied more pressure. Larry grimaced.

"It doesn't sound fair to watch people while they're in a bookstore."

"Was it fair of your beloved customers to just watch while you stood there with your hand cut open? All bets are off, y'know?"

Ed dried Larry's hand, took down some generic-brand bandages, dressed the cuts. They looked like they had closed. Weird, considering how they'd bled.

The two walked to the front of the store. A few customers glanced at Larry, as if ashamed of their apathy of a few moments before. At the counter, they found Vicki petting Groucho, talking to her softly. The cat seemed calm and happy.

Until Larry came near.

She bolted and hid among the stacks.

Ed stayed until a kind of normality took hold, shooting the shit with Larry and Vicki, watching customers. A young man in the theater section mouthed lines from plays, occasionally making sweeping gestures with his hand. Vicki dubbed him "Olivier." A fashionably disheveled young woman sat near the poetry section; her clothes were almost Dickensian. She made orgasmic faces as she leafed through dusty volumes of maudlin Victorian crap.

The normality was itself theatrical. Larry was upset and not doing a good job hiding it; Ed would have felt like shit if he'd left right after Larry's trauma.

As the sunlight faded, Ed left the store and headed toward the river.

Larry . . . he's such a kid, he thought. *So much like how Andy used to be.*

His kid brother, who'd taught him a dimension of despair that even Amelia could not. Ed's mind returned to his thesis; it raced ahead of his wishes, reflexive as a tongue probing an aching tooth.

Despair, he thought, *is the absence of Hope. Embracing Hope was the sin of Pandora, not curiosity. Can it not be argued that despair is a Mercy, actualized and fulfilled in Death?*

Ed turned and walked a few extra blocks to take the subway home, and so not pass over the bridge that called him to a Mercy of his own creation. Once seated on the train, he tamed the thoughts that had formed ahead of his wishes, ahead of his better judgment, placing them as beautiful imaginings in the hallways of his intellect.

Crossing beneath the river, his awareness in his memory palace, he knew peace.

IX

Saturday, 4:30 P.M.

She leaned on him, crying, in the deepening winter darkness. She wore no coat; her grief was tangible in the living-cold air.

He walked her down the aisle marked by piled ice to the waiting arms of her father. Her sobs were silent; her body shuddered with cold and anguish. She held her shaking hands before her as if they were injured, bleeding.

A whisper, choked, escaped her lips.

Paul could not make out what she said. Part of him knew that this was what should be.

Gently, he gave Jo to her father, who met his eyes and spoke a soft, "Thank you, Paul," as he eased her into the car.

In the time it took her father to walk around the car to the driver's side, Jo had misted over the passenger-side window with her sobs, her forehead against the glass. The mist made her look as if she wore a veil of fine silk.

They drove away, and Paul felt something that could be called at once remorse, guilt, and pride.

(. . . *killed him. You . . .*)

Cold wind swept away the feeling.

My God, he thought. *Who could have done that to Bill?*

He walked back to the building, down the corridors to the apartment. He'd left the front door open. The bags of Christmas presents he'd bought (along with his new pair of gloves) were just inside. His eye fell on the gift he'd bought for Bill, stacked atop the others in one bag; he shuddered.

(*You . . .*)

Paul had come home from the shopping center to find Jo curled in a fetal ball in the living room, the answering machine in her hands, clutched to her chest. The cords that had connected it to the wall had been pulled out. The casing was cracked, and fresh indentations and cracked plaster marked the wall near where it had been placed.

"Oh, Jo . . . what's happened?"

She did not hear him.

He went to her, slowly.

As his shadow fell upon her, she looked up and grabbed his overcoat like a wretch grabbing at the hem of a priest's robe, begging for benediction.

(A wretch, begging. A begging wretched piece of shit.)

He knelt, and she bolted upright, throwing her arms around his neck, mumbling, weeping, managing to choke out the words, *"He's dead . . . he's dead. . . ."*

He carried her to the couch, where she grabbed one of the cushions and clutched it to her chest. Paul went to where she'd dropped the answering machine, brought it to the kitchen, keeping her in his sight. The machine looked as if it might play. But he knew he should not do this.

Dreading to leave her alone even a moment, he ducked into her room, took her Walkman from her bedside, and removed the cassette of *Meet the Beatles* inside. He went back to the kitchen, pulled the standard-sized cassette from the answering machine, put it in the Walkman. Through the headphones he heard two messages from Jo asking if Bill had called the apartment. Then the slow and mournful voice of Bill's father, calling from New Jersey, told Jo what the Boston police had told him. Paul could hear the cries of Bill's mother echoing in the back of the recording.

(You . . .)

(Nigger parents. Nigger Bill had nigger parents. Should be used to this by now. What the fuck are they whining about?)

He pulled away the headphones and went to his friend, who had stood by him through the death of his mother, who had supported him at every turn since they had met.

"Jo?"

He touched her face. It was hot.

"Jo?"

"Bill . . ."

"I know. I know."

She brought her hands as fists to her face. She clenched her teeth as she drove her knuckles into her eyes.

"Oh, God," she said. "Who could . . ."

"Don't ask. Just mourn, for now. Just mourn."

Fists still over her eyes, she buried her face in the pillow. Paul, still in his coat, went to the kitchen to wet a dishcloth. After a few moments, when she had pulled her face from the pillow, he gently dabbed her forehead with the cloth. She brought her fists away. Before she could open her eyes he put the cloth over her eyes, trying to cool the fever of her grief.

She whispered, *"I love you, Paul."*

"I love you too, Jo."

He tended her with the mercy of comfort, until she fell into exhausted sleep.

He plugged in the phone, called Jo's parents. As he spoke to Jo's father, his voice not more than a whisper, Paul glanced out the back window to see Jo's car parked in its usual space. Jo must have waited for Bill in New Hampshire, and then driven back down to see if he'd been held up.

A few moments later, Jo woke with a small cry.

Paul went to her.

As the winter sun faded, Jo's father came to the door.

She held out her arms to him.

"Daddy . . ."

Paul stood aside as she cried herself out.

Then Jo's father asked Paul to help Jo to the car.

Now, the aloneness in the apartment haunted him.

(You fucking killed him.)

Now, the aloneness made a twitching in his heart.

He felt the call of the city as an itch in his blood, summoning him to the tranquillity of crowds.

(. . . killed him . . .)

He needed the quiet of the city, the silence of its roar and bustle to drown out one single voice in his mind. He told himself he needed to buy a new answering machine.

In lavender-grey winter twilight, coils of phone cord in his pockets, he passed a cardinal perched on a neighbor's bird feeder.

He tried to remember what it was like to be touched by beauty, but could not. His gloved hands gripped coils of cord in his overcoat pocket. He convinced himself he needed the cord to choose an answering machine, to make sure the cord and machine were of the same gauge.

On the subway, pressed close among his fellow city dwellers, the layered voices of the city deliciously flooded his mind.

But among the voices, one single, sour voice made him shudder as does the touch of spiderweb against one's face. The sour voice offended him, even as it called to him.

He got off at Kenmore Square, gritting his teeth. The city led him toward the voice, so that he might silence it.

Silence, among the throngs.

Feeding on the energies of the square, he sang "Silent Night" to himself as he sought the sour voice of the piece of shit who had accosted him earlier that day.

"Holy night . . ."

X

Saturday, 8:14 P.M.

Come back to me.*"*
     She had slowed her heart, her breath, so they kept pace with the flow of the River. She infused her mask of the murdered girl with an aura that recalled the sad beauty of fog. She moved as does slow wind through dead yellow leaves clinging to the branch.

"Come back to me."

The shuffling crowds did not see nor hear her; they were too taken by their bright and tinsel-draped desires to note the fine strokes she painted. Her call was silent, audible only to those few who chose to hear the sublime, who live in their dreams, only to forget them with each passing moment.

Her clothes were simple, save for one lovely and delicate thing folded near her breast. Among the crowds, full of ugly noises and thoughts, she called to the stricken man.

"Come back to me."

She infused the City with her cry, letting the River's blood carry her voice as it informed the soil and air. She called through the man's sickness, born of the City.

The man was near. His soul, his sickness and sadness, stood out like a speck of amber amid sand. Part of him resisted, or did not hear her call.

She drew herself into the drowsy scope of five human senses. She needed to find him among the streets; to go to him while he slept, as she had before, was not enough. She had to fulfill the song of the City in his flesh, show him the Mercy the City afforded.

Hours passed before she found him, drinking tea from a paper cup. He stood out of the wind in an alley, huddled over the cup as if over a fire. She willed her senses to accommodate his living sickness. She tasted the tea, felt the warmth of the cup in her hands. She saw the crawling movements of his disease within the cage of his ribs.

She entered the alley, unseen as wind.

She drew away the square of lace by her breast and placed it so that it hung over her face, held by the mist she willed around her. As the fabric draped, she wore away the sharpness of her features, as if she hid behind cold morning air touched with the color of distance. He looked up at her, and his eyes grew wide with wonderment and joy.

"Come back to me," she said with a voice infused with the resonance of angel song.

The stricken man gasped. The gasp would have brought forth a spastic fit had she not inhibited his cough reflex. His cup of tea fell smoking by his tattered shoes.

She tinted her skin with the color of stars, made herself glow with the halo worn by the summer moon. She willed the glow to pass through the weave of the garments she wore.

"I have missed you," she said, tasting his loving terror for the Beauty she had given him on her lips, the tip of her tongue, the back of her throat. She felt his tears building inside him.

She felt his need to speak, and also his shame that his voice was too coarse to speak as he wished it to.

His face was lit by her glow.

She placed two fingers of her right hand over his diseased mouth.

"Don't speak," she whispered.

And with that, she drew away her hand and lifted her veil, the one she knew he'd dreamt of.

"Come to me, for I have missed you," she said. She placed her hand on his chest with the gentleness with which a man would place his hand on the belly of his wife, many months with child. "Let me heal you."

The man let out a small choke.

"Shhh. Let me heal you."

She turned her head as she spoke, just slightly. And in turning her head, she sharpened her features and made splendid the star-glow she radiated. She saw herself captured in the polished black stones of his eyes.

Together, they walked the unseen paths of the city—the back alleys of Boston that have no name. As they emerged from one alley, she took his hand and let him share her vision.

She shared the darkened stars, the patterns of layered clouds as they drifted past the moon reflecting the City's light, reflecting the moon's light. She showed him the beauty of the City as she saw it, the profundity of her darkness.

He stumbled as she showed him the lovely patterns he had never seen before as moonlight struck the jagged edges of the rubble near his home.

She caught him. She wished to part his fragile intellect, find his true *Name* amid his hurting thoughts and lift it from the nest of quiet shame in which he carried it.

She carried him to his makeshift home, placing him on his couch of cast-off clothes as if he were a child, then entered the rusting metal shell, pulling the door behind her.

The air was thick with illness. The stricken man held a thick coat against his chest, looking as if he were ashamed to have her in this place. Gently, she pulled away the coat. "Let me heal you," she said. Distant streetlamps filled the metal hulk with blue glow; the light striking the cold window behind him gave him a faint halo.

The man nodded, then undid the layers of clothes that kept at bay the winter air, baring his breast to her.

She placed her hand upon his skin and pressed through his flesh, pressed through his ribs. He cried as she burned the disease from his lungs, as she killed the crawling things his tortured mind imagined his sickness to be. The sickness pooled in her palm and her immaterial flesh drank it, then carried it out of him, to be sweated out of the skin of her wrist, made inert.

She felt the clear breath he drew.

She felt his relief, his sadness that he could never repay her for the Mercy she granted him.

Pain . . .

A burning on her skin . . .

A stabbing on her brow, like that which the eyes feel upon staring into the sun . . .

Sudden voices flooded her mind.

A shadow on the window behind the man she healed.

For an instant, she saw a profound beauty as the glass shattered behind the man in minute patterns, brought into contrast by the blue glow of the City. Hands of the shadow reached in, something thin stretched between them.

Sudden voices . . .

Screaming across her mind.

The hands held wire.

The wire entwined around the stricken man's throat and he was pulled away from her, out the window, to the field of rubble.

Sudden voices . . .

Screaming in an idiot choir of discord across her senses.

An explosion of steam and blood.

She looked to her hand, saw skin, lung, and rib extending from her wrist like a bloody crab—the healed flesh of the man made one with hers as the rest of the man had been pulled away.

Through the broken window she saw the stricken man dying, twitching as the shadow garroted him, his heart pumping blood through the wound her hand had left.

The shadow dropped the man.

And the Succubus screamed with anguish, for she would never know his Name, never have his essence to complete her aria.

She moved like a sheet of rain out of the car, just as the sweet trophy of the stricken man's soul rose before her sight to join the shimmering light of stars overhead. She stepped over the man's split and steaming corpse to confront the shadow that had taken him from her.

The shadow resolved itself as a young man, staring down at the body upon the rubble from where he had stumbled backward. He still held his garrote in his black-gloved hands.

His gaze shot upward, to her killing hand still fused with the flesh of the dead man. His dumbfounded look became one of stark horror.

"Oh, Sweet Jesus Christ, what are you?"

The Succubus recoiled, slammed back against the rusted hulk *not* by the terrible power of the Name of the *Kristos,* but by the surging force of the Enfolded One as It rode the voice of the man It had possessed. The Enfolded One pressed against her awareness; her hearing filled with the sound of bending metal, and voices . . . idiot voices chanting, shouting, breaking the integrity of her identity. Dimly, she was aware of her head bleeding where it had smashed against the edges of broken glass on the car.

Inscribed upon the young man's aura was the great blind reptilian form of the Enfolded One: dragonlike, a pebbled worm, armored, its eyes glazed over and moist with a film like soft and rotting eggshells. A spur of the thing twitched and quivered in the young man's heart.

Rising, she saw It change to a sundering ocean of soul scurf, each fleck of foam a fragment of what had been in life a fragmented intellect. The young man was constant and unchanging as It changed, as is a prism as it refracts light around and through it.

The young man's Name screamed amid the idiot voices; his intellect, his soul, strove to retain its integrity amid the roiling black filth around and within it.

She was close enough to taste his Name through the idiot chants, "Paul," as she sprang to kill him . . .

. . . when a force churned through the ice and dust and rubble and pinned her to the ground with the sheer weight of its Will. She fought, until she knew the Will to be that of the One whom she loved more than any other in the wide expanse of Being.

"Father . . ."

PART FOUR

A Gaze Blank and Pitiless as the Sun

Chapter One

Tuesday, December 18, 1990. 10:15 A.M.

P aul sat in back of the Red Line train, head resting against the cold window as the train crossed the Longfellow Bridge. He whimpered. No one heard.

The repeated clatter of wheels was punctuated by the repeated sound in his mind of Bill's head thudding against the car door; with each thud of Bill's skull, Paul whimpered. Yet his muscles ached for the satisfaction of driving Bill's head forward, breaking it with a slam of the door. The satisfaction of grabbing his (NIGGER) jaw and twisting his (NIGGER NIGGER NIGGER) neck until it broke with such a happy sound (NECK BROKE NECK BROKE NECK BROKE LIKE A NIGGER NIGGER NIGGER ON A TREE).

And there also had been the satisfying smell of shit in the cold air (SHIT'S BROWN LIKE HIS FUCKING NIGGER SKIN) as Bill's twitching body lost control of itself.

(GOOD SMELL   It's wrong
GOOD SMELL   It's wrong
GOOD SMELL)   It's wrong

"IT'S FUCKING WRONG!"

Paul flinched, scanned the train.

Did anyone hear?

He glanced to the window he'd been resting against. There was no fog-clouding moisture from his breath upon the glass.

He'd not said

"IT'S FUCKING WRONG!"

out loud.

So he was safe now.

Even though he wanted to scream that what he was doing was *FUCKING WRONG!* to the whole world, and so gain small expiation.

A homeless man (SHOULD KILL HIM, TOO! DIRTY SHIT. DIRTY LAZY *CRAZYLAZYCRAZYLAZYCRAZYLAZY*CRAZY SHIT! LAZY SHIT!) sat a ways down from Paul, babbling softly to some creature of his booze-doused imagining at his shoe. And Paul knew . . . just *knew* . . . that if he chose to listen, he'd understand the delusional rants perfectly.

Paul had been invested with unwelcome empathy. There was a raging sea of emotions around him. *(around him. around him.)* Sundering. Yet each wave had a distinct VOICE.

He needed the VOICES to stop: the anxieties about losing the war; about winning the war; the despair of some; the exhilaration of others. There were the VOICES of those who liked the idea of Arabs dying under American bombs (IT WAS WRONG), but who'd never admit this was what they longed for. There were anxieties about being drafted; about *not* partaking in the war; about missing news coverage from the Gulf that would provide the catharsis of providing a *new* set of anxieties for the evening.

Even while he was assaulted by the VOICES, he longed to be near them, to be near people, to feel the voices packing themselves like a million blind and hungry maggots in his skull, pressing, squirming, behind his eyes, in the channels of his hearing, even the back of his throat. VOICES, made solid like maggots, eating and shitting and growing fat on his sanity. Why did it feel so comforting?

School wasn't crowded enough; he couldn't be there.

He had called in sick; "Bad flu," he'd said. The VOICES called him to the city, to the folds of its streets and alleys, to the comfort he could find entwined in a labyrinth.

Yet amid all that he sought to hear, what voice was his own?

"It's wrong."

What voice could he trust as that of his mind?

"It's wrong."

Paul looked up from the grey slush filthy floor.

The homeless man looked at him.

"It's wrong," said the homeless man.

The bitch had pulled out his heart.

Paul thought of his desperate run from the dead guy's car, past Fenway Park. From that woman who had wanted to kill him, she who clutched the bleeding clump of flesh in her fist, broken bits of rib protruding from her hand like the legs of a spider. Had Paul saved the homeless man in the car, saved him by garroting him as that bitch did some evil thing to him?

What was that shaking in the earth? Why had he felt such quiet in his mind as it descended, just before his desperate run across the field of ice and rubble?

Amid the clatter of the train, something touched Paul's awareness, spreading behind his eyes like a migraine. An ungodly fear took him, making his heart beat impossibly fast; he felt something twitch in his heart, like the thorny stem of a rose, stiff and unmoving as the strands of muscle clenched and unclenched around it. His hands became fists; his palms bled where his fingernails had dug into the soft flesh.

A young hippie couple at the far end of the train held hands and seemed to be huddled in some ritualized recitation. A wave of tarlike froth washed over the remaining scrap of what he'd known to be himself; a cacophony of VOICES crashed upon his intellect.

He tightened his tie, then buttoned and belted his overcoat, which still smelled of stale air and mothballs. The scent touched him in a way that quieted the VOICES a bit, while the pain in his heart made him wonder a moment if his own death was close at hand.

Dying on this train, amid all the VOICES might be kind of nice. Save for the voices of that couple . . .

II

Tuesday, 10:20 A.M.

O *ur Father, who art in Heaven . . ."*
    The young man huddles with his wife on the Red Line train as it careens across the Longfellow Bridge toward Porter Square, where he and she will catch a bus home. The backpack at her feet holds sweaters and shirts they have bought at a place near the river that sells defective clothes by the pound. The young man has not been called to work today on the pretext that there is nothing for him to do; he knows his hours are being cut to provide capital for Christmas bonuses, which Louie will distribute with great magnanimity to the union guys.

The young man and his wife whisper the Lord's Prayer to keep at bay the influence of the Enfolded One. The war and the "holiday season" are both fodder for the Beast, and the violent closeness of the Enfolded One a few days before has left them still shaken. The young woman has whispered to her husband that she feels that they are being hunted; he has admitted that he has the same feeling. The

Beast is taking lives and souls. Part of It is *very* near. They are ready to answer their Patron's summons, to counter the influence of the blind idiot.

"*. . . Hallowed be Thy Name . . .*"

Holding hands, they draw strength from each other.

"*Thy Kingdom come, Thy Will be done . . .*"

As they pray and invoke, the train speeds under Massachusetts Avenue, devouring and vomiting humanity at each stop.

"*. . . On Earth, as it is in Heaven.*"

At Porter Square, they emerge to the concrete plaza where the city fathers have erected a monstrous sculpture of bloodred metal consisting of a tower, atop which is mounted a mobile that turns like the arms of a windmill. To the young man, the thing looks like a thresher designed to harvest humans. He slips his arm around his wife's waist as they walk to the bus stop.

They reach home, and she places her key in the front door of their building. The young man thinks he hears bellowing at the periphery of his senses.

He does not tell his wife, but later he spreads crushed rock salt about the front and back door of the building. He appears to be spreading the salt to melt the ice on the sidewalks, doing the manager's job. Yet as he pours the salt, he speaks a Forbidding, and lets blood fall from a cut he has made on his thumb. The salt and ice drink his blood, making cold rubies in the winter sun, and he hopes this will be enough to keep at bay the terrible messenger he fears has come near his home.

III

Tuesday, 11:08 A.M.

She did not enjoy being so ugly.

The Succubus sat on the edge of the bed as the lover she knew as "Brian" died. Dried and fresh blood flecked his beard. He reached for her, and for perhaps the twentieth time, she shook away his fever-hot hand. The place stank of him, of the extract of a fragrant bark he dabbed himself with, of the weedy things he lit and smoked with practiced nonchalance.

Mimicking his nonchalance, she reached to the bed stand and picked up a pack of the finger-lengths of weed wrapped in paper, put one in her mouth and lit it.

She drew smoke; it was too sweet, thick with oils of spice. She grimaced, blew out the smoke. She ran her tongue over her crooked teeth and shifted her weight on thighs she had made slow and pale for the man dying before her.

"Help me," he managed to whisper.

She touched his burning face. His blues eyes contrasted nicely with the red of his skin.

"I am," she said softly.

With that, he began to cry.

She'd found him in a pub, surrounded by other youths who fancied themselves poets. Yet they had not the faintest spark of the fire that burns in a poet's heart. They drank ale and coffee; a few were accompanied by disheveled girls whom they showed off with the flair of bravos at a joust.

The Succubus left the pub to return as an unlovely girl, wrapped in a bulky sweater she had stolen in a café down the street. Holding a glass of ale, she insinuated herself at Brian's side.

"Hi," she said nominally to all of them, but truly only to Brian. "I was wondering if I . . . could join you all."

Later, she walked with him near the River and listened raptly as he instructed her on how to look upon the River and find its hidden beauty.

"I've never met anyone like you," she said.

She indulged his "sensitivity," which he was as proud of as some men are of their broad shoulders. He fancied himself a healer—the quality that had drawn her to him. He believed the sensitivity of his touch, the insights of his soul, could elevate a homely girl such as she to a great queen. She'd spent their first night together in his arms; they did not make love, for to do so would "cheapen what they had."

Last night, she tired of the game.

As he entered her, she had entered him, thrusting her hand into his chest, pouring into him the illness she had taken from the stricken man. She'd not expunged all the sickness from her body; some had been saved in her marrow. She had refined it, made it a vitriol.

She pulled out her hand, and began her death vigil.

"Help me," he managed to say again. He coughed, bringing a spray of scarlet to his lips.

"Darling, heal thyself." Out of consideration, she blew smoke away from his face.

He choked, mouthing what she knew to be a plea for mercy. She thought to explain that what he suffered was her Mercy, but thought the better of it. He could not understand a notion so poetic.

Brian's cat emerged from the darkened far corner and hissed. She smiled at it, made a swiping motion with her hand. It scuttled back into the darkness. She laughed. It had a sweet face.

Brian trembled. He'd begun to shimmer, to glisten not only with sweat but with the fiery energies of his cells coming apart. He, who thought himself a poet of the City, had taken the City into his being in the form a killing poem born of the River he'd thought so lovely.

She leaned over him and said, "You've taught me so much about Beauty. Thank you."

She kissed him, then cast off her mask. With her hand on his brow, she cooled his sickness enough for him to know that what he saw was no fever dream. She was flattered that a dying man, so weakened and sick, could still find her so desirable.

With impossible grace for a woman of flesh, she stood and walked to where Brian had stacked his black metal and plastic boxes that made music. She pressed the buttons she'd seen him press, and the room filled with music that he had told her was full of "the profound genius of the Celtic peoples."

She threw her ebony hair over one shoulder as she walked back to the bed, moving like fog and in time with the music. She climbed into bed and lifted him; she felt in his heart the hope that she would heal him. She slid behind him and placed her legs on either side of his skinny hips, then eased the burning man's back against her chest as she leaned against the headboard, keeping him upright so he did not prematurely drown in blood. She placed her scarlet hands upon the red skin of his torso, held him close, and softly kissed his neck, rocking him in time with the music.

"I've never met anyone like you," she said.

She reached into Brian's clouded perceptions, then manipulated the music as it registered in his mind. She changed the rhythms and sibilances so they became, for him, the music that she had heard in the realm of her Father. Brian arched his back, trembled not with fever, but with awe as he heard that which transcended the sublime, that which transcended Beauty as he could understand it.

What he heard infused his soul with the delicacy of despair. She held him closer as he trembled.

She placed the Truth of his death in his mind, not expressing it as words, for to do so would interrupt the music. She let him know, in his despair, that he was a mere substitute for the stricken man who had touched her, and who had so wrongly been taken from her. She let him touch her memory of the man with the noble heart, her sense of the magnificence of his soul. She showed him memories of Arthur, letting him taste the bitterness of poetry deferred.

Brian's last breath rose from his lips.

His despair-sweetened soul flowed into her slowly, as water flows from a handful of snow, to trickle along the palm.

His hand fell away from hers, to land among the sheets. She was touched that even while she killed him, he had weakly placed one hand over hers in a gesture of affection.

She placed him carefully on the bed, creating a plausible tangle of sheets among his limbs. She enjoyed a shower alone, working the handles as she'd seen Brian do. It would have been simple for her to cleanse herself through sublimation and sweat, but she liked the spray of warm water upon her skin.

She felt Brian twitch in her flesh as her skin sang with each droplet that stuck it.

Then she drew a bath.

Soaking in warm water, she took apart that which had been Brian; his memory, soul, spirit, and intellect became one with her.

Resting, she closed her eyes and thought of "Paul," the puppet of the Enfolded One who had taken the stricken man from her.

He was Its trophy that It had claimed in order to subvert what she achieved in the Living World, in order to subvert her Name. It had guided Paul to her; It had used him to take the stricken man from her.

She would have killed Paul if her Father had not extended his Will to stop her . . . for *had* she killed him, his soul would have dropped to Hell.

Paul, once a righteous man, would have been held up by the Enfolded One as a testimonial to Its might, to the completeness of Its contamination, to the victory of the Mob over Beauty. Her Father, the Unbowed One, would have sent her on her pilgrimage for naught; the profundity of his vision of Beauty would have been lost.

Her Father had forced an image into her mind as she'd sprung to kill Paul.

He had showed her Paul crucified upon the ribs of one of her Father's fallen allies, raised up against a false sky that shifted like a swarm of insects. The sky was made of the heavy, living *breath* of the Enfolded One in one of Its more debased forms. Under the sky was the Enfolded One again, Its churning black body cresting in waves; hidden within each wave were folds of dragon skin; hidden within each scale was the screaming face of a bile-enriched, weak soul.

Paul screamed, his aerial body dripping blood made black by the marrow of the bones he was nailed upon. The crucified soul became a standard for the Mob Mind as It sundered the onyx cathedral where the Succubus was to be granted her Name.

A righteous man, a widow's son whose soul had been nurtured as had been the souls of God's prophets, made a pawn of the Mob, made a tool to thwart the Unbowed One.

The Succubus pulled the surface of the water around herself, close to her skin, then stepped out of the bath, dry. The remnants of Brian's soul she had sweated made a residue on the water, an oily slick that glistened and drifted in patterns recalling the shifting layers of color in a peacock feather. Soon, the oil was gone.

She walked to Brian's bed, saw dust settling on his eyes. She helped herself to some of Brian's clothes, placing them in a canvas satchel, and prepared to again search for lovers. She had to quicken her pilgrimage, in order to return to Damnation with her Name before Paul's soul could be drawn to the waiting coils of the Enfolded One.

Brian had a jacket of brown leather. She tried it on, taking a moment to fathom the working of the zipper. She made her face that of the murdered girl, but gave herself the fullness of body that had belonged to the mask named "Jeannette." She thought to stop near the dead church and look upon the bronze angel she had painted with the ash of humanity. Perhaps, by facing a nemesis she had bested, she would find the determination to best Paul and his flailing Master.

As she left, she put food out for the cat.

IV

Tuesday, 2:00 P.M.

The bell struck the hour. Frank reached for the blood thinner in his coat pocket. The pills were small; he could swallow them without water, though not comfortably.

He shuffled along Beacon Street, a folder of glossy photocopies tucked under one arm. He'd gone to the Boston University library to search for pulp magazines he'd read as a boy. They'd been consigned to the blurry realm of microfilm reading machines. He photocopied a few of the stories he'd remembered from youth—the black-and-white illustrations, badly reproduced on paper like baking parchment, brought back the moments when he'd read them on his uncle's farm, brought back the bright taste of infinite summers.

Frank swallowed. The pills stuck—two pebbles behind his Adam's apple. He ducked into a deli near the corner of Mass Ave. and bought a bottle of juice. He drank it at a corner table, then left before succumbing to the temptation of the gloriously fatty foods there.

At the corner, a young woman— quite pretty— in a brown leather jacket with the ubiquitous student book bag over one shoulder was staring up at something.

He followed her gaze up to the facade of the renovated church and saw something he'd never noticed before: a bronze angel looking down upon the sidewalk, hidden behind the winter-dead trees. The walls were still soot-stained from the fire that had gutted the church years ago. The angel herself looked filthy, coated in ice and ash.

Frank resisted the urge to cross himself.

He felt eyes upon him.

The girl was looking at him. She gave him a mournful look, acknowledging in the unspoken language of strangers that they both have seen something ugly and shameful. Frank shook his head in silent agreement.

As he walked away, he saw the girl cross herself, as if she had felt his urge to do so as her own.

Feeling a pang of guilt, he walked to Newbury Street, his legs giving him trouble due to poor circulation. He stopped at a religious bookstore to belatedly buy an Advent calendar.

At the corner of Berkeley, he went to his church for confession in preparation for Christmas Communion. He put a few dollars in the alms box, lit a candle for his wife. With the Advent calendar sharing the folder that held blurred images from his boyhood, he went home to call his son-in-law about plans for Christmas.

Stepping out of the church, he felt a twinge in his arm that he made a point to ignore.

V

Tuesday, 4:27 P.M.

Cold winds came up as the day faded, blowing along the streets beside the Charles. The wind made Ed's eyes hurt, as if his contacts might freeze to his corneas.

The wind carried the air that hung over the frozen river. He wended his way to the bookstore, to snuff the call of the river to his withered soul.

The war, looming over everything, made the simple act of walking city streets a burden. Everywhere were reminders: blazing headlines; arguing undergraduates; the worried faces; the eager faces; yellow ribbons affixed to *everything*.

It made Ed sick, reminding him of that which had made his kid brother a cretin, of that which had put into stark focus the intellectual justification for suicide that formed the backbone of his thesis.

The banality of evil . . .

The store was empty when he got there. No one was at the counter. He heard boxes being shuffled and dropped, and Vicki singing softly to herself. The radio was silent.

He found Vicki, crouched low as she shelved paperbacks in the horror section.

She flipped her hair over one shoulder and gave Ed a look that reminded him pleasantly of Rita Hayworth.

"Hey, Ed," she said, and resumed shelving and singing to herself. Ed recognized the song as Alice Cooper's "I Love the Dead." She had five boxes of horror paperbacks around her. A few seventies-era *Exorcist* rip-offs stood out. The shelves she filled were almost empty.

"You're restocking completely?"

Vicki nodded. "Ohhhh yeah."

"The whole section?"

"Merry Fucking Christmas. You wanna go out and beat up Tiny Tim with his crutch?"

"How about the other guy with his ukulele?"

Vicki stood and leaned, quite nicely, against the shelves.

"Let me tell you something. When I first worked here, back when Groucho was so small you'd think she was a powder puff with feet, I went gung ho for Halloween. I aggressively bought up all the nifty horror stock I could find. Spooky campfire stories for kids, novelizations of old monster movies, out-of-print classics. Great stuff. I decorated the section with paper pumpkins and that cotton crap that looks like spiderwebs. The section looked like Elvira's set.

"We sold absolute *dick* out of the section. Nothing. I felt like Charlie Brown coming home with a bag of rocks. Jack was pissed . . . ooooh, he was *pissed*. Well, all that stock stayed up through November. Then, once the holiday season crept up on us, we got hit hard for horror. By the time Christmas rolled around, we couldn't keep the shelves stocked. It seems everyone has lots of anxieties around Christmas, dealing with the folks, the high cost of presents, and the high cost of emotional blackmail."

She reached down to the box closest to her and pulled out a stack of battered books. With a flourish, she shoved them on the shelves.

Ed looked. They were five copies of *A Christmas Carol.*

Vicki made a gesture over the Dickens like a game-show hostess waving her hand over some expensive trinket. "They sell like hot-cakes out of this section at Christmas. Like hotcakes. Nowhere else in the store. Just here. God bless us, one and all."

Ed leaned against the shelves, pulled out a clove.

"Jack here?"

"No."

He lit up.

"You wanna hear my Merry Fucking Christmas story? Couple of years ago, when I was starting grad school, I was short on cash. Comes with the territory, right? I was home for the holidays in D.C. My dad's a lawyer, and I *could* have just asked him for the money, and he'd have given it to me, no problem, but all my life he's been encouraging my kid brother and me to take care of ourselves. I found work as Christmas help in a *toy store* in a *mall* near one of the richest parts of town."

"It was a nightmare. It was like splashing around with an open wound while sharks had themselves a nice feeding frenzy all around you. But the real *coup de grâce* was when girls I had dated in high school came in with their paunchy older husbands and their brand-new *kids.* Oh, Vicki. It was a *special* pain. A Purgatory all my own. To this day, when I hear muzak of 'Here Comes Santa Claus,' I break out in a cold sweat."

Vicki pulled the cigarette out of Ed's hand and took a drag. As she handed it back to him, she whistled 'Here Comes Santa Claus.'

"Don't *even* joke!"

"Sorry."

Ed nodded at the shelves.

"How's business?"

"It sucks. People are too . . . too . . . I don't know, *depressed* to buy much."

"Yeah."

Ed took a final drag from the clove and put out the butt on the sole of his shoe.

"Jack got you working alone?"

"No."

Vicki turned to the shelves, fussed with the alphabetical sort.

"Larry at lunch?"

"No."

She shoved a few books off to one side with a thud. Groucho bolted out from behind a nearby shelf, looked at the two of them, and began chasing an invisible mouse.

"Is something . . . ?"

"Yeah."

"What . . . ?"

" *'Larry'* is pissing me off today."

"Why?"

She lowered her voice. "He's sitting in back sulking. I don't mind him blowing off work. *I'm* one to talk, right? But he's blowing off work, shuffling around the store. It's like he's . . . It's like he's had a *stroke* or something. I wouldn't give a shit if he were sick, but I think he's *choosing* to not be all there, like he's going out of his way to be a space case. I don't know why it's . . ."

Footsteps, among the stacks.

Vicki started shelving. ". . . And I wasn't about to let Dave drag me off to see *Rocky V*," she said. "And my cousin was talking about seeing *Look Who's Talking Too*, f'r Chrissakes."

Larry stepped out of the shadows near the poetry section.

He looked like a junkie stepping from an alley into the bright light of day. He had stubble on his face growing in thin lines, not patches. Larry had botched shaving, missing entire strokes of his face with the razor. He threw his arms around his chest, looking chilled.

("Eddie . . .")

Vicki turned from her shelving toward Larry, said, "Hey, Lawrence."

Then she turned to Ed and gave him a look that was at once apologetic and shocked. Her eyes said she'd take back everything she'd just said about Larry, if she could.

(He held up his swollen hand. "Am I gonna die, Eddie?")

Ed broke eye contact with her, said over her shoulder, "How're you doing, Larry?"

"I'm 'kay," said Larry.

He shuffled toward them, and the sense Ed had was of standing on a street corner just as a panhandler steps up.

(He took Andy's hand in his. It was like a coal. The skin was tight, and felt like rubber. "No, you're not gonna die.")

They stood, talking of nothing, until both Vicki and Ed had begun to affect, without realizing it, Larry's nervous rocking back and forth.

Larry turned to Ed.

"Uhhh . . . Ed? Could . . . I ask you something?"

Ed shrugged, a little afraid of what he would ask of him. "Yeah. Sure."

And Larry walked away, without indicating by way of spoken language or body language that Ed should follow.

Ed followed, giving Vicki a meaningful glance over his shoulder. Vicki called, "Hey, Lawrence?"

Larry stopped, turned slowly, not certain, it seemed, that his name had been called.

"Uhhhmm. If you want to leave early, I won't mind. Really. I'll close out the register for six o'clock."

Larry nodded.

" 'Kay."

Larry led him to a place where the bookshelves made an alcove like a phone booth closed on three sides. The true confession books and magazines were shelved here; Vicki had once told Ed that folks who bought that stuff were a little embarrassed, and liked to peruse the stock unseen. As Larry led Ed to the section, a lone customer walked out, passing Larry, not looking at him. The customer walked toward where Vicki shelved. Ed wondered if the guy had heard anything he and Vicki had said.

Larry leaned against a shelf. Ed did the same, facing him from across the three-sided booth. There was a grate between them, up high, above the shelves. Warmed air went up to the vent shaft.

"Ed?"

"Yeah?"

"Are you training to be a priest?"

A sick feeling spread through Ed's gut.

"No."

Larry weighed this a moment. Ed had a feeling that someone else was in the alcove with them—invisible, standing close.

"D'you know priests?"

"Yeah. I know a lot of them."

Distant mumbling came to their ears. Two people talking elsewhere in the store. Vicki and the customer? Two other customers who'd just come in?

Larry coughed dryly in a spasm, stopped suddenly.

"Are you okay?"

"Yeah. I'm okay. It's dry heat, from my apartment. Dries me out. Makes me sleep badly."

The feeling in Ed's gut got worse.

Larry muttered something that could have been *"Gives me weird dreams."*

"Why do you need a priest?"

"Hm?"

"Why do you need a priest?"

"Guilt."

"Why do you feel guilty?"

"I'm telling you because you know a lot."

"Why do you feel guilty?"

"Because you know a lot about watching people. Like Vicki. You both do. It's funny."

"Uhhhhmmm . . ."

"I was glad when my father died."

Ed felt as if he'd been punched.

"Larry I can't really . . ."

"When he died, I got money from the insurance. It was enough for me to move out and find a place here. Even if I didn't get money out of the deal, I'd still feel guilty. Because I'd still be glad."

Larry cast his head down and smiled the kind of smile an alcoholic makes as another drink is set before him that he knows he should not have.

"I'm going back."

"Where?"

"Providence. For Christmas. It'll be hell, because I gotta face my family and face that I'm glad he's dead."

The holidays, thought Ed. *"God bless us, one and all."*

"You don't have to go back."

"Yes, I do. If I don't, my family's going to take it as an admission of guilt."

Guilt? Of being glad?

"I'm afraid, Ed."

"That's okay. To be afraid."

For once in his life, Ed wished that Father Eugene Tomassetti, shit scholar, fuckhead of a thesis advisor, but pastoral counselor extraordinaire, were on hand to bail him out of this.

"I don't know who I am, anymore."

What in God's name . . .?

"Who does?"

Oh, that's great, Sloane! That's great. Why don't you waltz over to the self-help section and crack open a nugget of profound seventies wisdom like I'm OK—You're OK, *and do some kind of* Lectura Dante *from it? Way to go! Wow, five ethics seminars, and that's the best you can do? CHRIST!*

"Yeah," said Larry. "Who does?"

A new voice nearby, deep and resonant. Footsteps. Vicki's voice echoing among the shelves.

Ed and Larry looked up.

Vicki and her bear of a brother *(Dan? No. Dave! That's it!)* rounded the corner and peered into where they stood. Dave carried a brown grocery bag.

Vicki said, "Hey, Lawrence?"

"Yeah?"

"Umm. My mom had Dave bring over dinner for me. But I had such a big lunch, I can't eat right now."

"Oh."

"Do . . . you want it?"

"Yeah. Sure. But I don't want to take your dinner. I'll have just a little bit. Some."

Vicki blurted, "But you gotta . . ." Then she said, more softly: "Okay. I'll just have a little. I had a really big lunch."

"Uh-huh."

"And why don't you go home, too? I'll cover. Like I said. You can take the food with you. Maybe have a nap, or something?"

"Yeah . . . maybe I should go home."

Vicki and Dave walked toward the front counter. Larry followed. Ed noticed that Vicki carried Larry's jacket with her.

Ed slumped against the shelf and realized that cold sweat made a lovely scent (like that of a wet dog) when meshed with the raw wool of his sweater.

"Christ."

He followed them to the counter, where Vicki was unpacking the brown bag. The contents included almost a whole baked chicken in a bed of foil, a Tupperware container of salad, paper plates and napkins, and sundries like popovers and pieces of fruit. Vicki took a small bite of each, so that her paper plate looked like the picnic fare of a girl on a diet. The three didn't notice Ed.

"No, really, take it, Lawrence," she said.

Larry finally agreed. Vicki repacked the bag. "Now, just go home, Lawrence. Just go. Take it easy."

"Okay."

Larry put on his jacket. Stumbled toward the door.

"Hey, Dave, aren't you going the same way as Lawrence?"

The big bear looked, for an instant, as if he'd just been awakened from a nap.

"Huh? Oh, yeah. I'm going that way."

Dave followed Larry, towering over the guy like a walking tree.

As the bell over the door stopped ringing, Vicki fell into the chair behind the counter and put her hands over her eyes. "Oh, God," she said.

Ed walked to the counter, fished out a clove, and extended it to her.

"Hey, Vicki."

"Yeah." She pulled her hands away from her eyes. "Oh. Thanks." She took it.

Ed offered her a light.

"Thanks," she said again.

"Did you . . . ?"

"Yeah. I called my mom, and she had Dave bring the food over. She's always got a chicken in the fridge for us to gnaw on. The guy's catatonic."

"He's got some heavy shit at home to deal with. He's going back for Christmas."

Vicki blew smoke, frowned. "He told you that?"

"Yeah."

"He's never mentioned his family to me."

"I don't think I can blame him."

"Is it so bad that it could make him such a mess?"

"It's more than that. I *think* he's on antidepressants, and if he's just moved from Providence, then maybe his Rhode Island prescription has run out. He hasn't had the chance to get it renewed. He's got to go back to where his family lives to get the prescription that helps him to deal with what they throw at him."

"Merry Fucking Christmas," said Vicki. She frowned; Ed had the feeling she didn't completely buy his explanation. Which was fine. Ed didn't completely buy it either, but it seemed to make them both feel better.

She tapped ash off her cigarette. "That's pretty good guesswork, Sherlock."

"I like to think of myself as more like Mike Hammer."

Vicki laughed, and it was nice to see her laugh. She was so pretty. . . .

"Boy, dat Mickey Spillane," she said in a faux New York honk. "He sure is a swell writah."

Ed joined in on the routine. When Ed had first come into the store and laid Spillane's *My Gun Is Quick* on the counter, Vicki had grinned and let loose with the "swell writah" jazz. Ed had recognized it as a quote from *Marty*, and had come back with . . .

"So, whadda yah wanna do tonight?"

Vicki jammed the cigarette in one corner of her mouth.

"I dunno. Whadda *you* wanna do tonight?"

She dropped the New York accent.

"So, what *are* you doing tonight? Can I interest you in dinner?" she said with a tilt of her head.

Ed looked at her meager paper plate. He didn't want to take what looked like not much more than a snack for a big healthy girl like Vicki. He glanced up at the clock.

"No, I should get going."

Vicki seemed to think this was funny, for some reason.

"Where're you off to?"

"The gym. They've cut back the hours for exam period. I feel like I've been used like a punching bag. I figure I'll feel better after I've bashed a punching bag for half an hour or so."

She nodded, as if she'd expected what he'd said. She put out her cigarette on the heel of her sneaker. "Maybe some other time?"

"Yeah. Of course."

Later, Ed kicked through the snowy streets, coming home from the gym. He thought a moment about his guess as to why Larry acted so weird. He hoped that he was right.

The fear that he was profoundly and grievously wrong fluttered at the back of his mind. He squashed the fear, snuffed it as he would pinch a candle flame between his fingers.

The fear rose again.

Throughout the rest of the night.

VI

Tuesday, 10:15 P.M.

Paul, on his hands and knees, felt naked without the pressure of a tie knotted at his throat. The fumes of cleaning solution gave him a blinding headache. The pain was the only way that he knew to find quiet from the voices, and from the crushing loneliness of their absence. He dunked his brush in the bucket then scrubbed the last few tiles in the kitchen.

Suds fell from the yellow rubber gloves he wore. He was sure no trace of blood remained on them. The chlorine in the solution dissolved the blood away. All gone. No longer dirty, filthy, dirty.

(AIDS*BLOOD*AIDS*BLOOD*AIDS*BLOOD*FAGGOT*BLOOD*)

Paul breathed deeply of the fumes. The pain fisted in his brow, made his eyes tear and the inside of his nose burn. And the twitching in his heart fell still.

The blood was gone.

He glanced at the clock above the stove. He could call Catherine soon and plead for forgiveness. In that obliteration of self, he'd find yet more peace.

Over supper, she had vivisected him with her scalpel-precise tongue. He had nearly come with her disfigurement of his ego.

All because he asked her if she was sleeping with someone else.

As they prepared for their afternoon session of sex, Paul wandered to where she kept a large red candle that she liked to light for mood, and lit it. It had melted down considerably since the last time he and Catherine had had sex.

After the sex, over dinner served on tasteful plates on tasteful place mats, drinking fine wine from fine glasses, he'd asked her.

"Are you saying I'm not an *adult*? That I can't have some private aspect of my life to myself without you sticking your nose in it?" she said. "Are you saying that it's *any* of your business?"

Paul took a sip of wine, loving deeply this woman, wondering how he could ever have left her.

"No. All I'm saying is that nowadays, it's something people who sleep together should be up front about."

"You think I have AIDS? You think I wouldn't be careful? Oh God! How could you say that about *me*? Are you so insecure that you have to attack me? Am I just something you dust off and objectify just to give some guilt *you're* feeling about *your* foibles?" She honored him, acknowledging he was important enough to attack without first invoking Claire.

She slammed her frail, almost translucent hand beside her plate. The impact was less than that of an apple dropped to the tabletop.

"Answer me!"

Paul took a breath.

And said, "No darling. I'm just trying to be careful. It's been a long time since we've been together."

The results of this quietly stated fact were spectacular, ending with Catherine throwing his overcoat at him as he walked down the stairwell of her building. The obliteration of his ego was euphoric.

But it lasted only about half an hour or so.

He needed a new fix.

He wandered the streets, finding crowds, finding noise, finding the press of bodies, feeding on the sweet anxieties of war and war mania as voices echoed in his mind.

(Shoulda killed 'em!)

(AFRAID!)   (Fear the burning.)

(COWARDLY SHITS!)   (Enemy fear sweet.)

(Help me)

(You killed him.)

Paul reached into his coat pocket, squeezed his keys until they bit into his palm through his new gloves. The voices brought memories of the hippie couple. He'd followed

(. . . stalked . . .) them to their

building in Somerville, riding a cab behind the bus they took. But the doors to their building, front and back, filled him with irrational panic.

(Shoulda killed 'em!)

He'd gone home after that, but could not forget the hippie couple.

Something like small bubbles pulsed in the veins of Paul's temples. Each one had a voice. He wanted to press his fingers through the skin of his temples, squeeze them silent.

He'd thought of walking back to Catherine's for a tearful reconciliation when he passed a grovelike park on Boylston where, even in the cold, shadowy figures milled about among the trees, walking from trunk to trunk. The ten or so shadows among the trees, pacing to shake off the cold, were like the shadow of a single school of fish entwined among the trees.

Each one, part of a greater one. He was jealous.

He was angry.

They were butt-fucking faggot-whores, looking for tricks. Faggot-whores, who go on their hands and knees and take it for a buck. Dogs whose shit is thick and rich with come and AIDS.

(How can you say that . . .)

Paul went to a convenience store nearby

(. . . about me?)

and bought a pair of yellow rubber cleaning gloves and a small bottle of cleaning solution.

MAKE IT ALL CLEAN!

BE SAFE!

ALL CLEAN!

SOLUTION!

He walked the streets until he found, by smell, by the shadow of the shadows cast in the neighborhood, a building hidden by its own architecture. A place artfully paneled with weathered wood, disguised as something old and decrepit and

(DISEASED)

vacant.

Barely visible above the door, in Old English lettering, was the place's name. He knew then why he just fucking *had* to pick up a chunk of broken concrete, about the size of a baseball, in the alley next door.

He waited.

(RAMROD LOUNGE)

To go in would mean discovery. He'd be noticed. A new face. A remembered new face. Couldn't risk it.

(RAMROD LUNGE)

Better to wait.

For drama.

Like a theatergoer just before the curtain is lifted.

He didn't wait long.

The door flung open and a little guy nearly ran out the door, followed by a big guy.

The name of the place (RAMROD) pressed against his every thought.

Memory and awareness became jumbled mosaic.

The argument, loud and abrasive, between the two guys as Paul walked near them.

The little guy running off as the big guy bellowed and raged.

Paul walking with the big guy while his heart tried to beat itself free of the barb lodged in it that tickled and itched and tore.

The stink of the solution as Paul poured it over the rubber gloves as the steaming dead faggot at his feet still breathed through some habit of the body that would not stop until the body grew cold in the winter air.

The only clarity he knew was the pleasure of expunging the name of the place from his head by bringing the rock down on the base of the faggot's neck.

RAMROD!   RAMROCK!

RAM ROD

RAM ROCK   RAM

                                   ROCK

RAM ROD RAM ROCK

Using what the voices barked in his head to make them quiet, awhile.

He'd killed a fucking AIDS faggot. Saved him the bother of getting AIDS for his butt-fucking self.

True, he'd done himself a favor, too. Tasting the quiet in his mind was like tasting Catherine's wine.

Delicious, delicious.

He got on a bus a few moments later.

No one gave him a second glance.

Once home, out of his suit, in the pressing quiet, he'd begun to clean, craving more of the cleaning-agent headache and the peace it gave him. The simple nervous energy of repetitive movement helped, too. Oh, yes. It helped.

Hence, Paul's frenzied cleaning of every baseboard; every bit of molding on every door and doorjamb; the fur of dust on the refrigerator coils;

CLEAN, NO FAGGOT BLOOD CLEAN

                              the glass light fixtures; the

undersides of chairs . . .

He cleaned out his closet

CLOSETS

WHERE

FAGGOT FAGS

SHOULD

STAY

                         throwing out boxes of plastic models

he'd kept for some dumb reason since he'd been a kid and a few collages he'd made in college on a lark. He threw out an old worn book on identifying the birds of North America. It was beat up. Piece of shit.

He threw out old jeans and T-shirts decorated with the logos of bands he'd never really liked. Old sneakers. A denim jacket. He cleaned the grout between each tile in the bathroom. Clean, clean. Then murmuring came. Muted voices, not in his head. Coming out of the walls as he finished the kitchen floor.

The walls of the building were thin. TVs were being turned on, for the eleven o'clock news.

And with the dull thump of voices from TV speakers clicking on, clicking on, clicking on, in each of the units around him, Paul felt the war resonating, trembling along his spine, felt the war forming a cold clot of worry at the base of his skull.

He fell to his knees and breathed the fumes of the steaming bucket of cleaning solution.

The voices overwhelmed him, anyway. He *saw* the voices, refracting through his awareness, churning in the froth in the bucket.

He woke with the taste of blood in his mouth.

He'd bitten through his lip.

Slowly, he pulled himself out of the fetal ball he'd curled into.

He cried, knowing that he could not partake of the war.

Unless he found a way to fight it at home.

(SHOULDA KILLED 'EM!)

Trembling, he stood.

Glanced at the clock.

Reached for the phone, set nicely next to his new answering machine, to call Catherine.

VII

Tuesday, 11:30 P.M.

om and Dad had called just after eleven o'clock. They knew Ed for a night owl; they'd known since he was six, and he would not slow down until Johnny Carson had begun his monologue. Steve, Ed's roommate, pecked away on his computer in his bedroom as Ed sat in the living room, glass of beer beside him.

Mom and Dad and Ed had chatted aimlessly until Mom had asked, with a nervous tinge: "Ed? Are you . . . going up to see Andy this year?"

He took a sip of beer and after a moment said, "No, Mom. I can't. I really can't."

Mom and Dad had seemed to accept what he said, though with recalcitrance.

They said good-bye. Before the hang-up, Dad had offered again for Ed to come down to D.C. for the holidays. Ed told him he was just too damned busy, much as he'd like to.

Ed pressed down on the cradle, put down the receiver.

The click of Steve's keyboard, faint through his bedroom door, was almost soothing. Ed wondered what the hell it was like back in his dad's day, if roommates had to work on dissertations late into the night, bashing away on typewriters.

He wondered to what extent Mom and Dad saw what Andy had become.

("Ed'n'Andy," spoken as one word as they grew up. The Sloane boys, one year apart. Inseparable. Sometimes mistaken for twins.)

He wondered to what extent Mom and Dad chose not to see what he'd become.

(Dad, colleague of legislators and D.C. kingmakers; less-than-proud classmate of Watergate defense attorneys.

Dad renounced the expected lifestyle of a man of his position. He lived in the wooded area of Rock Creek Park, with its wide gorge that had allowed Ed'n'Andy to have Bradbury boyhoods.

While Dad's colleagues, upon hitting male menopause, dumped their wives in favor of twenty-five-year-old trophy brides, Dad would end his day at work—which usually began at 6:30 A.M.—by going off to the bathroom attached to his office and shaving a second time and dabbing cologne, so he'd be fresh for his wife.)

Ed could understand why his parents, particularly Mom, would choose not to dwell on Andy's chosen lifestyle.

(Mom, a woman of quiet grace. Working in housing long before it became fashionable.

She never let Ed or Andy take for granted what they had, often taking her sons to housing developments, through blasted neighborhoods where segregation's ghost loomed.

While Newark burned during the 1972 riots, Mom had set Ed and Andy down before the TV to show them that the news coverage did not explain what they, two kids, knew firsthand about poverty and the rage and despair it can inspire.)

Ed missed his kid brother. It was as if he'd lost him in an unjust war, or in a freak accident. . . . Perhaps he had.

(Building Mom's study. She was away for three days; Dad had made them conspirators. Ed'n'Andy had cleaned out the attic while Dad had bought lumber and rented the tools he needed. The three had worked steadily for three days in the D.C. heat. Dad had no moment of difficulty or doubt, as if the project had been something he'd worked out and had already built in his mind a thousand times over.

For Ed'n'Andy, it felt a heroic struggle to complete the study before Mom came home.

And surprised she was, coming home to see the refinished floor, the shelves, the new lighting, the air-conditioner and space heaters plugged into the newly grounded wiring.

Ed, standing with his brother and father, looking up at the single tear on his mother's cheek and seeing afternoon light coming in over the trees and through the attic window refracted in that tear so that it became a shining jewel, had never known a more peaceful happiness.)

Ed felt like shit that he hated his brother now. But Andy had re-created himself as a hateful thing. Maybe hating him was a way to maintain respect for him, a way to acknowledge all the work he'd put into being hateful.

(Last year, the moment. Amelia had left to tend her brother and his lover. Ed, hoping for some comfort, had gone to visit Andy—no . . . Andrew*—and stay at his new house. Maybe he'd get to know Andrew's new wife. He'd hoped he and his brother could go ice fishing, blow off steam by shooting the shit and hiking.*

What he got was a parade of Andrew's ostentatious purchases: his new car, his macho jock computer with color monitor and laser printer, his golf clubs. . . . Andy had never had the slightest interest in golf before.

The confrontation with the depth of his brother's banality occurred as Ed noticed, for the first time, that the work of abstract art in Andrew's living room was, in fact, a photograph. Ed walked closer to the photo, trying to make out what it was.

He was nearly pressing his nose against the expensive glass and metal frame when he realized that he was looking at an aerial photograph of his brother's new country club.

What the hell had Andy become that he'd join the ranks of the nouveaux riches *in such a grotesque way?*

Andrew had thrown away the person he was in favor of a mask. The mask became more important than the man. As the days passed, Ed saw that Andrew's wife was part of that mask, as much as Andrew was part of hers. The blowup came when Andrew asked Ed when he was going to grow the fuck up and stop spending his life counting angels on the heads of pins.)

Ed had known since high school about Arendt's concept of the banality of evil. But Ed faced now, in the midst of drawing together his thesis born of his own suicidal mind-set, the evil of banality. How it can so completely inform a society that it becomes immoral to live in that society. Suicide becomes justified, as it was in Masada. When he got back from his brother's, Ed—thinking of sleeping pills and frigid nights—had drawn together his thesis, knowing how Tomassetti would react to it.

Ed turned off the light, finished his beer, listened to the soft clicks of Steve's keyboard.

He thought about Larry in the darkness, and wished he could pray for the kid before banality took his soul and name away and replaced them with a mask he should not wear.

VIII

Tuesday, 11:43 P.M.

The snow was light— small flakes that did not fall with their own weight, but as accents to the currents of air wending through the city.

The Succubus made herself invisible in the cold air. She laughed and sported among the rooftops. She ran with silent tread along the railings of fire escapes, among gabled windows and castle-like turrets. She leapt from building to building, burning away—in her effort to remain unseeable—most of the élan that she had taken with Brian's soul. But what matter? Other lovers would come. . . .

Snow clung to her, making her a speckled shadow of a woman. She shook off the flakes, laughing.

She jumped to the facade of a baroque building of brick and curling black metal, alighting upon a gargoyle of cut stone that had not felt a hand upon it since it had been set there almost a century before.

She looked down, and saw the body that held the sick soul she had sensed.

She lay like a sphinx upon the gargoyle's back and watched the demented man at the crossroads circling a streetlamp as a moth circles a flame.

In the cold, in the snow, she whispered.

"Speak my Name."

The man continued his circuit around the lamp. She prodded his festering mind as a child prods a spider with a twig.

She drew a deep breath; the coldness of her body allowed her to inhale snow, unmelting, so that it tickled her lungs.

Slowly, she whispered.

"Speak my Name."

The man stopped and gripped the streetlight as a man who has run himself to exhaustion will grip the trunk of a tree.

He trembled.

"Speak . . . my . . . Name."

He grunted, and struck his head against the post.

She heard him as his mouth moved, as his voice, unused for weeks, awoke without his will.

"Tsssssssssssf," said the man.

She smiled and threw her head forward so that her hair, dusted with snow, fell as locks about the head of the gargoyle. She kissed the stone figure's head and laughed, then turned her attention back to the man.

"My Name. Speak it."

"Tsssssssssssiffffrrrrn."

The man leaned forward; spittle fell from his sore-covered mouth.

"Speak it."

He looked about in panic, so unsure of the intrusion in his mind, frightened of the clarity of the intrusion, the clarity of its imperative.

"Tssssiferne."

"Properly. So I may hear the music of it."

"Tssifoni."

The utterance, faulted as it was, sent a sensuous hunger through her.

"Shriek my Name."

The man sobbed, bit his filthy hand with crumbling teeth.

"Shriek my Name."

The man shook his shaggy head.

"Shriek my Name at this crossroad in my City. Shriek it."

"Tssifoni!"

The sensuous hunger became a burning sweetness, spreading beneath her skin.

"Again. Louder."

"Tssifoni!"

"Again."

The man fell unconscious upon the fifth utterance, and her Name echoed among the redbrick canyons.

The Succubus rested, elated, upon the back of the gargoyle. She rolled over, so that her back touched the stone figure's back, and looked at the night sky as it cried crystalline ice.

She had been prayed to, this night.

And the prayers had given her strength, had given her a new gravity that was buoyant; each syllable meshed with her being as a specter meshes with fog.

Two servants of her Father had been made aware of her, and had offered portions of their spirits to her in the form of ancient invocations. Their offerings were made richer by the love they shared, by the love that had infused the ritualized utterances that had made the Succubus strong and full of fire.

So moved, so full of joy, she had to caper and dance and fly and run through her promised realm. Hungry for more worship, she reached out for one demented who could offer her a taste of the adorations to come. Happy, looking to the sky that still filled her with awe and terror, she thought then to not wait to take another life, another soul. So soon after Brian, *could* she configure herself upon indulging a new cruelty, *could* she restructure the souls within her to accommodate another soul, and so reach another sphere, another realm ruled by an Insurrector?

Of course, she could. If she acted as Avenger, again, as the avatar of Tisiphone.

She reached out with her mind, leaving her body. A pigeon fluttered awake in its nest beneath the gargoyle and flew into the snowy night, unable to navigate without the sun to bear upon, but too afraid of her intrusion to stay in its nest.

She combed the city for a singular heartbeat, one that echoed the mournful cries of her brother imprisoned long ago in the flesh of pigs only to be drowned; a heartbeat she had first heard beneath her defaced and blasphemous rival cast in bronze.

She would avenge the imprisonment inflicted upon her brother by the *Kristos* himself.

IX

Wednesday, December 19, 1990. 12:34 A.M.

The sleeplessness of age, the taste of chamomile tea, and the quiet of a building huddled in winter night.

Frank looked at the photocopies he'd made of the pulps from microfilm. He missed how fresh and clean those real pulps had smelled when he'd bicycled back from the newsstand to open them for the first time, how wonderful it was to run his fingers over the chips of wood in the paper. That smell was probably lost, forever. A pile of pulps somewhere in an attic, or in an overpriced collector's store, would smell of yellowing paper turning into mulch.

Dan Turner . . . Conan . . . Combat Johnson . . . the Shadow.

Lord, how they had captured his imagination. He was afraid to actually *read* the stories; they couldn't be as good as he remembered them. But the illustrations took him back to that time of innocence, as did the simple sight of the typefaces and the ads for products guaranteed to give you a Roman nose or a he-man body in just six weeks, to relieve scalp itch, and to clear up blackheads and warts.

Frank stood to put away his teacup and change into his pajamas.

The pain struck his chest like a punch.

His hand went numb; he dropped the cup. He fell to his knees as his eyes teared. Constriction around his heart, a squeezing of his lungs. So sudden—*Oh, God in Heaven*—so sudden, without the warning shortness of breath. His chest felt pulled into itself, collapsing like a canvas bag. Movement restricted, he looked up to the phone on the end table. He could not stand. Could not crawl. Coldness in his fingertips, as if they had been thrust into snow. *Oh, God. Please not now . . . please not now, please not now.* He gripped the phone cord and pulled. The phone crashed by his head and he knew the deepest terror he'd ever felt, terror that the phone would strike him unconscious so he'd die without the dim chance of prayer as his eyes went forever black. He reached for the phone and dialed 911.

The emergency operator answered on the fifth ring. He tried to speak. With all his will and strength he tried to speak. Instead, he tapped the phone against the floor, weakly. Tapping a message as meaningless as the tappings of a branch against a window.

He heard the operator's voice, crackling, buzzing: "We are putting a trace on this call. If you understand, tap again."

Frank did, just as a new pain spread through his chest with the deliberation of fire through young wood. His jaw went slack. The voice of the operator became indistinct; Frank's vision blurred. His head pressed against the floor and he thought of Jenny and Susan, wishing that he could have said a true good-bye to them or that he had embraced them the last time that he saw them. *Oh, God. Please not like this, please not like this, please not like this* . . .

Three quarters of an hour he lay in pain and perdition. Three quarters of an hour he cried out for benediction, for mercy to an unhearing existence. He fought. He cried. He screamed soundlessly. He saw a bronze-red light, like that of dusk near half-frozen lakes reflecting the sky upon surfaces of wind-driven water and still ice. Sirens called in the distance. Frank felt sudden peace. The light shifted, as if its source were a lantern carried through the room by a person of slow and beautiful grace.

She stepped into view, a being of loveliness unknowable, loveliness that transcended the faulty medium of sight. She was no statue, no object of possible idolatry. She was that which had been cast in bronze, made knowable to the dying, and perhaps to the living.

The angel, dressed in silence, stood before him. She was still, yet shifting, as if she did not fully extend into the dimensions knowable by mere sight. She stood over him like a shepherd.

You are not alone.

Frank did not hear the words, but knew them in the way he knew memory.

The paramedics pounded on the door, calling. Frank watched the angel, looked into her eyes of indigo, and knew that he should not try to call out with his stricken and failing body. He had not locked the door; it was not his habit to do so until he went to bed.

The angel was with him in the ambulance, occupying the space that stretchers and equipment did, veiling her radiance lest the winter-dusk glow of her being be stained by the harsh light. Tubes were thrust into his throat, needles pushed into his veins. At times, the ambulance, the paramedics, faded in his sight, became grey shadows. But the angel remained, quieting his fear and pain, soothing him with the promise of hope and mercy.

Swerving lights, as he was wheeled to the emergency room. Harsh fluorescents. He was left a moment, wheeled to a corner of this warehouse of human suffering. The angel stayed with him, her hand upon his brow in that awful moment of forgottenness.

Then, men and women clad in linen stood over him, tending him.

Calling to him. The angel stood among them; they stood in the midst of her.

You are not alone.

He was invaded, prodded. Current stabbed his burning chest. He fell into a blackness without sheen, into a void without the form, shape, or lightness of sleep. He did not despair. The angel was near, at times parting the darkness with her light, holding him in the waters of her bronze-red glow.

Dawn. He was aware of dawn, of the arid pain in his mouth, of tubes pressing down his throat and the sound of the machine that monitored his heart. *Dawn had come:* he knew this, even in the windowless ward he lay in. He was alive in the breaking daylight, out of the deep night of desperation and fear and pain.

He opened his eyes to clear vision, to shining chrome and white walls. He was alone, in a room with three empty beds. Triage for the ICU?

Flickering like a candle flame was the angel at the foot of his bed. Her voice rang lovely, like a church bell, in his mind.

My brother.

Frank tried to swallow, but the tubes scratched him from inside. The bronze-red glow about her changed, shifted slowly to scarlet.

You must know my brother was imprisoned in flesh he could not tolerate, as you have in your heart flesh you cannot tolerate. My brother drowned himself, for despair. I desire despair from you, to partly make amends. Amen.

A stab of pain, a needle in his heart. The monitor beside his bed spiked. The scarlet of her glow grew deeper. Frank thought a moment of the shadows visible beneath lakes, made blood red.

This is the time of hope. This is the time of beauty, when coddled favorites of God such as yourself believe you may pass from out of the valley, out of the shadows. This hour is mine. You cannot hope. You are not alone. I am the cruelty of Mercy.

The needle of pain became a dagger.

Despair is sweetened by hope; I reclaim the hope I have granted you.

The monitor spiked, trembled. It beat fast as a rolling drum. Frank felt his heart tear. An image flashed in his mind of the implanted valve ripping free. He heard the sounds of screaming animals, smelled the stink of shit and the shocking cold of deep water.

His heart stopped. Doctors and nurses burst in. The monitor screamed an unchanging wail. In the corner of his sight he saw Jenny and Susan in the doorway, pushing, yelling, blocked by an orderly.

An outstretched hand as the curtains were pulled shut around his bed. A plaintive cry.

"Daddy!"

The sound of a door slamming as his chest was laid bare.

Amid the flurry as he died, the angel revealed herself, a thing colored of blood, black-haired, with a look of beatitude upon her lovely and cruel face. The doctors and nurses passed through her as they faded to imperceptibility, as she became sharper in his dimming sight, as the scream of the monitor faded to a distant echo.

In his despair, the blackness of death was made red as her skin.

Chapter Two

I

Wednesday, December 19, 1990. 9:25 A.M.

H e saw his father clutching his heart, falling in the hot sun, cursing him. Lawrence clutched his heart as well, felt a knife of pain driven through it, dying as his father died. For the first time, his father seemed pleased at something Lawrence did. Lawrence crawled through the grass toward him.

Held by the loamy smell of the soil, Lawrence heard, through the ripping pain in his chest, the screaming of animals.

He was among the animals as they squealed, as they charged into cold water. Their backs became barbed and humped in the shallows, grotesque. He tried to swim, but slashed his own throat with each stroke. He sank, streaming blood; he realized, with rage, that he was no longer in a human body. He bellowed soundlessly with his brethren, with himself, fractured into many.

. . . Through all, the rage of his father, cursing him.

Lawrence woke smelling of fear and sickness. He pulled the tangle of covers away and felt the pain in his heart return. A minute passed before he could move. Pockets of emptiness, of *otherness,* moved through his flesh, each like a small ghost wandering through the chambers of his body. He stumbled to the bathroom sink, splashed himself with cold water. The face in the mirror was as alien as that of a stranger peering from a window.

God, what's happening to me?

He walked back to bed, taken by sudden chill, *feeling* that someone waited for him among the covers. He wrapped himself in a blanket, rocked back and forth. His father, even in death, filled his life with dread.

("C'mon! What's wrong with you? Five-fifty an hour not good *enough for you? Huh?"*

He took a pull from his post–Sunday dinner beer.

"Don't know where I went wrong.")

Dad had gone wrong when his emotional blackmail misfired, costing him his life, according to Lawrence's family. Of course, his family could not accept this entirely, so the blame as to whose actions had cost Dad his life was shifted squarely on to Lawrence's shoulders.

("It's steady work! You never had steady work in your life. So you're gonna turn your back on it now, Mr. Smart-ass?")

Dad had decided Lawrence should be a janitor and forsake his two part-time retail jobs. Graft and kickbacks had seen to it that downtown Providence was being constantly rebuilt. Janitors were needed to keep that new office space in tip-top shape. The janitors were unionized, and Lawrence stood not a chance. Dad insisted that Lawrence go for an interview Saturday afternoon. Lawrence agreed; embroiled in what became the early stages of his breakup with Jacob, he wanted to keep peace in as many ways as possible.

As Saturday approached, Dad called Lawrence. *"Need your help, son!"* Oh, how jolly he sounded! *"Gotta take care of the landscaping Saturday!"* "Landscaping," never "gardening," even though all Dad "landscaped" was his postage-stamp-sized backyard.

"No, Dad," Lawrence had said. "I've got the job interview."

"Awwwwww, you can reschedule it for your old man, can'tcha?"

"No, Dad. I can come by after the interview."

"That'll be too late! C'mon! It'll be good for ya to get out in the sun!"

"No, Dad."

His father gave him a round of curses and slammed down the phone. When Lawrence told Jacob, he laughed.

Lawrence gleaned details of what had happened from the shrieking attacks by Angie; from the shit handed to him at every family meal since his father had dropped dead. Dad had worked himself into one of his trademark furies: *"Fuckin' no-good kid! Can't help his dad around the house! Fuckin' gotta do* everything *for myself!"*

So worked into a lather, having inspired terror among his wife and all others in range, Dad had chugged a six-pack. Or two. Then he grabbed tools from the garage to furiously uproot old plants so he could dig new beds in the brutal sun . . . in the close and humid air.

Lawrence saw, afterward, the lay of the garden where Dad had fallen. One bed had been only partly prepped—the old plants pulled out before the soil had been gouged. No careful pressing of the spade made these gouges. The spade had been stabbed into the ground.

Dad had a special emotional torture planned for Lawrence when he stopped by after the interview. Very special. But he was dead by the time Lawrence got there. The only clear memory Lawrence had of the aftermath was of Angie pounding her fat fists into Lawrence's chest as her dumb zit-faced bastard looked on with a smile.

Lawrence pulled the blanket closer, lay down. He was seized by a fit of trembling. His lungs itched; he wanted to cough. The ghost, the worry, walked again from the dark part of his mind and touched him softly: *Maybe you have AIDS.*

The trembling stopped. *God, what's happening to me?* he thought. He rolled over, pulled more blankets over himself. He remembered a dream in which he'd spoken to Ed about being glad his father was dead, yet the dream felt *tangible . . .* more real than it should be. As he stood, wrapped in a sheet, he wondered if he'd actually spoken to Ed.

Stumbling to dress himself, he heard the echo of a woman crying—sound carried by vents or conduits? Her weeping was soft, the tone of lamentation, and Lawrence knew in a way he could not fathom that she wept for a lover she would never know.

II

Wednesday, 10:16 A.M.

Made in China.
	He put it aside.
Another make, another brand.
Made in China.
Another.
Made in Japan.
"Made in Japan" used to be a joke. It used to denote inferior quality, back when we had a bit of fucking *pride* in ourselves as a country.

Paul put it aside. Picked up another rubber mallet.
MADE WITH PRIDE IN THE USA.

He felt the weight of it. It was right. So right. Twice as expensive as the others, but how could you put a price on *pride?* Paul paid for the mallet and left the hardware store, ready to fight the war on the home front.

III

Wednesday, 11:30 A.M.

S *he is here.*"
The young man embraces his wife, kisses her. They roll among the sheets, make love again. His wife touches his face and whispers again, *"She is here."*

A promise made, a promise kept.

Last night, in their fear of the Enfolded One, they had invoked the Unbowed One and had felt in the ether what could only have been the presence of their Patron's Daughter: gentle, loving, and strong. The Unbowed One had sent a Daughter, as he had long ago sent a Daughter against the Sons of Light in Qumran. In prayer, in meditation, the young man and his wife had felt her take strength from them, felt her make herself whole through their spirits. A Begotten Daughter, clothed in twilight, who shall veil herself in the squares of the cities.

As they had touched her, the young woman had cried, "The River!"

The young man had felt it too, holding his wife in ritualized embrace, contorted with her in flesh and spirit within the pattern of electrical tape that was a representation of their Lord's intellect. The Begotten Daughter drank of them and he felt the River, felt how it informed and shaped her and her identity. The young man felt the strength of the Charles, as he had not felt it since he'd been a boy.

They had both nearly blacked out. Exhausted, they pulled comforters around themselves. Sitting in candlelight, he looked upon the salt they had strewn within the geometric pattern in invocation of the *spiritus loci* of the Dead Sea; their Lord's throne was placed metaphorically in Sodom—in opposition to Qumran.

He held his wife close. "The River," he said.

She pressed her face against his chest. "I can smell it."

"You can?"

"Yes. I smell the water, the fog, the soil on the banks. I can smell the snowy wind that comes off the ice."

He kissed her.

"This is what we've been called to do," he said.

"And perhaps more."

He thought then of what had stalked them home, that which he'd driven away with salt and blood. Would they be called to bring It down? He was not certain he had the Will to slay a man, even if the man was a vessel of the Enfolded One. For now, it was enough that they knew what the Unbowed One willed of them: to provide strength for his Daughter, joined to the River. The battle with the Sons of Light entailed the Unbowed One mastering rivers, making them overflow with his Will and might and beauty. Would not a battle with the Enfolded One entail the same?

Once they had rested, they both stood and felt exhausted again. They stumbled to bed. In the morning, they made love and fell into a deep sleep.

Now they lie awake in the late-morning light. The day is more than half over, the sun due to set in a few hours—one of the shortest days of the year. She stretches, for herself, and for him. Her loveliness, even after eight years of constant and faithful marriage, arouses him madly.

He rolls on top of her, kisses her. She laughs, pulls his ear and says, "Nnnnnoo!" the way one would to a misbehaving puppy.

He flashes her a hurt look.

"We have to go shopping!" she says. "There's nothing in the house to eat!" And with that, she gives him a slight slap on his backside.

They get out of bed. She goes to shower while he goes to make her tea.

In the kitchen, he turns on the radio, quickly changing it from NPR to an oldies show on one of the college stations. He thinks of the profundity of what his Patron is doing, the journey he has sent his Daughter upon. From the airy realms of Damnation, following the inverted Tree of Life, she will rise toward Flesh, eventually reaching the Void that those on Holy Pilgrimage cross with Wisdom, yet she will cross with Ignorance. Yet Ignorance of what? What Ignorance can bestow upon her Flesh, with all its limitations, yet also allow her to *transcend* Flesh? Can he and his wife provide her the strength and adoration she will need for such a journey?

He takes down a canister of tea as the kettle rattles and clanks, and as Grace Slick sings of what one pill does as opposed to another.

Naked, enjoying that the apartment is well heated, the young man takes a broom from the kitchen to the living room and sweeps the Salt of Sodom he has laid within the configuration of their Lord's mind. The salt must be fresh each time it is used ritualistically; sea

salt would be best, but as Morton's is still less than fifty cents a container . . .

As he sweeps, he hears the shower going.

He is about to go back to the kitchen to fetch the dustpan he has
forgotten when the bathroom door opens.

The tread is wrong; the shower still runs.

He looks up to see atrocity.

A man has his wife in a hammerlock, pulling her as a butcher
would haul a carcass from the kill floor. In one hand, the man holds
a rubber mallet. His wife, naked, struggling weakly, has a livid bruise
across her forehead the width of an apple. The man is naked, his
penis engorged with rage, or desire, or both.

"I got your slutbitch."

The voice is that of the Enfolded One. He hears *chanting* within
the voice, a thousand thousand outraged, wounded cries of weakness
that together form a great Beast of blind ire.

"Got your slutbitch! Got her good!"

His wife tries to speak, her voice sounding as it does while she
murmurs in her sleep. She tries to gain her footing, but her legs
shake like those of a newborn fawn.

"C'm'n get her! C'm'n get your slutbitch!"

He is safe.

The young man is safe inside the pattern of electrical tape, within
the Will of his Lord. Yet tendrils of his Enemy's mind touch him. He
sees his wife taken into the maw of the Enfolded One. A trophy,
ripped apart and reformed by the many dragon mouths of the Beast.
Nuggets of her soul thrown about as nourishment for the thousand
discordant mouths within each dragon mouth, to be ingested and
shat out and eaten again, her intellect intact within each nugget,
screaming. The vision is a lie, it must be a lie, it is . . .

The fleshy vessel of the Beast squeezes his wife's neck in the crook
of his arm. "I hear it popping!" he says. "I hear her neck popping!"

In the kitchen, the kettle boils, whistles, drowning out the sound
of the radio.

The young man looks about. Behind his wife, propped by the
door to the kitchen, is their ceremonial sword. He drops the broom,
crouches.

His Enemy moves like rushing water. The mallet strikes him across
the temple and he falls. His Enemy drops his wife, and with both
hands brings the mallet down on the bridge of his nose.

Drowning in his own blood, his last thought is of his wife.

IV

Wednesday, 12:34 P.M.

Paul understood.

It is a violation that makes a rude object of that which has been created in the image of God, an abrupt destruction of the poem that is the human form. The loss of a limb is tragic caesura, the cutting short of a stanza. But to take the head is profound objectification; both head and torso are made so sadly incomplete.

The slutbitch was still alive as he hauled her like a sack of laundry onto the dais of scrap lumber. She was still trying to speak. Paul laid
(LAY THAT BITCH!)
her faceup, feeling guilty that he should get pleasure handling her as he prepped her for the blow
(GOTTA GET HEAD! GOTTA GET BLOW!)
The sword tingled in his hand as if it were coated with venom. For the second time, he wielded it, driving the blade through her creamy bruised neck as if it were soft butter.

Warm blood washed his feet and the feel of her hair as her head landed by his left foot was sensuous. Picking her up by the hair, he set her head next to that of her fellow victim.

Afterward, he tipped the wooden chair painted to look like a throne and decorated with fake jewels. Using a bit of the woman's lovely hair as a brush, he painted a mark upon the dais in blood, and took particular delight in destroying a figure made of salt with doll's eyes set into the face and a lead gimcrack of a big-titted woman with bat wings sprouting from her back.

While he worked, a barrage of hippie-era hits played on the radio. He chuckled as he picked up the heads, held them close to his face (the heads were *heavy*), and proclaimed, along with Jim Morrison, that he was the Lizard King, and could do *any*thing.

He set the heads on the sofa and made them watch as he pulled the electrical tape off the floor. The pattern made him sick to look at, much in the way the mark he painted on the dais exhilarated him. He stuffed their mouths with the electrical tape, painted the mark he'd put on the dais on their foreheads, then merrily defecated on a pile of salt in the middle of the living room.

He wetted a dish towel in the kitchen and cleaned himself a bit, agreeing with Mick Jagger that if you try sometimes, you *do* get what you need.

Going through the closets, he found expensive tools; the guy was a carpenter. Among the tools was a handcrafted whip. Oh, what he could have done if he'd known about these toys . . . to torture a hippie asshole with the tools of his trade. Mr. Skilled Carpenter hadn't had the foresight to fix things for himself. Little shithead had probably wanted his manager to take care of everything. Shitwhiner, with a slutbitch.

Paul pulled clean towels and washcloths from the closet and went into the shabby bathroom. The shower still ran from when he'd turned it on after stunning the stunning woman with the mallet. He cranked the hot water and washed. All the personal hygiene products were of the "all natural" variety. How could they afford this stuff and live in such a shit hole? Washing his hair with shampoo perfumed with nard seemed lavish.

He reached from behind the shower curtain to grab his trophies in their thick plastic garbage bag. He rinsed the outside of the bag so there was no trace of blood. Then he dried himself, dried the bag. He went to the bathroom window, opened it, reached up to ground level and pulled down his clothes and overcoat from where he'd left them folded in a cheap vinyl valise he'd gotten at his dry cleaners. Sick yellow leaves from the tangle of bushes fluttered in with the valise. The front and back doors of the building had still filled him with creeping panic. The *smell* of the hippies had led him to the side of the building, where a path had been beaten to the gas and water meters in back. Paul had looked at the window, seen that nails had been driven into the pane to keep it from opening wide enough for an intruder to squeeze through. But the wood was *rotten*. It was easy to pull up the window; the spongy wood yielded as the pane slid.

Tying his tie, he grinned as he heard Paul McCartney sing of how someone else had come in through a bathroom window. He pulled in his galoshes and slipped them over his shoes.

Carefully, he walked through the bloody apartment, stopping in the kitchen to shut off the radio. By the refrigerator stood a recycling bin full of newspapers and brown paper grocery bags. He helped himself to a grocery bag, put the garbage bag inside it, then opened the refrigerator and piled fruit and vegetables on top of the garbage bag. Camouflage.

Not knowing why, Paul carried the heads to the apartment door then looked out the peephole. Clear.

He pulled off the bloody galoshes and left them, then went into the dingy hallway. By the front door, he found a little girl playing with Barbies.

She smiled at him.

"Hi!"

"Hi, honey!"

She gave him a careful look that alarmed him not in the least.

"Are you a teacher?"

"That's right, honey!"

The girl smiled, pleased with how clever she was. Paul opened the front door, stepped out with his trophies. Whatever had made him sick about the front door had died, whatever energy that had fueled his dread was inert. He stepped along the salty front walk to wend his way to the bus stop, some blocks distant. He regretted he had to leave behind the galoshes; his shoes might get ruined. No one around here shoveled their walks.

Some neighborhood . . .

The little girl had looked as if someone had struck her across her nose. She had what looked like a fading bruise. Who could do such a thing?

Paul rode into the city, called for some reason to the river, then to the twisting streets. He got off the bus near Mass Ave., and was about to turn toward the presses of humanity among the shops of Newbury Street when the VOICES flooded his mind.

He ran to an alley and dumped off his burden, casting aside the brown bag and the camouflage of food. He put them in their plastic bag atop a garbage can, then ran back to the street.

He rode the trolleys until a whisper of his own intellect reasserted itself.

Back home, asleep, he dreamt of the woman he'd killed.

The sun had set when he called Catherine to expiate him from the desire and regret he felt.

V

Thursday, December 20, 1990. 3:45 A.M.

S he walked as an old crone among darkened streets. In a bag, she carried the insult inflicted upon her. She mumbled the orisons of a diseased mind, invoked the sweaty murmurs of the dispossessed. Those few who saw her averted their gaze. She emerged from the city's maze to the banks of the Charles.

Skirting the River's edge through icy fog, she saw a young man running toward her with the speed and grace of a deer. The vibrancy of his strength made a glow in the fog. Oh, that she could drink that glow as if it were wine, bathe in the glow touched by the fog. But she dared not, for she needed to be unseen and unnoticed.

The man passed her, ignoring her, unwilling to see any reminder of mortality. His glow touched her; she shuddered. Her aged hands were cold. The joints creaked, her wrists tired from her burden. Closer to True Flesh, she partly knew its limitations while wearing its guise. To attain and transcend True Flesh, she needed another soul; she would have then taken one lover for each sphere of the Abyss she needed to cross to reach Materiality, and beyond.

Earlier this day, upon her rooftop, she had felt a goddess: drunk on the despair of the man named Frank, drunk on the strength given her in prayer by the servants of her Father.

As dusk came and she prepared to walk the city, the strength granted her by prayer felt *close,* yet *sour.* Rotted. Like splendid fruit left too long on the vine.

She dropped to the alley, hearing the call of a soul she longed to heal with her cruelty. As she dropped, her aura became fetid, as if she descended lake waters clear near the surface, yet muddied toward the bottom.

She dropped through the ethereal shit of the Enfolded One, through Its secretions and corruption. Her features ran like wax; the face of the murdered girl gave way to her natural face. At the base of her building atop a garbage can, she found a bag of plastic.

She opened it and found desecration. Their foreheads had been painted with the mark of the Enfolded One. The bag was full of the soul stink of Paul, her Enemy's vessel. Enough of her Father's Will remained to mark the heads with beauty and strength, which made more ghastly the contamination of the Enfolded One.

She wiped away the marks of blood from the foreheads of those who would have loved her as would her own children.

She waited for deeper night to grant some peace to those who would have given their lives for her. When the moon was invisible, she walked as one whom the city made invisible.

And now she stood, wizened and stooped, at the place where she had killed the boy named Spaw. The hole in the ice where she had pulled him under had yet to freeze over. Under the slight rumble of late traffic on the bridge she looked about, then walked upon the ice, making herself light, still suffering pain and cold in her hands, and gave the remains of her Father's servants to the River. She felt them carried toward the sea, felt the River wash away the ugliness of the Enfolded One.

"Please come back!"

She hoped they, so newly baptized, would not lose all their essence to the maw of the Enfolded One.

"Come back toward me! Please? Can you hear me? Ma'am? *Ma'am?!*"

She turned to see the young runner standing on the slanting, icy rocks—hand outstretched. He looked so lovely, enveloped in the glow of his health in the fog. She stood upon the waters, touched that her savior would call out so.

Trembling, she stepped toward him. She filled her eyes with confused fear, then slipped on the ice, quickly regained her footing.

"Come to me. That's good! Come to me!"

She made herself dense with each step, making the ice creak. She held her hands before her, made them shake pathetically. The runner took her hand, one foot on the ice. She let him pull her to the esplanade as she let out a sob.

"It's okay," he said. "It's okay."

His glow of health was wonderful. He had no forlorn sadness in him, no poetry. But he was beautiful and strong; she wanted comfort.

Kissing him threw him in a stupor. Holding his body, like the work of a master sculptor, was like holding a dream actualized in flesh. She ran her crone's hands over his body, pushing them through the fabric of his sweat-moistened clothes. He sighed, and she felt the hardness of his arousal. She whispered by his ear, "Thank you. You are kind."

She left her savior stumbling by the River. He walked to a young tree and put his arms about it, trying to support himself.

The Succubus walked along the River. With each step she turned back time, making herself again the murdered girl. The comfort of the embrace she'd stolen had allayed her sadness and rage.

Comfort . . .

At her home, in her natural form, she looked upon the dawn and the new fire it struck upon the Hill. She thought of Salvation and kindness, and realized Absolution was the weapon she must take up against her Enemy.

She buried herself in snow, then warmed it with her body. The partly melted snow refroze as ice. Without breath, with her body cold, she slept; the faint light of the runner's aura glowed in her glassy casement. She saw it from behind the lids of her eyes.

There was a stirring, as if a voice called her from below.

VI

Thursday, 4:37 P.M.

The room was crowded with ghosts.

There was a weight in the air. He thought of sickrooms, of hospital wards in Dickens novels, of the withering of souls. The worst nightmare he'd ever had was of being an Auschwitz survivor who'd returned to see the piles of hair, of shoes, of bloodstained clothes. He'd been overwhelmed with grief, drowned in the weight of souls inscribed into the soil, the splintered wood. He'd fallen to the ground, tearing his hair, his clothes. The smoke of the chimneys had carried memories of suffering as particles of soot, and those memories—strands of black milk in the air—accused him as he breathed them in . . . as they touched his skin as would dust. Memory of that nightmare crashed upon him as he hefted Larry toward the bed, bearing the kid's weight on his shoulder.

"Stay with me, until I sleep."

"What?"

"Stay with me, until I sleep."

Oh, Christ. I'm not strong enough for this.

"Okay," Ed whispered. "Okay."

He eased Larry onto the bed then pulled off his shoes. The air was dense, *old*, but *alive*, haunted. Ed felt weak; he wanted to turn around, to see if a crowd of living shadows would be visible before fading to nothing.

"Promise? You'll stay?"

"Yeah. I promise."

There were no chairs in the bedroom; the only light filtered from the entryway. Ed reached for the nightstand, not willing to keep his vigil in darkness. Larry didn't notice as he clicked on the light. By the lamp were two battered Perry Mason books.

Vicki had called Ed at his office, having gotten the number from the campus directory. He'd been grabbing a few books he needed; ten minutes earlier or later, she wouldn't have found him.

"Get over here," she'd said.

"What for? I bounce a check?"

"God damn it! Get over here!"

"Where are you, the store?"

"Yes, I'm at the store. I need you. Get over here!"

Over the phone, Ed had heard a distant voice, getting closer. Larry?

Vicki switched personae.

"Yes," she purred, as she did whenever she dealt with a pain-in-the-ass customer. "Yes, I'm afraid that book is out of print. Would you like me to put a search on it?"

"Okay," he said. "I'll be right over."

"Thank you for calling, and have a merry Christmas!"

When he arrived, Vicki threw her arms around him. Ed jumped: too weird. Nice, but too weird.

"C'm on over here," she'd said. There was fear in her voice—*fear*, in this girl, who could push around her hulking brothers as if they were grade-school kids, who could stand up to condescending Harvard profs as they expounded on things they knew nothing about, who could wring apologies out of MIT frat boys for staring at her chest. She led him to the counter.

"Lawrence is acting weird."

"Yeah, but—"

"No. *Really* weird. He tried to kick Groucho, and when I yelled at him for it, he said he didn't remember. He's mumbling a lot. In different voices . . ."

"What, like he's impersonating somebody?"

"No. It's always his *voice*, but the speech patterns are weird."

Ed thought of something, remembering Larry's cuts that had closed: "Is he speaking different *languages*? Does he sound like he's translating in his head from another language before he speaks?"

Vicki frowned, then jabbed a little dagger of ice in his heart by saying, "Maybe," instead of a proper and sane, *"No."*

"Where's—"

"Jack's out going over some estate stuff. But if he comes back, Lawrence will be f—"

"I was going to ask, 'Where's Dave?' "

"He's at work. I can't find him."

"Have you asked him about medication?"

"Dave?"

"No! *Larry,* f'r Chrissakes!"

"And how does one casually ask if your pal is a loony, and would he like a happy pill?"

"Sorry."

"It's okay." She leaned against the counter. "I need you to take him home."

"I'll do it," he said.

Walking to Larry's apartment, Larry had leaned on Ed, then stumbled a few steps before leaning on him again, as if they were lovers. A few jar-heads and jocks they passed looked like they'd enjoy a bit of sport at the expense of two fags. Along the way, Ed could have sworn that Larry had lost his sight a few seconds. Outside his building, Larry clutched at his chest but then righted himself. As Larry tried to get his key in the front door, Ed took the key to open the door himself. Larry's hand was cold as a dead person's, even though he'd just taken off his gloves. In the elevator, Larry had coughed, dryly.

Christ, thought Ed. *Does he have cancer, or AIDS? Is he having some kind of systemic shutdown?*

Mundane illnesses were forgotten as Ed brought Larry to the bedroom and felt the press of dead minds against his own. Among the crowd of dead minds, he felt one, feminine, that seemed to call to him. It was *familiar,* like something that he'd once longed for. Ed caught a whiff of river air, thought of the presence he'd felt in the alcove as Larry spilled his guts.

He sat on the side of the bed, watching Larry.

And as the clock of a distant church struck five, Larry was still. Leaning close, Ed saw that he still breathed.

Larry's mouth moved, slightly.

Ed tried to make out if he said anything intelligible. The words he murmured had a meter; he could make out that much. Then Larry enunciated more clearly.

It sounded like an old form of German. Not modern. Middle High? Gothic? Where the hell could Larry have picked that up? Larry muttered then in something that could have been Old French.

No! thought Ed. *I'm not going to entertain so stupid an idea. I'm not. And even if he is speaking some kind of Old German or French, that proves nothing. It proves abso-fucking-lutely nothing.*

Ed stood. The air felt clear—the crowd of ghosts gone. The "ghosts" had just been Ed picking up on Larry's weird vibe. Now that Larry was asleep, the weirdness was gone. Period.

Ed thought, against all propriety, to go to Larry's medicine cabinet and see if there were any prescription bottles on the shelves. Or maybe in the trash. Then he'd go to the library, pull the *Physician's Desk Reference,* and . . .

Larry was in REM sleep.

His eyes fluttered, his lips moved, the words he spoke became more clear, though Ed could still not make them out.

And as he dreamed, Larry sank deeper into his mattress. Far deeper than a skinny kid should sink, as if all the ghosts, the aerial bodies Ed had felt in the room, had . . .

Oh, for the love of Christ, *Ed! You live in the twentieth goddamn century! Start living like it! Just put all the moldy crap you study back where it belongs! You are not Saint Thomas Bloody Aquinas, so stop thinking like him! Stop this Millennialist bullshit. . . .*

Larry fell into a deeper sleep. He relaxed. His weight redistributed. QED, Dr. Van Helsing. My anemia diagnosis stands. Could you get rid of all this garlic, please, or should I see the AMA about suing you for malpractice?

Ed left, refusing to feel helpless about a situation he knew could not exist, refusing to violate Larry's privacy. He closed the door to the apartment, checking that it locked behind him. He decided to go back to the bookstore, wait until Vicki did the six o'clock checkout, and then extract a few beers in payment out of her. As he hit the streets, night air came howling off the Charles.

A succubus, Ed. What the fuck are you thinking?

VII

Thursday, 10:30 P.M.

I *need you.*"
In deep twilight she had dreamt that the man with the noble heart had come close by. She broke out of her shell of ice, desperate for strength, desperate for the fulfillment of another lover.

She searched, found the soul she had touched the day before— that she had been on her way to take when she had found her Enemy's taunt. With true night, she left her body to find that soul, the last she would need to reach the fullness of Materiality, and so transcend it, crossing the Void. Once she had been made a thing of the Material realm, she could confront her Enemy who Possessed a Material body.

In less than one hour, she had found and bedded the lover she sought. His name was "Tim," and he was sadly and profoundly ugly.

"I need you."

She kissed her lover's mouth as he entered her.

She arched her back, pressed her torso against his, held him tight.

"I need you to be beautiful for me."

She kissed him again, and with her lips and tongue she felt the shifting of his teeth as they straightened out of their natural crookedness. He pulled away from her, but she would not let him go. His jaw broke as his teeth reconfigured themselves; she kept blood from pooling under the skin, kept his jaw from swelling.

"Be beautiful for me."

She pressed her hands against his face. Bone melted like sugar, reformed. His round, child's face took pleasing angles. He twitched as she spaced his eyes apart, moving the lobes of his brain as she did so. She changed the color of his covetous eyes from dull brown to vibrant blue—shifting the configuration of the thin proteins in his irises. His mouth was open; the snapping and shifting of his sunken ribs and sloping shoulders echoed in his esophagus and throat.

"Be strong for me."

Ribs and shoulders filled out; ligaments stretched, joints reconfigured to give weak limbs the sense of being finely toned; layers of fat compacted within the striations of muscle, creating the illusion of years of hard work or exercise. Sweet tears from his new eyes fell upon her face.

He was paralyzed, his spine stretched to give him stature. She eased him out of her, gently laid him upon his back. Enough nerves remained intact for him to do what she needed.

Before she mounted him, she ran her hand over his new face, loosening stubble from the follicles, wiping away whiskers, giving his skin newly shaven smoothness. With him inside her, she joined her vision with his, allowing him to *see* his broad-shouldered, narrow-hipped perfection, allowing him to *see* the body and beauty he had always desired.

The Succubus bathed in the warmth of his frustrated vanity until it spread as fire through her loins. She shared the fire with him. Joining her gaze with his, she drew his soul into her as she stopped his heart.

His intellect was intact in the fore of her mind. She slid off the bed and pulled from under the mattress the glossy booklet of pictures from which she had drawn her exaggerated body. The images had deeply inscribed his erotic imaginings. In the pictures, the woman she had made herself to resemble made love in various ways with the beautiful man she had recast Tim to resemble. Tapping Tim's memories, she compared her work to the images before her, to the images of Tim's desire.

She had done well.

Tim's body was bruising, the joints swelling, round like heavy fruit. Tears of blood ran from his eyes. His restructured ribs fell with the weight of his flesh. Dressing herself as the murdered girl, dressing herself in clothing, she thought a moment as to what might happen when the man Tim lived with came home.

She decided it did not matter, and went back to her own home. In her natural form, she broke apart Tim's soul and began to tremble.

The time to cross the Void had come.

VIII

Thursday, 11:52 P.M.

L awrence woke with a start, tumbled out of bed.

He kneeled, like a child saying evening prayers, pressing his face against blankets that stank of his own fear.

(*"Didn't I promise?"*

Thrusting . . . the pleasure of being entered, the soothing, gliding, wonderful pressure of his lover inside him.)

Had he dreamt it, or was it memory?

(*"Didn't I promise?"*

Lawrence purred in reply: "Yes.")

A wish? He wiped his face with a sheet smelling of fever.

(*In the midst of lovemaking, Lawrence saw through Jacob's eyes,* became *Jacob, felt as did Jacob. He saw his own sweating back and leaned forward to kiss himself. In the midst of all, he smelled earthiness, the close air of a fox's den.*

And as Jacob, inside Lawrence without protection, he knew that he'd been exposed to HIV. And he did not care that he had lied to his lover.)

No, damn it. I'm negative. I got tested. I'm okay. Lawrence stood, looked at the clock; he didn't remember coming home from work. Had he gone at all? He must have. He was dressed. His shoes were at the foot of the bed. He must have stumbled home in a fog.

He was hungry. He went to the kitchen and opened the fridge; he knew he had cheese, some bread. Baked chicken? When had he baked a chicken? It wasn't bought at a store or a barbecue place.

He closed the fridge, his hand trembling. The cold pockets of emptiness again walked through him; he couldn't eat.

He went to the living room and sat. His dream . . . the *barrage* of dreams he'd suffered, the visions of death and blindness, the tearing of his heart, the sense of drowning, the urges to suicide. . . . Was he

going mad? Was he displacing hidden grief over his father's death?
No. Perhaps . . .

He called Jacob.

"Hello . . ." The voice was not his lover's.

"Uhh . . ."

"Yes?"

"Is Jacob there?"

"Who wants to know?"

"Lawr . . . It's . . . Lawrence."

"Oh, and how *are* you?"

"I'm all right. Is this . . . Is this Roger?"

"Hmmmmm. Yes."

"Is . . . Jacob there?"

"He's out getting ice. Should I have him call you tomorrow?"

"Tomorrow" . . . the bitch . . .

"No. I'll try later."

"I *bet* you will."

With that, Roger hung up.

Roger . . . a notorious slut. Part-time street hustler. Known to go
off to New York for rough stuff in the few leather joints still open.
Known to fly into rages. Roger . . . Mr. Wrong. An integral part of
every fag's death wish.

Lawrence knew, then . . .

His dreams were born of Jacob's death wish; it called to him, part
of him wished to make it his own. Jacob was in search of the ultimate
Drama, rewriting his life as a tragedy.

Lawrence could not deny the attraction. Maybe he should give up
his fight, embrace the emptiness, and go back to Providence, to par-
ticipate in the Drama of Jacob's death as a caretaker. . . .

He tried to conceive of a way to expiate the sin of that thought
when a vein burst inside him. On the floor, bleeding through eyes
and nose, he twitched as the residue of the souls of six men and an
infant, cold pockets of emptiness, shifted and reconfigured within the
template of his spirit, his intellect, within the ghost of himself he carried as a shell within his body.

IX

Midnight

Naked, moving as mist and wind, she smoothed the snow of her rooftop as one would smooth a tablet of wax. She flowed over perfect whiteness, writing her journey, her inner configuration of souls, upon the snow. She had begun her pilgrimage from the realm of her Father, the Unbowed One, from his Kingdom in Hell that echoed the Worldly creation of God's Kingdom; *for this point of beginning* she wrote a mark in the snow. Around the mark she made an impression, rounded as if made by a sphere of glass pressed into the snow.

Her first lover—Andrew—whom she had slain with the Instability of his needs, with the longing for nurture that such Instability inspired: she had taken him in the realm of her Mother, sweet Lilith. The child, Troy, she had taken in this realm, as well—a victim of the Instability of his mother's beliefs. She made a new mark and impression above the mark of her Father's realm.

Arthur, taken in Lust; John (who forsook his name for "Spaw"), taken out of his Greed for power over women, belonged to the realms of the Shining One and of the Angel of Poison, respectively. She made two more marks, parallel, above and to either side of the mark she'd made for Lilith's realm.

Brian—taken by the Inharmony of his soul without poetry (a surrogate for the stricken man she had lost, whom she had wanted to take by releasing the Ugliness the city had placed inside him). Brian belonged to the realm of the Giver of Judgment; this mark she made between and slightly above the last two.

Frank, whom she took with Cruelty, belonged to the realm of the Fiercest in Despair. This mark she made above and to the left of the Giver of Judgment's.

Tim had died for the Apathy he held for his own flesh. Parallel to the mark of the Fiercest in Despair, she invested Tim with the mark of the Adversary, the Giver of Knowledge.

And there, she left the wind and collected herself in flesh.

And there, in flesh, she broke apart Tim and took him into herself, making her configuration complete, attaining True Flesh for the first time, crossing the Void to a Materiality of her own.

Like widening rings in a pond, her awareness reached outward.

The crystal of the snow around her crashed, shattered, became a wall of surging cataract. In a state of nonbeing—yet still intangibly one with her body—she was crushed, burned, her ashes scattered. A roll of thunder fell upon her like a great stone. A rain of burning metal, shifting, colors like a thin layer of oil upon windswept water, fell upon her. Ice the color of lightning became her blood; receding lights of red and green entwined with her flesh. The bite of strong wine spread beneath her skin. Her spine became a sword. Her teeth melted and ran like wax.

She crossed a chasm of burning Ignorance, upon a bridge made of hair.

She drew into herself a *spark* that had, once before, been hers—the spark invested by God in the body she had once occupied in fleshy life.

She looked out across the rooftop, toward the hill she had seen upon the first dawn of her pilgrimage, to the River that connected to the sea that had caught her upon her fall. Knowing that she had lived before—having now earned the devastating knowledge that her Father had intended her to earn—she pulled the Divine Spark she had stolen close to her heart.

Once mortal . . .

Once living . . .

She now moved as one partly resurrected, transcendent, her very existence a profound blasphemy, a mockery of those Saved Dead who will walk in Flesh at the End of Time. As one Damned, she had stolen back her Grace.

Burning, an angel newly terrifying, foretold by no prophecy, she saw around her the influence of the Enfolded One as a raging sea washing through the city, stronger than she had ever seen It before. Or, perhaps she saw It now with stronger sight than she had possessed before. Burning, with her shining trophy nestled by her heart, she drove her newly tempered Will into that sea.

She found Paul, the Widow's Son, whose soul had been nurtured by birds.

She touched his entrapped soul; doing so was like thrusting her hand in a furnace to touch a nugget of gold. She withdrew. On her knees, thanking her Father, she pledged to cheat the Enfolded One of Its trophy as a minister of Stolen Grace.

PART FIVE

Towards Bethlehem to Be Born

D *eep Winter Morning.*

He feels the warm body next to his. Even in sleep, he knows no respite from the need to obliterate his deepest sense of self, for his breathing is synchronized with hers.

Aware, he watches himself, distant, mourning, remembering whom he has forgotten. He sees the roiling of alien dreams in his mind, the lies he has told himself to keep those dreams in check. Victim of opposing and concurrent wills, Paul haunted himself, a splinter of himself looking down, as the dead are said to look upon their bodies before rising. He can heed no such call now.

His mind shifts to a level of dreaming closer to wakefulness. He is pulled back toward himself, to the cold filth of his ruined intellect. The voices begin, and had he the physicality, he would weep.

He is not yet completely sundered by the voices as he comes partly awake. He rolls on his back, and through half-closed eyes, with a mind only partly imprisoned, he sees a small miracle announce itself.

A fiery small creature, hovering on wings beating impossibly fast. A living thing crafted with God's most profound Love, that proves the magnificence of the Will that had thought Creation. The creature once meant more to him, though, as a talisman of an earthly love that has been lost.

The creature is an intrusion, *pushing aside his wretchedness, reminding him of a past before his fall to irredemption.*

He drifts to painful waking, the sane scrap of his awareness drawn into the noise of alien thought.

Paul awoke, next to Catherine.

Why had he dreamt of a hummingbird?

The dream had been an ugly thing, pressed with cold fingers into his mind. He was about to wake Catherine for a bout of dysfunctional lovemaking when a shadow moved in the hallway.

He stood, naked, ready to defend Catherine and her lovely pale thinness from any NIGGER that might have broken in. NIGGER Santa was about to get a surprise. . . .

He followed the shadow to the living room, where it resolved itself as nothing, joining the shadows of branches that crossed themselves upon the hardwood floor. He looked to the windows, saw the sun coloring the sky of this, the day before Christmas. There was a scent in the air, one that should have given him comfort, yet which instead filled him with a profound guilt.

He dressed, left Catherine, walked home in the light of the rising sun.

Chapter One

I

Monday, December 24, 1990. 7:11 A.M.

A ngel of Death, she has marked him through the senility of his
Possession, through the mumbling of his shattered mind. Holding the spark of Creation she had stolen from the Forge of God, she
followed him.

In breaking daylight, as the east blushed rose while the rest of
heaven was still adorned in blue, she who had lived before followed
the tool of her Enemy. She had given herself to his Salvation as a
bride gives herself to her groom. His memories, his dreams snuffed
by the Blind Dragon . . . she had tended them from afar, ignited
them softly, like the wick of a candle, that she might curse the darkness in his heart.

Paul walked streets that had informed his mind in childhood. She
thrust a thread of her awareness into a cardinal singing in a tree
some blocks distant. She willed it to alight upon a branch before
Paul, to sing its magnificent song. From behind, blocks distant, she
saw his shoulders stoop, saw him hang his head in shame.

Paul turned; she thought he might recognize her and her mask.
He walked a few steps, then turned right— toward a sanctified structure she smelled, that she felt upon her skin, soft as the wing of a
moth.

She followed, sensing the nature of the comfort he sought, sensing that each drop of his blood trembled with fear, with shame, with
the longing for assoilment.

Paul entered the church, running to the great arched door the way
a child will run to his mother's hem. In the house of one of her Enemies, the Enemy she sought to confront would be weakened. She
left Paul there; soon she could grant him her Beatitude.

II

Monday, 7:35 A.M.

The quiet terrified him, filled him with the weight of grief. The quiet had a rhythm; it shifted, it moved as does the seam of a cloud. It stammered the truth he could not bear to hear.

Paul looked toward the font where he had been christened. The stations of the cross were images with less meaning than placards seen out of the corner of the eye. He knew they should mean more to him.

He went to a bénitier, dipped his fingers in cool holy water. He thought of holding a sword, of being hurt by holding the haft. A memory? His fingertips itched, as if he'd touched a poisonous plant; his forehead itched from where he had touched it with holy water to—

"Can I help you, son?"

Paul turned to see a young priest—thankfully, not one he knew.

"Mass isn't until eight," said the priest, not unpleasantly. Paul winced.

"I need to confess," said Paul. He carried the weight of sin, but not the memory. "Badly. I need to confess."

The priest, not yet forty, frowned. He was not jaded enough to tell Paul to wait until after mass, or to come back at a regular hour. Paul smelled the ever-present priest smell of strong coffee and morning cigarettes on his breath.

"Aahhhhh. Come this way."

He led Paul to the confessional. Paul entered the right-hand booth. The panel slid open; even through the grate, Paul could smell coffee and cigarettes. And cologne?

"Forgive me, Father, for I have sinned. It has been . . . a year? A *year*, since my last confession."

"Yes, my son?"

"I have . . ."

(Not cologne . . . booze.)

". . . disgraced myself before God."

(Not that what I've done is half as disgraceful as a drunk priest.)

The priest took a deep breath. His stink came through the grate as he exhaled. "It is in God's power to forgive us all."

Paul shifted, undid his overcoat in the midst of the fever flush that had taken him. The weight of sin hurt to carry. Yet he could not articulate his sin, and so be granted forgiveness from God.

(How does God forgive a stupid MICK priest who boozes before breakfast?)

"I have broken a commandment." Yes, Paul must have broken a commandment to feel so wretched, to have a soul so grievously injured.

"There is a New Covenant with God."

"Yes, but I . . ."

(. . . WAS DOING GOD'S WORK.)

Paul pressed his hands against his temples, forced fingers into his flesh. Memories of blood, a woman's hair on his feet. Wetness. Crunching bone.

High notes came from close by the altar: the organist practicing. Paul felt the vibration through the confessional. The notes conflicted with the words pressing into Paul's thoughts. He had done God's work. He'd done what was right. He just wished to be free of the weight he carried.

"But I am *not* truly sorry for what I have done."

"Then . . . then I cannot grant you absolution."

(*Ego te absolvo . . .*

. . . ego te . . .

WHERE DO YOU GET THE

EGO TO JUDGE US?)

Paul smelled Catherine's perfume, her femininity, clinging to him. He wanted the obliteration of his sense of self. *That* was the absolution he sought, the contrition he needed to enact.

The venomous itch he'd had on his fingertips as he placed them in the stone cup of piss-water by the door was now on his face, in his mouth, in his lungs, along his limbs and torso. His throat felt swollen with poison, closing up. If he regretted what he had done so righteously, he could be free of it, be free of the poison.

"I . . . want to . . .

(. . . MAKE YOU SORRY, YOU DRUNK DUMB MICK!)

. . . *be* sorry."

Paul put his hand on the grate. It was made of cheap wood, like rattan. He could punch through it and grab the faceless bastard passing judgment on him in his comfortable darkness.

(DUMB DRUNK MICK! DUMB DRUNK!

DRUNK DUMB!)

The organist continued practicing. Paul heard footsteps. The congregation? No, too early. The choir. Yes. The choir coming to warm up.

"If you want to be sorry, then you already are sorry, but can't say so to yourself."

Sorry . . . for so much blood? Am I sorry?

The organist stopped. Muffled voices drifted from outside the booth. Paul heard greetings, rounds of "Merry Christmas." One voice rose above the others. The choirmaster, directing, shouting orders with a tone of good humor.

(It's wrong.)   *(It's wrong.)*

"I don't know how many selves I have."

Paul pressed harder on the grate It creaked. Fluttering sounds from the main chapel: pages being ruffled.

The priest coughed, stammered.

"I don't . . . I don't really know what you mean."

(YOU WILL.)

(It's wrong.)

Paul pulled his hand away from the grate as if it were burning hot.

"Neither do I," said Paul, and left the booth.

In the brighter light of the church, Paul blinked as he pulled his overcoat closed. A few members of the choir glanced his way. Paul walked to the side door. The priest stepped out of the confessional just as the choirmaster played a single note on his pitch pipe.

The choir broke out in *Adeste Fideles.*

Harmony hurt Paul more than had the silence.

He passed the bénitier, pushed against the door, grinding his teeth; his molars felt as if they would crack. The priest was two steps behind. Outside intruded on his senses as he crossed the church threshold.

Paul turned on his heel, raised his hand.

"No, Father," was all he said.

It was enough.

The priest stood in the cold, his breath misting in the air. Paul walked on.

At home, Paul wondered if he could have done what the voices had impelled him to do with his bare hands.

III

Monday, 11:35 A.M.

Lawrence stared at the ceiling, wondering how he was going to pay next month's rent.

A few nights before, he'd awoken in a pool of blood. He'd run to the mirror, seen the mask of dried brown. He gingerly touched his nose, to see if he'd tripped and broken it. Nothing. He moved it side to side. The lack of pain terrified him.

He called a cab, went to the emergency room, was warehoused in a locker of human suffering. Gunshot wounds went past. A thin old man, mostly naked, mostly blue, was pushed in by firemen. A girl about his age came in with a grouchy bastard yelling at her for cutting her finger. She sat and held up her hand—bandaged in a dish towel—as if trying to get a teacher's attention. Her blue eyes were full of tears. She shifted her weight, and Lawrence saw she was pregnant. A guy of about thirty sat near, his jaw swollen, mouth stuffed with cotton. A beer mug in his hand was full of melting ice; in the ice were four bloody-white nuggets: the man's teeth.

He'd been there three hours, was about to leave, when a nurse called him to an examining room. A doctor not much older than he came and shone a flashlight in his eyes, looked in his ears, looked at his nose.

"Nothing's wrong that I can see."

He called in the eye, ear, nose, and throat specialist.

He found nothing wrong. Lawrence looked at the clock; he had to be at work in five and a half hours. An hour after that, he was told that he should come in for a CAT scan.

"How much is that?"

"Your insurance should cover it."

"I don't *have* any insurance!"

The doctor gave him a look, as if Lawrence had just admitted that he was illiterate.

"Oh, then I guess we should just watch and wait."

Yeah, I'll just keep you on retainer. Or, how about I work as your caddie, and if I start bleeding on the green, you take care of me then?

Lawrence went home, called another hospital's "Dial-a-Nurse" service.

"Well," said the nurse. "It could just be broken blood vessels. But these really are emergent symptoms, and you should come to the emergency room. . . ."

Today, Lawrence had gotten the hospital bill: three-hundred and thirty bucks. To have the specialist look him over had cost extra.

"Merry Fucking Christmas."

He had a few weeks to pay. But Tom's theft had damaged his finances much more than he had imagined. To use the insurance money from Dad . . .

He didn't want to. He could, but didn't want to. The worry about money was a sour feeling, collecting in the pit of his stomach, as was the worry that the bloody nose was something more serious than broken blood vessels. (*Had* he bled from his eyes? *Had* the blood over his face only come from his nose?)

The trip to the hospital had marked him with bad dreams. Amid the jumble Lawrence remembered was a terror of being under the hospital lights, the sense of probings in his chest, of his heart being squeezed by a cold fist. The terror gave way to a hopeless, soul-killing ache as the harsh hospital light gave way to darkness, soon eclipsed by bloody red.

Lawrence got out of bed, finished dressing. He had today off. Maybe if he stopped by the store, business would have picked up enough that Jack would let him work extra hours. Maybe . . . The store had been a tomb. Vicki, who'd worked for Jack longer than any human being on record, had gotten as her Christmas bonus a discount coupon for a steak house she couldn't get to without a car. Yesterday, she'd waved the offending coupon at Groucho, who took swipes at it. "Merry Fucking Christmas!" she'd yelled, as Groucho finally shredded it. Lawrence also had to worry about whether or not *Vicki*, not just Jack, would let him work. She'd been seeing to it that Lawrence had nothing to do, not even checking stock. When Lawrence did something on his own initiative, she'd chewed him out mildly, pulling rank as assistant manager.

Lawrence had just put on his "Christmas lumberjack shirt," an Eddie Bauer flannel of red and green plaid, when the phone rang.

Lawrence picked up—expecting it to be Vicki—and regretted not letting the machine answer as he heard, amid the telephone static, the clang of dishes and pots and barking, familiar voices.

Angie shrieked, *"God damn it, Lawrence, where are you? Mother is worried SICK!"*

IV

Monday, 12:44 P.M.

Ed Sloane walked his memory palace. His physical self rode the bus from Cambridge over the Harvard Bridge. In his hand, unseen, were the index cards that he used to write notes for his thesis. He conscripted the information from the cards into images in his palace.

In a new alcove, he imagined a woman standing by an open chest. An iron bar had been used to force the chest, the lock of which was broken; the woman held a dove close to her face.

Pandora, holding the last occupant of her Box of Curses (though, in fact, it had been an urn): Hope. The box had been pried *open.* . . .

The question Ed wished to pose, represented by this imagining—"Is Hope a deadly sin? All deadly sins are based upon pride, *and is it not prideful to assume Hope is granted from on High as a beneficent act?"*

Oh, Tomassetti's gonna love that one.

His awareness still in the compartments of his intellect, Ed remembered to breathe. He continued his masonry of thought.

He tried to make the face of Pandora that of the woman who had played Ophelia in Olivier's Hamlet. *But her face shifted to that of Amelia, filling him with shame and remorse.*

He turned to the next alcove.

Here, a carved figure of Eve as depicted upon Cathedral bas reliefs. She stood before a mirror, in which was reflected Mother Mary. Beside this tableau stood Pandora again, this time before a mirror that reflected nothing.

If Eva *could be reversed, redeemed and made* Ave, *how do you redeem Pandora, the woman created as "the gift to all?"*

Ed wished he knew how to answer that question.

The bus rocked; he withdrew from his memory palace, looked out the window, pulled the stop cord. Getting off, he grabbed the bag he'd put on the seat next to him, then walked the half block to the bookstore. There, he found Vicki brushing Groucho, who had perched by the register. Tufts of cat hair littered the counter. Beside the piles lay a red-and-white Santa hat.

"Hey," she said.

"Hey. What's with the hat?"

"I was wearing it, until I realized how stupid I felt. No one's here."

"Merry Fucking Christmas."

"Brush Groucho for a second."

Ed took the brush. Vicki reached for a bag on the chair; it was from the pet store across the street.

As Ed brushed, Vicki pulled from the bag a small pair of felt antlers joined by a length of elastic. She slipped them on Groucho's head while Ed brushed her butt. As soon as Ed stopped brushing, Groucho batted off the antlers, then scampered away.

"Worth a shot," she said, pulling tufts from Groucho's brush.

Ed picked up the Santa hat.

"No one's here?"

"No."

Ed put on the hat.

Vicki said, "Something's missing," then patted tufts of cat hair onto Ed's face. His facial stubble held the tufts like thistle burrs; they fell off as he smiled.

"Worth a shot," she said.

"Yeah." Ed reached into his bag, pulled out a bottle of wine festooned with a ribbon. "Merry Christmas."

Ed thought Vicki blushed.

"Thanks." She looked at the label, gave it a long appraisal. "I wish I knew *dick* about wine, so I could be impressed."

"If you knew *dick* about wine, you wouldn't be impressed. I just happen to like it."

"Good enough for me."

She reached across the counter, her sweater clinging most agreeably, took the hat from Ed's head and put it on herself. Then she reached under the counter and gave Ed what had to be a videotape, wrapped in green foil paper.

"Merry Christmas."

"It'd better not be a fob for my watch, because I sold it to buy you a brush."

"I know that story. It's the first recorded 'Merry Fucking Christmas.' "

"I think the first recorded 'Merry Fucking Christmas' was when Saint Nicholas found three kids chopped to pieces in a tub of brine."

"Stop one-upping me, Sloane, and open your damned present."

Ed pulled off the wrapping. It was a noncommercial VHS tape. The label pasted on the side read, in handwritten green and red letters (with a tiny sticker of mistletoe, to boot), KISS ME DEADLY.

"Is this . . . is this the movie where they change everything from the book, and have Mike Hammer chasing down a box of isotopes, instead of dope? The one with Ralph Meeker and the guy who played Dr. Cyclops?"

From under the stupid hat, Vicki flashed a pretty smile.

"Yeah. That's the one."

"I *love* this movie! How'd you get it?"

"My cousin has cable. I had him tape it for me off one of the classic movie channels. I saw the listing in the paper and thought of you."

"Oh, jeez, Vicki. Thanks!"

"Don't mention it."

Ed almost leaned over the counter and kissed her. Instead he reached into the bag and said, "*This* is for the hardest-working employee in the store."

He set a can of tuna, decorated with a ribbon, on the counter.

"She'll love it. Ahhh, did you get anything for . . . Larry?"

"No. I kind of felt weird. I don't know the guy."

Vicki shrugged. "Maybe you got to know him too well, acting as his impromptu shrink?"

"Yeah. Maybe."

"So, what're you doing for Christmas Eve?"

"I don't know."

"You don't know?"

"I kind of hate Christmas."

"This makes you special? Just go check out the horror section. It's the only thing we've been selling. What're you doing tonight?"

"I was going to stay home. I got the place to myself. I was hoping to enjoy the quiet, then go to the corner bar and tip a few."

Vicki dropped her shoulders, then gave Ed the kind of look one would give an eight-year-old caught in a transparent lie. "And that's it?"

"Yeah."

"Did you ever see the *Happy Days* when Fonzie spent Christmas Eve alone, eating ravioli from a can?"

"And Richie Cunningham got him to spend Christmas over at his place? No, I can't say I ever saw that episode."

Vicki reached over the counter and punched him in the shoulder. Her small fist was strong; it *hurt*. If the blow had hit him in the mouth, he'd have lost a tooth. The dumb Santa hat fell off her head.

"Don't be an aaasshole, Sloane! Why don'tcha come to my Mahm's house with me?" Vicki slipped into a heavy Boston drawl, then dropped it, just as quickly. "There's going to be an incredible spread. Eggnog. Booze. A fire. C'mon. Don't pull a Fonzie on me. You *know* how my mom cooks."

Ed drummed his fingers on the counter. His shoulder throbbed.

"Okay, okay! I'll come."

"Ahhhmmm . . . What *I* should say now is 'You're welcome.' Maybe you should have said something *before* that? I'm not certain. Can you help me on this one?"

"How about 'Thanks'?"

"Ooooooh! You're good, Sloane. That grad school stuff is working wonders on you."

"It was either that, or 'Does your mom have a fireplace?' You said there'd be a *fire,* I just wanted to make sure . . ."

"Yes, my mom has a fireplace. No chimney, though."

"Good. Seriously, though. Please promise me there'll be no group viewing of *It's a Wonderful Life?* I'm so sick of that movie."

"No promises. But if an aunt or a cousin turns it on, you're not required to watch. We can go on the back porch and drink beer. My uncle Al always brings sparklers and firecrackers. We can set some off."

"Fair enough."

"Come back here at six-thirty. That's when I'll close up. I want to make sure Groucho has enough dry food and water to get her through to the day after tomorrow."

"All right. Six-thirty. How'll we get there?"

"We can take the subway. I'm a cheap date."

"Uhhh . . . How about if I bring cab fare?"

"If you want to be chivalrous, sure."

"Uhhh . . . Okay."

The day was dying when he left the store; the sun was low over the bridge crossing the Mass Pike at the end of Newbury, looking as it does in black-and-white photos. Fashionably dispossessed twenty-somethings shuffled along Mass Ave., all in black, of course, all broken-looking in some way. Ed became aware of how he himself must have looked, should anyone take note of him.

Then Ed retraced the route he'd taken a few days before, knowing that unless he checked on Larry, he might incur another burden born of moral paralysis to bear along with his betrayal of Amelia.

V

Monday, 3:16 P.M.

sound cut the air. Lawrence started.

He'd never heard it before. He leaned back in his chair, heart pounding against his chest. The hospital bill fell from his hands to the floor. He had been staring at it, worrying. That must have been *hours* ago, judging by the light. Had he an awareness of *lyrics* in his head? As if he'd been in one of the Portuguese neighborhoods in Providence, hearing pop songs in a language he didn't know, yet which had stuck in his mind?

What *was* that sound, the smoke detector?

It screeched again. He whipped his head to the left. It was the buzzer by his apartment door. He went to the panel, pressed the talk button. "Y-yeah?"

The voice from the primitive speaker was like that of astronauts radioing from the moon. *"Larry?"*

"Ed?"

Silence from the speaker; Lawrence took his thumb off the talk button.

". . . ing through the neighborhood. Thought I'd stop by and see how you were doing."

"Uh . . . Come on up. I'm in apartment ten-oh-five."

Lawrence hit an unlabeled red button on the panel; he hoped it worked.

He went to the mirror in the bathroom, smoothed out his hair. He felt drunk with depression about his money, about going to Providence, about . . .

A knock at the door.

Lawrence answered. "Hey, Ed!"

Ed looked, for just a moment, like an animal who did not want to enter a place where it suspected a trap. He crossed the threshold and seemed to sag, as if a new weight of fear had been placed on his shoulders. Lawrence was about to ask him if he was sick when Ed said, "I just wanted to see how you were doing."

"I'm . . . I'm *fine*. Thanks. I . . ."

Lawrence turned his gaze downward, trying not to give Ed any indication of what he felt, or *why* he felt what he did. Still gazing downward, he stepped around Ed and shut the door.

"Don't be a jerk," said Ed. "You're *not* fine."

"Yeah. I'm not." Lawrence still cast his gaze downward, then lifted it suddenly. "How'd you know where I lived?"

Ed seemed afraid, as if the trap had been sprung.

"Vicki told me."

Lawrence knew there was more to it than that, but didn't pursue it. He needed whatever comfort and company he could get, even if it was from a man whom he wanted, and whom he'd never have. Ed and he stood where Tom and Lawrence had tumbled across the threshold, kissing. Lawrence, not welcoming the irony, stepped to the living room.

Ed said to his back, "So, what *is* up with you?"

Lawrence fell back into the chair, too depressed to say anything that meant anything.

Ed stood in front of Lawrence, unzipped his leather jacket, shifted nervously as he said, "No offense, but you look . . ."

Ed's gaze went down. Quickly, he reached for the bill where Lawrence had dropped it.

"You went to a doctor?"

And as soon as he said that, Lawrence could tell that Ed regretted even so inadvertent an invasion of privacy.

Lawrence nodded, held out his hand for Ed to give him the bill. "Yeah. I went to the emergency room. I had . . . I had a . . ."

"You don't have to tell me."

Lawrence *wanted* to tell him. Wanted to tell him, *Maybe I have a tumor, and I'm scared to death, and would you please hold me and make the fear go away?*

"I'm okay," he lied. "The doctor said I should come back for more tests." A half-truth.

Ed pulled at his sweater collar. He didn't believe Lawrence, that was plain. But he accepted what he said as true enough. Ed looked in pain, as if the air of the apartment hurt to breathe, as if he had a stabbing headache that faded as soon as he felt it. He reached into his jacket and pulled out a pack of cloves. "D'you mind?" asked Ed.

"No."

Ed lit up and said, "There's something else, maybe?"

The sweet smoke was relaxing. Lawrence let go, as much as he dared, and told him *minimally* about the emotional blackmail of going back to Providence, about his money trouble after the hospital visit.

"And I don't have enough cash to get a round-trip ticket and be able to eat the rest of the week." As Lawrence stopped speaking, he sighed. To unload, even just this bit, was like pulling a splinter from his psyche.

"I got money," said Ed. "But are you sure it's *good* for you to go to Providence? Y'know, mentally?"

How did Ed know that his family was that fucked? Lawrence hadn't told him just how *truly bad* things were at home.

"I kind of *have* to go."

"Because of the thing with your father's death, right?"

Ed blew out a puff of smoke. Lawrence was about to ask him how the hell he could have known about his father and all the attendant grief of his death when, refracted by the dying winter sun, Lawrence thought he saw two grey faces drifting, contorting, stretching in the dissipating smoke. He grabbed his head, felt something painful, cold, and empty shifting inside him—something he'd felt before, maybe in a dream. The feeling passed as quickly as it had come.

"You okay, Larry?"

"Yeah. I'm fine."

Ed knelt by Lawrence's chair. The Drama Queen in Lawrence thought how much this was like Ed getting down on his knees to propose.

"Look, I got about a hundred bucks in my pocket. You can have it. That'll cover a round-trip to Providence, easy, and it should even cover cab fare back to Boston if you're completely trapped, or if you want to get the fuck out of the house and check into a motel. Pay me back whenever."

Ed pulled out the money, and the little suppressed Drama Queen whispered that this was a bit like having Richard Gere come to save him, come to take him away and take care of him.

Lawrence took the money, smiled.

"Merry Fucking Christmas," he said.

Ed laughed.

"Merry Fucking Christmas."

VI

Monday, 4:16 P.M.

Twilight came, invading the streets.

The Succubus prayed, for strength, for purpose, for resolve. Her voice sounded as chimes, as church bells, as wind. None living could hear her. Her voice, nonphysical, informed by the burning spark inside her, echoed off the coping she knelt against as she would kneel against an altar. An hour before, her meditation had been broken by a voice that might have been a phantasm, a longing made into figment, a pressing upon her senses. The voice *could* have been that of the man with the noble heart, lost to her on the bridge, now impossibly close. She could not be distracted by such longing, and fell upon her knees, calling to her Father.

She prayed in the advancing night.

And as daylight faded, her prayer was answered with a vision. The burning violet of dusk changed, as if each particle of light shifted in unison, reflecting bands of a spectrum that had yet to touch the Earth. The sun became the color of claret, and she was aware of the red sun not low in the east, but high overhead, as at noon.

She felt the awful weight of her Father's Will. She was surrounded by Revelation, a Benediction lifted above the desolation of Damnation for her, her Father's nation, to see. The Revelation was a covenant—a promise of what he would forge once she had completed her pilgrimage in his Name. Gaze low, seeing nothing but the brick coping before her in the new light, she looked up slowly, as a visionary would, expecting to see the face of Him who had been the Focus of her ecstatic desires.

The building, the coping, the city faded to wind. She was presented with her Father's Triumph: his victory after long centuries; the end of the Exile inflicted upon him for his refusal to exist as a slave. She saw the fruition of what her Father had begun in the initial heartbeats of created history.

She saw the *End* of history, a history so often and so rudely violated by the Tyrant with His petty and miraculous intrusions. This was the End that brought no Rapture, no irenic apocalypse, no grand and pompous display of destruction. There was just the Earth, enduring and enduring, holding air that had been breathed by the shuffling trillions who had walked her surface. The stars shone through the indigo of noon sky, the moon reflected the red of the cooling sun. Everywhere is the beauty of despair, the terror of the omnipresent sublime. All the patient, suffering Earth has mellowed, all the rough edges of stone have been worn smooth by rainstorms and seasons without number.

This is her Father's realm, the realm he had first sought to create before the Earth had cooled. Under this dim and dying sun, humanity endured, her Father husbanding their souls that shall never be resurrected, drawing all humanity to the loveliness of his aesthetic despair. And with the strength that possession of these innumerable melancholy souls would grant him, her sweet Father would thread other suns into rosaries of blasphemy, passing them through his fingers as he rewrote the song the Tyrant had denied him.

In the vision, she stands upon the still waters of a lake, its waters reflecting colors that did not exist in the world where she had begun her pilgrimage. This is Boston, her realm within her Father's realm, after the waters of the River, so full of anxious worry, so full of the city's pain, have long overflowed their banks—part of her Father's victory. The lake bleeds into the still sea without interruption. She can see this through the ancient light, across the darkened miles. The Hill upon which she had seen her first dawn is now but an islet on the lake. The weak and silent sun can now no longer reveal its voice upon its rounded peak. The towers of Boston are gone. Beneath her— preserved under icy fathoms— are the streets of Boston, carpeted with silt full of the pain that informed the waters over millennia. The City endures under the lake, counterpoint to the City that existed agelessly under the burning waters of the Dead Sea, counterpoint to the other City near the Dead Sea where her Father's Enemies had dwelled.

Her Father's victory, over the Tyrant.

In a world where so few lived—where the fires of reckless passion could not be kindled within those who live under a cooling sun—the Enfolded One could not reign, could not contaminate the still and lonely beauty of this still and lonely existence. She looked to the moon, so close, so visible next to the red sun overhead, and she knew the Blind Dragon would be imprisoned forever before the bloodglow of the moon's face.

A cold wind came across the lake, making the surface tremble, making her heart tremble. The vision faded while the wind endured. As the coping and brick resolved in her sight, the beauty of the vision endured in her heart, then faded with the wind.

The Succubus stood, so achingly lovely in the translucent light that she acquired a light of her own, soft as that of a candle. She looked upon her City; the Enfolded One raged amid the frenzy of war, amid the contortion of spirits driven by panic and blind fear and emotional blight. She dressed in darkness, then walked to the recession of her rooftop. This night, which she had chosen for her battle, she would not drop to the alley below. She would fall, willfully and pridefully, in the manner in which her Father had fallen. Near the ground, she arced slowly and set herself upon her feet so lightly that the snow and gravel did not yield to her weight.

Stars revealed themselves to her as she walked the City, seeking her Enemy. They, too, would belong to her Father.

VII

Monday, 5:32 P.M.

Paul ran, bloody hands held before him.

He had punched and punched and punched the kid, while a group of bystanders watched, transfixed, feeding him. They would have done nothing until the boy was dead. Then still perhaps, they would have done nothing.

Paul had bumped into the kid near Copley Place. He had wrapped himself in the psychic and physical labyrinths of the city, trying to find an inner safety, trying to find comfort. But there was the feeling that he was being watched, and the sense that he had forgotten something profoundly important. He went from restaurant to restaurant, having cups of bland and overpriced coffee, then from bar to bar, having glasses of beer

(MADE THE AMERICAN WAY), one after the other. But the places were achingly empty. Crowds were gathering at the shopping complexes; he sensed how in pain and panicked they would be. He left his beer unfinished and went to Copley, to the temple of frenzy.

At the entrance of the complex, on a small plaza of brick, he saw a kid, no more than five-six, peering at the headline of the *Boston Globe* displayed in a newspaper vending machine. He stuck his skinny ass out into the paths of those on the sidewalk as he read. Paul passed near enough to hear the kid say: *"Fucking war."*

Paul grabbed the kid by the shoulders and pulled him away from the vending machine. The kid wore glasses: the red and green and blue lights of the complex reflected in the lenses. Paul saw himself in the lenses, then batted the glasses off the kid's face with a slap.

He felt a crowd gathering at his back, felt the comfort of others, felt the empowerment they gave him with their passive collective gaze. Paul said through clenched teeth: "Wha'd you say?"

"Nothing."

"You got something against freedom? You got something against our protecting human rights?"

"No."

The kid's teeth would have cut Paul's knuckles to the bone had he not been wearing gloves. The crowd gathered, became thicker around Paul and his victim. He was about to smash the kid's head through the vending machine when something *like* conscience touched him, when a thought not his own entered his mind and quieted his rage. He heard something like birdsong—the kind one hears in summer twilight, during long dusks.

He dropped the kid to the snow, where he covered his ruined face and sobbed. Paul looked to the crowd. They were one being, made suddenly silent, watching . . . *part* of him. When he ran, they did not block him. None followed. Blocks away, he cast aside his bloody gloves; his hands were bloody beneath them. He walked a few blocks; the cold air had made his lungs raw as he ran. He took to side streets, caught a bus that dropped him near the apartment, then ran again.

His hands ached as he turned the key in the lock. He slammed the door behind him, threw bolts, put on the chain. He pulled off his overcoat, let it drop, threw his jacket, his tie, his shirt on the chair Jo had salvaged from her parents' house. He stumbled to the kitchen and washed his hands, letting the blood flow onto the white enamel. He cleaned the cuts with mild soap.

Movement, behind him. He turned quickly, walked to the doorway, hands still wet—the water still running. He hoped that the police had found him, that they had traced him, had come to punish him. Nothing. Nothing there at all. He returned to the sink, washed his hands again, then put ice on the swollen knuckles. In the bathroom, he put disinfectant on the cuts, bandaged the deeper ones. He went to the hall closet and pulled down a comfortable sweater. He had the sense that Jo's pile of linens had been knocked askew, and wondered if he had disturbed her stuff while in one of his . . .

The voices echoed in the distance, coming closer. The silence of the apartment filled him with dread. His mind longed for the press of the voices in his mind. He craved obliteration and the pain of nonbeing. Night called him. The bars would be full of the dispossessed this night, full of the unwanted who would not be missed.

(THEIR LIVES WOULD NOT BE MISSED.)

It would be easy to find a lonely person this night

(FIND 'EM, FUCK 'EM UP!)

and bring them here. Oh, the work he could do. The peace he'd find in their suffering. The twitching began in his heart. Maybe . . . maybe

the *greatest* peace could be found with Catherine. Could be found in the taking of her life.
(TAKE BACK THE LIFE THE SLUTBITCH TOOK FROM YOU! SLUTBITCH HAS BEEN FEEDING ON YOU!)
                                                                    It's wrong.
(TAKE BACK! MAKE HER TAKE BACK ALL THE SHIT THAT SLUTBITCH HAS SAID TO YOU!)
                                          It's wrong.
      (TAKE BACK! PAY BACK!)
   Paul gripped the closet doorknob. It was glass, multifaceted. He pulled it from the dingy brass grip.
   (It's wrong. You killed him, Paul. You killed him. It's wrong.)
   Could he cut his way to freedom through his own flesh? Could he find peace by gashing artery and vein? Would he carry the filth and the guilt of all he'd done with him into death?
      (CUT THAT CUNT FOR WHAT SHE DID TO YOU!)
   It's wrong.
   Without his will, his hand brought the glass to his eye and he peered through it.
   Fractured sight. To see so much in so many ways *yet with one vision*. Facets upon facets, refracting so many images. He turned away from the closet, looked at the living room. The fractured sight made it tolerable to see what he would have seen with the painful sight of being *one*. He, himself, felt wonderfully shattered.
   Paul sighed. Breath rattled in his chest. He began to hyperventilate. The peace of being shattered called to him.
CHANTING VOICES
                  CHANTING VOICES
                               CHANTING VOICES
   . . . piled in his mind. They compressed and expanded and did not impel him to violence, but gave hint of peace born of shrieking discord. Shattered hearing, with shattered vision and thought. With no scrap of the hated self.
   The way to such freedom was to cut himself out of his body. He would be shattered. He would be broken into fragments, like brittle clay thrown against stone.
   He pulled away the glass. He realized he'd fallen to his knees. He knew what he had to do. He'd smash the glass knob and cut his way to obliteration, become one with the voices, feel their weight in every aspect of his being.
   From his knees, he was about to crawl to the tub and smash the glass against it . . .

. . . when silence intruded.

The silence gave him peace, filled him with a sense of the Beautiful he felt in his tortured soul.

A scent came to him, a scent that had once filled him with a deep and profound love, a scent that he had last known the worst, most painful night of his life.

Tears filled his sight.

A shadow fell upon him.

"Paul."

VIII

Night

The iron bars passed through her and she forced her scream through the metal. The metal sang and creaked, as it did for short moments in spring while the ground around it thawed and the metal settled upon the shifting earth.

The iron contorted her scream until it became like the grinding of rusted hinges meshed with the sound of soft crying.

Am I whole? O my Father, help me. Am I whole?

Trembling, she looked down toward the spiked bars of the great iron fence that she'd forced through herself. The cold iron had bled away the poison within her. The poison ran into the soil; she saw it flow as a spilled liquor of green fire into the ground that still held a residual trace of sanctity, saw it flutter to nothingness and evaporate. Her hands, blood-red, hung toward the ground. She wondered when she had lost her human form.

She pulled herself from the bars, leaving scraps of her flesh upon the spear-like points. She dropped like clothing falling from a line, feeling *pain* upon falling for the first time. She was held by winter darkness in the shadow of tall office buildings—empty this holiday night—overlooking the graveyard. She crawled to an alley, to find deeper shadows.

Under a loading dock, she trembled, then wept as she closed her wounds and, through her skin, retook the blood that had soaked her clothes. She had left her coat outside Paul's apartment building, along with the clothes she had to cast aside in order to move as a draft through the windows of his home. Had she the strength to become mist, she would flow into an empty apartment and take a new coat. Yet she dared not give up her body, so ravaged now that until she had healed awhile longer, she would not risk dissipating it.

"Mother?"

Paul's word had touched her with the physicality of a lover's hand. She had extended herself more deeply into Paul's mind, trying to shift in his perception, trying to bring forth the scent of the woman—now dust—to his awareness. She bent the light around her, making her image shift and shimmer like a reflection in running water. She let the purloined sheet she wore as a burial shroud fall to her shoulders, so that Paul might see the withered flesh, the burning tumors upon her diseased skin like pebbles thrown upon grey paper, the few pathetic strands of hair on her head.

"Paul. Child, what have you done?"

The look in his eyes wounded her. His mind's voice, as he burned with shame and grief, speaking of his sins, drowned her. From his knees he fell forward, hung his head. Amid his roiling thoughts, she felt the Enfolded One. She pressed deeper into Paul's mind; it was like thrusting her hand into an urn of broken glass.

The Enfolded One reached for her, Its will a leprous distillment. She flowed against the screaming current of Its shattered thoughts, the filth of Its mind. The chambers, the valleys and gates of Paul's mind were rife with Its contamination, rife with Its abominations. She coursed through like quicksilver. Paul snapped his head back, trembled, wept.

"Mother. Help me. Please."

She felt his cry, felt the agony of the debasement of his soul.

"Help . . . me . . ."

It flowed out of him, not exiled, not exorcised. *It* flowed, warping his aura in Its image, rearing Its heads. She longed to turn away, to flee. It reached for her with Its many-eyed, blind stare, Its many-mouthed hunger, Its rage of many voices. The barb of one of Its tails twitched in Paul's heart. The barb had blossomed there, grown as do thorny vines in rich soil. The thorns pricked and stung as they twitched—she *felt* this through her joining with Paul. She could not pull them from him and so guide him to Heaven, *away* from Damnation, *away* from where he would be Its trophy.

Paul reached up, begging for absolution. The Blind Dragon had infused his spirit with its venom. Were she to kill Paul as she pulled the barb from his heart, he would still be the thing's trophy.

The Beast trembled with rage; It bunched Itself, ready to strike, ready to flow like black floodwaters and attack her. It bellowed with all Its voices. The force of the bellow struck her like a blow. She fell to her knees; her shroud fell away, showing the livid scars where her breasts should have been. She felt Paul see the scars, saw with his eyes how he saw the scars, felt the grief the scars brought.

Through the weight of that grief, through the force with which it cut through the tangle of bestial thoughts in his mind, she found the well of Paul's dreams. There was Beauty within. She lunged for his Beauty; the Enfolded One screamed. She gave Paul the still quietude of the vision her Father had given her—the peace, the melancholy.

The screaming voices fell silent.

She heard the quiet of his mind and withdrew from him.

"Mother?"

Paul's eyes were unseeing as she rose above him; he was drowning in a river of forgetfulness, forgetting the feeling, not the *fact* of what he had done.

"Confess, Paul," she said, enticing him toward his own innate righteousness, toward Salvation, toward Heaven. "I have wept in death for your soul."

"I can't confess."

She touched his burning face with her grey parchment hand. She let herself cry with pity for this man who had been the plaything of so ugly an intellect, and who would be again if he did not find his Redemption.

Not wanting to harm him, yet knowing she must, she reached into his breast and pulled at the barb lodged there. To touch this dole of the Enfolded One burned her hand; she did not allow herself to feel the pain.

"Oh, God . . . Oh God in Heaven forgive me . . . forgive me for the butchery. Forgive me for the blood and the pain. Forgive me for the anguish and humiliation. Forgive me for offending You and turning my back on Your Love. . . ."

His voice fell away into deepening prayer that could not be given form in words, only in the soft sibilances born under a whisper. Hand still by his heart, still kneeling, she lifted him with her free arm across her knees in the way the mother of the *Kristos* held her Son in death.

"Are you sorry for what you have done?"

Paul blinked as tears streamed down his face.

"I give you Absolution . . ."

She crushed his heart; the barbs pierced her hand.

". . . and Peace."

He twitched a short while. His tortured soul ascended, free of the unnatural burden of the Enfolded One, rising as does shimmering heat from a fire.

The Succubus rose, let drop his body.

And the Enfolded One lashed out, no longer contained by Paul's soul, no longer limited by the flesh It had occupied.

In her mind, It roared like thunder. It raged. She held It, fought Its idiot call while longing to join with It, to wrap herself in Its filth.

Fighting Its call, she dressed herself in clothes she found in the apartment and stumbled into the hallway, still wearing the withered body of Paul's mother. The venom burned like a spray of holy water, made sand of her blood. The tumors she had set into her skin twitched; her hand that had touched Its barb was marked with stigmata that leaked not blood, not lymph, not *spiritus,* but a mixture of the three that dried to dust as soon as it beaded on her palm.

The night air helped her to focus, to realize what she had to do. She passed scores of people who chose not to see her—a sick older woman, poorly clothed on a night of killing cold. They, taken by the Enfolded One in their need for a war that was naught but a promise of the Apocalypse they did not deserve or earn, were blinded from concern.

She needed sanctity, a poison to counteract the poison within her. Graveyards, churches, synagogues, and mosques were all too strong for her to go near. The murdered church offered her no means to ground the Beast inside her. Her one recourse was the graveyard that was itself mostly dead. She followed the back alleys to where she could climb the black iron fences hidden beneath the dark office buildings and forced herself onto the spikes.

Cold iron had brought quiet.

The Succubus shifted her weight. She was not so well healed as she had thought. Her body settled around her wounds. She smelled of blood; not all the essence she had leaked upon the bars had been re-absorbed. She put her hand over her chest, felt the closing scars through the shirt she wore. She wished to go home, to sleep, to heal. To pray and thank her Father. To steel herself after this victory for the completion of her pilgrimage.

Breathing deeply, she reformed herself into her favored mask, that of "Jeannette," that of the first living woman she had become. She changed herself slowly . . .

. . . and threw her head back screaming into the unhearing ether, her wounds reopening as the woman she had been in life two centuries before stepped forward in her awareness. She drove her fist through the concrete loading dock as her scream became eclipsed by the roar of a dragon. The Enfolded One had insinuated Its contamination into the ghost-shells of the souls she had configured within her, weakening her, harrowing her flesh. She felt barbs blossom in her own heart. She screamed again, retreating within her own mind from the Beast that hunted her through her own intellect. Inward, inward . . . she found a chamber of her mind that was safe, on the threshold of her dreams, where Beauty lived.

Within that chamber, she found Lawrence.

IX

Night

Holding on to the overhead bar on the subway, Larry arched his back as if someone had stabbed him from behind.

"Jesus Christ! What's wrong?"

Larry met Ed's eyes.

And Ed felt the crowd press close, heard a roar that could not have been the roar of the train. The train shuddered; Larry fell against him. Ed caught him, one armed, holding on to the overhead bar. He looked at Larry's back, expecting to see a protruding knife. Larry grabbed Ed's shoulder, righted himself, met Ed's eyes again. The crowd looked at them, not caring, seeming to gain strength from whatever plight they suffered. Larry said softly, close to Ed's face, as would a lover: "Help me."

Larry became heavy, so heavy that his small frame could not possibly contain the weight he bore. Ed thought his arm would break. *Aerial bodies, forced into flesh; the weight of ghosts, joining with Larry's spirit, packing themselves tight into the shell of his soul.* It was all medieval horseshit, but Ed could think of nothing else to explain how . . .

Reptilian.

Through his coat and clothes, Ed felt something press against him using Larry's body, Larry's unnatural *weight*. It surged, it flexed like the powerful backs of snakes. It was rough, like the skin of a crocodile. The roar came again, over the sound of the train, and Ed felt the reptilian coagulation on Larry's being tremble with the sound.

"Christ!"

He heaved Larry off him as the train slowed to a stop. The kid fell, grabbed the back of a train seat before he lost his balance. The passengers stared, dumbfounded, the way a movie audience would stare at the screen. Their gazes had a *cold* weight, like deep ocean waters. Larry stumbled to the doors as they slid open. Ed followed.

The platform crowd closed around Larry before Ed could step from the train. The kid was gone, swallowed. Ed shoved his way to the far wall. As the train pulled away, Ed realized that Larry had left his overnight bag behind. He scanned about. Larry made his way to the stairs, walking against the flow of the crowd descending, seeming to need to be in people's way. Ed followed, pushed his way through the crowd.

Before he reached the top of the stairs, he saw Larry going through the turnstile. When Ed got to the turnstiles, there was no sign of him. Ed sprinted up the stairs leading to the street.

No sign of him in either direction.

Ed walked from the subway kiosk. The cold hurt, felt like subzero temperatures. Wind, like that from the Arctic, howled down the street. It bit, made his eyes tear. But those around him—shuffling amid the Christmas Eve gaudiness—did not bow their heads, did not block the wind, nor draw up their collars. The wind wasn't natural, it did not come off the river.

He ran into the wind, defying it.

Half a block ahead, a cluster of humanity gathered around some focus—like in news footage of bodyguards protecting a VIP from sniper fire. The crowd. Larry wanted the crowd. The crowd wanted *him*.

He ran harder, slipping on the ice. The air scraped his lungs and throat. He saw the cluster of humanity enter the sprawl of the Copley Place shopping complex. Heart pounding, Ed followed them, half a minute behind, pushing through the revolving doors.

The sea of humanity filled his mind with idiot murmurings. As if a million chanting idiot voices tried to silence one million others.

Ed fell into a corner of the windowed entryway, whimpering. Slowly, as if coaxing limbs made weak from paralysis, he brought his fists against his ears and for the first time in long agonizing months, prayed for God to help him.

X

Night

As Jeannette, she walked the shifting streets, the forgotten back alleys. She fought the urge to join the crowds, to let herself be taken by them, for they would take apart her mind, her intellect. The

Enfolded One would entangle her in the riot of their voices and they would circle her, like a current or eddy around a stone, eroding her. By dawn, nothing but wind would remain.

Her identity, her shattered, rended self, was reasserted after centuries of death, after an eternity of torment interrupted by the Will of her Father in defiance of the Divine Justice that had thrown her to the Lightless World.

(As a little girl, she walks the streets of a great city just before dawn. She follows officers of the guard as they ring bells behind the carts of garbage collectors. Tired, broken people, like herself, march to their stoops and pile their trash. She runs ahead of the guard, ahead of the garbage collectors, pulling what morsels she can before the officers shoo her away. Sometimes dogs beat her to the morsels, and she is bitten. The guards laugh, and say it serves her right.)

The Dragon has entwined itself around the branches with which she has connected the souls within her. Memories, awakened in flesh, of her first life have come before they are meant to, before the sweet concoctions of her Father have come to full fruition. To simply *know* what she had been had given her strength, but not enough strength to bear *memories* of what she had been.

The Succubus leaned against the brick wall of an alley and wept. She called to the soul she had found pristine within herself, in the sphere where her dreams dwelled.

"Help me." She spoke in the manner of prayer.

He did not hear her, but she felt him. He infused her with his spirit. She felt him as a warm glow, the kind a girl feels in her heart while she thinks of her first love.

(He serves the New Caesar, this handsome man who leads her from the camp. She has traveled far from the choking city of her birth. He takes her hand, and his hand is the strongest she has ever felt. Never has she seen as much green as she has in these splendid fields, nor has she smelled such clean air. She is giddy, and hopes to become his favorite. She balks at the sight of the church, still smoking. She balks at being led within, along the aisle, like a bride led by her groom. The altar is uncomfortable against her back, she is blackened by soot. He pays her with jewels pried from the chalice, and she feels like crying, but can't deny the call of a handful of bright wealth. She believes, in the dying light, that she can see herself reflected in one of the bright faces. Tears, and the need to hide the jewels, never allow her to be certain.)

The Succubus walked a few paces, then fell against a cold grey Dumpster. The smell reminded her of how she'd lived as a child, before her alchemical resurrection. She pushed the Dumpster into the alley wall. Particles of bloody-stone brick flew upon impact.

"Help me."

She was not heard. The man who had touched her in the realm of dreams had been poisoned by the Dragon, through her. She needed to make him hear her call, her plea.

The Dragon roared again. She felt a snapping in her arm, blinding pain. Fighting the roar, she had convulsed so violently that she had broken her own arm.

She stumbled onward, forcing her arm to knit, too weakened and too imbued with True Flesh to simply become mist and re-form healed. As she left the alley, snow began to fall. In the changed city-light, in the forced quiet of snow, she found enough peace to look upon her arm and see that it had healed wrongly, crookedly, for she had not thought to set it before willing it to knit.

She could find no way to gain enough leverage to break it and reset it. She fell back into the alley, curled into a ball, and wondered how she could be so horribly forsaken.

Lawrence frolicked among the masses, feeding off their anxious anger, their group frenzy. Singles bars in the complex were packed tight with well-heeled professionals who had no family but what they could find among other professionals, who wallowed in their self-imposed exile, convincing themselves that this was the holiday atmosphere they had *always* wanted. Their voices vibrated in his mind, and he liked how this vibration drowned out his thoughts.

He ambled to the bar, loving the feel of eyes on his back, loving the press of bodies near the service area as people clamored for drinks so that they might eventually find company this Christmas Eve in the form of meaningless sex.

When the bartender turned to him, Lawrence said without thought, "Beefeater! And tonic!"

His heart raced. He looked about. At a few tables, obvious office parties that had migrated to the bar were in full swing—full of drunken power games and coercions that he could feel, even at a distance.

He was partly aware of the bartender slapping down the drink before him. He threw the guy a five, left the drink, and felt the pissed gazes of the patrons around him as caresses. Under the bustle and hubbub, he moaned with pleasure.

He walked to another service area, to stand in line and feel bodies and minds and voices close to him. He'd waited ten minutes before he realized that he should wend his way back to the gay bar. Oh, to be surrounded by people so willfully dispossessed, to be around people packed so tightly in a bar in defiance of Christmas convention, to be around so many who would use the occasion as a great pity party, liberally dousing their beers with tears. He could go back and maybe find Tom there, and indulge in the act of picking him up so that he might be victimized again. . . . That he could find such delicious obliteration of his ego excited him so, his knees trembled.

He forced his way out of the bar, to the great shopping complex. By the bar entrance were lines for the mall's multiplex. He looked up to the posted schedule; the line before the ticket stile was to see *Rocky V*. The patrons were beefy meatheads, like the military guys who'd come into the store. A *Rocky* movie—where jocks could find vicarious pleasure in seeing Stallone beat the shit out of somebody as the music swelled, as the crowds on screen cheered Rocky in a way that let the movie audience claim the cheering and chanting as their own. All that cheering—a displaced cheering-on of the troops as they kicked Saddam's oily Arab ass. Should Lawrence go to the movie and feed on that cheering?

No, the energy at the gay bar would be even richer.

Lawrence almost skipped through the mall, jostling people, planning in his mind the most crowded route he could take to the gay bar. Tom would be there. He'd have to, a predator like him? All those vulnerable queens and fags longing for company? Longing for a romantic story of how he'd met Mr. Right on Christmas Eve, when Tom was Mr. Wrong? Lawrence reached the street. The air smelled heavy with snow. He hurried as he realized how greedy his back was for the feel of Tom's weight upon it. After a few blocks, there were no Christmas crowds to be found. No one felt close enough for him to find and follow.

He'd made it to a quiet section of Boylston Street just as the first flakes fell, just as pain that he felt as the snapping of the bones of his upper arm screamed across his intellect. He stumbled, cried out, then braced himself against a streetlight. He grabbed his biceps, wondering if he had been shot from a passing car, afraid whoever had shot him was rounding the block to finish the job. No blood. The pain did not fade; his arm looked uninjured.

Then through the pain, changing in layers, he felt a comfort he had never known before. He felt something stir inside him, felt it break free, trembling, as a young bird would break free of its shell.

Through his pain, he realized he had sought this comfort his whole life.

A voice touched his mind, soft. Softer than the touch of the snow alighting upon his hair.

"Help me."

The voice felt as if it had come from the city itself, from the wind coming from the river.

"Help me."

Lawrence looked up at the halo cast by the streetlight upon fluttering snow falling around it.

Beautiful.

XI

Night

I *got too close,* thought Ed. *I got too close, and whatever is messing with Larry messed with me. Now what the fuck are you gonna do about it, Sloane?*

The shopping complex was the size of a great museum, and packed as some market scene out of a DeMille epic. He'd edged his way into a pickup joint, gone to the theater complex and bought a ticket to scan about the lobby, sneaking in as many theaters as he could before being thrown out by two ushers. He'd have gladly beaten the crap out of them if he hadn't been so deeply afraid of what he faced this night.

He ducked into a quiet corridor by the theaters that held a bank of phones and a cluster of rest rooms. A red EXIT sign shone over a door at the far end. He leaned against one wall, slumped to a squat. He put his hands on his temples, rubbing them.

Jesus Christ in Heaven, what am *I dealing with?*

He pressed his eyelids gently; what he wanted to do was press in his knuckles deeply and massage his tired eyes that had just read hundreds, maybe *thousands,* of faces as he'd tried to find Larry. But if he did that, his contacts might slip under his eyelids.

Whatever it was that was messing with Larry was . . . it was evil, *God damn it. Just admit that, Sloane, and maybe you'll come out of this okay. Now, just* think. *For the love of God, use your head and* think.

Pressing his hands over his eyes, he withdrew to his own intellect and approached his memory palace slowly, to compensate for the fear in his heart and the noise around him. Ed walked through the woods he envisioned around the palace, woods like the ones around his childhood home. The seven walls encircling the palace were of great blocks of granite; the stream circling the palace was of jeweled blue. Through the portals of the seven walls lay the atrium, full of flowering plants, carpeted with grass so vibrant it looked as if it had been enameled.

Aware of the wall pressing against his back, aware of the drone of voices and footsteps just outside the corridor, Ed thought: *It's not a succubus, or any medieval misogynist thing like that. That'd explain part of what's messing with Larry. A succubus would need a stable male element to pack him full of ghosts over time. If Larry were that element, he'd be dead by now. Succubi just don't have male progenitors, alchemical fathers that remain part of them. It doesn't happen, Doctor Van Helsing; there's no precedent. That's assuming this isn't all ergot-spawned bullshit. It's a demon you're dealing with. Now get to work.*

From the atrium in his memory palace, Ed looked to a door like the one to his boyhood room; beyond were his personal memories. Another door, very ornate, was guarded by an Angel standing upon rubble: the Angel of History before a corridor of History. Boethius' Lady Philosophy guarded another door. The door to the far left was adorned with images of the sun and moon transposed over each other in mutual eclipse in alchemical union: the door to Esoterica. It had been a long time since Ed had opened this facet of his memory.

A kid screamed in the mall; its high-pitched tantrum echoed through the air.

Ed opened the door to Esoterica. He went past the images of Alchemy, past icons of ravens, serpents, alembics, and creatures of burning fantasy. Adjacent to the hall of Alchemy was a hall that held glowing configurations of the Tree of Life and the attendant angels of each sphere according to various scholars. Each configuration was imagined as made of stained glass, illuminated by noon sun. Just past the Tree as envisioned by Luria—a Tree that held burning sparks, Divine Sparks, within its spheres—was the Tree of Darkness, the inversion of the Tree of Life, as realized by Kohen. The Tree's spheres were marked with their attendant demons and vices. Ed went past this tree to a door marked with the Seal of Solomon and pushed it open.

Within were demons.

He looked to the alcoves along this hall, all placed to the left.

Here, a demon of stone with the body of a powerful man and the head of a unicorn. He was carved as if in midstep, and carved oaks stood about his twisted form.

At the demon's feet were orchestral instruments.

Amduscias, the Walker Among Trees, Infernal Lord of Orchestral Music.

No reason to link anything to him.

In the next alcove, a creature at once like a man, yet also a chimera of other beasts. The demon looked to be caught in a slow dance. At his feet were arranged an archer's bow, made useless by a cut string; pipe rolls of vellum tied with red ribbon; a map of a section of the Potomac, soaking wet, as if the river of paper had overflowed its banks.

Belial, the Worthless One, or the Unbowed One. Lord of Dance and the Rhetoric of Infernal Law. Infernal Lord of Rivers, which will overflow in his triumph.

No, the demon-wind (if that was what it was) had not come from the river, but from the direction of the sea. Belial has nothing to do with this.

The next alcove: a demon with the body of a man, face of a lion, wings of an eagle. A map compass at his feet, with a fan placed along the line marking the southwest.

Pazzuzu, Lord of the Sirocco, of the southwest winds. No, the wind had come from the east. Too cold to be a desert wind. Can't be him.

Next alcove: a great bas-relief in terra-cotta. A blurry image, eroded by time. At the foot of the great slab of clay: a ball; the letter Z carved in wood; a bull made of stone. Set apart from these: a fly caught in amber; a miniature of a market stall, full of produce; a shattered pair of boy's glasses.

Baal Zebul, Beelzebub, the Lord of the Flies. Syrian god, or Baal. A lord of commerce worshiped in marketplaces, where sacrifices were made to keep flies at bay from food products.

Baal Zebul drove the flies with wind. Larry was carried to a place of commerce. He'd tweaked as the subway passed beneath Copley Place, through earth that supported what is nothing but great temple to Baal Zebul. *Jesus Christ in Heaven, help me. I'm not strong enough to face this.*

Ed went on through the hall in his mental palace.

The next alcove held a chaos-monster of stone: a great serpent erupting out of a roiling sea.

Beneath the monster: a blanket bunched and compacted within itself; a monitor lizard with bloody sockets for eyes; a paperback copy of Hobbes, like the one Ed had had as an undergrad.

Leviathan, the Enfolded One, the Blind Dragon. Embodiment of the . . .

"What *the fuck're* you doin', ya shit?"

Ed opened his eyes just as the booted foot came at him; he rolled out of the way.

From the floor, he looked up to three jocks, just out from *Rocky V,* at a guess. The one who had tried to kick him stood on point before the others, who grinned as they egged on their alpha male. The alpha male had his jacket open to reveal a T-shirt emblazoned with an American flag. Underneath were the words: TRY AND BURN THIS, ASSHOLE!

"You a faggot?" said the alpha male.

Being pulled from his memory palace left Ed dazed. He felt as he had when he'd touched the *reptilian* thing that had clung to Larry. Voices pressed on his head. Voices, he realized through his fog, like the buzzing of flies.

"You crouched down there looking for some dick to suck in the men's room?"

Ed brought his mind into focus. The buzzing in his head got louder.

"Answer me!"

The jock brought his leg back for a kick.

Ed rolled toward him, slammed into the leg the guy stood upon, knocked him over while he was off balance.

Ed got up, kicked the guy in the knee while he was down. His two pals stepped around him. Ed grabbed the smaller of the two and shoved him into the other. Both fell onto their buddy, who rolled on the floor holding his injured knee.

Ed looked up, ready to run.

At the end of the corridor, in the main mall, a crowd had gathered. They moved forward. Ed felt their eyes on him as if he were under a single gaze: all eyes melded into one vision. Many eyes, one gaze. Segmented sight. Like a fly . . .

"Jesus."

The smallest guy was up; Ed threw the hardest punch he had ever thrown into his jaw.

Ed ran away from the crowd, past phone banks and rest rooms, to the red glow of the EXIT sign. The heavy door swung open as he slammed into it; Ed grunted with the impact. Cold air, snow all around him. Heavy footsteps behind; the door swung closed. He slammed into it again, from the other side this time, as his pursuer was on the threshold. The guy bellowed: the fire bar had caught him. He stumbled through the door, stooped over. Ed punched him, at a downward angle, in the left eye.

He was half a block away before he looked back. He let the snow hide him as he stumbled to the side streets. On a street he did not know, he gathered snow from the hood of a car and pressed it against his face.

He cried then, realizing that this was the first moment in his life that he had known terror.

XII

Night

The crowds called, and the strength of their call smothered the pain in his arm. He could hear—in a way he had not known he could hear, the bustle of crowds in a hotel bar—three blocks distant. To go there, for a quick fix of the press of humanity, to drink the liquor of war anxiety, to taste the self-pity and bitterness of Christmas Eve exiles, could sustain him until he made it to the gay bar and found Tom, or someone like Tom, on the prowl. Maybe he could find a Mr. Wrong at the hotel . . . a closeted married man out tonight to punish his family, a man who would in the morning treat Lawrence with delicious contempt. But Lawrence saw Beauty in the falling snow, in the lights of cars as they passed, in the night color of brick and in the cold grey of the winter sky. Lawrence felt a poetry fluttering in his chest like the wings of a bird.

The lights of cheap Christmas decorations *touched* him in a way he knew they shouldn't, made him feel as he'd not felt since he'd been a boy and his gaze had yet to be jaded by pain and belittlement.

In his mind, amid the noise that called to him, soft words: *"Where are you?"*

Had he asked, or been asked?

Lawrence stumbled to a car, pulled off his left glove, then pressed his hand into the fresh snow on the hood. The cold against his palm was a new feeling, sexual; it moved him as only dreams had before.

Something stirred in his heart. He knew the feeling, not as something he'd known in life, but that he'd known in the infinite understanding he had been blessed with before coming to full awareness, before his soul had been inscribed into sinless flesh. The feeling and the need to deny the feeling eclipsed each other in a waltz. He needed to deny the feeling because it seemed so unreal, so unlike what he'd hoped his whole life it *would* be.

How could this be love with no object, with no focus of his longing gaze? How could this be love, disembodied? Born of his soul and his soul alone, as if it had touched a shifting reflection of itself?

"Where are you?"

Lawrence made a fist, held the snow tight. The pain returned, creeping through the flesh and bone of his arm.

He thought, through the willful voice of consciousness: *Love, how can I feel love?*

The Succubus shuffled through the snow, holding her malformed arm, expending strength in suppressing the Blind Dragon's influence. She had walked the maze of Beacon Hill, walked the narrow streets of brick, where the buildings blocked the light of the moon that touched the sky behind the snowing clouds. She knew it to be a sickle moon, like that which had been in the sky the first night she had been reborn upon the Earth, that had been in the sky as she rose, resurrected, from the foam of the sea to touch land for the first time in her new existence between life and death.

The fire she had seen upon Beacon Hill on the dawn following that night, she now realized, would have been nothing but shadow among these narrow streets: here, upon the hill, the sun was made silent.

"Love, how can I feel love?"

The lone voice in her mind, yet not her own, gave her comfort. She answered the voice, answered the soul of him who had dwelled within her, spoke the poetry that she herself longed to hear.

"I am half your soul. Make my soul gentle with the touch of yours. Heal me through your wounded spirit, so that I may heal you, beloved guardian of my heart."

He withdrew. . . .

She felt him close within himself, felt him retreat into the shadowed realm of her own intellect on the borderlands of dreams.

"No. Please, no."

The narrow winding streets brought her close to the River. She called to her Father, invoked the strength of the Unbowed One as best she could with her shattered will. But her Father was lost to her. Then, moving through the dark valleys of her mind, she felt mem-

ory come upon her, echoing as does the tolling of church bells
through the walls of a city.

*(On narrow streets, as a girl, so small, she runs to where her father lies
under the wheels of a fine carriage. His legs are crushed; the hooves of
the horses have battered the face that she loved. She runs to him, runs to
him, her small legs unable to carry her fast enough to his side so she may
give him comfort as he lies in terror. He extends his hand, but before she
takes it, it falls limp. Her father's blood flows on the street, drunk by filth
and straw, by spaces between the paving stones. She picks up his hand
from the street that drinks his blood like sweet wine and it is already
growing cold in her grasp. Two of her aunts come to carry her away as
her mother falls to the ground, pulling her hair, shrieking. As her aunts
take her away, she kicks and screams, knowing that her father needs her,
and that she cannot help him.)*

The memory brings tears, and she cries out with a soundless voice
for her second and terrible Father. None living hear her, though a
few nearby take a sudden chill that they cannot be rid of, no matter
how they try.

XIII

Deep Winter Night

Ed Sloane lit the last cigarette of his life.
     What will I do when I find him?
He looked across the great divide of the city: Huntington Avenue. On the far side "things got bad," in Boston parlance—the forsaken neighborhoods, where the Boston of Symphony Hall gave way
to the Boston of crack houses and gang war.
     Standing in the falling snow, Ed touched the unearthly terror he
felt, became aware of it meshing with mundane urban anxiety that
seemed petty, threatening mere bodily existence. What he faced this
night found expression not only in threats to his person; the three
who assaulted him, the crowds that *watched,* were part of something
larger, more malignant . . . soul killing.
     What can I do when I find him?
Ed crossed the street, afraid he might be crazy, and more afraid
that he might not be.
     I can't face something so old, so primordially evil, for the love of God.
There was no traffic. The quiet, the awful quiet of late Christmas
Eve, which once would have been a source of comfort, now made

him more afraid, pressing cold fingers upon his back. Ed crossed into a different night, toward the world of urban exile his mother had taught him about.

And if that's not what I'm facing, then I'm a nutcase; I'm facing my own insanity. Larry's eternal soul is at stake. What's my sanity against that? A good doctor and a batch of happy pills can get you back your sanity.

He stepped onto the curb. Throughout Boston, stores were closing; last-minute shopping frenzies died down. Larry would have to come here if he were influenced by Baal Zebul, demonic lord of commerce . . . called the way he'd been called to Copley Place to feed on the energy of humans doing transactions.

Reasonable assumption, Ed. Assuming you're not completely full of shit, and aren't suffering some kind of folie à deux *with Larry.*

Ed finished his cigarette, walked away from Huntington Avenue. Within a hundred yards, he was walking through the Boston no one wished to admit existed: a ghetto isolated by the city fathers by careful rerouting of transit lines and restructuring of postal zones. The city within the city, made invisible to tourists and polite white citizenry by carefully placed and zoned tall buildings and billboards.

The few passersby gave him wonder-filled looks. As Ed pulled up his collar, he realized most white boys who came here to buy drugs probably drove. He passed ancient town houses of blasted brick, sagging with neglect. Debris spilled from front doorways onto the filthy snow paths beaten into the sidewalks. Burned and gutted buildings stood beside vacant lots choked with tall winter-dead weeds. The lots were full of cast-off refrigerators and stoves, rusted hulks of cars, rotting furnishings. Ed thought he saw a man asleep on a cast-off couch slowly buried by snow. On closer look, he saw that it was not a man, but bundles of clothes.

The wind blew snow into his face and eyes. The few lights on in the tenements only added to the emptiness, gave it a weight that pressed against his sight.

Baal Zebul's realm, like the realms of desolation legend told of, where dragons lived.

Larry *would* come, to these forsaken streets to walk among forsaken people, where suburbanites and college kids came to buy drugs, partaking of oppression by patronizing it. Drug traffic was the only commerce on these streets, the only transactions taking place in Boston this late. Baal Zebul's realm, a desolation created by commerce: the commerce of drugs, and the commerce of trickle-down oppression.

In a few doorways, Ed saw piles of human shit. The Lord of the Flies was also the Lord of the Dunghill.

The unshoveled sidewalk had become impassable. Ed walked along the curb, facing traffic. A car came at him from the gloom, a man and a woman staring at him through the windows as they passed, dumbfounded.

Carefully, Ed withdrew part of his mind from the desolation, separating his mind to two tasks: following the twisting street, and standing before the mnemonic device for Baal Zebul in his memory palace. Walking among chunks of filthy ice, he also stood before the graven idol. He touched the edge of the alcove Baal Zebul occupied, an edge that shared a wall with the alcove of Leviathan, the Enfolded One. Baal Zebul's alcove swung open on hinges so intricate they could not exist outside Ed's imagination. Beyond the alcove, a small corridor held particulars of what Ed knew about the demon.

Something bodiless came at him, in his mind and upon the street.

He felt it, as he had once, while walking a creek bed, felt a winter-heavy wind coming toward him. It blew among the treetops, giving itself shape as a breaking wave of glistening new-fallen snow knocked from the branches. Yet what came toward him now wasn't a cascade of snow. It was the very desolation of this place—*awakened*—surging through the street.

Ed stumbled, froze.

In his mind, something charged him through the darkened corridor he'd opened, something not his own mind, something that . . .

Headlights coming at him through the snow, quickly, with purpose.

Voices descended, crashing through the corridors of his mind, thick as the darkness of the night. Ed smashed closed his awareness of the memory palace, closed off that part of his intellect, choked it. His will drained; a cold hand entered his heart and pulled the strength from him. He felt the cascade of spiritual noise that had overcome him in Copley Place. Hopelessness became thick in his veins, suffusing his flesh with the clammy feel of wet earth.

The headlights bore down. Something that was not him screamed in his intellect, made a pain in his mind like the crawling of ants in a wound. He tried to move. Buzzing greyness, shadows of fever-dream, warped the street before him.

The car stopped ahead of him along the rubble-filled street. An old four-door. Dented. Paint peeling.

Headlights went dark.

"Oh, God. No."

Something raked his mind, tearing, like talons across silk. A smell, foul, like that of the reptile house at the zoo. The stink had a warmth; it did not come from the snowy air.

The car doors opened.

Gripped by the cacophony in his mind, unable to run, unable to cry for help that would not come, Ed saw urban nightmare made flesh as five youths, in baggy gangsta clothes, piled out of the car.

Something shuddered, breathed, and twisted in his mind. In the delirium of his senses, Ed saw—for an instant, silhouetted against the snow—the five emerging out of the car like the snaking heads of a dragon rising up from its body.

Incarnate.

The voices in his mind were made incarnate by what stood before him: urban nightmare, made real by the fact that it was a nightmare, with a sense of shifting, partial reality behind it. Cop-show nightmare. TV-newscast nightmare.

The five stood a moment with the body posture of challenge. Ed couldn't hear what they said. The cadences of their speech became one with the throng in Ed's mind; they shimmered in his hearing in time with what twitched in his head like a serpent hatching from its egg.

The smallest, youngest of the five, strutted like a rooster before the open passenger door, gun held high, displayed for the approval of his friends.

Gun held high.

Glinting in the dim streetlight, glinting in the snow.

Gun held high.

Ed was transfixed by the gun; it winked like an eye. He longed for the opiate stare of that eye, longed to receive its fiery gift. To the cheers of the other four, the kid lowered the gun at Ed. The eye became metal, became again the weapon it was.

Ed screamed and went for the gun.

As a dead man, he had nothing to lose.

His scream silenced the voices as he slammed into the kid, knocking him against the open car door. The force slammed the door shut. The thing in his head bellowed, slashed at his mind, tore his thoughts. Ed defied it, translating the defiance in his mind into violence enacted by his body. Ed twisted the kid's wrist and broke it.

The gun fell as Ed smashed the kid twice in the neck with his elbow. Ed's hand went numb with the second blow. He kicked the gun under the car.

He pulled the kid around in front of him, back against the car door. The kid weighed nothing. He was thirteen, at the most.

A sawed-off shotgun was pointed at him, held by another kid of about eighteen. The three other gangstas stood at the shotgunner's back, out of the possible spray of buckshot.

Ed looked the guy in the eye. The bellowing voices rose in his mind, telling him he should *die,* telling him to not fight.

Ed shouted the voices down.

"So what *the fuck* are you going to do? You gonna shoot me? You gonna maybe shoot your little pal here?"

Ed's shouts cut the desolation, cut the alien presence in his mind, quieting it. The silence frightened him; it was silence that could be broken by a shotgun blast.

The kid squirmed. Ed hooked his arm, with its numb hand, around the kid's throat and yanked the kid's head up.

"Don't make me break the little man's neck."

Why am I doing this macho movie bullshit? This makes no sense. This is the fantasy. The fiction. Not real.

The guy raised the shotgun, level with Ed's head.

Ed's fear changed in a way he couldn't understand, because what he was afraid of had changed in a way he couldn't understand.

"You ain't got the *baaaaallllls,* White Boy," the gunman said. The guy's voice was real, not a phantom sound. His voice carried violence and hatred, but *human* violence and hatred. Ed matched his voice.

"And you ain't got *aiiiiiiim,* shithead! What? Who the fuck are you? You think you can blow my head off nice and clean? Go ahead, you stupid fuck. Or are you too much of a pussy to shoot a guy while standing on a sidewalk? Would you and your little *girlfriends* like to get in your car and shoot me? Or is looking a guy in the eye when you kill him too much for you?"

What the fuck am I doing?

The gangsta with the shotgun took a step toward Ed, getting a cleaner shot.

Ed bellowed loud enough to wake the block. "Don't try it!" The guy stopped in his tracks. Ed bellowed again. "Don't even fucking *think* about it!"

This is all movie bullshit. Bruce Willis bullshit. Maybe this is the bullshit they live. I'm matching it.

Over the blood pounding in his ears, Ed heard windows opening along the street. Human voices; Ed fought the urge to hear them as the bodiless voices in his head. In the building behind the four gangstas, lights came on in the windows.

"Put the shotgun down."

"Fuck you."

The kid squirmed again; he was crying, his body twitching with sobs. Ed tightened his grip around the kid's neck. Tingling went up his hand to his elbow as he closed off the kid's windpipe.

The kid reached with his good hand to his throat, trying to say something.

"I hear his neck popping! You wanna wrap this kid in a body bag for Christmas, shithead? Put the *fucking* shotgun down on the *fucking* sidewalk!"

I'm no fucking hero. I'm no fucking hero.

Ed saw only the barrels, two points of deep empty blackness, coming toward him in the snow.

Ed heaved the kid into the gunman.

The guy stumbled on the icy pavement as the kid fell on him. He tried to catch the kid with his left hand, keeping the shotgun raised toward Ed with his right.

Ed tackled the guy while he was off balance, falling in a heap with the gunman and the kid. With everything he had, before the other three could jump him, Ed drove his numb fist into the crook of the gunman's elbow.

The guy's arm jerked.

The shotgun went off as the three other gangstas fell on him. One screamed as he fell to the ice, holding his bloody ankle.

The blast made the other two jump back.

Ed grabbed the weapon from the gunman's useless arm and started swinging.

Ten minutes later, across Huntington Avenue, covered with sweat and vomiting in an alley, Ed could not fathom how the fuck he could still be alive. Sirens wailed in the distance. Through the alley, Ed saw an ambulance scream down Huntington, turn right at the corner. Wiping his mouth, Ed trembled as he followed the alley to a nameless access road behind a restaurant.

Ed limped down the alley, the ugly backside of a line of posh restaurants. He thought he was crying again, but realized that he'd lost a contact lens in the fight; his left field of vision was a blur. Snowfall became an unearthly white glow.

He came to a chain-link fence with a locked gate. Past it was a way out to a main street. Which street, Ed could not tell. Dumpsters of rotting food brought gorge to his throat, despite the cold, despite that he'd already puked his guts out.

He grabbed the fence, tried to pull himself up. His limbs were quaking. He closed his eyes, calmed himself. Larry was out in this city, a kid whose soul was endangered. To ignore Larry's terror would cost Ed his soul. Ed, and others close to him, had suffered enough for his moral paralysis. No more. He'd no longer allow it.

He looked up with his bisected vision to the slit of sky above the alley, to the quiet snow, falling lightly. Then he climbed the fence.

As he brought himself over the other side, a wind surged down the alley. The stink of the Dumpsters changed, became the stink of something alive.

It was like liquid.

A flash flood of shadow crashing down the alley.

The necks of a many-headed dragon; an image reflected upon the surface of water holding its integrity as the water rushed.

Ed hung on the fence, crucified, as the demon he faced punished him for defying its screaming, shattered will.

XIV

Midnight

She leaves the green fields, returns to the city. She senses death will take the camp, and follows carts bearing wounded, dying soldiers. She pays her way on her back. A kerchief taken from a dead soldier holds the jewels she has been paid. She will build a life for herself with these stones, even in a city so hungry and full of anxious fear as this.

She sleeps in graveyards. Even the worst vagabonds forsake preying on those who sleep upon sacred ground. The graveyards are full of fires lit by the dispossessed, who warm themselves sitting on piles of bones.

Hunger is everywhere. She realizes she is with child. At night, she walks the quays, hoping to earn a few sous upon which to live while she has a fortune hidden in her skirt.

One quay brings her to where the river angles sharply at the tip of the Isle of the City. The place interrupts the river; boats and punts are piled *here like autumn leaves piled in a shallow stream. She looks upon the bridge crossing the river here, noticing the grotesque faces of stone lining the bridge's underside.*

Transfixed by moonlight playing upon the stone faces, she is unaware of the man until his weight crashes upon her back and his arms are around her chest, crushing her.

She is pulled to the steps leading from the quay to the river, her screams unheard. She is thrown to the steps and kicked, punched, violated. She tries to push the man off, to cast him into the river. Angry, he smashes her head against the steps.

Dawn comes. She is bleeding. She has been robbed of the stones that were to give her a new life.)

The River brings no peace.

She is so terribly alone, stalked through her own mind by her greatest Enemy beneath Creation.

The Succubus had thought to give herself to the River, to go upon the ice and cast herself under its cold mantle. As she had come near the bank, the memory of what she had suffered beside another river half a world away and lifetimes ago drove her from the banks. Now she walked the esplanade, suffering where she'd once found strength.

She felt the moon set, felt the loss of the moon's unseen beauty behind the clouds behind the snow-filled air.

An ache spread through her face, a coldness suffused the bone beneath her eye. She raised her hand to the right side of her face and touched the mask, "Jeannette"; on the left side, she touched the face of the murdered girl. Uneven hair, entwined with two different textures, fell across her brow. Her left eye shifted as the skull around it changed shape, made a socket too large for the eye it held. Air filled the vacuum around and behind the eye. The tears she shed made the eye burn madly. As she pulled her hand from her face, her red skin melded with the skin of her mask—like different-colored waxes flowing, melting into each other.

Something burned away the integrity of her body, spreading as does the brown that runs before flame as it burns paper.

"Make it stop!"

The Dragon coiled through her intellect—devouring—its many heads shifting in unsynchronized layers, like schools of fish turning against one another in the same waters. Her awareness broke apart as did the stability of her body. Her thoughts ran like quicksilver as something melted near her heart.

"Make it stop!"
The thought was not hers.

Lawrence burned. The fire inside him had voices. It spread across his back. It blackened his ribs, made them press against his chest like splintering wood.
"Make it stop!"
He threw his head back.
"Make it stop!"
He brought his hands to his forehead as he realized he was on his knees, as the glory hole before him came into focus, as the cock thrust through the glory hole jerked and leaked a stream of come to the bathroom floor.
The voice in the next stall rang out: "Aw, shit!" The stall wall shuddered as the man on the other side punched it with all his might. "You little *bitch*!"
The fire spread through Lawrence, whispering, murmuring, down his arms to his hands; his fingers constricted, tendons pulling tight, as if the fire dried them out. The bass throb of music pounded the bathroom walls.
The door to the next stall opened. The voice said again, "Little *bitch*!" Lawrence knew whom he'd encountered in the anonymity of the glory hole, knew whom he'd sought out and found without volition.
Lawrence stood. His knees shook; the pain in his upper arm again cracked through flesh and bone. He braced himself against the stall as the door swung open, almost hitting him in the face.
Tom stood there, shocked.
Then he laughed.
"So, who's the little safe-sex bitch now?"
He reached into the stall and slapped Lawrence. The blood rushed to his face, making fire upon the fire under his skin.
Tom grabbed Lawrence by the shirt.
"We got some unfinished business, princess. Slip me the wrong key? Pull away before I can dump my load, you little tease?"
He shook Lawrence with his wiry-strong arms, then pulled him out of the stall. Three men stood in the corner, entwined. One lifted his head to look at the drama unfolding, then, as if deciding for the other two, turned back to the coil of limbs and necks.
Tom looked to the three and grinned. Lawrence trembled with the fire inside him. The press of voices insinuated themselves in his every thought.

"Unfinished business, princess," he said.

"Make it stop."

Tom snorted. Gave Lawrence a little shake. "Just getting started, princess."

He pulled Lawrence toward the sink. Lawrence looked down drunkenly, saw that Tom had not zipped his pants. His cock thrust through his fly, getting hard.

Tom held on to Lawrence, reached for the liquid soap dispenser, slathered soap on his cock.

Lawrence watched, dumbly, realizing he wanted this obliteration of himself. To lose himself would be to lose the pain of the voices, to quiet the fire. He looked up.

Past Tom, he saw himself in the mirror over the sink.

He saw himself.

Screaming, shouting down the voices, he thrust his fist past Tom's head, into the mirror. The glass shattered, sprayed the back of Tom's head.

"What the fuck?!"

Lawrence broke away, ran into the crowd of the Christmas dispossessed in the bar. The press of bodies called him. Blood streamed from his hand. He stumbled into the entryway, violet with black lights.

He ran past the bouncers into the night.

A block away, in the snow, still burning, still bleeding from his ruined hand, he realized he'd left without his coat.

Knowing he could die in this cold gave him his first moment of real joy since coming to Boston. In death, he would be free of the voices.

Cars went past. There was a hospital nearby, the one he'd been to the other night. He could have his hand fixed, then get a cab home from the hospital. Ed had given him enough money. He could live through this night, if he chose.

"Beloved?"

Lawrence looked to the sky, saw the swirl of snow, saw the loveliness of the grey sky. The voices fell quiet. The fire cooled. He longed for *her*, whom he had heard in his mind. He longed for the music of her voice, the gentleness he sensed abided in her heart, gentleness that abided for *him*.

Lawrence watched his blood fall upon the snow. Gently, with trembling fingers, he pulled bits of mirror from his knuckles.

He spoke.

"I'm afraid."

"You have guarded my heart. You have kept me safe, without know-ing so. For that, I love you. I shall always love you."

Lawrence wept. For the first time in his life, with a certainty he had sought his whole life, he knew a declaration of love to be true. She, this angel who touched him and gave him such comfort, could not lie to him.

Love.

The joy of it spread through his heart.

"Fight what torments you. Fight it with the Beauty you see and taste and feel. It is mine, and I share it with you, beloved guardian of my heart. It is my gift."

With the joy she brought, he saw a new Beauty in almost every-thing he saw. Even in the blood that stained the snow.

"Come to me," she called. *"I weep among the sighs."*

Surrounded by the stillness by the River, the Succubus saw, for the briefest moment, what her distant love saw.

The sight churned forth the pain of more memories.

(She has a bed of straw in the basement of an inn. The quiet is terri-ble, and she knows that now she is as alone as she has ever been in her life. She has drowned her child, needing this quiet, taking its life by laying her arm over its face in the night. The innkeeper knows what she has done, and lets her stay, for she is a fine whore.

Later, she steals linen from a drunk wash maid, then wanders to a part of the city where some still have bread. She washes herself with the linen, and seeks a household where she can wet-nurse. But winter comes early, and before she can find such a house she is caught in the first snow, still wet from washing herself. She takes sick, and none will have a sick wet-nurse. The consumption takes her, and she dies before spring, coughing upon the snow; the last thing she sees is her blood, frozen to ru-bies upon the ice where she lay.)

Where was he, her Love? Where was he who could deliver her from misery? She longed to throw her arms around him, to be loved and comforted, to lie upon his breast and so be free of the howling clatter that assaulted her.

"Save me," she called over the still River, over the sleeping city. *"Save me from the prison of my body, save me from this quiet torment. I languish. Save me from the Beast that torments us both."*

"I love you, and I always will."

XV

Deepest Night

E d destroyed his life behind him as he ran.
He destroyed beauty, knowledge. He destroyed that which he loved.

He did not look back.

In his body, he shuffled, surrounded by filthy wind that might or might not be the product of his own madness. In his mind, he ran through his palace, obliterating the shapes and forms he'd given his memories as he went, destroying the framework he'd given his mind lest the demon gain dominion over it.

He ran through the grassy courtyard. The Beast spilled forth, translucent, screaming. A great shadow like a crocodile fell upon him as he opened the door guarded by the patroness of philosophy. The statue shattered behind him. A marble bust of Plato melted like wax as teeth snapped at his back. A bust of Socrates, a bust of Aristotle, gone, as were the rooms they guarded.

Bricks, mortar, and stone flew apart; Ed felt the Beast's glee that Its prey destroyed that which he loved. Hot breath on his neck, poisonous. Ed ran on. Ahead, a door marked with an engraving of a branch, heavy with ripe fruit. Ed pushed through, destroying all that he'd learned of Augustine. Cities of God and Cities of Earth blasted to dust. Ed wept at the loss.

In his body, Ed felt his pulse race, felt it thunder in his head. The blurred vision of his left eye became the vision of his palace. In his right, he saw the brutal city, saw that he'd made his way to a main street.

All he knew of Isidore of Seville, destroyed. The Beast bellowed. A thousand idiot voices rode Its roar; each one called his name in unclean sibilance. Ed ran on. Great dusty tomes holding the wisdom of Peter Lombard, destroyed.

Ed ran on.

He lost Peter Abelard as a room of bright tapestries erupted in flame.

Hildegard von Bingen shattered with figurines of porcelain and a great window etched with stars.

Roger Bacon splintered with a room of marvelous devices made of wood.

Saint Bonaventura, a miniature hill blown apart.

Christine de Pisan, a torn veil.

Saint Dominic, a great torch, extinguished.

Thousands of hours of reading and thought, of learning and synthesis, obliterated.

A room guarded by a gentle man cast of stone, Saint Francis, holding a bird's nest where his hands met in prayer, eradicated.

Past the rubble of this room a door loomed, inscribed with a great serpent devouring its own tail.

Ed pushed against it, felt claws rake his back, while on the street his physical self fell against a lamppost, gasping.

He pushed through the door, slammed it shut.

He turned, saw the door melting, as would an image in a photograph dropped in solvent.

"No."

Leaning against the lamppost, he whispered, "I defy you. I resist you." He turned his gaze downward, pulled out his right contact lens, cast it to the ground. He willed his vision to blur. Drew himself completely into the realm of his intellect.

The room he stood in was full of symbols of the sun and moon, full of fantastic creatures cast in stone, of dragons, griffins, chimeras. Bas-relief images of knights defending great furnaces, of crows and sphinxes. Glass vessels of various types on shelves and tables. A black Madonna stood near a peacock made of multicolored blown glass.

The door bled and bubbled. The Beast liquefied Ed's will, his memory, his thought and imagination. Chanting voices, screaming, filled his awareness.

"I draw the line here, you piece of shit."

Despair would be too easy. He would not indulge it, for he knew now that despair was the weapon of his enemy.

"I know you. I know your name, you fuck. I know you."

The Beast bellowed as it raped his mind.

"I know how to kill you."

He willed the image of the Dragon Uroboros onto the pummeled door.

The dragon must obliterate itself.

Come for me, you piece of shit. You killed my brother, you took his soul. You nearly killed me with the hopelessness you've sown. You've taken almost all I've ever loved. Come for me, you piece of shit. You've contaminated my world. You're the blind idiot. Stupid, too stupid to lie, you can only spout. You spit poison without the craft of a lie, for as soon as you formulate the lie, you believe it. I know you. You are not the dragon of life and power, you are not the dragon of the Earth. This dragon does not devour itself. To kill it, you must destroy yourself, you must burn out its filthy influence.

The door folded inward.

Ed willed his palace to nothing, unlearned all he had stored with a storm of fire.

A sound like a gunshot rang out on the street.

A few came to their windows to look, saw only a drunk young man stumbling through the snow.

By morning, none would remember.

XVI

Deepest Night

I *hurt."*

The silence of a city.

"I can heal you."

The stillness of brick, the solidity of darkness cut by streetlights.

"Help me to be near you."

They knew the music of voiceless things, saw beyond the tarnished sad mirrors of mundane sight. As dreamers, they became what the other dreamt.

"Let your voice go forth, let it touch me as light touches the spirits hidden in gems. Touch me with distance, and so draw me near."

Drinking of darkness, as of water. Drinking of each other, to quiet enemy voices. New shoots, taken in sudden frost—each other's soul became as longed-for sunlight.

"I'm afraid. I am so afraid."

Pulse, and beating of hearts, made counterpoint to the stilled voices. Pulse, and beating of hearts, run slow as the patient River, quiet the anxious song of troubled spirits.

"Forgive me."

The River called.

XVII

Ending Night

Where're ya goin', punk?"
Like two sharks.

The young cop circled close, stroking his nightstick as if it were his cock. The other cop, fat, older, and red-nosed, circled farther out, an approving look on his puffy face. Their big leather cop jackets creaked in the winter-night silence.

Boston cops. The kind who live for dealing out grief.

The younger cop grinned as the door-mounted light on the squad car, parked across the sidewalk in Ed's path, made a halo behind him through Ed's blurry vision.

"Where're ya goin', punk?" he said again.

Boston cops. The kind who make people set to testify against police corruption disappear. The kind who loot markets owned by Blacks and Koreans who've set up shop in White neighborhoods. The kind who like, especially on holidays, to give out the old B'n'R treatment—"beaten and released"—to relieve Christmas stress induced at home.

No more.

Ed had lost too much to the Beast that influenced these men, to the demon that had made a smoking Hell of Ed's mind. Ed would have no more of Its torment, no more of what It spread throughout the world.

No more.

"Who're you calling 'punk,' *junior?*"

The young cop stopped and smiled, unable to believe Santa had given him such a cocky, dumb fuck to beat up. He gripped his wooden dick, teeth flashing in his happy grin.

"Hey, Griff!" he called to the fat cop. "Wouldn't you call that verbally assaulting an officer of the peace?"

The fat cop stopped, eclipsing the light mounted on the car door, and rubbed his chins sagely.

"Why . . . *yes.* Yes, I *would* call that verbally assaulting an officer. We can't have any of that, now. Can we?"

Layers of fat shifted on the cop's face as he smiled.

"Ohhh, nooooooo. We can't," said the young cop, taking practice swings with his baton, "have any—"

"Fuck with me. I'd love it."

The cops stopped grinning. Ed was supposed to be scared. Because if he wasn't scared, the cops would have to give him a *real* beating. Not just a fun one.

"Fuck with me. I'll get your asses in Walpole. Fuck with me. My daddy's a law professor. Civil rights law. Fuck with me. Dean of Harvard Law School's gonna post my bail. It'll be a Christmas present. My dad's his best pal. Fuck with me, and you're gonna give me every paycheck you ever take home for the rest of your lives. Fuck with me."

The young cop slumped. His fat coach shoved junior aside.

"You cocksucking rich little . . ."

Ed got in his face, like a drill sergeant.

"What'd you say to me? Huh?"

Ed smelled the reptilian smell, again. He let it inspire no fear in his heart.

He locked his eyes on the piggy eyes of the fat cop.

"I don't think I heard you! Say it again!"

The fat cop stepped back.

"Say it again! Say it! And I'll fucking own your fat, doughnut-stuffed ass!"

He took a step toward the cop.

"Say it!"

The fat cop walked backward, toward the car.

Ed pressed his luck; he had to or the stare-down would not work. Like a grade-school teacher, he said, "Now where you are going, Officer?"

Junior had backed toward the squad car. To make a radio report? To get a shotgun?

Ed kept it up.

"I said, 'Where are you going?' This ain't over. Because *tomorrow,* I'm getting an apology from you both. *Tomorrow,* I'm gonna be at the precinct house; you both are gonna give me an apology in front of your desk sergeant. Bright and early. Or am I gonna have to make my daddy wake up his pal on Christmas Eve?"

As the cops pulled away, Ed heard, just faintly, the itching sound of voices echoing in his head. He snuffed them. Pinched them to extinction, consigned them to the abyss. The smell faded, was carried away by the wind.

He found a reasonably dry stoop, sat, brought his hands to his face. He did not need to see the sky over the buildings around him to know that the east was growing pale; he sensed it in the way that he once could, as a child in sleep, know when his parents looked in on him. Yet what he sensed now was not comfort.

Dawn was coming. Dawn was when the tides turned, when the course of battle changed. Dawn brought a new day, and Ed had failed, this night—Larry was still lost in the sea of the city. This was a time for fear. This dawn brought a dread he had never known. He closed his eyes and prayed as he never had before.

Ending, he said aloud, "Please God . . . forgive me, my weaknesses."

XVIII

Dawn

L awrence moved as smoke through the streets.

His mind touched every corner, every facet of the city. He had an awareness of the city, felt it as he had before only been able to touch the soft spirit of deep woods.

Lifting light.

Red flowing, making itself visible in brick. Night grey changing to the pale shadow grey of day. Black made itself livid in the dried blood on his hand. The snow had stopped, and Lawrence realized that he had heard in the snow a hidden music. The silence was profound; the silence was an ache. He called to his love, to she who was close in his mind, yet so painfully distant in flesh.

"I'm afraid of the day."

She touched his mind with her words, as a kiss would touch his lips.

"The morning comes, and with morning, I will be far from you. The city will wake. The voices of the city will keep us apart. We will not hear each other, and the vulgar voices of the Beast will take us."

Lawrence knew what she said was true. The city trembled as it woke, shaking like the back of a great beast roused to anger from sleep. His mind, touching now so many corners, so many cold and secret places, would be shocked by the riot of other minds.

"I cannot bear to be apart from you. I cannot bear to not touch you as we are touching now."

Lawrence trembled, thankful that the cadences of his mind were being spoken with a voice time could not corrupt.

"I feel the birds stirring in their nests. I feel the beating of their hearts

as they stir from the stupor of winter sleep. The dawn birds will sing their winter song, and we shall be apart."

"No."

"Did you hear, my love? Did you hear the sound of snow, did you hear the music it wrought?"

"Yes. I miss it. I miss it as I will miss you."

Lawrence saw he was in Back Bay, saw he had made a circuit to the street near his home. Brownstones gave hint of coming day; light reflected in windowpanes grew pale. He felt weak. This night of cold air had spread itself in his flesh; the cold lived beneath his skin. He would die from this night. His body would wither, as surely as his soul would wither under the weight of brutalizing voices.

He said: *"I need the sound of snow. I need to share the music. With you."*

"I feel you. I feel you as I would feel the new skin over a closed wound. I feel you. I need you. I need to be with you before our song is lost. Come to me, before dawn keeps us apart."

Lawrence followed her voice, followed the pull in his heart.

"Come to me."

Lawrence followed her voice, followed each echo her voice made upon the canyon walls of brick.

"Come to me, for I need you."

He stumbled to the far end of Newbury Street and saw, through the lightening darkness, the outline of a woman standing on the corner before a great church that towered over the brick shops around it. The church was of vast blocks of grey stone, a place of shifting tones among the awakening reds of brick.

Lawrence went to her along the aisle of snow. Upon drawing near, he saw that she was wounded, that she had a complexion sallow. That her eyes were askew, her face unmatched with itself, that her hair was stammered, of two colors and textures.

Yet for all that, she was lovely, filling him with deep desire and a longing for the comfort the living cannot know. As his gaze fell upon her, as she limped toward him the few steps that kept them distant, she changed. Her twisted limbs made themselves right, her skin took a blush, her hair became jet-black.

With a voice Lawrence heard in the air, not in his mind, she said, "My love." Her words were like music. She stepped toward him, kissed him, and as Lawrence kissed her, he felt her lips become full, felt the unequal shape of them become matched.

She embraced him, her breath upon his neck.

"I can't live without you," he said. "I can't."

A fragrance came from her hair, of spring air and fresh wind from a hillside. He felt her body fill and shift as she pressed herself against him, felt the reconfiguration of her bone and flesh.

She brought her face away from his neck, met his eyes.

Lawrence nearly wept at the sight of her beauty, wanted to drown in her eyes, wanted to taste the burning rose redness of her skin that had blossomed from the initial blush that had touched her face.

"Nor I without you."

The street was empty, but Lawrence heard and felt the city awakening. Like distant thunder, coming closer, he heard the torturing voices that would take him from Beauty, that would deliver him to an obliteration of self he could not bear.

"Help me."

"We shall help each other. We shall heal each other. We will share our own comfort and joy separate from the rest of existence."

With that, the red angel of his heart, she whom he loved, and whom he would always love, amen, gently pulled his wounded hand from around her and ran her fingers over the deep cuts. The wounds closed, the pain faded.

Lawrence sighed with the release from the pain.

She turned her eyes upward, toward the church.

"Look."

Lawrence saw, etched against the lightening sky, a faint glow of blue about the church—a shell, translucent, shaped like a robin's egg.

"There is our peace," she said.

Quickly, with impossible grace and beauty of movement, she undressed and cast aside her clothes. Her beauty informed the very sublimity of Lawrence's sight, had a weight that filled the spirit that transmits light.

"Share peace with me. Share love with me."

She took his hand, led him to the church steps. They ascended to the door. The shell of blue light touched the walls of the church, churning against the door.

"Put your hand upon the lock," she said.

The voices grew louder, more angry. They were no longer distant. They loomed close.

Lawrence put his hand on the lock. She touched his arm, and he felt part of her move through the solidity of his arm, felt her press through his palm. The lock tumbled, the door swung open partly. Lawrence saw into the darkened church entryway.

She ran her hand along his arm, touched his face. Lawrence kissed her palm.

She said softly, "I now give myself to you, forever," then told him the Name that she had once had in life, the Name she had forgotten in death, and in second life.

"I am Lawrence."

"You are Lawrence, my love."

"You are my love."

The voices grew closer.

She threw her arms around him, kissed him.

In a few moments, partly free of his clothing, Lawrence entered her while braced against the door of the church.

Together, as one, they fell across the threshold.

She drew him into her being as she was obliterated. Lawrence felt the salvation hidden for him within her heart as she, and he, consigned themselves to an oblivion of dust.

XIX

Morning

E d heard the church bells for sunrise mass cut short, and he knew. Ed heard sirens wailing in the silence of Christmas morning, and he knew.

He ran through the streets, through the borders of Back Bay. He came to the church, saw the small crowd, saw the ambulance, saw the paramedics pick up the limp and partly clothed body of the young man he had sought to save and carry it from the church doorway— as if from a funeral—down the steps to the silent ambulance. On the church threshold, Ed saw something like gossamer piled in a configuration like that of a body. He ascended the steps to look more closely, but was blocked by a policeman stretching crime-scene tape about the doorway. A soft wind came, warm, like that which would carry light spring rain. The flecks of gossamer blew away, whispering with sad voice, moving like the front of a winter storm. What the flecks whispered was lovely, though Ed could not fathom its meaning; he could only glean from the scuttling intonations. He thought a moment of the flow of a river.

Soon the flecks were gone.

"May you know peace," he whispered.

Later, he sat in the church to attend Christmas mass. He sat at the back pew. After mass, the priest found him there, crying in his sleep.

Gently, carefully, the priest woke him.

Shaking, Ed reached out his hand.

The priest took it as Ed whispered, *"Forgive me, Father. For I have sinned."*

In the empty church, Ed made his confession.

The priest, trembling, gave Ed solitary communion.

It was late afternoon when he reached home.

He shaved, showered. Then lay awake in the darkness.

He reached for the phone, dialed.

"Ed?" she said.

Epilogue

That morning, Jo, accompanied by her father, went to the apartment she shared with Paul to bring him over for Christmas at her
parents' house.

She found him dead, in a rictus on the living-room floor. Shrieking in her grief, she fell to her knees by his body and beat it with her
fists. Her father pulled her away as she again fell to her knees and
screamed at the injustice of a world that would take from her the two
men she had loved the most.

Lawrence's family did not allow an autopsy. They buried him, an
embarrassment, and never mentioned him again. Angie saw to it
that all Lawrence's possessions were burned or sold, so as "to not
upset Mama."

Vicki heard of Lawrence's death when her brother Dave—who
had read of it in the paper—had called her at work to tell her. She
closed the bookstore and wept, holding Groucho close, knowing
that she would miss, for the rest of her life, the frail young man she
had known only a brief while.

Jacob fulfilled his need for drama and death. Alone, unmourned
in an AIDS ward, he died some years later. His last thought as his
lungs fell still was of Lawrence gently lifting him from his ravaged
body.

The Unbowed One, Belial, Father of the Succubus, mourned as he
had never done since the first flaring of the sun for his Daughter who
had martyred herself for him and his cause.

The Succubus, she who had been damned and died and lived to
find again the Name she had always had . . . she was made free of the
concerns of flesh, was made free by an obliteration transcending the
death she had already traveled.

The echo of her soul moves now across human minds, free from her promised Name, free from the Name that had been forgotten. Second death made an *ave* of her being. She lives among some as a memory of comfort, as the quiet beauty some know in the first moment of snowfall, as the soft splendor some feel upon waking, and knowing they are loved.

And Ed Sloane, knowing that the demon he faced moved upon the Earth exerting Its Will—which he had come to know as no other person who has lived has known Its Will—recognized the frenzy of the war that ushered in the next decade as a sacrifice made in the demon's honor. He watched as It wallowed in the deserts near Nineveh, watched as It bellowed and came and wallowed in the blood spilled by hundreds of thousands of deaths.

With this recognition, he found the strength to face other such demons, found the strength to face them and the human weaknesses that feed them: the foibles of the human intellect, collected since the Fall.

With this new knowledge of Evil came a new knowledge of Good. He found the strength to heal himself, found the strength to pray. In this way, his soul had been made whole.

Though there are still a few nights each year that he wakes up screaming.

Acknowledgments

Acknowledgments for a first novel are never so much for the existence of the novel as for the existence of the writer.

Therefore, I must thank the late Lee Marshall, who told me to shut up and write; Chris Abbey, who told me to shut up, quit grad school, and write; and Gretchen Schork, who told me to shut up and write. I must thank Dennis Costa, Rheinhold Schumann, and Tom Glick for teaching me how to research and think. I must thank Janet Berliner for taking seriously a young punk she met in a Vegas hotel lobby; Janna Silverstein for her insight and support in that same Vegas hotel lobby; Ellen Kushner for her devastatingly good advice; P. D. Cacek for telling me to shut up and write; Phoebe Reeves for telling me to get the draft done; my partner in crime, "Cowboy" Bob Fleck; Juris Ahn and Michael Gibbons for supporting a fellow Buffalo expatriate and telling him to shut up and write; David Honigsberg for smashing Kabbalistic insight into my skull; Monique Mayer for her abiding, patient love and friendship; Tina Jens, for being a true pal; Judy Dodge, for doing the impossible; John Lavin and Brendan Peterson for being there; Jenna Felice for her inspirational bungee-jumping; my agent, the redoubtable Don Maass, for going to bat for me; the redoubtable Jennifer Jackson for handing Don the bat; Bridget McKenna and the NadaCon crowd for kid-glove handling a tiresomely tortured *artiste*. I must thank my fellow Millennialists, Greg Kihn and Tananarive Due.

Finally, I must thank my editors at Tor—Melissa Ann Singer for hearing my pitch and Debbie Notkin for telling an unshaven guy who hung out in her bookstore, skimming books he couldn't afford, to shut up and write.

"Or else . . ."

dawnsong@mindspring.com
www.mindspring.com/~profmike